DCI HARRY MCNEIL SERIES

BOOKS 1-3

JOHN CARSON

DCI HARRY MCNEIL SERIES

Return to Evil

Sticks and Stones

Back to Life

Dead Before You Die

Hour of Need

Blood and Tears

Devil to Pay

Point of no Return

Rush to Judgement

Against the Clock

Fall from Grace

Crash and Burn

Where Stars Will Shine – a charity anthology compiled by Emma Mitchell, featuring a Harry McNeil short story – The Art of War and Peace

DCI SEAN BRACKEN SERIES

Starvation Lake
Think Twice
Crossing Over
Life Extinct
Over Kill

DI FRANK MILLER SERIES
Crash Point
Silent Marker
Rain Town
Watch Me Bleed
Broken Wheels
Sudden Death
Under the Knife
Trial and Error
Warning Sign
Cut Throat
Blood from a Stone
Time of Death

Frank Miller Crime Series – Books 1-3 – Box set
Frank Miller Crime Series - Books 4-6 - Box set

MAX DOYLE SERIES
Final Steps
Code Red
The October Project

SCOTT MARSHALL SERIES

Old Habits

DCI HARRY MCNEIL SERIES

Books 1-3

Copyright © 2021 John Carson

Edited by Charlie Wilson
Cover by Damonza

John Carson has asserted his right under the Copyright, Designs and Patents Act 1988, to be identified as the author of this work.

This is a work of fiction. Names, characters, places, brands, media, and incidents are either the products of the author's imagination or are used fictitiously. Any resemblance to actual events, locales, or persons, living or dead, is coincidental.

Without limiting the rights under copyright reserved above, no part of this publication may be reproduced, stored in or introduced into a retrieval system, or transmitted, in any form, or by any means (electronic, mechanical, photocopying, recording, or otherwise) without the prior written permission of the author of this book. Innocence is and

All rights reserved

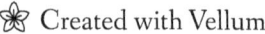 Created with Vellum

RETURN TO EVIL
DCI HARRY MCNEIL BOOK 1

ONE

MAY 1999

Jill entered through the side gate of the cemetery and hurried along the track that ran parallel to the road behind the high wall. The old caretaker's house was over on the left, but she took a fork in the road and went right. There was a small hill here which blocked the view of the house.

Their meeting point.

She slowed down and started to cry.

Then a figure stepped out from behind a large gravestone.

She caught her breath and jumped. And then recognised him. Her boyfriend.

'Oh, thank God you came,' she said, running to him and throwing her arms around his neck.

'Of course I came.'

It was dark now. Spots of rain fell through the canopy of trees. Most people would be scared to come into a cemetery after dark, but Jill found it peaceful and comforting. *You don't have to fear the dead in here,* she had told a friend.

Her boyfriend's arms felt good around her. 'Did you tell your wife about us?' she said, then pulled back to look him in the eyes.

'Not yet. I promise I will. The timing has to be just right.'

'I know. I understand. I can't wait until we're a family.'

'It's going to happen soon.' He held her close again.

Then they parted and she stood looking at him. 'I told my dad I'm pregnant.'

'You did what?' A look of anger passed over his face.

'Please don't be angry. He was drinking again. My mother is God knows where, so I just blurted it out. I told him we're going to go away together.'

'Jesus. These things take time to plan. We can't just rush into it. It's called *adulting*. We don't want it to go pear-shaped.'

'Don't talk to me like I'm a child.'

'You're fifteen. You *are* a child.'

'Don't talk like that! I'm going to be your wife. When I'm old enough, we can get married. We'll have our baby.'

They both heard the shouting at the same time.

'Jill! Where are you?'

'Oh my God. He must have followed me.' The shouting

got closer, then they saw the torchlight cutting through the darkness.

'He's coming. He knows we hang out at the old house here.'

'Stay calm,' her boyfriend said. 'Just tell him you're meeting a friend here and you'll be back home soon.' He slipped away into the darkness, out of sight behind a large gravestone.

'Are you still there?' she whispered.

'Yes. Stay calm. I'll be right here.'

'*Jill!*' The light picked out her face and blinded her. 'There you are. What are you doing here?'

'Just go home. You shouldn't be here.'

'*I* shouldn't be here? You're the one who should be home, waiting to explain to your mother!' Jill's dad was swaying and she could smell the drink on him.

'You're drunk. Go home.'

'You're coming with me.' He reached out and grabbed her arm, but she pulled away, her nails catching his arm.

'You're not my real dad!' she spat.

'Jesus. You listen to me: you get home right now!' He stepped forward, but tripped and fell, banging his head on a gravestone. He lay unconscious.

Jill's boyfriend stepped out from behind the grave.

'I think he's dead,' she said, putting a hand to her mouth.

The boyfriend reached down and felt her dad's neck for a pulse. 'He's alive. He's just out cold.'

'Thank God.' She looked at the love of her life and thought how much she loved him. Then she looked down at the prone figure of her father.

She didn't see her boyfriend come up behind her with the little stone vase, didn't see him swing it. All she felt was a sharp pain in the back of her head. The whole world swam in front of her eyes and she couldn't stand straight. Her legs buckled and she fell, landing close to her father.

She lay there, unable to speak. She felt hands under her armpits and then she was being dragged, away from her father. Now she was lying sideways across the grave. What was going on?

Where was her boyfriend?

She saw the hands on the gravestone above her; wanted to move but couldn't. She heard a grunt of exertion.

Her last thought before she died was, *The baby!*

Then it was all over.

TWO

PRESENT DAY

'Slow it down a bit, pal. My head's about to explode,' Blinky said from the passenger seat of the Transit tipper truck.

'If you toss your bag in here, you'll be cleaning it, mind,' said Joe 'Rats' Ratcliffe. He slowed the work truck down as it bounced into the cemetery. The ride-on lawnmower and other grounds-keeping tools rattled about in the back of the trailer and in the bed of the truck.

'I should have taken your advice last night and capped it at six pints. Never again.'

'I told you, but oh no, you knew best.' Rats drove the small truck straight ahead. All the film crew's vehicles were parked up on the left, round the side of the cottage – caravans, vans and big production vehicles that looked like converted coaches. All the ancillary things that went with making a TV show.

'There's Honey Summers over there,' Rats said, pointing.

Blinky was in the back of the cab, groaning. 'I don't know what the fuss is all about with that one.'

'What? Are you daft? She's one of the hottest actresses on TV right now. I for one can't wait to see this show when they finish it.' Rats swerved away from a gravestone as he put his eyes back in. They were on the gravel track that led down into the lower part of the cemetery.

'It's not going to be on TV until next year,' Blinky said. 'And slow down. It feels like I'm on a rollercoaster.'

'Look at you. What a state. I don't want you skiving off and leaving me to do all the work.'

'I'll be fine. I have my flask with me. Filled with black coffee.'

Blinky groaned again as the truck stopped.

'You want to use the strimmer first while I use the lawn-mower?' Rats said.

'Is this the face of somebody who gives a toss?'

'Come on, get up. The fresh air will do you good.'

Rats jumped out and opened the back door while Blinky tried to get up. 'That's it, boy, up and at 'em!' Rats shouted.

'Jesus. I'm going to run you over with that mower when it's my turn.'

Rats laughed and clapped his friend on the shoulder as Blinky got out and stood on shaky legs.

'Jesus, what's that smell?' Rats said.

'It's not me.' Blinky looked around.

'I hope you brought a spare pair of skids,' Rats said, walking round the truck. Then he stopped and put an arm out as his friend came to join him.

'What's wrong, Rats? You see a ghost or something?'

'Look. There's a lassie there. Lying on the grass.'

'Is there somebody with her?'

'I know I don't wear glasses like you, but my eyesight's not that good that I can see through gravestones.' Rats looked at his friend and shook his head.

Shoes were hanging off the feet and Rats could see red toenail varnish Low-hanging branches and bushes and a large headstone blocked their view of the girl.

'Do you think there's a couple round there going at it?'

'Have a word. It's just gone ten.'

'Oh, there're opening times for it now, are there?'

Rats looked at his friend and shook his head. 'If they were going at it, then don't you think the sound of a diesel engine might have made them sit up and take notice?'

'I'm going to have a look.' Blinky walked towards the gravestone, looked round and retched. Then he turned to Rats, wiping his mouth with the back of his hand. 'Call the cops.'

THREE

The sky was overcast now, bringing with it a cold wind. Perfect weather for being in a cemetery.

'Jesus, what a way to go,' Detective Inspector Frank Miller said. 'Just when we think we've seen it all.'

'Nothing surprises me anymore,' said Detective Chief Inspector Harry McNeil as they stood inside the large forensics tent. 'At least it must have been quick.'

A large gravestone, grey and lichen-covered with age, was lying flat on the top half of the woman. Only her bottom half was showing, the very top of her jeans soaked in blood.

They stepped out into the cold. It had been warmer earlier, but Edinburgh's weather liked to play games.

The forensics team were doing their thing and had been scouring the scene all day. They would lift the gravestone soon and give her some dignity.

Miller wasn't wearing an overcoat; he'd thought he didn't need one when he left the house that morning. He was shivering slightly.

'Come and walk with me over here, Frank.'

Harry started walking away from the scene and Miller followed him.

Harry stopped at a gravestone near the site of the old caretaker's house, which had been pulled down in the past few years. Miller stood looking up at a gravestone that sat on an incline. The stone looked like a monument rather than a death marker. The small hill blocked the view of the demolished house.

'What is it about this cemetery, Frank?' Harry said. 'The things that have gone on in here, you would think it's the only cemetery in Edinburgh. Why this place? What draws people here?'

Miller blew his breath out. 'It's such an old place. Whoever designed it made the front of the catacombs look like the front of a castle. It draws you in. Draws the darker side of some people.'

Harry turned to face Miller. He was standing between two gravestones. 'She died here. Jill Thompson. Twenty years ago this summer. She was fifteen years old. Found crushed to death under a gravestone, right where I'm standing. She was murdered and nobody was ever caught.'

'I remember being here too, but I was only a boy,' Miller said. 'She was just a child, not much older than me.'

'That didn't stop somebody from killing her.'

Both men stood in silence for a moment before Harry spoke.

'You ready for this, Frank?'

Miller looked at him, and thought of a young girl whose life had been ended prematurely in a cold, dark cemetery twenty years ago.

'I've never been more ready.'

'Then let's do it.'

FOUR

FIVE DAYS LATER

Harry McNeil was looking in the bathroom mirror when his girlfriend came and stood in the doorway.

'Your tie's squint,' Vanessa said, smiling at him.

'My head feels squint.' He fiddled with his tie. 'There should be a law against Monday mornings.'

'I told you to go easy last night. What with it being Sunday and you having to get up early this morning.'

'I was just being sociable. It's all Stan's fault.' McNeil looked again, but his tie was still squint.

'For goodness' sake, I have four-year-olds in my nursery who can do a tie better than that.'

'Give one of them a call. Maybe he can come along and do this one for me.'

Vanessa stepped forward and turned him to face her. 'You're going to blame Stan for getting you drunk?' She fiddled around with the tie. 'Anyway, isn't his retirement party next week?'

'It is. Last night was just the two of us. Stan was giving me some last-minute tips. He'll be showing me the ropes for a couple of weeks until I head the department.'

Vanessa shook her head. 'You've been a copper for over twenty years. A lot of miles under your belt. And you're only forty. I don't think you need tips on being a detective.'

'Easy. Forty in two weeks. Or had you forgotten?'

'No, I haven't forgotten, smarty pants.'

'Harry doesn't feel well and you're playing games,' he said. 'Harry wants sympathy and paracetamol. And more coffee.'

'No, yes and there's some water in the kettle. And while you're at it, tell Harry to get a move on. We don't want him to be late on his first day.'

'First day back on regular duty after being on the ghost squad for four years.'

'I've never heard you call Professional Standards that before.'

'It's just one of the names the others call us. Sometimes we have to be like ghosts, appearing when we want to and when we're least expected.'

'It's going to be a big change for you, but let's not forget the C word.'

Harry raised his eyebrows.

'*Chief*,' Vanessa said. 'Detective *Chief* Inspector Harry McNeil.'

'It does have a certain ring to it.'

'Stan is going to be proud of you.'

'He's a good guy, although he likes a wee drink to himself. I can't keep up with him at times.'

They left the bathroom and went through to the kitchen, where Harry poured himself another coffee.

'Didn't Stan drink on duty?' Vanessa said.

'It was something over nothing. I was lead investigator on that. Somebody dropped him in it, but he was off duty. They were trying to get back at him.'

'Don't get me wrong, Stan's a nice guy, and I know you two go way back. It just seems a coincidence that three months after that happened, Stan's retiring.'

'He'd been thinking about it for ages. They needed somebody competent enough to head up the cold case unit, but nobody fitted the bill.'

'Until Stan put in a good word for you. You two are as thick as thieves.' She gave him a kiss.

'You're not wearing a wire, are you? Recording this conversation, trying to incriminate me?' He smiled, but something in the way she'd spoken had suddenly put him on guard.

'Yeah, so don't try to make a run for it. The building's surrounded.' She laughed. 'I'm so glad you got the promotion. And you just have to walk down the hill and you're right at HQ.' She scuttled about getting her things together. 'See you at dinner. No, wait, it's parents' evening. I won't be home until later.'

'You own the nursery; why can't you just let the teachers do it?'

She smiled a sad smile and shook her head. 'I wish. But don't worry, there are some microwave dinners in the freezer. You won't starve. And remember to give Frank a call.'

She blew him a kiss and left her house.

Remember to give Frank a call. DI Frank Miller. Harry was still renting Frank's flat around the corner, the one Frank had owned with his first wife, Carol, who was now deceased.

He spread out his copy of the morning paper, *The Caledonian*, and started reading through it, but his mind wasn't on that day's news.

Vanessa's flat was in Learmonth, looking down the hill to the Comely Bank bowling club. Round the corner from where he lived.

The club was where they had met. A birthday party was being held there and they had been introduced. That was almost eighteen months ago. Now they spent most nights at her place, but sometimes Harry wanted the solitude of his own apartment. Vanessa had talked about him moving in permanently and she had asked him to talk to Frank about giving up the flat.

He knew he should be thankful for having Vanessa in his life, but it was just a big step.

His mobile phone rang. It was Stan.

'Harry! I just wanted to call and wish you the best of luck.'

'Thanks, Stan, but you did that last night. And how are you not lying in bed with your head over the side, trying not to choke on your own vomit?'

Stan laughed. 'Years more experience than you, laddie. I've already had a big fry-up and I'm meeting my mucker tonight for a sesh. Sorry I'm not going to be there to show you around, but they have me going to talk to somebody in HR about my upcoming retirement. Waste of time, if you ask me, but rules are rules, I suppose.'

'Don't worry about it. I'm sure one of the others can show me around.'

'Just remember what I told you about them.' There was silence for a moment. 'You don't fancy coming along for a pint tonight, do you?'

Harry hesitated.

'It's okay if you're busy,' Stan said.

'No, it's fine. Vanessa is working late anyway.'

'Great. Diamonds at eight?'

'I'll be there.'

'Good man.'

Harry disconnected the call. Another sesh with Stan. Vanessa would lecture him again, no doubt. He'd stay over at his own place tonight. Maybe go into work tomorrow without a tie. Or buy a clip-on.

He didn't want to get dragged out to the pub with Stan every night, but he had few friends as it was. The friends he had had on the force at one time now gave him excuses when he wanted to meet up. Four years in Standards and they treated him like he was the Grim Reaper.

Nobody could blame them, least of all Harry.

Outside, summer was knocking on the door. He unlocked his car and got in. It was a Honda CR-V. It had been his wife's, but she had let him have it in the divorce settlement. She had been quite happy to take the house, but the thing whose value was going rapidly in the opposite direction? That he could have. He still told people it was his wife's, in case they wondered why he was driving a girl's car. *Mine is in the garage,* he would tell them.

Morag had got the house, sold it and moved with their son, Chance, to Fife, where her family lived. That had been after the argument which led to her brother coming across and clocking Harry one. If it hadn't been for the can of pepper spray and his extendable baton, Harry might have been in a worse state.

It had ended without any charges, thanks to Harry getting the upper hand.

Harry pulled out from the kerb. It would be a five-minute

drive down to Fettes HQ, if he got through the green light first time. Which he did. Walk there indeed. *Do I look like the sort of bloke who likes to exercise?*

Then he was pulling into the car park off Fettes Avenue, behind the Waitrose store.

It had been a long time since he had set foot in this building. It looked like an office block from the seventies that had somehow missed the wrecking ball. No doubt one day some developer would be drooling over it, especially since the neighbour across the road was Fettes College, a prestigious school. The one that Tony Blair had gone to, though Harry didn't think that would hold bragging rights these days.

He passed through security and headed upstairs to the cold case offices. And when he stepped into the incident room, he found a giant of a man about to throw a computer out the window.

FIVE

'When they said the computers use Windows, I don't think that's what they had in mind,' Harry said, standing looking at the big man.

He turned to Harry. 'Oh, hi, boss.' The man grinned and put the old monitor down on a desk. 'I was just telling the others that you can use anything to work out with.'

'It's all fun and games until somebody loses an eye,' Harry replied.

'Even a couple of cans of beans could get your arms started.' The man nodded vaguely in the direction of Harry's biceps, an unspoken insinuation that Harry still paid the gym membership but didn't frequent the place.

'Well, I've had my beans for the day. The coffee kind.' Maybe he'd start walking to work after all.

'Ignore him, boss,' a young woman said, getting up from

behind her desk. The others in the incident room looked at her.

'I'm DS Alexis Maxwell. Everybody calls me Alex. Except him.' She nodded over to the big man. 'DC Simon Gregg. Everybody calls him Simple, except his mum.'

'Welcome, boss.' Gregg shook Harry's hand.

The phone on Alex's desk rang. She answered it, spoke and hung up again.

'And we call her Alexa, like that Amazon woman. *Alexa, answer the phone*, that sort of thing.' Gregg turned to Alex. 'Who was on the phone?'

'It was the village again. They're still looking for their idiot. I told them you were busy.'

Gregg made a face.

Harry reminded himself to tell Stan at the pub that night that a better heads-up would have been appreciated.

He looked at the others.

'This is DI Karen Shiels,' Alex said.

Harry nodded to the woman, who looked to be in her forties. She gave a grim smile back.

'These two gentlemen are retired detectives, brought back to help out the team. George Carr and Willie Young,' Alex said.

'It's a pleasure, gentlemen,' Harry said, and the two older men nodded to him. He looked around at them all. He was sure they already knew who he was, but he didn't want any ambiguity.

'I'm DCI Harry McNeil. I spent the last four years in Professional Standards. I haven't investigated any of you, as that would have precluded me from heading this department, so I don't know any of you personally, but I hope to get to know you better. Any questions?'

None.

'If any of you have a problem with me being in Standards, speak up now or forever hold your peace.' He looked around at them each in turn, but none of them said a word.

'Good. I now pronounce us boss and team. I will be working alongside DCI Weaver for a couple of weeks until he retires, then I'll take over the reins. I need another coffee and then we can sit down and go over the case. DCI Weaver told me there's a case ready to go, so let me get some caffeine and we can get started.' He turned to Alex. 'Can you show me where the canteen is?'

'We have a kettle,' Gregg said.

'I'm sure the boss doesn't want to drink our coffee before putting money in the kitty,' she said, and walked out of the incident room, Harry following.

'I had a read of your profiles last week,' he said as they made their way downstairs. 'They didn't go into details as to why you're here. All the files told me was your names, age, rank and where you were stationed before you came here.'

'DCI Weaver didn't tell you about us?' Alex replied, scepticism in her voice.

'He was going to, but I told him I wanted to get a first

impression for myself.' They walked towards the canteen. 'So, what's your story?'

She cleared her throat as they went through the door and stood in line for breakfast. 'I punched a prisoner. He was handcuffed, but he headbutted me. According to witnesses, as I bent forward, he tried to bring his cuffed hands down on my neck. I knew I was in trouble, so I punched him hard between the legs.'

'Seems fair enough to me,' he replied as they shuffled along the queue.

'He was the Lord Provost's son.' Alex ordered two bacon rolls, one to be bagged. 'One for the Jolly Green Giant,' she explained. 'Six foot six and acts like he's five, but we love him.'

'I can see how he could come in handy if we need a door taken down quickly. We can use him as a battering ram.'

'He's a sweetheart.'

Harry ordered a bacon roll as well, and they took them and ordered two coffees. When they reached the cash register, Harry paid. 'Mark this day on your calendar. The boss is not always going to be this generous.'

'Duly noted,' she said, smiling. 'You want to sit at a table?'

'What about Gregg's roll? It'll get cold.'

'That doesn't matter. I've seen him eat worse.'

They caught an empty table, Harry not wanting to ask what worse things the DC had eaten.

'DCI Weaver said I had to sit down with you all, one by

one, and get the lowdown on why you're here, in the cold case unit. But that's a waste of time,' Harry said. 'That's why I'm delegating to you. If you're comfortable with that.' He took a bite of his bacon roll. He didn't want to put ketchup on it, just in case it squirted out on his tie. God forbid he would have to put another one on. Maybe switching to a bow tie in future would be the way to go.

'Of course I am.' She took a bite of her own roll and washed it down with coffee. 'Look at us, like we're out on a first date. And you paying for the meal. You're going to give me a reputation, sir.'

'Your reputation precedes you,' Harry answered. 'What did Weaver have you call him?'

'Stan, or boss. Whatever we were comfortable with. Except in front of other officers – then it was boss, or DCI Weaver. What do you want us to call you, Harry?'

'Cheeky. But Harry is fine. Same rules apply, though.'

She grinned. 'Of course.'

'Now start off by telling me about yourself.' He ate and drank and listened.

'When I made it to detective sergeant, I thought I was heading in the right direction, promotion-wise, until the Lord Provost incident. Just my luck, he was good friends with the Edinburgh commander. Not Jeni Bridge, her predecessor. I was transferred to the cold case unit, which I thought was just for older detectives waiting out their time till retirement. Seems I was wrong.'

'Perceptions can be deceiving at times. I was shanghaied into Standards, and at first I didn't think it would be too bad. Turns out you get treated like you're the one caught with the can of petrol after the orphanage was burnt down. But tell me more.'

Alex nodded. 'I was stationed at the West End before I got sent here, two years ago. I'm twenty-nine, been in the force since I was eighteen. I was in a long-term relationship until a year ago. It didn't work out. We were engaged to be married, had bought a house together, but after we split up, we sold the house, and now I've bought a flat in the Stockbridge colonies –'

Harry held up a hand. 'We've gone a little bit off-topic. This is not your pitch for Tinder.' He smiled at her red face.

'I'm pulling a beamer here, aren't I?' she said.

'Yes, but I'm pretending not to notice.'

'Right, Stuart Gregg. Twenty-five. He left his post on a surveillance job, and the person he was supposed to be looking out for left and they couldn't find him. The same guy went on to rob a bank and he stabbed two workers.'

'I hope Gregg had a good excuse.'

'He did. He got a call saying his wife and baby daughter had been in a car accident.'

'Were they okay?'

'They were both dead on arrival at the Royal.'

'Jesus.' Harry looked at her. 'And they put him here as punishment?'

'Yes,' Alex replied. 'The brilliant commander.'

'What's the deal with Karen?' Harry asked, finishing his roll.

'She had a breakdown. She had reported a senior officer for sexual assault. Nobody listened. She got into an altercation with the officer at the police club. She had gone there with some friends. The officer cornered her and she hit him. In self-defence, but the commander didn't see it that way. That was a year ago.'

'You're telling me this officer attacked a junior officer, and now Karen is here? What happened to the senior guy?'

'Nothing.'

'As a former investigator, that hacks me off, let me tell you,' Harry said.

'It happens.' Alex finished her roll.

'Not to my team it doesn't. Nobody better put a hand on anybody else. You have me on your side now.'

'I appreciate that, sir.'

'And I know about the two older guys in the office. Weaver did tell me about *them*. A couple of good guys.'

'They have a wealth of experience,' she said as they got up.

'Experience counts for a lot,' Harry said.

They made their way back to the squad room. As they entered, Gregg now had Willie Young above his head.

'Then you would just slam the bastard down on the deck and kick him right in the you-know-what.'

'Mother of God,' Harry said, shaking his head. 'Please tell me this isn't a daily occurrence.'

Gregg put the older man down. 'Just showing them a bit of self-defence, boss,' he said, grinning.

'Next time the village is on the phone, tell them to come and collect him,' Harry said.

'Your office is over there, sir.' George Carr pointed towards a door.

'Thanks. I'm also going to take a desk out here. There seems to be a few spare.'

Everyone eyed each other. 'That's not what DCI Weaver does,' Young said, looking ruffled after his bit of audience participation.

'Well, now I'm going to be in charge, so I think I'll have a desk out here as well. That way I'll hear what you're saying about me, and as it won't be behind my back, I won't have to hear it second-hand in the canteen.'

Alex smiled. 'Now why would you go and spoil all the fun?'

Harry sat down at an empty desk. 'Somebody go and get the file so we can start work.'

'It's not that easy, sir,' Carr said. 'Things have changed. Commander Bridge was on the phone. This one is going to be different.'

'In what way?' Harry asked.

'It has similarities to the death that occurred last Wednesday. I assume you heard about it?'

'The girl in the cemetery? Yes, I heard about it.'

'She was killed in the same way as a girl who died almost twenty years ago.'

Harry looked at the others. 'Why do they think they're linked?'

'You'll be liaising with DI Frank Miller, sir. He'll tell you. They want you and Alex at the mortuary. Right away.'

SIX

Miller was at the mortuary with DS Steffi Walker. 'What happened to you?' he asked her, looking at the bruise round her eye.

'I know, I'm a clumsy cow. I tripped on the cat and fell into the ironing board.'

'Might be an idea to get Peter to iron his own shirts, now that he's moved in with you.'

'He does. He told me he ironed his shirts when he had his own place.'

Miller smiled. 'Maybe add a little bit more water to your drink?'

'I wish.'

Harry McNeil walked in with Alex, and Miller turned towards him.

'Good morning, sir,' Miller said.

'Good morning. This is DS Alex Maxwell.'

'DS Steffi Walker. We've been told that we're working on this case together. That's why we're all here,' Miller explained.

'Okay. Sounds good.'

'Good morning,' Professor Leo Chester said as he came into the PM suite.

'Good morning,' they replied like schoolchildren.

Kate Murphy and Jake Dagger came in behind the professor and they all exchanged pleasantries.

'I asked you to come here today because there is news. The girl, Trisha Cornwall, was murdered and that changes everything,' Chester said.

'What are you marking as the cause of death?' Harry asked.

'The gravestone was estimated to be twenty-two stone,' Kate said. 'It did horrific damage to her insides, but we did our best to measure her height and she was around five-six. Her features were completely deformed, as you can imagine.'

The detectives agreed they could imagine.

'We've been working over the past few days to try to reconstruct as much of her as possible, and we found a round hole in the back of her skull,' Jake Dagger said. 'Not immediately apparent, but when we put the skull together, it was there. It looks like she was hit by something blunt and round, like a hammer. Nothing on the gravestone could have caused that damage, so it had to have been inflicted before it was pushed over onto her. Cause of death: blunt-force trauma.'

'Seems a bit like overkill,' Harry said.

'We've all heard of psychos who stab somebody seventy times in a fit of rage,' Alex said.

'That seems to be the case here,' Miller agreed. He turned to Harry. 'Commander Bridge will want a rundown of things. I'll meet you up at the station, sir?'

'Okay. See you up there.'

Miller and Steffi left by the back door and drove to the station, further up the Royal Mile.

'You're quiet today, Steffi. Usually, we can't get you to shut up.'

'I had a busy weekend, sir. Just doing things around the house. And I had a few drinks with Peter since he had the weekend off.'

'Do you ever go down to the police club?'

She looked at him. Such a sad look on her face, he thought. 'No. We don't go there. Sometimes we go out with some of his bus-driving colleagues.'

Steffi said nothing as Miller pulled the car into the rear car park, driving through the vennel under the old building.

Alex pulled her car in and parked next to him.

DS Andy Watt was standing outside talking to one of the uniforms. 'Here they come, the backshift,' he said as Miller and Steffi got out of the car.

'Fuck off, Andy,' Steffi said, brushing past him and going through the back door.

Watt looked at Miller. 'I'm taking that bottle of aftershave back. The saleswoman said it would attract women like bees to honey, not make them tell you to fuck off. What a swizz.'

'Some men just have it naturally, Andy.'

'Seriously, boss, what's wrong with her? She's always up for a bit of banter. And what's with the eye?'

'She said she tripped over her cat and hit the ironing board.'

Watt gave Miller a look. 'She doesn't have a cat.'

'Maybe she got one. Maybe Peter had one and took it with him.'

'And I ride a unicorn to work.'

They started walking to the back door. 'Just don't mention I told you.'

'You got it.'

'This is DCI McNeil and DS Alex Maxwell. They're working on the gravestone case,' Miller said.

They went up to the investigation suite on the fourth floor and were directed along to one of the conference rooms.

Detective Superintendent Percy Purcell was head of CID. He was waiting with Edinburgh Division Commander Jeni Bridge.

'Sit down, everybody,' Jeni said. There was a jug of water in the middle of the conference table with glasses around it.

'DCI McNeil and DS Maxwell are from the cold case

unit,' she said, 'and I've invited them along here today because I was in a meeting at the Crown Office last week, discussing the body that was found in Warriston Cemetery on Wednesday morning. And its similarity to a cold case murder.' She looked at Harry. 'I was informed by Professor Chester at the mortuary that it's now officially murder. Blunt-force trauma to the back of the head. The woman was in quite a mess and it took a few days to reconstruct her skull.'

Purcell leaned forward. 'As you are all aware, MIT are called out to any scene like last Friday's discovery as a matter of course. Just in case. Now we've had confirmation, we can look at this case through a different set of goggles.

'First of all, the victim's name was Trisha Cornwall. She came from down south and her next of kin have been informed. The Metropolitan Police are talking to the family to get some background. But the reason you're here, DCI McNeil, is because of the similar case to this one from twenty years ago. You'll be lead investigator on this case, with DI Miller riding shotgun. You'll be working with DCI Weaver in your cold case unit.'

Harry looked at him. 'The only information I was given this morning was that we would be working with DI Miller. My team member didn't go into any details of the case.'

'It concerns the unsolved murder of a young teenage girl back in July 1999. Jill Thompson. Have any of the older members of the team heard of this case?' Jeni asked.

'I have,' Harry said. 'I was in uniform. I hadn't been on the force long.'

'I have,' Miller said. All eyes were now on him and he felt like he was on a game show. 'I was brought up in Warriston Road. The cemetery was our playground during the summer holidays. We used to play football there and ride our bikes about in safety. We watched them filming the first *God Complex*. I was ten at the time.'

'Did you know the victim?'

'No. I mean, she came to our street with her friends, and they would hang out near the trailers that the TV stars stayed in between filming. I knew *of* her, but my friends and I didn't hang out with them. She stayed along the other end of Warriston Road.' He looked at some of the others. 'For those of you who don't know the area, Warriston Road is split into two; the allotments and crematorium are between the two parts. Jill lived in the Ferry Road end. I lived in the St Mark's Park end.'

Jeni nodded, then turned to Purcell. 'If you could get everybody up to speed.'

'Certainly.' He opened the folder that was sitting on the table in front of him and extracted a sheaf of papers, which were passed around. Crime scene photos from back in the day.

It was hot and stuffy in the room. Miller reached over and poured himself a glass of water. Looked down at the gravestone lying on top of the girl. From 1999. It could have been the same scene from a couple of days ago.

When everybody had copies, Purcell started reading. 'But as for our original victim, Jill was fifteen at the time of her death, and three months pregnant.'

Harry looked at the photos of the young girl. She was pretty, with a nice smile, and he could see why a young man might be interested in her. Or some perverted older man.

'Known boyfriend?' he asked.

'Yes. There was talk of a boyfriend, and she had written about him in a diary. That means nothing, of course, but somebody had to have got her pregnant.'

'Who found her?' one of the detectives asked.

'There was a young man who lived in the street. A loner. No girlfriend, no real friends. He was a teenager, around the same age as Jill.' Purcell looked at Miller again.

Miller nodded. 'I knew him. Graham Balfour. He would hang out with me and my pals despite being a bit older. I think he was around fourteen at the time. A bit weird.'

'We took the liberty of doing some preliminaries on this. Balfour still lives there, according to the voters' roll,' Purcell said.

'Does he have a record?' Harry asked.

'He's a registered sex offender. Pissing in public. But that's all,' Jeni said.

'Times have certainly changed,' Purcell said. 'Drunks all

over Edinburgh would use a hedge after being in the boozer and nobody said a word.'

They were all looking at him.

'I'm not condoning, like.'

'Anyway,' Jeni continued, 'I would like Miller and his team to go and talk to the film crew, who are back today. There was a security guard on duty on Wednesday, but he saw nothing and heard nothing. And McNeil can take DS Maxwell and go through the old murder with DCI Weaver and the rest of his team.' She looked at Harry. 'You will both work with Miller here at the high street until told otherwise.'

'Yes, ma'am.'

'Any other questions?'

'Is there DNA from the first crime scene?' Miller asked.

'Yes. It's being taken to the labs. DNA has moved on quite a bit in twenty years, so they'll do their thing.'

Harry put a finger up. 'How did they come to the conclusion that Jill Thompson was murdered?'

'By the position of the body,' Purcell said. 'And the height of the gravestone. Distance, her weight and the weight of the stone. Children have been killed by climbing onto gravestones which have then toppled over, but we did some research last week and all the victims in the UK were small children. When the stones toppled, their feet were off the ground, so it was harder for them to jump clear. And the stones were bigger than them, so when they fell back, the stone was big enough to cover most of their body. Jill's body was in a completely different position than if she'd been climbing on it. Therefore, it was determined that somebody pushed it on top of her.'

'No sign of a hole in her skull like this new victim?'

'There was nothing in the pathology report.'

'Right,' Jeni said. 'Miller, you and DS Walker are going over to interrupt filming in the cemetery. McNeil, you and DS Maxwell are going to interview Graham Balfour. Your team can go through the old files from the Thompson murder. Bring Weaver up to speed when he gets back from his retirement interview. Any questions?'

Nobody had any.

'Good. We'll use the incident room for liaising. Get to it, people, and I want a daily report. But I'd like DI Miller and DCI McNeil to stay back, please.'

Miller and Harry stayed while the rest stood up and filed out.

'Right, before you both go off anywhere, Chief Inspector, I want you to go and meet a counterpart of yours from Northumbria Police. Detective Inspector Charlie Meekle. He'll be off the Newcastle to Edinburgh train' – she looked at her watch – 'in an hour. Waverley of course. Take DI Miller with you.'

'Why's he coming here?' Harry asked.

'We asked him to come up here and give us some input. He was on the original case, twenty years ago. Tell him that he answers to you while he's up here. Do I make myself clear?'

'Very.'

'Right. Off you go.'

They were dismissed from the room like little boys. Outside in the corridor, Harry took Miller aside.

'I just wanted a quick word, Frank.'

'No problem, sir.'

'Sir? Christ, I've been a DCI five minutes. Don't bother about that stuff unless it's in front of the others. You and I go way back.'

'It's good to see you back on regular duty. Keeps you out of mischief,' Miller said, smiling.

'I can only hope.' Harry turned around to see his DS standing further along the corridor, looking at her phone.

'How's your new team?' Miller asked, looking at the young woman.

'They seem a decent bunch, to be honest. Stan Weaver ran a good team, but retirement beckoned. He's away in a couple of weeks or so.'

'You're one of the lucky ones, Harry. Some of the others from Standards go downhill. Or else spend the rest of their careers as loners.'

'Norrie nae mates. I had few as it was, but after I joined Standards they always had an excuse when I asked them to go for a pint. Except you. My landlord.'

'Is that what you wanted to talk to me about? The flat?'

Harry hesitated for a moment. 'Vanessa wants me to have a word with you about giving it up.'

'And you're hesitant.'

'I am. I don't know why; I spend most of my time at her house. It's just that the flat is…my sanctuary.'

'It's all the same to me, Harry. If you want to give it up, that's fine. If not, that's good too. But I can see why you're hesitant.'

'You can? Mind enlightening me?'

'You would be moving into a house that's Vanessa's. Yes, it would be your home, but not your *house*. That's the difference. In the back of your mind, you're not sure about taking the leap, in case for some reason it goes sour. And if it did, you would have nowhere to go. Nowhere to run to.'

'Jesus, you're wise beyond your years, Frank.' Harry smiled and clapped Miller on the arm. 'How about a pint? Tonight?' He knew he was supposed to be having a beer with Stan, but that wouldn't be a couple, it would turn into another full-blown sesh. Time to give Stan a call and take a rain check.

'Sure. Somewhere that other coppers don't drink?'

'I'll give you a call.'

'Do that, Harry.'

'And if Vanessa sees you and asks –'

'You talked to me about the flat.'

'Good man. Now let's go and pick up that DI.'

'I'm just going to grab my coat. I'll catch up.'

Miller walked away and Harry headed over to where Alex was standing.

'We go way back,' he said to her.

'None of my business.' She looked around. Nobody there. 'But do I get invited along for a pint?'

'No, you bloody well don't. What if I was seen out drinking with another woman? Are you trying to get me divorced? Again? Before I'm even married to her.'

'I never got you divorced the first time.'

'You're going to be a delight! I just know it.'

Alex smiled at him. 'And they said you were going to be grumpy.'

'Who did?'

'Nobody.'

SEVEN

They drove down to the railway station, Miller behind the wheel. No cars were allowed in the station, which never failed to amaze Miller. They were allowed through because they were police, and they parked the car with a police sign on display.

They stood on the platform waiting for the train to come in, and it obliged ten minutes later. It was the King's Cross to Aberdeen service, and people started to get off in droves.

'He's here now,' Harry said as they looked along the platform.

'How can you tell?' Miller asked.

'He's the big, tall guy carrying a tartan suitcase.'

'Maybe it's just somebody who's patriotic.'

'Or somebody wanting to impress the heathens,' Harry said as the man stopped before them and put his case down.

Meekle looked to be in his fifties, with a rough beard that had long ago started to turn grey.

'You two must either be trainspotters or waiting for me.'

'Charlie Meekle?' Harry said.

'Aye. Or you can call me *Inspector* Meekle if you like.' He spoke in a thick Glaswegian accent, not the Newcastle one they had been expecting.

'I don't like. I'm DCI McNeil. DI Frank Miller. Let's try not to get off on the wrong foot.'

'Aye, nae bother, sir.' Meekle looked at them. 'You might be wondering why I'm not talking in a Geordie accent.'

Miller wanted to get moving. 'My money's on you've been watching *Still Game* on the way up so you can fit in.'

'Good answer, but this time you'll have to settle for second prize. I'm originally from Glasgow. Worked in Edinburgh, but transferred down to Newcastle because I felt like it.'

'Right, so now we've cleared that up, let's get a step on. We've a murder to deal with,' Harry said.

'You want to pick up my case?' Meekle said to Miller.

'Not really.'

'What way is that to welcome a guest?'

'As the boss said, we have a murder to investigate. If I wanted to carry a suitcase, I'd be working at the Balmoral.'

'Suit yourself.' Meekle picked up the case. 'I'm staying at the Radisson in the high street. We could drop my case off, then go to your station.'

Harry was walking ahead. 'Bring it with you. We'll call you an Uber later on.'

They walked to the car. 'How long since you were here?' Miller asked.

'A long time. Big changes, I'm sure.'

Harry got in behind the wheel, saying nothing to the inspector.

'You won't recognise it then,' Miller said.

As they drove down to Warriston Cemetery, Meekle looked out the window of the car like a tourist.

'Boy, that was quick. I was just settling in for a road trip,' he said as he got out of the car. 'Will my case be okay in here?'

'I don't think anybody's going to touch your Y's,' Harry said.

'Good point.'

EIGHT

Harry McNeil stood watching the scene unfold before him. Honey Summers ran between some gravestones and hid behind a large one, before stepping out and putting her hand up towards the man chasing her, and then the man stopped, grabbed his throat and fell to the ground.

'Cut!' the director shouted, and all the crew started moving.

The man on the ground got up, dusted himself down and walked away.

'This brings back memories,' Meekle said.

'I should hope so,' Harry replied. 'That's why you're here, after all.'

Meekle ignored him.

'Good job, Dustin!' the director shouted.

'Who's the pretty boy?' Alex Maxwell asked. She had

driven down with Steffi Walker while Meekle was being picked up at the train station.

'That's Dustin Crowd,' Steffi said. 'You into sci-fi?'

'No. You?'

'Well, I know I'll be watching the original show before they put the new one out, but I can already tell this one is going to be my favourite.'

'I got a list of names and told the producer that we'd like to interview everybody who was here on Wednesday,' Steffi said to Harry.

'Okay. Maybe you and DI Miller could start by talking to Honey Summers. I'm going to take Alex to talk with Graham Balfour. Inspector Meekle, keep an eye on things out here.'

A PA showed Steffi and Miller into the trailer, which was a bigger, American version of what they called a caravan. This was like a house on wheels.

The actress was waiting for them, still in her costume. She was sitting at a table, smoking. Dustin Crowd sat opposite.

'They'll be banning smoking in here next,' she said. There was a glass next to her. She picked it up and took a sip from it.

'We'd like to ask you a few questions about last Wednesday, if you don't mind,' Miller said.

Honey shrugged. 'It's fine. It wasn't me.'

'It wasn't you what?' Steffi said.

'Who murdered her.' Honey gave Steffi a look that stopped just short of *obviously*.

'What did you think of my performance?' Dustin Crowd said to the detectives after they were introduced to him.

'You'll excuse me if I don't ask you to sign my tie,' Miller said. 'We're here to talk about the girl who was murdered last week. Trisha Cornwall.'

'Oh, her. She used to hang about here.'

'You know her, then?'

'Oh yes. There are fans, and then there are nutter fans like her. I made the mistake of answering one of her questions on Facebook and she turned from a fan into a stalker. And boom – next she wants me to be her baby daddy. Same with Randy, our director; he did the same. And some crew members too. She wouldn't leave us alone. I rue the day I answered a Facebook message from Trisha Cornwall.'

'Did you ever sleep with her?' Steffi asked.

'That's a bit personal, isn't it?'

'So is murdering somebody,' Miller said. He couldn't fathom why women would fall at this man's feet, although he was starting to imagine the man falling at his feet after he'd clocked him one in the pub.

'I didn't murder her,' Dustin said.

'Sorry if we don't take your word for that,' Steffi said. 'You might have to convince us otherwise.'

'I don't have to convince you of anything. I'm innocent. End of. This is not a trial.'

'How about a trial by public opinion? What happens to your career when people think there's a possibility that you're a killer? You'll light up the Internet with that one. And even if you're not, and we get the real guy, mud sticks. Your name will forever be out there, and this murder will hang around you like a bad smell.'

'Alright. I met her last week. She wanted a signed shirt. That was Tuesday. She told me if I didn't want to sign the shirt, she could always post things on Facebook about me, and I'm talking about personal texts.'

'You could have got a lawyer onto her,' Miller said.

'Trust me, I just wanted her to go away. I met her and gave her a signed shirt.'

'And then she did go away, permanently.'

'I did not kill her. I have an alibi, which I will happily provide.'

'Where were you late Tuesday into Wednesday?' Steffi asked, looking at both of the actors.

Dustin looked at Honey. 'Go on, tell them.'

Honey made a face at him like she'd just stood in something. 'Schmoozing with some of the investors. We were at a function, all of us. Dustin, Carruthers – he's one of the investors – a whole lot of other people. We were there until late. Then we went back to the hotel. My PA drove me and one of the writers back.' She looked at Miller. 'We had drinks in the hotel bar before I went up to my room. Alone. Dustin went to his, then we spent the night together. We've been an item for a little while now.'

Miller nodded. Her story sounded plausible, but she was

an actress at the end of the day. 'Surely people in the hotel would see you going into the one room?'

'We have two adjoining rooms. People *think* we're in two rooms.'

Dustin was grinning. 'Honey and I will be making an official announcement later, and that will only add to the frenzy about the show.'

'When you've been filming scenes in the cemetery, have you noticed anybody strange hanging about? Watching you?' Steffi asked.

'Take your pick. Usually, they're lonely old men, looking for an autograph, hoping to be invited in here for a quickie.'

'And that's just me,' Dustin said, laughing.

'Give over,' Honey said, not amused by his joviality.

'Were you here on Tuesday during the day?' Miller asked Honey.

'No, we were filming around the old town. Down by Holyrood.'

'What about you, Mr Crowd?' Steffi asked.

'Listen to you; Mr Crowd! Call me Dustin. We're all friends here.'

Miller looked at his notebook. 'How many producers does this show have?'

'Five, I think, but they're not all here. Carruthers Wellington stays here, so he can report back to the other investors. The director is here today, Randy Kline. You might want to give him the third degree. Randy by name, randy by nature. And the second unit director, Mike Peebles.'

'My colleagues are talking to them now. But do you have many fans here asking for autographs and such stuff?'

'All the time. They're always creeping about, but it's to be expected. Oh, don't get me wrong – without fans, we don't have a job. But some of them go one step too far,' Honey said.

'Like?' Steffi said.

'Like thinking they can take you out to dinner or home to meet their mother. Some want an autographed pair of panties. Preferably with me still wearing them. Most of them are fine, but some of them are creepy.'

'Well, if you do see something strange, or you remember anything, please call me.' Miller handed her a business card as he and Steffi stood up to leave.

'You too, Dustin.'

'I will indeed, my good man.'

Outside, some of the crew were wandering about.

'What did you think of her?' Miller said. It was getting warmer now, a hint of what the summer might bring. A few clouds scudded about, as if deciding whether to change direction and come over to piss on them or not.

'Calls herself talented,' Steffi said. 'What talent does she have? She can memorise lines written by somebody else, and be told where to move and how to say those lines by somebody else. Big deal. Another overpaid moron who should look for another job.'

Steffi's breath was coming in gasps now.

Miller looked at her. 'You need a cup of tea.'

'No, I don't,' Steffi said, making a face.

'I could do with one. There's a catering van along the way. I'm sure they could spare us a tea.'

Steffi let herself be led away. Miller knew something was wrong and hoped his DS would talk to him about it.

He looked around him, not wanting to turn his back on any of the film crew or actors, since any one of them could be the killer they were looking for.

NINE

'Graham Balfour?' Harry McNeil said to the face peering at them through the crack in the door. He was holding up his warrant card for the man to see.

'Who's asking?'

'I am. DCI McNeil.'

'What do you want?' Balfour's voice rose, echoing off the concrete steps in the hallway. They were on the top floor of the two-storey building. s

'We just want a word. Or would you prefer we stood and talked here? And if you shut the door on me, I will come up with some excuse for why I need to enter your house with a warrant.'

'Fine,' Balfour said, stepping back and opening the door wide.

Harry and Alex stepped into the lobby and Harry turned

to watch the man shut the door. *Never turn your back on them if you can help it.* And that was when he was only investigating dodgy policemen.

'You'll excuse me if I don't offer you a cup of tea,' Balfour said, leading them through a door on the right. The living room.

'That's fine. I don't usually drink a lot of tea on duty. I never know when I'll need the bathroom.'

'Och, here we go. That was a long time ago. I'd been out drinking, and I had to go. I mean, there's hardly an abundance of toilets in Edinburgh and the ones that are open stink like nothing on earth. I got caught out. And a patrol car was passing. You know the rest, obviously.'

'We want to ask you a few questions about an incident in the cemetery last Wednesday,' Alex said.

'Okay. Sit down if you like.'

Harry didn't like, preferring to stand. He'd be able to reach his extendable baton faster if he stood. He regularly practised drawing it out in the bathroom. *No pointing in having a baton if it gets caught in a hole in your pocket, Harry, my old son,* Stan Weaver had said to him one day. *There's nothing more dangerous than a dirty cop.*

Alex sat down while Balfour sat opposite, on the settee.

Harry looked out of the front window for a moment. This detached block of flats had been built at a right angle to the houses next to it. Like it had been an afterthought to the builder, back in the thirties. It seemed like the block had been stuck into St Mark's Park itself.

Harry watched as a young mother supervised her child in the playground opposite. Beyond that, trees bordered fenced-in football fields. Further over on the left was a gate that led into allotments.

He turned to face Balfour. 'Where were you on Tuesday night, Graham? You don't mind if I call you Graham, do you?'

Balfour shrugged. 'What do you mean, where was I?'

Harry held out his hands. 'Seems a pretty straightforward question to me. I mean, were you at work?'

'I don't work. I was with some friends.'

Harry already knew the man didn't work, but he had wanted to hear how Balfour would answer. 'What do you do with your time?'

'Not that it's any of your business, but I go job hunting during the week.'

'Were you in the cemetery on Tuesday?' Harry asked.

'Yes, I was.'

'Doing what? Job hunting?'

'Trying to get Honey's autograph. On a piece of paper, not on her panties. You know some guys actually ask for that? I mean, Christ, I can't even imagine.'

'Not your thing?' Harry said, still staring at the man.

'No, it isn't. But Honey's autograph on the cover of a DVD of her latest movie is. I can sell it on eBay.'

'Did you see anybody else there?'

'The dead woman, you mean?'

'Yes, that's who we mean,' Alex said.

'Yes, I saw Trisha. She hangs out with us. Or did. There's a group of us.'

'Did you see anybody suspicious hanging about?' Harry said.

'Weird, you mean? Half the people watching that show being filmed are weird. But my group and I, we're always respectful.'

'Group?' Harry said.

'My friends. We go all over the UK autograph hunting. It's how we make money.'

'You can't make a living from that, surely?' Alex said.

'Not just autographs. Memorabilia. Get them to sign something and the value shoots up. Especially among those sci-fi geeks. Like, if I got Honey or Dustin to sign a T-shirt, I could make a good few quid off it.'

'They must get bored with you asking?'

'Trust me, they can't tell one face from another. They'll sign anything just to get us to go away.'

'I want to ask you a few questions about Jill Thompson,' Harry said suddenly, seeing if he could throw Balfour off-kilter.

'Jill? That was a long time ago.' Balfour stared at the wall for a second, as if picturing Jill Thompson's face there.

'You know why we're asking, don't you?' Alex said.

'Of course I do. She died the same way as the woman last Wednesday.'

'Don't you think that's strange?' Harry said. 'Same thing, twenty years apart?'

'Why would I think it strange? People go into the cemetery all the time for one thing or another. Never anything good after dark.'

'Do you go there after dark?'

Balfour gave him a look that suggested he thought Harry was winding him up. 'Junkies. They're the ones who go in there. Not like when I was a kid. We used to play in there. Football. We'd take sticks and batter at the giant hogweed that used to grow there. Climb up the ivy to the top of the walls. Play hide and seek. We had fun. Then those older folks discovered it and turned it into a pit. But what did you lot do? Nothing.'

'You were close to Jill then?' Alex said, ignoring Balfour's barbed comment.

'Not well enough to get her pregnant. Sometimes we hung out. I told the detectives all this back then.'

'I know,' Harry said. 'I read the report. Fourteen-year-old you told the investigators you and Jill would play in each other's houses.'

'Hardly playing, Inspector. We would listen to records. And it wasn't just the two of us; several of us were always there.'

'Did she tell you she was pregnant?'

'No. I read it in the papers.' Balfour held up his hands. 'It wasn't me. I first went with a woman when I was sixteen. A married woman would have some of us guys round and let us have at it. Her husband was a truck driver or something.'

'Did Jill ever tell you she was sleeping with somebody?' Alex said.

Balfour looked between the two detectives. 'No. A friend of hers did. But she swore me to secrecy.'

'What was his name?'

'She didn't tell me his name. Just that he was older and married, but he was going to split up with his wife. He had to be careful, because his wife was jealous and he already had a kid, but he was going to leave her and then he and Jill could move in together.'

'Move in together?' Harry said. 'She was fifteen, man! How could she move in with a man? Technically, he was a rapist. At the very least, he was taking advantage of a young girl.'

Balfour sat back further on the settee. 'I'm just telling you what her friend told me. I agree with you. And we were all shocked when she died.'

'What about some of the other girls she was friends with? You ever talk to any of them?'

'There was Alice. Her best friend. They were thick as thieves. Then, when Jill died, Alice wasn't around anymore. I think she moved shortly after.'

Harry remembered the name from the file.

'Do you know if Jill ever talked about her family? Anybody she had a problem with?'

'Are you kidding? Jill was Little Miss Goody Two-Shoes. Or she wanted everybody to think of her that way. Her mother was very strict. If Jill was five minutes late for dinner, her mother would go ballistic. I think maybe Jill rebelled because of it.'

'Are you planning on going back to the cemetery?' Alex asked.

'Of course we are. As I said, it's how I make a living. Plus, you never know, Honey might accept my invitation to dinner.' Balfour grinned at Harry.

There's more chance of her accepting a dinner invitation from the Yorkshire Ripper.

Outside, Harry looked over to the park, imagining fifteen-year-old Jill hanging out with her friends. Like a fifteen-year-old girl *should* be doing.

Not getting ready to move in with a married man.

They went back to the cemetery and arrived just in time to see Charlie Meekle get into an altercation.

TEN

Randy Kline blew cigar smoke around the living room area of the trailer. An older man was there too, sitting down. 'That's all we need,' Kline said, pacing back and forth, 'a dead body near the set. Was it foul play?'

'Yes. She was murdered,' Miller said.

'We need publicity, of course, but not the wrong kind. This is history repeating itself.' Kline stopped to stub the cigar out in an ashtray that was already overflowing.

'It'll soon go away,' Steffi said.

'Will it? I don't think so. Type *God Complex* into a search engine and you'll see the details of the first murder. It follows the first show like a bad smell.'

'We need to know if you saw anything strange going on last Tuesday into Wednesday.'

'Sit down, please.' Kline waved his hands in the direction of some seats and sat down near the two detectives. 'You know we're filming a sci-fi show here, with all sorts of strange people going about in costume? Nobody strange would stand out.'

'You allow members of the public to observe,' Miller said.

'We do, but we have stewards keeping them at bay. Most of them just want to watch, but some of them want more.'

'Any of the actors or crew complain about anybody?'

'No. But you could ask him,' Kline said, nodding to the small man who had just come in.

'What's up?' Mike Peebles said.

'They're questioning everybody about the woman who was murdered last Wednesday.'

'That's certainly going to put this show on the map,' Peebles said.

'You do know a woman is dead, right?' Miller said, standing up.

'Of course I do. But we were just talking about that last week,' Peebles said, nodding to Kline. 'We were thinking of ways to get better publicity for the show.'

'And what better way than to shove a gravestone on top of a woman?' Kline said. 'Except we didn't do anything like that. We were talking about getting stars to tell us how big a fan they were of the original show, so we could do a YouTube video.' He looked at Peebles. 'And if you stop talking like a dick, the police might not take us in for questioning or give us a going-over.'

'Oh, stop getting your jockeys in a knot. It's free coverage in the paper.' Peebles walked into the kitchen area and opened the fridge. Took out a bottle of Coke. 'I bet her highness is frothing at the mouth.'

'Honey is upset, yes, if that's what you mean.'

'Where were you on Tuesday night?' Steffi said. 'Save us having to come back here with an Alsatian so it can grab your nuts. Just before we give you a going-over, of course.'

Miller threw Steffi a look.

'If you must know, we were filming in Perthshire. Some outside scenes at a castle.'

'He was,' Kline confirmed. 'They were up there with some of the actors.'

'We stayed in a manky wee hotel that served black pudding you could play hockey with.'

'You were all together from Tuesday night until now?' Miller said.

'No. Despite rumours in the, we actually have time off between filming. The crew and actors finished Tuesday evening, and they're not due to be filming again until tomorrow, up the high street. So they can do whatever they like. As long as their arses are back where they're supposed to be, we don't chain them up in a dungeon.'

The door suddenly burst open.

'I found this guy sniffing about outside.' Meekle pushed

the man into the main area of the trailer. Harry McNeil was with him.

'Shovin',' the man said to Meekle, turning round as if he was going to have a go.

'Welly, I think you're sniffing around the wrong trailer. Honey's is further down,' Kline said, grinning.

'What are you doing here?' Miller said, recognising the man.

'Relax, Inspector. It's our very own Carruthers Wellington. Our man in the middle.' Kline turned to Meekle. 'He's our liaison with one of our big investors.'

'Why were you creeping about outside?' Peebles said. 'Nebbin' at our conversation.'

'For your information, I was not *nebbin'*. I was waiting.'

'What do you need, Welly?' Kline said.

'Look, if this police activity is going to affect the show, I need to know about it. The investors will not be happy if they find out somebody's been murdered and somebody here is in the frame for it.'

'You can tell them that investigating this murder is more important than your filming schedule,' Miller said.

'Easy for you to say,' Wellington said. 'I have people I have to report to.'

'Let's just deal with it, then move on,' Kline said.

'If any of you think of anything, please let us know.'

'What do you make of that Carruthers Wellington?' Harry said when they were outside.

'I know him,' Miller said. 'He's obviously using a fake name. He's Adrian Jackson's nephew, Brian. Nothing to worry about.'

Harry trusted Miller, but thought he might run the man's name through the system anyway.

'I feel like a spare prick at a wedding,' Meekle said to Weaver as they stood in line to get a coffee at the catering trailer.

'Well, I'm here now, and thank Christ they had the good sense to ask you up here for your opinion. I'm sorry I wasn't at the station to pick you up, but I had to talk to somebody in HR about my impending retirement. Waste of bloody time.'

'Don't worry about it. We've got our ears to the ground.'

'What can I help you with?' the caterer said.

'We'd like two coffees,' Weaver said. 'We're detectives. Mind if we ask you a question?'

'Naw, fire away. You want a couple of bacon rolls? Pizza? The production company pays for all of this.' The caterer smiled at them.

'Go on then,' Meekle said. 'Bacon roll, ta.'

'And you, sir?'

'Same. Easy on the ketchup.'

'The condiments are right there, sir.' The caterer turned to a female assistant. 'Two bacon rolls.'

'Coming right up,' she answered.

'What's your name, pal?' Meekle said.

'Tom Robinson. Owner and operator of Robinson Catering.' He smiled and swept his hand around. He went to the large urn and poured two coffees.

Weaver looked around to see if anybody was listening, but they were the sole customers. 'Do you get any of the show's fans coming to you for food?'

'Aye, some of them try it, but they get nowt. Food's only for the production crew and actors. Some of them cheeky sods try and tell me that they work here, but if they don't have a badge, they don't get served.'

'Any of them stand out?'

'One lassie. Well, I say lassie, but she's no spring chicken – though she dresses like she thinks she is. Always hanging about with a daft laddie, but again, he's no' a laddie. Looks like he's in his thirties, but always wears one of those graphic tees. They're always here, looking for signatures.'

'You wouldn't happen to know this guy's name, would you?'

'Graham. I heard the lassie call him that. Right pain he is. He's always hovering around here, trying to get free scran. I told him to piss off. And then one day I saw him getting into a real fight with the woman who was murdered.'

'Do you know what they were arguing about?' Weaver asked.

'Not sure. I was busy. I thought I heard the woman say

something about somebody being pregnant. I thought he had maybe got her up the stick or something.'

'Thanks.' The detectives walked away, well out of earshot.

'I told you,' Weaver said, then bit into the roll. Meekle said nothing.

ELEVEN

Aileen Rogers sat and had another glass of wine. Looked at her phone again, at the text message that was there. It made her smile.

Looking forward to seeing you tonight.

She read it over and over, and each time she looked at the words, they sent a shiver through her. She couldn't call him, just like he couldn't call her. Spouses on both sides stood in the way. It didn't matter. Chatting online had been the beginning of a journey that was going to end in them both leaving their partners. Texting him – sometimes *sexting* him – was the middle step.

He had asked her if she had told anybody, and she'd promised him that she hadn't, but he didn't understand how women worked. She'd told her best friend. That wasn't telling somebody, in woman-speak. That was just nature.

He'd told her that if he got caught, his wife would hurt them both. But once he was away from her, they could start a new life. She couldn't wait.

She closed the text and called her friend. 'Janice. He texted me that he wants to meet tonight. I am so excited.'

'Well, you go, girl. You deserve to be happy after all you've been through with that twat.'

'It's been on the cards for years. I warned him a long time ago. But would he listen? No. So fuck him.'

'Nobody will blame you, Aileen. Least of all me. But please be careful when you go with him.'

'What do you mean?' Aileen said.

'I don't mean anything. I'm just saying be careful. You haven't actually met him, have you?'

'That doesn't mean anything. We've talked for hours. I feel like I've known him for years.'

'You've not exactly talked, though, have you? I mean, chatting on the web and texting isn't actually talking. You could have been talking to one of those robocall things and you wouldn't know it.'

'Jesus, Janice, tell me what you really think. And I don't think that's how robocalls work. Besides, we have spoken on the phone.'

'When?' Janice exclaimed. 'You never told me that.'

'When he was able to. When his wife wasn't around. I spoke to him last week, and he sounded even better than I imagined.' Aileen felt a mixture of elation and anger.

'Still. You can never be too careful.'

'Anyway, Drew will be in any minute, so I have to go.'

'Do you want me to come along with you tonight? I could sit in a corner and just watch.'

'No, that's fine, Janice. I'll be okay.'

'Well, if you're su–'

Aileen cut her off mid-sentence and threw her phone down onto the couch. What a cheeky bitch! *Do I want you to come along and sit in a corner of the pub? No, I do not want you to come along and get your fucking cheapies when I'm out with my new man.* That was Janice bumped from now on. There was no way Aileen was ever going to tell that slag anything again. Janice was one to talk; she'd gone outside with one of the blokes they worked with at the Christmas night out and dropped her scants for him.

Aileen thought she might just be dropping her own scants for her boyfriend tonight. There was only the slightest bit of doubt creeping about in her mind. His name. He had told her to call him *Buddy* when she had asked him. Oh yeah? What the fuck was that short for? *Buddington?* Or maybe it was what his wanker pals called him in the pub when he arrived and they were all pleased to see him. *Budster!* they might shout, clapping him on the back and wanting to buy him a beer as if he'd just crawled through a raging inferno and rescued two puppies. Or successfully shagged some bint he'd met online.

Aileen shook her head. Janice was getting in her brain

again. Debbie Fucking Downer. She didn't know why she hung out with her anyway. Just like in a marriage, trust was everything in a friendship. She could trust Janice not to say anything to Drew, but after tonight it wouldn't matter.

She heard a car door closing outside their house. That would be Drew home now.

He came in, loosened his tie and put his briefcase on a chair.

'What's for dinner?' he said.

'Whatever you want to take out of the freezer and put in the microwave,' she said, getting up, and took the wine glass and phone with her upstairs.

'Fucking bitch,' he said.

Oh, you don't know the half of it, she thought, ignoring him.

She went into their bedroom and locked the door. She was going to get ready for the love of her life and Drew wasn't going to ruin it.

TWELVE

Harry McNeil was sitting having a beer in the St Bernard's bar in Stockbridge when Frank Miller walked in. There were spots of rain on his jacket.

'Jesus, just when I thought it was the start of a warm spell,' Miller said, standing over Harry's table. 'Same again?' He pointed to the half-empty pint glass.

'I'll get them,' Harry said, but Miller waved him away and got two lagers before sitting down opposite his friend.

'Cheers, Frank. It's not true what they say about you.'

'It is, Harry.' Miller laughed. 'Just don't tell Kim.'

'Your secret is safe with me.' He drank some of his own lager. 'I wonder what she was doing up here?' Harry said.

'She lived up here, apparently. Just moved here a few weeks ago.'

'They have an address for her?'

'They said she was staying with a friend in Leith. Uniform have been there, and the friend says she moved in with a man she met online. Trish was going to give the friend an address, but she hadn't so far.'

Harry drank some more of his pint. 'You'll want to talk to this woman tomorrow. See if she can remember more when she's not quite as upset.'

'I'm thinking it was maybe Graham Balfour, over by the cemetery. How did you get on with him when you spoke to him earlier, sir?'

'Knock that *sir* pish off, Frank. Jesus, I've known you long enough. And Carol, remember?' Carol was Miller's first wife who was also a detective and killed whilst on duty.

'Sorry. Old habits and all that.'

'Anyway, we spoke to him. He's a bit of a wido as well as a weirdo. He and his cronies make their living from getting autographs and the like. He was hanging about the cemetery with the other members of the anorak brigade. And he told us he knew Trisha and she would hang out with him and his mates.'

'It puts him at the scene, if nothing else.'

Harry drank some more, then looked at the door, as if expecting it to open.

'You told me Vanessa is giving you a hard time about the flat,' Miller said.

'She wants me to give it up, as I said. To be honest, I'm not ready. Simple as that.'

'Have you tried talking to her?'

Harry shook his head. 'No. I'm always putting it off. I was even going to say I had signed a lease and it was for a year, but she might see through that.'

'Building the foundation of your relationship with a lie. It can only crumble, Harry.'

'Jesus. I only hope my son grows into a man like you. Little sod will probably end up inside, knowing my luck.'

'But tread carefully, my friend. You don't want to throw away a good thing on insecurities. I'm not telling you how to live your life, but go into this with your eyes wide open. What if you decided not to give the flat up and you split up – and then missed Vanessa so much, but by the time you realised this, she'd moved on?'

'Christ, listening to you is like eating cheese before bed.'

'Just giving it to you straight. Just don't go home pished tonight and try to talk to her about it.'

'Not going to happen. She's got parents' night at her school so I'm not going to be staying at her place. I'm going to stay at the flat.' Harry drank some lager. 'Just saying I'm going back there feels good inside. I know that sounds horrible, but your flat is my home. I'm comfortable going there.'

'I get the feeling Vanessa isn't.'

The door opened and in walked a familiar face. Miller couldn't place her at first; mid-twenties, black jeans, wearing a light raincoat.

'Christ, it's Alex,' Harry said.

Miller snapped his fingers. 'Alex Maxwell, your DS.' He should have paid more attention to her in the meeting earlier that day.

'Jesus, don't go shouting it.' Harry tried to disguise his face with his pint glass, but Alex looked over. She was unsure whether to join them, so she went to the bar and ordered a drink. G and T, Miller guessed.

After getting a drink, she approached their table. 'Hello, sir. Didn't see you there.'

'Yes, you did. You just didn't want to buy us a drink,' Miller said, smiling.

'Nothing gets past you.'

'Grab a seat if you like. It's Harry's round next and he mentioned doubles and I don't think he was talking about a tennis match.'

Alex grinned and sat down. Looked at Harry. 'I didn't know this was your local, Harry.'

'It isn't. I was just having a pint with Frank.'

She looked at them. 'I can leave you be.'

'Don't be daft,' Miller said. 'We were just discussing the case, but we won't be meeting like this every night. As much as I'd like to.'

'You married, sir?'

'That's a bit forward, isn't it, Sergeant?' Harry said.

'Oh, I was just –'

'He's pulling your leg,' Miller said. 'Yes. And I have two daughters.'

'That's nice.'

'What about you?'

'Still waiting for Mr Right.'

Both men looked at each other. *Mr Right doesn't exist.*

'Jesus, here's Stan Weaver,' Harry said, looking at his watch.

The DCI saw him and walked over to the table. 'Where the hell have you been?' he said. His breath stank of beer and he was swaying about.

'The time just got away from me, Stan.'

'That's one thing I like, McNeil: punctuality.' He was slurring his words and he pointed a finger at them all.

'It's only eight twenty. I would have been up in five minutes.'

'Bollocks.'

'Hello, Stan,' Alex said, smiling at him.

'It's DCI Weaver to you. Little upstart.'

'Surely about to be ex-DCI?' she answered, still smiling.

'Don't get smart with me, Maxwell. I still have two weeks in that department, so don't forget it.' His face was starting to get red. Miller and Harry ~~both~~ stood up.

'What? You both want to go boxing with me?' Weaver spluttered, trying to remain upright.

'You're going to get lifted in a minute, Stan,' Miller said. 'You don't want to start off retirement in a holding cell, do you?'

'Who do you think you're talking to, Miller? I worked

with your dad. He was a real copper. Not like you bunch of pen-pushers.'

Harry put a hand on his arm. 'Come on, Stan, you've had enough.'

'Take your fucking hand off me. I don't need you to tell me how much I've had to drink.' Weaver pulled his arm away and staggered back out. As the door opened, they could see another man waiting for him. The man looked in and then the door shut quickly. Charlie Meekle.

They sat back down.

'He'd better not be waiting for me outside, Frank, thinking he's got Meekle for company and they can set about me. I've had my fair share of fighting dirty coppers and that pair of bastards will get it, big time.'

Miller put a hand on Harry's arm. 'Weaver couldn't fight his way out of a wet paper bag right now. I don't think they want to go fighting. If they do, they're both finished.'

'Aye, you're right.'

'Well, don't you boys know how to show a girl a good time. I feel like I was auditioning for a new series of *The Sopranos – UK Style*.' Alex smiled and sipped her G and T.

'Stick around. I'm sure there's going to be more.'

'I do like a bit of cabaret. And something to eat. Either of you boys fancy buying a girl a bag of nuts?'

'You're a cheap date.' Harry stood up. 'If this was a date. Which it's clearly not. I just meant –'

'Dry roasted, Harry, please,' she said, grinning.

'That was a lot of fluff you told me about Weaver letting you call him *Stan*, wasn't it?'

'Yes, Harry.'

'I bloody well knew it.'

She laughed as Harry made his way to the bar.

THIRTEEN

Peter Hanson pulled into the terminus at Balerno and checked the bus was empty of passengers. It was.

He belched as he rubbed his stomach. Fucking fish supper. They were getting more expensive and the portions smaller. He knew he should hit the gym, but he couldn't be arsed. One week of earlies alternating with a week of the midday shift or backshift. It was hard to get into a routine. That was his excuse anyway.

He opened the back door of the bus and kicked an empty Coke can off. The damn thing had been rattling about there for hours. Those messy pigs couldn't just take their own shite home, could they? He would ban half of them from coming on.

His old man had been a bus driver too, before he croaked it. Hanson smiled as he remembered some of the stories his dad had told him. Back in the day, the coffin dodgers would all be lined up at a bus stop, then a voice from one of the control inspectors would come over the airwaves, telling them it was nine a.m. This was the time the pensioners could come on and put twenty pence in the hopper to use with their bus pass. Not a minute before nine, nor a minute after five, in order to let the workers get on. His old man would get to a stop close to nine and they would be like cattle trying to get on, and he would open the door and shout to them it wasn't nine yet. He wouldn't let them on. Instead, he would shut the door and drive off, seconds before the inspector announced the time over the radio, letting the old folks rage at him.

Hanson didn't think he could do that, but his old man was a right bastard. He had pulled his bus over outside Ocean Terminal one night on the backshift, told one of the passengers he didn't feel well and promptly had a massive heart attack. He was dead by the time the ambulance crew got there.

Hanson wasn't going to be in the job long enough to drop down at the wheel of a bus. He was going to get himself into Police Scotland and his girlfriend was going to help him. Even if it meant him being a special constable first. That was always a way of getting in the back door.

If his girlfriend could do it, then so could he. He sat down on one of the seats and took his mobile phone out and called her number. No answer. He tried the house number. Nothing. Nada. Zip. Fuck all. He wondered if she was getting it from one of the neighbours or something.

Fucking bitch.

She'd better not be out drinking with her pals again. Hanson had warned her about that. Drinking during the week with that Julie one. She was a bad influence. Well, he would just have to do something about that.

He heard a knock at the front of the bus. He put his phone away. Fuck sake, there was still another ten minutes before he was due to leave; they couldn't stand outside?

He got up as the knocking started getting louder.

'I'm coming,' Hanson said, imagining himself in a police uniform and taking his baton out to the person who was knocking on the door.

FOURTEEN

Aileen Rogers was standing outside The Dining Room restaurant down on Commercial Street when she heard the ding coming from her phone.

'Please don't tell me you've got cold feet,' she said in a whisper. She took the phone out and had a look at the screen.

Do you mind if we change plans slightly? I'd rather eat somewhere else if you don't mind. I'll explain in two minutes. Just round the corner. I'm waiting. Get a taxi and I'll give you the money. It's going to be worth it!

She felt a chill wind rushing along the wide, long street. It used to be filled with distilleries or something, but now it had businesses, including this new restaurant. *Fuck.* She'd told Janice they were coming here, and now that they weren't on speaking terms, if Janice found out, she would have a bloody good laugh at that. Aileen could imagine her so-called friend now: *Where did he take you? McDonalds?*

She sent off a quick text. *Where will I tell the taxi to go?*

Harvey's. It's just along from Malmaison. Just tell him to drop you off at Malmaison – he might not know Harvey's.

B right thr. xxx

A taxi came along a couple of minutes later. Even though Malmaison was just round the corner, Buddy was concerned about her safety and didn't want her to walk. What a gentleman! Drew would have had her walking.

'It's not a big fare, but I'll give you a decent tip,' she told the driver. 'My boyfriend just wants me to be safe.'

'No problem, love. The small trips add up at the end of the day.'

He drove along Commercial Street, turned left onto The Shore and drove down to the end where the hotel was. She handed him some notes.

'Thanks, love,' the driver said.

She got out and the black cab rattled away. There were some people about but nothing like it would be at the weekend. Then her heart sank. What the hell?

Opposite the hotel was Harvey's restaurant. And it was closed.

'Boy, do I feel like an idiot,' she heard a voice say behind her, then she felt a hand on her shoulder and she gasped and spun round.

A man was standing smiling at her. 'Aileen?'

'Buddy?'

'The one and only. But my name's Theo. I had to be sure you were genuine. No offence. I just got here. The taxi driver didn't know Harvey's had closed down.'

He held out his hand for her to shake. She felt his strong hand in hers. His smile showed perfect teeth.

'There are other places.'

'Indeed there are, Aileen. I was thinking about the floating restaurant down there, the Blue Martini.'

'Oh, I've heard of that, but I've never been.'

'It keeps the riff-raff out. Shall we?' He held out an arm for her to hook hers through, and they walked through the cool evening air to one of the boats moored on the Water of Leith.

Two doormen stood at the canopy at the end of the walkway that led up onto the boat. Aileen wondered briefly if they were going to have any trouble getting on, but Theo was dressed in a suit and looked immaculate, with his beard neatly trimmed and his hair combed into a fashionable style.

She saw him smile at the two men. 'Gentlemen, good evening.'

The men were used to sizing up people in a heartbeat and one of them smiled at him. 'Good evening, sir, madam.'

Theo indicated for Aileen to go up first. She smiled and thanked him. Drew would never have done that.

Inside, the bar was cosy. Background music played, but

not some of that rubbish they played nowadays. This was just setting the ambience of the place.

Theo led her over to the restaurant entrance and a maître d' smiled and showed them to a table overlooking the river.

They ordered drinks and looked at the menu.

'I can't believe we're meeting like this,' Aileen said.

'It's a good thing, though, yes?'

'Of course.' She reached a hand over and put it on his. 'I've been stuck with a husband who treats me like dirt for a long time. I needed to meet somebody who appreciates me. You know, when I was talking to you online, I felt that I'd known you for years.'

'I feel the same way.'

They ordered food and talked and laughed. Aileen hadn't felt so comfortable in a long time.

'What do you normally do for fun?' Theo asked her.

'Fun? I don't know the meaning of the word. I don't have fun anymore. Not with Drew anyway. I do meet up with a little group once a week. That's about as exciting as my life gets.'

'What sort of group? No, let me guess: the Circus Clown Appreciation Society?'

She laughed. 'Is there such a thing?'

'I have no idea. But you haven't said yay or nay.'

'It's a little drama group. We put on plays and the like. Just for fun.'

'Do tell me more!' Theo said. 'This is so exciting.'

'It's just for fun. But there's nothing like the rush you get when you're up on the stage in front of people, complete strangers who are enthralled by our performances.'

'That is indeed an achievement. I wouldn't have the guts to stand up on a stage and give it yahoo. I'd be shaking like a leaf.'

'I'm sure you would be fine under pressure.'

You don't even know the half of it. He smiled at her.

'I'd like to use the ladies', if you'll excuse me.'

'I'll be here.'

They were sitting at a corner table and the lighting was very atmospheric. Theo took a little vial of powder out and quickly poured it into Aileen's drink.

She came back and they drank and laughed.

The waiter brought Theo a steak, well done, while Aileen had chicken parmesan.

And yet, even by the end of the meal, Aileen still didn't know much about Theo. But she planned to change that. Drew was out with his friends and she thought it would be exciting to take Theo home with her.

He had other ideas.

They walked back round to where he had met her. It was dark now and colder.

'Can I give you a lift?' he said.

'That would be fabulous,' she replied, but then she stopped. 'I thought you said you came here in a taxi?'

'I have to confess, it was a white lie. I wasn't sure how this would go tonight. I've been out with a few women, but most of them were...a disappointment. Undesirables.' He made a face and smiled, putting up a hand. 'I'm not saying I thought you were like that, but if things didn't go smoothly, I could just get in my car without offering you a lift, as you'd have thought I came here in a taxi.'

'I never thought of that,' she said, her smile slipping. 'I thought we knew each other well enough, although we've only talked online.'

'Please don't be offended, Aileen. I get on with anybody and like to have a good time, but some of those women weren't who they said they were. I'm guilty of trusting somebody right off the bat. You included. But this is just a safety net.' He smiled, stepped closer and took her hands and gently kissed her on the lips.

She looked around to see what car he was driving and saw a white van.

'I have an idea,' Theo said, 'and please feel free to say no, but would you like to come home to my place and have a drink or two?'

Aileen sucked in a breath and practically hauled the van door off its hinges. 'Would I?' She jumped in the van eagerly.

Theo had once had a boyhood friend with a glass eye, and they had all teased him about it, saying it was made of wood. *Wood Eye.* Aileen's comment made him think of his friend, now a distant memory, separated by time and life.

'No funny business, I promise,' he said, getting into the driver's seat.

'No funny business? I was counting on funny business.' She laughed and started to mumble. 'I'm...such a lightweight when...it comes to drink.'

'Luckily, I haven't had too much. Well, let's go then.' He smiled and squirmed inwardly at her banging his van door shut. This wasn't a classic Jag – not a classic anything really – but it was his.

Aileen yacked on as they drove from Leith up Ferry Road, and down Warriston Road. He stopped outside the side gate of the cemetery.

Aileen's vision was so blurred, she could hardly see. The world was swimming around her. 'Are we there?'

'Yes. There's the gate to my house,' he said, laughing inwardly.

They left the van and walked through the gate. 'Up this way. I want you to meet somebody,' Theo said, and Aileen started walking. 'When we were talking online, you said you were very unhappy with your husband.'

'I am. I haven't been happy for a long time.' She was slurring her words now and holding on to him for dear life.

'Then I am the man to solve your problems. I am here to make you happy. You see, sometimes when people are unhappy, they just don't know where to turn.'

'I know.' They were walking side by side, and she turned to smile at him. 'I know I'm going to be in a happier place.'

'Oh, you are. I can guarantee it.'

They were walking along the track and Theo dropped back slightly.

'Don't keep me in suspense,' Aileen said. 'Who am I going to meet?' Her eyes were practically rolling.

'Your maker,' Theo said, and brought the hammer down on the back of her head.

FIFTEEN

'It's good to see you smile,' DS Julie Stott said to Steffi Walker.

'I'll second that,' said DS Hazel Carter. The two detectives raised their glasses to Steffi.

'It's being out with you two drunken reprobates that makes me smile,' Steffi said, grinning. They clinked glasses.

'I've just felt a bit down recently,' she said.

'We're always here to lend an ear,' Hazel said, and then she smiled even more when the door to Logie Baird's opened and in walked Kate Murphy.

'Ladies, let me get a round in,' Kate said, eyeing up their glasses.

'I won't argue with that, Kate,' Hazel replied.

Returning from the bar, Kate sat down with the drinks.

'Having a drink on a Monday night. Rock 'n' roll lifestyle or what?'

'Andy let you out then?' Julie said.

'Indeed he did. He says I should get what you Scots lassies call *blootered*.'

'It doesn't sound the same with a London accent,' Hazel said, laughing.

'Hey, I'm trying!' They all laughed. 'But Andy doesn't complain when I go out without him. He knows which one of us cuts up people for a living.'

'Who's got the kids, Hazel?' Julie asked.

'Bruce and his wife.' Hazel held up a hand. 'I know, he went through the mill, but he's fine now. And his wife is great.'

'And the kids are okay staying over?' Kate said.

'They are. Bruce will make sure they get to school okay in the morning.'

The next couple of hours passed in a flash, and at the same time a woman was stepping into a cemetery, Steffi Walker was stepping into a taxi.

'Logie Green Road,' she told the driver.

It was straight down Broughton Street and round the corner to her flat, which was accessed by walking through the stairwell and out through the back door.

There were only two flats here, one on either side of the door. The automatic light came on and she had her key out.

She opened the door, knowing she wasn't going to be disturbing Peter as he was on the backshift.

She got in, and before she had a chance to put the hallway light on, a figure stepped out of the bedroom.

SIXTEEN

'Carruthers Wellington?' Adrian Jackson said, turning back from the living room window in his nephew's flat. It was in one of the new apartment blocks built on the old Royal Infirmary site. It overlooked The Meadows park, which sat between there and Marchmont. Loved by muggers everywhere after darkness fell, which it now had.

Brian shrugged. His live-in girlfriend – Rita Mellon, older than Brian – looked at Jackson and gently shook her head in an *I told him* way.

'Carruthers Wellington?' Jackson said again. 'What kind of fucking name is that?'

'Look, hang fire, okay?' Brian said. 'Sit down and I'll explain.'

'Sit down? Are you sure? Just in case the old gin-swilling bastard falls over? Stop being so fucking antisocial and get me a drink. And none of that watered-down pish you give to everybody else. Get the good stuff out for your uncle before he puts his walking cane round your head.'

Jackson had already taken off his signature bowler hat. He sat down on one of the leather settees and looked across at the woman. 'Rita, please. I rely on you to keep our Brian on the straight and narrow.'

'I told him, Adrian. I said, what kind of a stupid name is that? Investments are supposed to be low-key. But does he listen?'

'Clearly not.' Jackson looked over at Brian, who was standing at the drinks cabinet with his back to the room. 'If you're slipping something into my whisky, you know things won't end well, don't you?'

'Jesus, Adrian, I'm not trying to kill you. The most I do is put laxatives in chocolate. But not for you.'

'I'll have somebody put something in you if you ever do that to me.' Jackson reached out, took the glass of whisky and sniffed it.

'You know I love you, Adrian. I would never –'

Jackson held up a hand. 'That's enough of that pish. Just tell me what's happening now.'

'Right, it's too late to change my name, because they know me down there. But it doesn't matter. We're getting a two hundred per cent return on our money, but more importantly, we have fifty per cent royalties on merchandise. I had the accountants go over it and we stand to make a small fortune.

Plus, the solicitors have made sure we're the only investors for the next two series.'

Jackson sipped his whisky and smiled. 'That's my boy. I can't believe they didn't make further series last time round. But we'll make sure they do this time.' He put the glass on the table. 'Let's talk about the elephant in the room.'

Brian looked over at Rita. 'That's not very nice. And she can hear you.'

'Cheeky sod.' Rita glared at him. 'He's not talking about me!'

'I'm just kidding.' Brian was smiling, but the other two knew he wasn't joking.

'The elephant in the room is this woman they found murdered in the cemetery where the production is taking place,' Jackson clarified.

'The production crew are worried, of course, but there's no talk of stopping,' Brian said, taking some of his whisky.

'There bloody well better not be any talk of stopping. I've sunk a lot of money into this and production is indeed going on. Remember one thing: I have other business partners and they won't be happy. Robert Molloy especially, although Kerry Hamilton is also a fierce one when she gets going. So if there is any restlessness among the ranks, let's quash it right away.'

'I think we could use it to our advantage,' Rita said. 'Everybody likes a bit of controversy. Or some ghoulish goings-on. We can capitalise on a woman being murdered right where the filming is taking place by advertising the fact. Something like, "Filmed where a real-life murder took place." That could be on the DVD packaging.'

'That's brilliant, Rita!' Jackson said, picking his glass up again. He finished the whisky. 'Let's have lunch tomorrow. We can put our heads together and see what else we can come up with.'

'What about me?' said Brian.

'Sorry, boy, I don't dine with anybody called Carruthers.' Jackson stood up. 'I'll come round about twelve. Wear something expensive. We're going to be eating somewhere upmarket.'

One of his bodyguards was waiting in the hallway outside the door. Jackson had spent twenty-five years in an American prison and he never took his safety for granted.

Especially now that there was a murderer running around.

SEVENTEEN

Fight or flight. Steffi Walker hadn't shirked away from a fight at any time in her job as an army combat medic, nor during her police career so far, and she wasn't going to back down from a fight in her own home.

She slapped the hallway light on, prepared to have a go with the man who had just come out of her bedroom.

'Peter! What are you doing?' she said, relaxing as she saw her boyfriend standing there.

'Where the hell have *you* been?' he said, walking across the hall into the living room.

It was a small flat, with the kitchen off the back of the living room. He headed in there and poured himself a whisky, but by the looks of him, he already had a head start.

'Why are you home so early?' she asked him. 'You weren't supposed to finish your shift until after midnight.'

'So you went out gallivanting? I thought you'd be in. I called from the Balerno terminus and got no answer. I was worried sick. So I called control and they sent a replacement driver.'

'I told you days ago I was going out with some of my colleagues.'

'I don't remember that. But is it too much to ask you to stay in when I'm working?'

'It is, yes.'

He was quick. She didn't see the back-handed slap coming. His hand connected with the side of her face. Then he pushed her hard sideways and her head hit the doorjamb of the small kitchen.

She lifted her hand, but he reached out and grabbed her by the hair and banged her head against the doorframe again, harder this time.

'You forget I was in the army too, bitch.'

'Let me go!' she yelled, but her vision was out of focus and she was finding it hard to think.

'Or else what? What is little Steffi Walker going to do about it?'

He jerked her head down further now, and she could feel the blood running from her cut lip. She couldn't speak.

'I didn't think so. Bitch!'

He threw her down onto the floor and kicked her hard in the stomach. She gasped, trying to scream, but the pain was the last thing on her mind: he'd kicked her so hard she couldn't take a breath and she started spluttering, thinking she was going to die.

'I'm going out and I won't be back tonight,' Peter snarled, standing over her and pulling a coat on. 'You think about what you did tonight. You understand?'

She didn't answer him, still struggling to breathe.

'I said, do you understand?' he screamed.

She nodded and he kicked her a few more times, on the legs, on the back, on her arm. Then he simply turned and left.

At that moment in time Steffi was more frightened than she'd ever been abroad, serving with the British army. She thought she was going to die in the doorway of her kitchen, the one her dad had helped her finish. In that second, she thought about calling him, but then her brain kicked into gear and she remembered he was dead.

She had nobody in the world now, and she was going to die alone. She'd be with her dad soon.

After what seemed an age, she managed to take a breath. There *was* one person she could call.

Slowly, she tried to get her mobile phone out of her pocket and she finally managed it. The device was on the floor and dazedly she managed to get the contacts page open.

Steffi hit the dial button and got her finger on the speaker button, just before she passed out.

She didn't hear the voice at the other end calling her name.

EIGHTEEN

Harry McNeil woke up with an uneasy feeling. Nothing he could put his finger on right away. He realised what was wrong when he had showered and was making coffee.

He was in his own flat and he'd missed a call from Vanessa.

He had assumed she would know he had come here when he didn't turn up at her place, though of course no one would have known had he been abducted by aliens on the way home. He'd have been poked and probed by the time anybody realised he was missing.

He poured a coffee and debated whether to wet some cardboard and pour milk on it or eat the bran stuff Vanessa had bought him. Either one had merits as they both tasted the same, but at least the bran had some raisins in it.

'Vanessa,' he said into the phone, talking to the voicemail.

'I just came here last night as I'd had a few pints. Call you later.' He hesitated, wondering if he should add 'Love you' to the message, but didn't in case somebody else heard it, and he ended the call.

Another uneasy feeling, like he got when he had to go to the dentist after procrastinating and the prospect of saving the tooth was anywhere between *We'll do our best* and *This is going to hurt me more than it's going to hurt you.*

Vanessa was pissed off at him – that was clear. He got up from the little table in the living room and pulled the net curtain aside, like an old woman trying to avoid the people selling religion who were coming to the door. He could see Vanessa's house across the other side of the bowling green, and her car was gone.

He sat back down and finished the cereal. He was sure she would call later, probably at the most inappropriate time.

He was about to leave when his phone rang. 'Vanessa?' he said, thinking that she was maybe using the office phone as her name hadn't come up on the caller ID.

'It's me, Harry.'

'Who is this?'

'Alex. I told you last night I'd pick you up to drive you to work. I'm sitting downstairs.'

'Okay. I'll be right down.' God, that was all he needed, some young woman coming to his flat. Tongues would no doubt be wagging.

He checked the mirror after brushing his teeth. His tie

didn't look like a dog had chewed it first. He nodded his approval and made his way outside. It was chillier, but the sun was trying to get out of its pit, while the wind was skelping the arse off some clouds. No doubt it would be snowing by lunchtime. Welcome to May in Edinburgh.

He looked around for Alex, realising he didn't know what kind of car she drove. Then she honked the car horn. She had rolled down the driver's window of a shiny little BMW and was waving to him.

Christ, all I need now is for Vanessa to come booting round the corner and see me and I'm toast. He didn't wave back, electing instead to duck slightly and pretend he didn't know Alex until he slipped into the passenger seat.

'Why don't you get one of those clown car horns? I'm sure some of the neighbours round the corner didn't hear you.'

'Good morning to you too,' DS Alex Maxwell said, all smiley and bouncy, like he was taking her out on her first driving lesson. 'Is that what your girlie CR-V has? A clown car horn?'

'It's my wife's car, Sergeant,' he said, buckling up. '*My* car's in the garage.'

'Oh yeah? What do you drive?'

'Never mind what I drive. That's not part of the inspector's exam, which you should be more concerned with,' he said as she drove off. The car had a new-car smell.

'There's not much chance of promotion when you land in the cold case unit.' She turned onto Comely Bank Road.

'I wasn't too pished last night, was I?'

'I have no idea. I finished my drink while you stayed with Frank –'

'DI Miller,' Harry interrupted.

'...and I was in bed by eleven. You, I can't account for.'

'I found Weaver. He was waiting across the road for me, full of apologies, slavering about how he hadn't meant it. I didn't have a drink with him. I told him to go home and sober up.' He turned to look at her as she drove through Stockbridge. 'What was he like to work with? I mean, I know him from going to the pub, but I only briefly worked with him in the past. What was he like on a day-to-day basis?'

'Stan was okay. He was a stickler for the rules.' She briefly looked at him. 'He liked a drink, though.'

'You ever see him drink on duty?'

'No. And would I have dropped him in it if I had? No, I wouldn't. We have to trust one another, Harry, and shopping your boss to Standards doesn't get you a *Blue Peter* badge.'

'You're too young to remember that show.'

'There's always YouTube. When all else fails, there's always YouTube. And Netflix when your next-door neighbour gives you his password.'

She pulled into the car park at the side of HQ. 'Your girlfriend giving you a hard time? Tell me to mind my own business if you want.'

'Mind your own business.'

'Aw, come on. I'm not a gossip. I just feel that we should get to know each other better.'

'Why? You going to name your firstborn after me?'

She laughed. 'You already know about me, don't you? You know I turn thirty in a few weeks. You can come to my party. Maybe we should have a joint birthday party, with you being the big four-oh soon.'

'I'll be celebrating mine by taking Vanessa out for a nice meal.'

'No big party?' she asked as they walked across to the entrance.

'Again, none of your business.'

'If you do have your own party, I'll come along, and I promise I won't spoil it by telling everybody it's nearly my birthday.'

'This is two mornings in a row I've come to work with a headache. I'm begging you to stop talking now.'

She laughed as they walked along the corridor. 'If you put a tenner in the kitty, you can help yourself to a coffee in the incident room.'

'I'll get one from the canteen and see you up there.'

'I take sugar in mine,' she said with a smile.

'I don't care what you take. Go put a tenner in the kitty.'

He went into the canteen and tried calling Vanessa again – not that he wanted to smack of desperation, but the suspense of not knowing whether she was pissed off at him was killing him. He knew he would come out with some flannel about having gone home to his place because he didn't want to disturb her.

He took the coffee upstairs.

DC Simon Gregg had lifted a whiteboard off the floor.

Jesus, here we go again.

'Day two of the workplace Olympics try-out?' he said.

Gregg looked puzzled for a second. 'I'm just moving the whiteboard over here, sir.'

'Right.' Harry took his jacket off and sat at a desk. 'Where's DCI Weaver?'

'He's not here.'

'I can see that, Simon. Anybody know where he is?'

None of them did. 'Great. Willie, why don't you give me a rundown before DS Maxwell and I have to go up the high street.'

Young flipped through some papers on the desk before him. 'We went through the witness statements from back then. They all said Jill talked about having a boyfriend but didn't give a name. They thought she was making it up, even when she told them she was pregnant.'

'And Jill's parents?'

'Divorced. They moved away shortly after their daughter's death.'

'We can talk to them later, if it comes to that,' Alex said.

Harry drank some of his coffee. 'Any results from the DNA that was sent to the lab?'

'Not yet,' came the reply from DI Karen Shiels.

Harry felt his headache start up a boot-thumping dance in his head. He took a packet of painkillers out of his pocket and washed two down with some coffee.

'Out on the lash last night, sir?' Gregg said.

'"Out on the lash" is reserved for young blokes like you. I prefer to have a few sociable beers.'

'You're not that old. What are you, early forties?'

Harry ran through the gamut of expletives, but wanted to keep his blood pressure down for the sake of the headache. The boot thumping had already started and he didn't want to introduce the orchestra.

'Thirty-nine.'

'Oh, right.' Gregg looked at Harry for a moment like he was waiting for the punchline, but when none came, he turned away.

Not even had the decency to pull a fucking beamer, Harry thought, about to roast him but chucked his empty coffee cup in the nearest bin instead.

'I think it's time we got up to the high street, sir,' Alex said, tapping her watch.

Just like Vanessa would have been tapping her watch last night, no doubt, if he'd actually made it back to her place. *What time do you call this?*

'Right. We'll report back with any findings we have,' Harry said as Alex led the way out.

'You want me to drive?' she asked him as they crossed the car park through a chill wind.

'Silly question, Sergeant. Do I look like I could manoeuvre a pool car through traffic without us having to write an incident report at the end of our shift?'

'That's true.'

They got into a scabby Ford that smelled of fish and chips and sweaty socks.

'God knows what goes on in these cars,' he said, cracking a window.

'Surveillance, I think.'

'They eat from the chippie, then do a bit of Morris dancing or something?'

'It's the "or something" that worries me.' Alex drove through Stockbridge, up Frederick Street towards George Street.

'Still not spilling on the home situation?' she said with a cheeky grin.

'There's nothing to spill, Sergeant, and keep your eyes on the bloody road.'

'I told you all about my ex and how we bought a flat together. Fair's fair, Harry.'

'It's DCI McNeil for you from now on. Giving me that spiel about how Weaver let you all call him Stan. I'm surprised you didn't embellish it by telling me he bought you all a drink on a Friday.'

She made a face like she should have thought of that, but said nothing. 'Anyway, I just wanted to say, if you ever want to talk –'

'I don't.'

'Let me finish. I was going to say, if you ever want to talk, you can sod off and bore somebody else with it.'

He looked at her for a moment before she laughed. 'Should have seen your face,' she said, heading over Princes Street and up The Mound.

'No wonder Weaver wanted to retire. I'm sure it was a toss-up between that and an early grave.'

They parked in the car park behind the station and walked in through the back door.

'Do you miss this place?' Alex asked.

'No, not really. I can hardly say it was on a par with a funfair.'

'Or visiting a brothel.'

He shook his head. 'Do me a favour: before you get to work tomorrow, make sure you've taken your meds.'

'That sort of remark could land you in front of HR. Or Professional Standards.'

He was looking at her back and couldn't see her face. Then she turned and smiled at him.

He held up a hand. 'Don't tell me: *should've seen your face.*'

NINETEEN

Miller woke up feeling that somehow he'd gone to bed the night before and somebody had broken his neck in his sleep. He was in a chair. He managed to move his head to one side and saw a figure lying in the bed to the side of him.

Light was shining in from behind the blinds. He didn't know where he was.

He gently moved his head from side to side, easing the stiffness, and then he remembered: Steffi!

He got up and used the bathroom. A nurse had said there was a room that was used for families who needed to stay overnight and had let him sleep there, promising to come and get him should things change. She had given him a travel toothbrush and a little tube of toothpaste. He just needed a coffee to function. He found one down in the canteen.

'How's she doing, Doc?' Miller asked as he came back

onto the ward. He felt chilled inside even though it wasn't cold in the hospital.

'She's bruised and has a slight concussion, which is bad enough, but I was told there was blood on a doorjamb, so we're working on the assumption that her head was hit against that. She was lucky. I've seen worse brain damage from a lesser strike. She's going to hurt for a while, and I want her kept in for a couple of days for observation. But again, she was very lucky. This time.'

'She's going to be alright, though, isn't she? Long term, I mean.'

'I'd put money on it, though nobody can ever say a hundred per cent. But yes, I'd say so. She had a severe beating, but nothing is broken and the bruises will heal. I can't speak for the mental scars.'

'Can I go and see her?' Miller said.

'Not too long. She's still in pain.' The doctor walked away.

Miller walked along to Steffi's room and found her sitting up, attached to a drip. There was a bandage round her head and she was hooked up to a monitor too.

'I thought I looked bad until you came in,' Steffi said, her voice raspy.

'Jesus, Steffi,' Miller said, looking at her.

'Nice to see you too.' She looked at him. 'No, it really is.' Then she started crying.

'Come here, you big girl,' he said and went over to the

bed. He hugged her as best he could before gently pulling away.

She sniffed and took the paper hanky Miller had handed to her from a box by her bed.

'What happened, Steffi?' he asked her.

'It was something over nothing. It's not a big deal.'

'Of course it is. You called me, and if you hadn't, God knows what would have happened.'

'I'm not pressing charges, Frank. I can't.'

He leaned closer. 'Who was it?' He knew, but he needed her to tell him.

'It was Peter, of course. You already knew that. But listen, he was just upset that I was out and didn't hear him calling from the Balerno terminus. He was worried.'

'Has he ever done this before?'

She swallowed like her throat was getting dry and Miller poured her a little glass of water. She tentatively took it and swallowed some. 'Yes,' she said, putting the glass down.

'How often, Steffi?'

'He just has a bit of a temper, that's all. It's the stress of driving the bus all the time. You know, people shouting at him, threatening him. He doesn't mean it.'

'Stress?' Miller said. 'Just like our job?' His muscles tensed with anger.

'He'll be fine when he's on the force with us, I'm sure. He said we knocked him back before, but he's got it all under control now.'

'He wants to be a copper?'

Steffi nodded. 'He's ex-army, like me. He'd be good in uniform.'

Miller put a hand on hers. 'You rest. I'll post a couple of officers at your door.'

'There's no need.'

'That was an FYI. It's happening, Sergeant.'

When two uniforms appeared, Miller said goodbye to Steffi and stepped out of the room. He spoke to the uniforms before he left. 'You do not, under any circumstances, let her boyfriend near her. He tried to kill her last night.'

Both men stood up straighter, maybe at the prospect of giving Hanson a lobotomy with an extendable baton.

A fucking copper? Miller thought as he made his way along the corridor. *Over my dead body.*

He knew Steffi was making excuses for Hanson. It was the classic domestic violence syndrome. Miller called his wife at home.

'It's out of her hands now. That went beyond a domestic last night. That was assaulting a police officer. Maybe attempted murder, if we can get Norma Banks on board,' he said.

Miller knew his mother-in-law, a procurator fiscal, could throw the book at Hanson.

'I'll talk to her, Frank. Just make sure Steffi's safe.'

TWENTY

They were in Kelty, a twenty-minute drive up the motorway, which would have taken longer, Harry thought, if Alex hadn't been driving like Stirling Moss.

'This isn't your fancy wee German sports car you're in,' he'd said, sure his life had flashed before his eyes a few times on the way up.

'We'd have been here even quicker if it had been,' she'd replied, smirking.

'If you were my daughter, you'd be bloody well grounded by now. No pub, no phone, no nothing.'

'I'm a first-class driver.'

'Says who?'

'Says me.'

'Did you read that in your horoscope this morning?'

Harry stretched his back. Not only did the pool car stink, it had all the comfort of Fred Flintstone's car.

His son also lived in Kelty, a few streets away, and the thought of his boy not living with him anymore made him wish he'd been a better husband.

His phone rang as he stood out on the pavement, looking down at a corner shop near the roundabout, where a few ne'er-do-wells with hoodies on were eyeing up the car. He prayed they would nick it.

'Harry? It's Frank Miller. We've got another shout to go down to Warriston Cemetery. We have a second victim.'

'Jesus. Under a gravestone?' He waited while Miller spoke to somebody, his voice muffled now as if he had put the phone against his jacket.

'No, different this time. I'll explain when you get back. Can you come over here when you're done with that woman?'

'Will do.' Harry hung up, the wind ruffling his hair. Kelty was a windy town, just off the motorway and exposed to the elements.

'Bad news?' Alex asked as Harry knocked on the woman's door and waited for a response. They'd called ahead to make sure she would be in and she'd promised she would.

'What gave it away? Me saying "under a gravestone"?'

'Just asking. And if she offers us Tunnock's Teacakes with a cuppa and there's only one, I'm going to eat it. And I hope there're only rich teas left for you.'

'Your father obviously spared the rod, but yes, it's bad news. There's another victim in the cemetery. DI Miller wouldn't go into details.'

'I wonder why Frank's keeping things close to his chest?'

'It's *DI Miller* to you. How many bloody times do I have to tell you?'

'Sorry, Harry.'

'Jesus.'

This flat was in a block of four, with the door on the outside, up a short flight of concrete steps. The woman answered the door and pulled her cardigan closed, as if the chill wind was ever-present.

'You're a hard woman to track down,' Harry said.

'I got married after...well, you know...'

Harry nodded his head, indicating that he did indeed know.

'Come in,' Mrs Dignan said, stepping back.

Harry and Alex stepped over the threshold and immediately went up a short flight of stairs into the flat proper.

'Would you like some tea and biscuits?' the woman asked.

'Yes, please, that would be great,' Alex said.

'I hope it's all rich teas,' Harry whispered to Alex. 'That would teach you.'

'I hope you like custard creams?' Mrs Dignan said a few minutes later, coming in with a tray.

'You shouldn't have gone to the trouble,' Alex said, not meaning it and looking at the plate to see if there was a teacake lurking there that had maybe fallen out of the box, but there were only custard creams.

Harry took the coffee and added milk. 'How long have you been using the name Dignan? If you don't mind me asking.'

'I stopped being Mrs Thompson four years after Jill died. Our marriage didn't survive. It died the day Jill did. Although Charlie and I weren't married in the traditional sense. Jill's real father died before she was born, and then I met Charlie. Jill was born two months after I met him, but he brought her up as his own. That's why I had the name Thompson and he was Meekle. But we were husband and wife in every other sense, even though we hadn't signed a piece of paper.' She sipped her cup of tea, ignoring the biscuits.

'I'm sorry to dredge up the past,' Harry said as Alex palmed a biscuit like a magician and ate it quietly.

'I figured you would be coming round again after I saw it on the news about that poor girl.' Mrs Dignan looked at them both in turn. 'I'll do anything I can to help you catch whoever did this.'

'Thank you.'

'You don't think it's the same man who killed Jill, do you?'

'All we're working on right now is that the manner of death is similar. We can't rule anything out at this point.' Out of the corner of his eye, Harry caught Alex catching some crumbs in her hand. *What are you going to do with them?* he wondered. Then she answered his unasked question by swiping them onto the tray.

'We know Jill was pregnant at the time of her death,' Alex said, as if 'the big crumb incident' hadn't happened. 'Do you know if she had a regular boyfriend back then?'

'Good God, no!' Mrs Dignan answered, and Alex wondered for a second if she was protesting about the disposal of the crumbs. 'No, she would never have had a boyfriend at that age. I know some girls do, but not Jill.'

Alex softened her voice as she carried on. 'Mrs Dignan, I know this must be hard for you, but Jill was obviously seeing a boy. Did you ever hear any of her friends talking about him?'

Dignan took a deep breath and let it out. 'No. I never really had much to do with her friends. I wasn't the *cool* mum. They all liked to hang out at that other house. The one where anything goes. I hated her going there, but it only caused a fight when I protested, so most of the time I said nothing, just to keep the peace.'

'What house was this?' Harry asked.

'The one near the park, on the other side of the walkway. The Balfour house.'

'Graham Balfour's house?'

'The same one. I did not like that boy at all. He was a weirdo.'

Still is, Harry thought but kept it to himself. 'Why would Jill go there?'

'Because of the Balfour girl. She was their leader, the one

they all wanted to hang out with. They would go to her house and do God knows what. I smelled smoke on Jill a few times, so I think the Balfour girl encouraged them to smoke.'

'Do you think that Graham Balfour could have been the boy she went with?' Alex asked.

'I doubt it. He was one of those boys who was borderline mental' She looked at the two detectives, as if saying the word out loud would be cause for them to put her in handcuffs. 'I know we're not supposed to use that word anymore, but it's true. He was. He acted like he was daft. I hated Jill going near him and warned her not to, unless the sister was there.'

'Did he ever touch Jill, to the best of your knowledge?' Harry asked.

'No, not that I know of. I think she would have told me. But that little Balfour besom would have encouraged Jill to go with a boy, I'm sure.'

'Did Jill ever mention anything about going to watch the filming in the cemetery?' Alex asked.

'Did she ever! I can't remember who was in that stupid show – some smarmy sod who shoved an old wig down his shirt front to make himself look macho. Made him look like a monkey more like.'

Harry flipped open a notebook and pretended to read from it. He didn't want Mrs Dignan to think he was a fan of the show, which he had been. He'd been in uniform at the time, but he'd been into sci-fi big time.

'Randy Kline?' he said, as if he'd just read his own notes.

'That was it!' Mrs Dignan said, snapping her fingers. 'Randy bloody Kline. What did he go on to do? Nothing. I haven't heard of him again, have you?'

'He went behind the camera. He's actually directing the remake of *God Complex*. So I heard, through the investigation,' Harry quickly added in case either woman thought he was a member of the Kline fan club.

'I don't know how old he was at the time, but he had to have been in his late twenties. Dirty bastard. If her father had thought for one moment that Kline had touched Jill, the only thing he would be directing now is his wheelchair.'

'He was twenty-four, according to the report I read,' Harry said.

'Same diff. He's still a dirty bastard.'

'Do you know if Jill ever had any direct contact with Kline?'

'I heard the girls whispering in Jill's room one evening, on one of the rare occasions they actually came over. Jill said she wanted to meet Kline soon.'

'Wanted to, or was going to?' Alex prompted.

'I think she was at the stage she just wanted to meet him in person, like she had a schoolgirl crush on him. I don't know if she ever did. But I told the police all this at the time.'

'I'll look for the original report,' Harry said.

'Have you spoken to Trisha Cornwall yet? I don't know if she got married, mind, so she might be going by another name, but they were good friends too.'

Harry looked at Alex before carrying on. 'No. Trisha's dead.'

'Oh, I'm sorry. She might have been able to throw more light on it. I know the police spoke to her at the time, but you know how you remember things much later.'

'I have people looking through the old reports.'

There wasn't much else Mrs Dignan could tell them, so they left.

Outside, the sun was out, but the persistent wind was still there, blowing Alex's blonde hair round her face as Mrs Dignan closed the door softly behind them.

'I can't believe you ate a biscuit,' Harry said as they walked down the short flight of stairs and got in the car.

'Why? I work out. I can burn it off.'

'Are you suggesting for one minute that I can't?'

'Of course you can, Harry.'

'I can.' He shook his head and put his seatbelt on. 'What do you make of this Kline guy?'

'I think you know more about him than you're letting on,' she said, starting the car. It rattled like a bag of spanners as she drove up the road. The car hadn't been touched while they were away; not even the neds had taken a fancy to it.

'I'm a fan of the show. I knew Kline was back directing, that's all. I saw his name in the report. He was questioned but was quickly ruled out.'

'Ruled out by who?'

'Probably his lawyer. Back then, Kline was a pretty big

deal, so his face was everywhere. In mags, on TV. If he was messing around with Jill, he must have been very careful about it.'

'Maybe he invited her into that caravan thingy they hang out in, in between takes.'

'The Americans call them trailers.'

'It's a fancy caravan. My mum and dad used to have one. Dad loved pissing off the drivers behind him when they drove up north.'

'Do they still drive it around?'

'Nah. They fly to Spain nowadays. Let somebody else do the driving.'

'Can't fault that logic. Now, I'm going to let you do the driving, back to Edinburgh, down to Warriston Cemetery. Grab something at the drive-through first. Harry's starving.'

'That's not going to be a thing, is it?'

'What?' he said as she got on the slip road for the M90.

'This talking-in-the-third-person stuff.'

'Harry doesn't want to talk about it.'

'You're annoying.'

He grinned at her. 'Harry doesn't seem to think so.'

TWENTY-ONE

The charred body hanging from the tree in the little walled-off section of the cemetery had been photographed and videotaped. The ground beneath the hanging corpse was burnt.

'This is worse than the last time,' DCI Weaver said, coming up behind them. DI Charlie Meekle was by his side, like an ever-present lapdog.

'He stopped at the one killing twenty years ago,' Harry said.

'I know that.' Weaver glowered at him.

'I wonder why this time round there's a second victim,' Frank Miller said. He'd seconded one of the other sergeants on his team to help while Steffi Walker was in hospital.

'Well, DI Miller, I know about this, as I was the lead investigator on the case twenty years ago. While you were running about in shorts. Did you read up on the last case?'

'I lived through it.'

Weaver looked puzzled. 'What?'

'I lived over there,' said Miller. 'I was only about ten or so when the girl was murdered here the last time.'

'Were you one of those wee bastards who used to climb up on the wall next to the caretaker's house and shout abuse at us?'

'I don't remember doing that. It was probably some of the older boys.'

'Aye, I'll bet.' Weaver turned his attention back to the woman, who was slowly being lowered down. Meekle stood close to him.

DI Maggie Parks walked over to Harry. 'There was a handbag on the ground nearby. The driving licence is for a female, so for now we'll assume it's her. Aileen Rogers is the name on the licence. The pathologist can confirm or deny later.'

'This is DI Meekle, up from Newcastle,' Harry said. 'I don't believe you've been introduced.'

'Good to meet you,' Maggie said without much enthusiasm.

'It's *sir*,' Meekle growled with his tough Glaswegian accent.

'This is DI Maggie Parks, pal,' said Harry. 'And if I ever hear you talk to her like that again, your arse will be put on a train back down south so fast there will be friction burns on the seat. Do you understand me?'

'I do indeed.' Meekle looked at Maggie. 'My apologies, Inspector. It won't happen again.'

Weaver looked at the DI but didn't say a word.

Miller looked at the charred figure, hanging from the tree by its neck. The sun was out, making the scene seem surreal.

'How come the rope isn't burnt?' Meekle said.

'It's a steel rope,' said Maggie.

'I was asking Miller there, to see if he knew.' Meekle turned to her with a smile. 'But getting you to answer for him is cheating. Just so you know.'

'Just keep your mind on the job, Meekle,' Harry said. 'And I want a full report on the Jill Thompson case from you later.'

'Rest assured we'll be swapping notes, sir.'

DS Hazel Carter took Miller aside. 'Sir, we ran a check on Peter Hanson. Lothian Buses said he called them up and said he had a family emergency. He told them his uncle was in a car crash last night down in Cumbria, so he'd be off for a few days.'

'Let me guess, he doesn't have an uncle in Cumbria?'

'He doesn't have an uncle. Period. I called his ex-wife and she told me. His work also said the address they have on file for him is Steffi's place. His mum and dad are dead, and the house they had was sold years ago.'

'So where the bloody hell is he?'

'Maybe he's on the run. He must know we're all looking for him,' Hazel said. 'I think he's hiding somewhere so he can get to Steffi. So he can talk to her and persuade her not to press any charges.'

Miller's jaw tightened at the idea. 'You may well be right.'

He turned when they started to lower the corpse. The SOCOs gently laid her on the ground, out of respect.

Maggie crouched near the figure, once a human being, now reduced to a black hulk. She shone a little torch on the head. Then she stood up and addressed Harry.

'I can't say for definite, but she looks to have a round hole in the back of her head. Just like the last one.'

'So burning her would have just been for show, if she was already dead,' he said.

'Looks like it.'

Alex came across to Harry. 'I had a call from the tech guys. They got into Trisha Cornwall's phone. She sent two texts the evening she died.'

'Do we know who to?'

'The phone company were on the ball; there were a load of texts and calls to one number in particular before the last texts. That number belongs to Randy Kline, one of the directors.'

'And the other one?'

'Graham Balfour. The guy who was a suspect in the original murder twenty years ago.'

'Sounds good to me. I'd like another crack at him. He's hiding something, I'm sure of it,' Harry said. 'I'll go with Alex and talk to him again.'

'I can come with you,' Miller said.

'We'll do it, Miller,' Weaver said. 'You stick to this woman here. Meekle, stay with Miller.'

Meekle nodded and Miller turned to look for Hazel Carter. He saw her and walked over. 'Contact our recruitment department and have them red-flag Peter Hanson's name. *Do not employ.* Explain to them why.'

'Will do.'

'We can walk if you like, sir,' Alex said to Harry. 'Balfour's place is just over there.'

Miller heard her and looked along to the end of the cemetery extension. He remembered climbing up a huge gravestone when he was a boy and it was time to go home for dinner.

'Fine by me. Our car is boggin'. God knows what those surveillance boys get up to in there.'

Weaver looked at Miller like he wanted to rip his head off but strode away after Harry.

TWENTY-TWO

'That was bad patter,' Weaver said to Harry as they left the cemetery and started walking along the pavement. He looked at Alex to see if she was listening, but she was walking ahead.

'What are you talking about, Stan?' Harry said.

'It's *Stan* now, is it? Been a fucking DCI for five minutes and respect goes out the window?'

'Jesus. Give me a break. If you've got a problem, spit it out.'

Weaver stopped so suddenly that Harry thought the DCI was going to smack him.

'Spit it out? Okay, I fucking will. I've given you the benefit of my wisdom when it comes to running the cold case unit. Took time out of my life to have a drink with you, and how do you repay me? Go drinking with your new pals instead of meeting me like you said.'

'For God's sake, get a grip of yourself. I was late, that's all. What else have you got to do with yourself? You're a widower. You can have a drink anytime, especially now, since you're about to retire. I don't see the big deal.'

'Don't you talk about my Nettie like that! Who the fuck do you think you are, McNeil? Just a jumped-up DI who nobody wants to work with.'

'I want to work with him,' Alex said, coming back towards them.

'Who asked you? You're another loser. You're just a wee hoor who'll never make it up the ladder without giving it to McNeil here.'

'That's enough, Weaver. You're going to cross a line here.' Harry thought he smelt drink on Weaver's breath.

'You'll never come up to my standards, you jumped-up little...' Weaver grabbed hold of the front of Harry's suit and drew his fist back. Harry stood his ground.

'Go ahead, Stan.'

'What then? Run back and grass on me, you snivelling wee shite. Once a rat, always a rat, eh?'

Weaver pushed Harry away and started to walk away.

'Where are you going now, Stan?'

'Mind your own fucking business. And remember one thing: until I retire, *I'm* in charge of this department.' Weaver turned to Alex. 'I want a full report from you, Maxwell. I want to know everything about Balfour.'

Weaver stormed off, not looking back, going back the way they had come.

Alex's face had gone red. 'Well, he can whistle for it. Talking to me like that. Who does he think he is?'

Harry straightened himself up. 'I think he drinks too much.' He patted her on the arm. 'Come on, let's go. Weaver won't be around much longer.'

It was actually warm now and Harry was sweating by the time they crossed over the footbridge adjacent to the old bridge that spanned what was once a railway line and was now the Leith-to-Broughton cycle lane.

'He might not even be in,' Alex said.

'He is,' Miller said. 'I just saw the curtain twitching on the side window, the one facing us. He must be looking out to see if he can see anything that's going on in the cemetery.'

When they got into the communal stairway, it felt good to be in the shade. Upstairs, the front door was ajar.

'It's open!' Balfour shouted from inside.

Harry led the way in, ready for combat, but none came.

'I made some tea. I saw you coming.'

'We know,' Harry said.

'Jesus, this is exciting,' Balfour said.

'Exciting?' Alex said. 'A woman is dead.'

'Exciting for us, I mean. This is our business.'

'No, it's *our* business,' Harry said.

Balfour indicated for them to sit. The place was quite tidy for a bachelor.

Alex sat on a leather couch, while Harry took a chair, making sure they could see Balfour in case he suddenly came at them with a sword or something.

'I want to know why you didn't tell us about Trisha Cornwall texting you the night she died,' Harry said.

'I told you I knew her. She was part of the group. I wasn't hiding anything.'

'Sit down, Mr Balfour.'

Balfour sat on a dining chair at the small dining table.

'She was murdered, and you were probably the last person to speak to her,' Alex said.

'I would think the murderer was, wouldn't you?' Balfour replied.

'Don't be pedantic,' Harry said. 'Why was she texting you before she died?'

'Should I have a lawyer present?'

Harry stood up. 'Listen, Balfour, you are our number-one suspect. We can either talk here, or we can take you to the station and keep you there for hours. Your choice.'

Balfour grinned and held up his hands. 'Alright, alright. No need to get tetchy.' He paused as Harry sat back down. 'The thing is, Trisha was unstable. And by that, I mean she would attach herself to somebody and find it hard to let go. She was all-in when she found a new friend. She wanted their friendship to be exclusive. Then she would pester that person. Emails. Texts. She was a real pain in the arse. When you were friends with her, you were *hers*. And if she asked you to start messaging on Facebook, look out. God forbid you spoke to somebody else.'

'She was a stalker, in other words?' Alex said.

'Oh yeah. I told her, you're daft doing that. We ask people for autographs, but Trisha took it a step further. Always wanting exclusive friendship. Then she got entangled with Randy Kline. You need to go and ask him. He friended her. I mean, Trisha was nice looking, don't get me wrong, but so is a Rottweiler. As soon as Kline thought he was on to a good thing, she had her hooks into him. She wouldn't leave him alone. I told her she was being stupid, but what do I know?'

'Did she ever talk about meeting Kline in person?'

'Of course! By God, the woman was insatiable when it came to stalking celebrities. Her crowning achievement was when she was served a restraining order. She had been stalking an author and wouldn't leave him alone. I'm surprised she didn't get a hammering before now. She was like a nice, delicious-looking cake on the outside, but full of maggots on the inside.'

Harry raised his eyebrows at Alex. *Maggots*. 'Did you see her on the night she died?'

'I did. Early evening. We were hanging about in the cemetery. Autograph hunting. But there was a group of us and I was never alone with her. My pals and I were together, then we came back here – without Trisha, I might add.'

'Did you know Aileen Rogers?' Harry asked.

Balfour looked into space for a moment, like he was

looking at the calendar on his wall for inspiration. 'Nope. Doesn't ring a bell. Why? What's she done?'

'She's dead.'

'I'm guessing she was either killed in the cemetery or was left there.'

The detectives were silent for a moment. 'Why would you say that?' Harry asked.

'I saw the flames last night. Late. I didn't call the fire brigade or anything. I thought they were filming a scene for the show. You know, the one where the woman gets burned to death? They're following the original script quite closely, and putting their mark on it, of course. So when I looked out and saw the flames, I thought that was pretty good.'

'What time?' Alex asked.

'After ten. Something like that. But let me ask you: that's two deaths like the characters' deaths in the script; do you think he could be following the original script? If so, then that's not the end of the deaths.'

Harry didn't answer. He knew from the original show that four more people died a painful death.

Including the policeman who was investigating the case.

TWENTY-THREE

The man walked slowly through the tall grass, his dark suit a stark contrast to the shades of green. He looked up to the sky, his arms spread wide.

The woman lay on her back, her hands tied behind her. Her clothing hadn't been touched. He looked down at her now, his blazing eyes piercing into hers like pinpoints of sharp light.

He brought his arms down and smiled at her. He could have been a lover come to rescue the damsel, if it weren't for the hammer he was holding in his hand.

A slight wind ruffled his hair. He didn't take his eyes off her as he got closer. He knelt down, maintaining eye contact.

'It's not going to be long now,' he said. 'I'll make it all go away. I'll take you away from this. You won't ever have to suffer again. You won't ever have to suffer those fools again.'

She couldn't hear him. She didn't struggle as he put the

rope round her neck and started hauling her upright, the rope sliding easily round the branch of the large tree. When she was above the pile of dry branches, he lit it and stood back, watching as the flames crept ever closer to her skin.

'Cut!' Randy Kline shouted. 'Good job, everybody. Dustin, that was amazing, as usual.'

Kline turned away as Dustin Crowd helped the actress to her feet.

There was a small crowd of onlookers out of sight of the cameras and a cheer went up when Dustin was finished. He smiled and bowed in their direction.

Harry was standing with Alex and Miller.

'Where did Weaver go?' Harry asked Miller.

'I thought he was with you?'

'He was, then he flew off the handle and stormed off. If ever somebody needed to retire, it's him. Just as well he's going in a couple of weeks, or he'd be booted out the door.'

'What happened?'

'Just an altercation. I've recommended officers be fired for less when I was an investigator. Where's Meekle?'

'I have no idea.'

Honey Summers walked over to them and stopped in front of them. 'Inspector Miller? I just wanted to talk to you in private.'

'This is DCI McNeil. He's in charge of the investigation.'

'We can step out of the way and talk,' Harry said.

'I'm scared, Inspector.'

'Scared of what?' Miller said.

'Somebody here.' She looked around to make sure they weren't being overheard. 'I heard somebody talking. About killing somebody.'

'You need to tell us who this was,' Harry said.

'I'm not sure who it was.'

'Who were they talking to?' Miller said.

'I'm not sure. I didn't hear another voice. Maybe they were talking on the phone?'

'We can have somebody shadow you while you're working here if you feel unsafe,' Harry said.

'That would be good.'

'I can assign one of my female officers.'

'Thank you.' Honey made to turn away but stopped. 'Somebody said that a woman had been burnt to death in the small extension part?'

'We can't go into details,' Harry replied.

'She was hit by a hammer,' Honey said. 'Then he hung her up and set fire to her corpse, with a little bonfire underneath her.'

'Did you see something?' Miller said.

'It's in the script,' she said, looking into the distance. 'The girl under the gravestone. The woman being burnt. Both of them had a hammer to the head first, so he could manipulate them. It's how the women in the script die. They're killed by God.'

'God?' Harry said, getting an uneasy feeling.

'Somebody with a God complex. That's where the title of the show came from. I won't give the ending away, but my character's next. The actress who was just being murdered by Dustin Crowd? She's before my character. Then I'm next. He puts a bag over my head to kill me. That's how my character dies.'

Harry looked at her, at the worry lines on her face. Without make-up, she looked normal, and he could see the natural beauty in her. 'Did you know the women who have been murdered? Trisha Cornwall and…' He hesitated. 'I can't say her name before her next of kin have been informed.'

'Trisha Cornwall was a bitch. I told Randy, if you sleep with her, you'll never get rid of her. But what do I know? He had his way and then she came back at him like a leech.'

'Do you think he could have killed her?'

'I don't think so. You never truly know somebody, though, do you?'

Harry thought about Stan Weaver. 'Anyway, Miss Summers, are you going back to your trailer?'

'Yes. I'm supposed to be getting made up by my personal make-up artist in the make-up trailer, but she hasn't shown for work, so one of the other girls is going to do it. Aileen's never late for work, but Randy will fire her for sure.'

'Aileen who?' Harry said.

'Rogers. If you see her, get her to get a move on. But I can't see her coming in to work now.'

'Me neither,' Harry said as Honey Summers walked away. Aileen Rogers would never turn up for work again.

TWENTY-FOUR

Mike Peebles peeked through the curtains in the trailer. 'They'll come looking for you. It's only a matter of time.'

'And then what?' Randy Kline said. 'That mental cow was asking for it. Stalking people like that. Didn't she have a boyfriend or something?'

'She did, but obviously his manhood wasn't in the eye-watering category.'

'I bet she didn't tell him she was messing around.'

Peebles stepped back from the window. 'You couldn't help yourself, though, could you? I mean, you couldn't keep it zipped up just one time.'

'Christ, what are you now, my dad?'

'Fine. I'm only trying to help. You fairly fucked off after that last scene, but what do I know? And what was Honey doing talking to that copper?'

'I couldn't tell. I was too busy fucking off, according to you.'

'Well, you were, Randy. You know they're going to come and talk to you and they're going to assume you killed that stalker bint, and Aileen.'

Kline looked at him. 'Who's Aileen?'

'The woman who looked like she'd been on a spit. The cooked one.'

'Isn't she the make-up woman?'

'One of them, yes. But I heard some talk. They think it's her.'

'That's the second one killed who's associated with this show. I know Trisha was a nutter, but she was connected through me,' Kline said.

'Now she's dead.'

'Mike, this is going to put us on the map. There's already a buzz on Twitter and Facebook about the show, what with me starring in the first one and directing this one. We're going to go viral.'

'You'd better hope so, or else Carruthers will go back to whoever is bankrolling this project and tell them we're a couple of con artists.'

'Speak for yourself. And that half-brain should have just stuck to using his own name,' Kline said.

'You know who's behind this, don't you?'

'I couldn't care less to be honest. I'm making a good wage from this and I'm going on to better things.'

'*We* are going on to better things.'

'Yeah, yeah.'

'However, we need to focus on the here and now, not having our names on the Hollywood Walk of Fame,' Peebles said.

There was a knock at the door. 'That's either Honey deciding she should stop fighting her feelings for you, or it's the coppers, who are going to ram a truncheon up your hole until you confess to being a lunatic murderer.'

Peebles opened the door and was relieved to see neither Miller nor Harry had their truncheon extended.

'Mr Kline, we'd like a word,' Harry said, standing just outside the trailer.

'Well, can it wait? My assistant director and I are going through some technical stuff.'

'No, it can't.'

'We can finish up going through the shooting script later, Randy,' Peebles said.

Kline looked at him and stuck two fingers up. 'Right, you'd better come in.'

Miller and Harry entered, followed by Charlie Meekle, who had reappeared as suddenly as he'd disappeared, citing bathroom issues.

'We'd just like to talk to you about Trisha Cornwall,' Harry said.

'Have a seat.' Peebles indicated for them to go through to the living room area.

Where? Harry thought. They glanced around, then sat on the small settees on either side of the slide-outs. These were parts of the trailer that extended out to make the room more spacious.

'I was expecting you,' Kline said. 'You'll know by now that Trisha was a stalker.'

'We do,' Meekle said. 'Looks like somebody wanted to shut her up.'

'Not me. She was nothing but a pain in the arse, but I wouldn't want that to happen to anybody.'

'We saw that she had texted you on the night she died.'

'She sent me a few,' Kline said, not denying it.

'Twenty-one, to be precise,' Harry said.

'A couple. Twenty-one. It's all the same. They got the same response: I told her I wasn't interested in seeing her again.'

'You slept with her,' Meekle said, his lip curling in disgust, 'and then you told her to sod off.'

'We get a lot of groupies hanging about, believe it or not. They start out wanting an autograph of the stars – although describing them as stars is pushing it – but then they want to become friendly with the crew. They think that by sleeping with them, they'll get an introduction. The crew take advantage if you ask me. They know fine well that there's no chance of the stars going out with a fan.'

'But a director getting it away is always a possibility.'

'There's never any promise made or implied.'

'It doesn't seem that Trisha saw it that way,' Harry said.

'Trisha was her own worst enemy. She slept her way through the crew. They all talked about her. Don't get me wrong, she was an attractive woman, but what went on inside her head made her daft.'

'Did she ever talk about Jill Thompson?' Meekle asked.

'Yes,' said Kline. 'She was Jill's best friend, back in the day.'

'Did you meet Trisha the night she died?'

'No. I told her she needed to calm down and to stop texting me, that I was busy with the filming schedule and it was over.'

'What about you, Mr Peebles?' Harry said. 'You ever meet Trisha?'

Peebles shifted position on his seat. 'Of course I did. She was never away from here. Always trying to get an autograph. When Randy knocked her back, she came to me, asking if I wanted to go for a drink. I told her to bog off.'

'How did she take that news?'

'She was pissed off, so she went back to annoying him.' Peebles nodded at Kline.

'Yeah, thanks again for that, mate.'

'Where were you both last night?' Harry asked.

'Working here,' Kline said. 'Then we went for a couple of beers, and then I went to the hotel where we're all staying. Had some more drinks at the bar and went to my room.'

'I was with him right up until we went to our separate rooms,' said Peebles.

'Where are you people based out of?' Meekle asked.

'Livingston. We used to have a studio here in Edinburgh, but it was getting too expensive. Now we have a place out in West Lothian.'

'Can you think of anybody else who Trisha was stalking?' Harry said.

'There was a member of the sound crew. She got her claws into him, bombarding him with Facebook messages, demanding to know why he didn't write back to her and questioning why he was talking to other women. Exactly the same way she was treating me. We were her personal toys and could only answer to her. He told her to sod off.'

Harry looked at him. 'Thank you for your time, Mr Kline. If you think of anything else, give us a call.'

'He's basing his killing methods on the script,' Peebles said.

'What?' Harry said.

'The way those two women have been murdered? That's in the script. It's how God kills them, or the man who thinks he's God. The character has a God complex, deciding when they should leave Earth for Heaven. They have a problem in their life, and he ends their life so the problem is solved, in his eyes.'

'How many people die in this script?' Meekle asked.

Kline paused for a minute. 'Seven.'

'Do you have a copy we can read?' Harry asked.

Kline walked across to a cupboard and took three copies out. 'Have one each. But do me a favour?'

'What?'

'Don't give one to that tosser Graham Balfour. He's already got two, both signed by some crew members.'

The detectives left the trailer, knowing they had a blueprint for murder in their hands.

Mike Peebles made sure the police were out of earshot. 'Do you think they know?'

'How can they?' Kline said.

'Somebody might have told them.'

'Not much chance of that now, thank God.'

Peebles nodded. 'You got caught once. Twice was careless.'

'It will be fine, Mike. You'll see.'

'I hope for your sake you're right.'

TWENTY-FIVE

'Have you seen Weaver?' Harry said to Miller.

'Not since earlier.'

'God knows where he got to.' Harry watched Meekle get into a car and drive off. 'Keep your eye on him, Frank. He said we were going to exchange notes and he hasn't called me yet. He'd better be in my office first thing tomorrow or else he'll be back on the train heading south.'

'Will do.'

Harry waved Alex over. 'Frank and I are going to the Royal to see how Steffi Walker is doing. You want to come along?'

'Sure.'

Miller gave Hazel Carter the keys to their car. 'Tell me you know where that bus driver prick is,' he said.

'Not yet, sir. Sorry.'

They got in the car, Alex behind the wheel, and headed up to the Royal Infirmary.

'Hanson's vanished off the face of the earth,' Miller said. 'Christ, I wish we knew where he was staying.'

The traffic was light and they made good time.

There were two officers guarding Steffi's room, different ones from earlier. They nodded to the detectives and stood aside.

Miller opened Steffi's door and stopped for an instant. 'Hey there,' he said.

She was looking at him, watching his eyes for a reaction.

'It looks a lot worse than it is,' she said, her voice sounding weak and hoarse. Her face was black and blue, the bruising having worsened throughout the day. Her head was wrapped in a bandage and she was still wired up to machines.

'Thank God it's only temporary,' Miller said. He mentally kicked himself for not seeing the signs when Steffi had had a mark on her face.

None of them asked her how she was feeling. They could see how she was feeling.

They made small talk for a little while.

'Listen, I don't want to put the wind up you, but we haven't found Hanson yet,' Harry said.

'I'm not pressing charges, sir,' she said.

'He's not going to stop, Steffi.'

'Have you heard from him?' Miller said.

'Christ, what is this? The three of you come in here and

get my blood pressure up? It was a domestic and it got out of hand. He won't do it again.'

'We just want you to know we're here for you, Steffi,' Alex said, sitting down on the bed and holding her hand.

'I know that, but this is personal. He won't do it again.'

'Did he tell you that the time before, when you came to work with a mark on your face?' Miller said.

'Please don't take this the wrong way, sir, but would you all just please piss off?'

The two detectives looked around awkwardly for a moment.

'We care about you, Steff,' Miller said.

'I know, Frank, but I'm tired.'

And scared? he wanted to ask, but he kept quiet.

'Why don't you two go and get a coffee. I'll meet you downstairs in the canteen,' Alex said, not budging from the bed.

Harry nodded and ushered Miller outside. They both heard Steffi starting to cry as they shut the door.

TWENTY-SIX

Later on, Harry McNeil sat on his couch with his feet up. He had brought files home from the office and was looking through them, trying to work out the puzzle.

His phone rang.

'Harry. Fancy a beer?'

Stan Weaver. *Christ.*

'Not tonight, Stan. I'm going through some papers.'

'Jesus, laddie, she's got you under the thumb and you're not even married.' Weaver said it with a slight laugh, but there was an undertone.

'We're busy right now.' Harry meant to use a light tone, but it came out a bit harsher than he'd wanted it to.

'Listen, about today –'

'I let that go, because you're going to retire, and you're

probably stressed, and I've had a lot worse done to me. But if you ever talk to one of my team like that again –'

'*My* team!' Weaver shouted. 'They're still my team! And you'll what, Harry? Get your pals onto me? Well, here's a news flash: you haven't got any.'

There was silence between the two men and Harry could hear the background noise of the pub. Weaver was well on the way to getting blootered again. Then Harry heard another voice, like somebody was talking to Weaver.

'*Don't take any guff off him. He pretends to be your pal, but there's a sleekit side to the wee bastard.*'

Harry thought he recognised Meekle's voice. The man must be standing next to Weaver, egging him on. *Not so wee,* Harry thought, but he didn't correct Weaver's friend.

'Well, you have yourself a good night, Stan. Give Meekle my best.' Harry hung up as Weaver started calling him names.

He had just set his phone down when it buzzed. He thought it would be Vanessa, asking him again if he'd talked to Frank about the flat. *No, I haven't talked to him, alright?!*

This was the second of three nights of parents' meetings and Harry was glad. Not that he didn't enjoy Vanessa's company, but sometimes he just liked to be on his own for a wee while.

He huffed out his breath, annoyance starting to grip him. *Why can't you just leave me alone for a little while?* He knew he shouldn't be thinking like this, but he needed some space.

To kick back and read a book. Or watch some Netflix. *Or read some death reports.*

He picked up his phone and read the message: *You eaten yet?*

Alex.

No. You? He put his finger over the send button and hesitated. Why had he immediately answered her? It had felt natural, like he was talking to a friend. That was one thing he liked about DS Maxwell: she was very easy to get on with, and he was enjoying working with her.

Fancy a Chinese? My treat.

Come to think of it, he was hungry. He'd popped the tab on a can of lager and had some crisps with it. Now he was famished.

Lemon chicken, fried rice, plz. He hit send without any hesitation this time.

Fifteen minutes. Get the kettle on.

He sent her a smiley face. The last time he'd sent a text to his son, the boy had told him he needed to get with it, to use shortcuts when he was texting. He wondered what the shortcut for *fuck you* was. Not that he would use it with his son, but it might come in handy for Stan Weaver.

And then he felt the tiniest pang of guilt. Should he be doing this while his girlfriend was at her school yakking to parents about how little Johnny was just wonderful, when all the time little Johnny was a potential serial killer who thought nothing of cutting the curtains or drawing on the walls with crayons.

What is there to be guilty about, Harry? he asked himself. *Working with a colleague? Everybody has to eat. And just because you're eating in your flat, that's nothing to get jealous over.*

Although, had it been Frank Miller who had suggested bringing the food over, Harry would have not-quite-politely declined.

Fifteen minutes in reality became twenty-five.

'Sorry I'm late,' Alex said when he opened his door to her. Her hair was wet from the sudden downpour that had started just minutes earlier. 'There was a queue. Who would have thought it would be so busy on a Tuesday night?'

He could see her shirt was wet as well. 'I could have come down and given you a hand,' he said.

'It's fine,' she replied. 'You don't have a hairdryer, do you?'

'I do. Not for myself, but my girlfriend keeps one here in case she stays over. Which is never, since she lives just across the road. In the cupboard under the bathroom sink. I'll dish up.'

She gave him the bag with the food and they stood awkwardly for a moment.

'I don't know where your bathroom is,' she said, smiling.

'Oh. Straight ahead.'

They turned away from each other, and a couple of minutes later, Harry could faintly hear the hairdryer going.

He hoped she would dry her shirt too, instead of asking him for a bathrobe. Christ, that would be all he needed: Vanessa coming home early to find another woman drying herself like she'd just taken a shower.

His phone rang again. Vanessa's name was on the screen. 'Hello,' he said, going through to the kitchen. *Please don't hear the hairdryer.*

'Hello, honey. Listen, I felt bad about not being there having dinner with you, so I thought I could bring something in if you don't mind eating a bit late?'

'Oh, don't worry about that. I fixed myself something. I wasn't that hungry, so I'll be fine. I'm just reading through some work stuff.'

He gently set the bag of food on the countertop, trying not to let it rustle.

'Are you at your own flat?'

He hesitated, looking for a loaded question. 'Yes.'

'Okay. I can come round and see you later.'

'Of course. I'll be here.' He looked at the clock; at least an hour and a half, maybe two hours before she finished.

The sound of the hairdryer died.

'Right, I'll let you go. See you soon. Love you,' she said.

'Love you too,' he replied, and wondered, not for the first time, if he was just saying the words out of habit. He switched the kettle back on.

He'd hung up before Alex came into the kitchen, looking more presentable.

'I hope your girlfriend won't mind that I used her hairbrush too. I don't have nits.' She smiled.

'That's fine.' *Trust me, she'll never find out.*

They dished up the food and sat at the table in the living room overlooking the bowling club, which had a lack of players. 'Rain stopped play,' he said, nodding down to the bowling green.

'I think that's cricket.'

'I know that, Sergeant. It was merely an observation.' He smiled, not wanting her to think he was admonishing her.

'My ex used to like bowling.' She looked at him and laughed. 'Sorry. Every conversation won't be about my ex. It was just a thing he liked to do.'

They continued eating, washing the food down with two cups of coffee. 'I was reading through the old case file,' he said.

'Anything pop out?'

'One thing. They filmed in the cemetery for just over a week last time. Nine, ten days, something like that. Exactly the same timeframe for this part of the shoot, but there was only one murder. Why have there been two murders this time?'

'Different killers, would be the obvious answer.'

'But is it? I'm thinking that maybe it's not. Something about this stupid show is making this guy kill women connected to it. I was checking, though, and the two recent victims weren't connected to the first show twenty years ago.

The only connection is that Trisha Cornwall lived near there before her family moved to London, and she would hang around the cemetery with the others.'

Alex nodded. 'Why was Jill Thompson killed twenty years ago? The connection is the show itself: they were filming the first one back then, and as soon as filming starts on the remake, a killer strikes again. Somebody with a grudge?'

'Could be. I'll get the team to co-ordinate with Miller's team and see who was at the cemetery last time.'

They ate in silence for a few moments, and Harry's heart missed a beat when he thought he saw Vanessa's car turn into their street.

'Does your girlfriend know I'm here?' Alex asked, as if reading his mind.

'How could she? She's working late.'

'We have things called mobile phones these days, Harry.'

'It's Chief Inspector.'

'Sorry, sir.'

He shook his head at her, smiling. 'Should have seen your face.'

'Touché. But tell me a little bit about yourself.'

'It's not very interesting.'

'Tell me anyway.' She put her knife and fork on the plate and finished her coffee.

'Well, I was married young, and I have a fifteen-year-old son. I got divorced, and my ex-wife and son moved to Fife to be near her family. In Kelty, where we were today. Her brother hates me, and we got into an altercation one day. I battered him after he attacked me, and I've never seen any of her family again. I go and see my son every couple of weeks. He's a great kid, but he's being poisoned against me by the wicked witch from the north.'

He finished his meal and sat and stared out of the window for a moment, thinking back ten years to when his boy was just little. Good times.

He turned to look at Alex. 'Now tell me a little bit about yourself. I already know you were engaged and your ex dumped you and you sold your flat and moved to the colonies. In fact, I know most things there are to know about you.'

'Oh, this is like going on a dating site. Not that I would know, mind, but I've heard some of the others talking about it.'

'Yeah, sure you have.'

'When I first met you yesterday, you didn't strike me as being annoying,' Alex said. 'But now I'm going to re-evaluate my opinion of you.'

He laughed. 'Carry on.'

'Like you, my life story isn't very exciting. I left school and wanted to join the police, so I was over the moon when Lothian and Borders accepted my application. I worked my way into CID, became a sergeant and belted the Lord Provost's son. The rest you know.'

'I don't know what your boyfriend did for a living.'

'He's a fireman. Fire*fighter*. I came home one day and

found him giving a fireman's lift to a female recruit in our bedroom. We went our own ways after that. Five years ago.'

'That must have been tough.'

'Not as tough as Gregg losing his wife and child.'

'True.'

They cleared the dishes and sat in the living room, going over the case.

'It all boils down to the *why*, as you said. Why would anybody want to kill people connected with the show?' said Harry.

'I think we can rule out an irate fan.'

'We need to try to find out who the father of Jill Thompson's baby was.'

'Do you think it was Randy Kline?' Alex said, some of the notes on her lap.

'If it was, he's certainly not saying.'

They carried on reading, Harry keeping an eye on the clock.

TWENTY-SEVEN

The doctor walked with confidence along the corridor and turned right towards the room. Two police officers were standing guard.

'Give me a shout if you need a coffee and I'll have somebody bring you one,' he said with a smile to the officers.

They nodded as he took his stethoscope off and opened the door. Nobody else was in the room, only Steffi Walker, sleeping.

The doctor lifted the chart. He didn't know what he was looking at. After all, he'd only been a doctor for ten minutes.

Peter Hanson put the chart back and stood looking at Steffi. He knew he didn't have long before the officers outside would wonder what he was doing and come in to investigate.

'Wakey, wakey, sleeping beauty.' He gently shook her arm.

She woke with a start and Hanson released his grip.

'You must have been in a deep sleep. Were you dreaming of me?' He smiled at her.

'What are you doing here? How did you get in?' Then she saw the doctor's coat he was wearing and the stethoscope.

'I wanted to see you, but they all think I'm a monster, Steffi. I mean, I know I lost my temper. I admit that.' He took a step back and held his hands up. 'But I've thought about it, and how stupid I was. I mean, really, really stupid. God, I lifted my hand to the woman I love. What kind of a fool does that make me?'

'You need to go, Peter. It won't look good for you if they catch you in here.'

'They won't let me explain, that's for sure. That's why I wanted to see you in private. Steffi, I love you and I'm sorry for what I did. It won't ever happen again. I don't know what came over me.'

'You need help.'

'I know and I'll get help. I'll go and see somebody. I promise. I just want us to start afresh.' He looked at her face, saw the tears streaming down her cheeks. 'I want to come home.'

'I don't know. You hurt me.'

'It won't ever happen again.'

'You said that the last time, Peter. You begged me for another chance. I gave it to you.'

'It was a mistake. It won't ever happen again, I promise

you. I love you, Steffi.' He leant over and kissed her. 'Can I come home?'

She hesitated for a second before answering. 'Yes.'

'Thank you.' He turned to look at the door. 'I need to go before they wonder what's going on. I love you. Call me when you're leaving the hospital and I'll come home to you.'

As he turned and made for the door she asked him, 'Where are you staying?' But he opened the door and slipped out without answering.

TWENTY-EIGHT

'Don't worry,' Rita Mellon said to her boyfriend, Brian. 'I'll be fine.'

'It's not you I'm worried about. I mean, we don't even know this guy, yet here you are, going out for dinner with him.'

Rita finished putting her lipstick on and adjusted her bra through her blouse. 'He's sound if he knows Adrian.'

'I suppose. But what if he takes a fancy to you?'

She laughed. 'Brian, love, I've been around other men before. I can spot a letch a mile off. I have managed to interact with men in the past without sleeping with them! What do you think I did when I was married to Malkie?'

Mad Malkie Mellon was Rita's ex-husband, whose current abode was the Bar-L, a notorious Glaswegian prison formally known as Barlinnie.

'I wish you wouldn't mention him,' Brian said, sipping his whisky. He was a good bit younger than Rita, but the two of them were inseparable.

'I can't pretend I wasn't married to him. Besides, Adrian assured me that somebody over there has had a word with Malkie and he won't ever be giving me trouble again.'

'Very reassuring, but I still worry about you.'

'Come here,' she said to him, turning away from the mirror in the living room. She gave him a hug. 'No kiss; I've just put my lippie on.'

'I suppose a quickie before you go is out of the question?'

She playfully slapped his arm. 'He's waiting downstairs for me.'

'Be good,' Brian said, and she left the apartment and took the lift down to the lobby. She loved living here with Brian and was grateful to Adrian Jackson for providing the flat for them. If he wasn't married and Brian wasn't his nephew, then maybe...

Downstairs, she looked around, but saw no car. No flashy motor anyway. Then she got a text. *Damn car broke down! Could you get an Uber to the restaurant? So sorry! Harvey's in Leith.*

She texted back that it would be fine. She thought about going back upstairs, but then Brian might think this was her fault and insist on coming along. She could handle this, and this investor was important to Adrian. Theo had told her in confidence that Adrian was having doubts about this project, but if he, Theo, got on board, they could make a killing with the merchandising.

She didn't want to mess this up for Adrian.

She got an Uber five minutes later.

Theo was waiting outside the restaurant for her. He was a fit-looking man, maybe in his forties. He had slick hair and a dark shadow on his face, like no matter how many times a day he shaved, he would always have this five o'clock shadow.

'Rita?' he said as she stepped out of the car.

'Yes.' She smiled at him. His handshake was firm and dry.

'I must apologise again. I really don't know what's wrong with the car. She's a classic car, but recently she seems to be playing up. I need to buy a new one. I'm awfully embarrassed.'

'Think nothing of it.' She looked at the restaurant. It was closed.

'I can't believe this place is gone. I know somebody who invested in it.' He looked at her. 'The Blue Martini is just along the way. We can get a table there, I'm sure.'

He ushered her inside and they were shown to a table that Theo had booked days earlier.

They made small talk until they each had a glass of wine and had placed their orders. Then Theo took his phone out and switched it off. 'I think it's just rude when people are in a business meeting and their phone goes off. There's a time and a place, and having a financial meeting isn't one of them.'

'Oh, yes. I agree.' Rita took her own phone out and switched it off.

'I'll switch it back on later, but right now it helps one to clear the mind and deal with the matter at hand.'

'Absolutely.'

Their food came and Rita thought it smelled magnificent.

'Once again,' said Theo, 'I contacted you directly as Adrian had mentioned he had you on board and you were the brains of the outfit. He was getting the jitters, so to speak. We had a meeting and I mentioned that my partners and I might be interested in coming aboard. And to be honest, after I read about the original show, I was hooked. Of course I then remembered when it came out and how successful it was. This time we can hit America with it, big time. You see, the one big advantage we have now is streaming TV, like Netflix.'

Rita smiled and nodded at the appropriate times. She had a feeling the deal was already done and Theo just wanted to spend some time with her.

'So, what do you say?' he asked her. 'Does it sound like a plan? Us coming on board?'

'I don't see why not. I'll talk with Adrian and he can get the financial side of things worked out with his team of accountants.'

'Great. As I said, I think Adrian just needs that little push. Now, what do you say we order some champagne?'

'Oh, I'm not sure. I don't usually drink much.'

'Listen, this dinner is a business expense and it would be

absolutely remiss of me to not have at least one bottle at the table.'

'Go on then.'

Theo smiled and indicated for the waiter, and he came back with the bottle.

'As long as I don't end up dead drunk,' Rita said.

Just dead, Theo thought, and they clinked glasses.

TWENTY-NINE

'Of all the fucking stupid things you've done, this one has bells on it,' Adrian Jackson said, pacing about Brian's living room. 'Just as well I called.'

'I didn't know, for Christ's sake. Rita was dealing with this because this guy had her convinced that she was doing you a favour by talking directly to him.'

'What exactly did she say?' Jackson had taken his bowler hat off but was still using the walking stick.

'She said they had been talking, that he wanted to discuss investing in the show as everybody stood to make a lot of money, but you were getting cold feet. He said they should talk over dinner.'

Jackson stopped the pacing. 'Try her again.'

Brian called Rita's number and it went straight to voicemail. 'Nothing. It's dead.'

'Let's hope *she's* not.'

'Don't talk like that, Adrian, for God's sake.'

'Go through everything that happened tonight, again.' Jackson sat down.

'She said he had texted her and he would pick her up downstairs. She left, and then she said he had sent her a text to say his car had broken down and so she had got an Uber. I tried sending her a text a little while ago but got no answer. I wanted to call her, just to see that she was safe, but her phone is off.'

'This is a nightmare.'

'Are you sure you're not dealing with another investor?' Brian said.

'Of course I'm bloody well sure. We don't need other investors in on this. Are you daft?' Jackson stood up again. 'Molloy is going to go off his fucking nut. I'll need to call him.'

'I called Uber and they wouldn't tell me where she went. Privacy and all that.'

'Fuck that for a game of soldiers.' Jackson called Robert Molloy and explained the situation.

'Get yourself round here, Adrian. I'm at the hotel.'

'I'll be right round. Five minutes.' Jackson hung up. Molloy was at 'the hotel', which meant his hotel on North Bridge, the one he owned with his son.

'Come on, Brian, and for God's sake, let me do the talking. We don't want Michael Molloy acting like he's on crack. When he's in one of his moods, people usually start losing body parts, especially if they've shagged him out of money. Stay calm, and if you *do* have to talk, just look like you're an idiot. Which shouldn't be too hard for you.'

THIRTY

The champagne had tasted good, Rita had to admit. But she made a point of not getting drunk. She didn't want Brian to get the wrong idea when she got home. But it had gone straight to her head.

'How about we go along and have a look round the set now?' Theo said to her.

They were standing outside. It was dark and cold now, a breeze coming in from the Forth just across the way.

'It's a bit dark to be messing about in a cemetery, don't you think?'

'I know it's dark, but the film crew will be there. It's not as if they all go home for the night and leave all the stuff. Besides, I heard them talking and they said they were filming in there tonight, so there's going to be plenty of people about. What do you say? Maybe we'll get an autograph or two.'

'Oh, okay then. But I want you to take a photo of me there so I can show my boyfriend.'

'Deal.'

She giggled to herself. Her head was swimming a little bit. 'That champagne must have been strong.'

'It was an 'eighty-two,' he said as if he knew what he was talking about. He figured Rita wouldn't know the difference between a bottle of champagne and a bottle of shampoo.

'Rita?' he said.

She looked at him.

He pointed to a white van that was parked just past the restaurant. 'It's all I could get at short notice. A friend of mine is a builder and he let me borrow it.'

She hesitated for a moment, but the champagne had loosened her inhibitions just a bit. Enough to accept a lift in a van.

'Oh, I suppose so.' Rita climbed into the Transit, hoping she wouldn't get her clothes dirty, but it looked clean. In fact, it was an unusually clean van, nothing like she'd expected the inside of a builder's van to look.

Theo got in and they drove away from the shore. He headed up towards Warriston. He drove past the crematorium and parked outside the side gate.

'There's security, so we'll have to be careful,' he said.

'Why can't we just drive through the main gate?'

'What with the murders, they've tightened up security. They might not let us on the set. But I want you to experience it.' He jumped out of the van and walked across to the gate. She got out on unsteady feet.

'It's padlocked,' Rita said.

'I've never met a padlock yet that couldn't be broken, Rita.'

That's when Rita got the bad feeling. She was standing looking at the gate when she turned around – and saw Theo coming at her with the polythene bag in his hand.

Her instinct was to scream. Which she did, loud and long.

Theo rushed her and put the polythene bag over her head. She struggled against him, but he was too powerful for her. He started to drag her back to the van.

Rita reached up to his face and dug her nails in, feeling something come away.

She didn't hear the other man shouting, but Theo did.

'Oy! What are you doing?' The man was standing further up, near the gates to the crematorium.

'You want some of this?' Theo shouted back.

'I'll give you some of *this*, ya bastard!' the man said, and then Theo saw the German Shepherd he had with him. The man started walking towards him, and the dog started barking and snarling.

'Let her go or I'll set the fucking dog on you!'

Theo watched as the man bent down to unclip the lead. He weighed up his options: try to get Rita into the van before the dog could run down here, or cut his losses.

Guessing how fast the dog would be, Theo pushed Rita roughly away from him and jumped into the van and drove away. He looked in the mirror and saw the man hadn't let the dog go, but was running towards Rita, the dog's lead in one hand, a mobile phone in the other. Theo didn't put the lights on so the man couldn't see the licence plate. Only when he got over the bridge into the other side of Warriston Road did he risk the lights.

'Too bad, Rita, we could have had a good thing going. I had the very gravestone picked out that was going to crush your skull to pieces, but never mind. There's always next time.'

THIRTY-ONE

Robert Molloy was sitting behind his desk, a glass of brandy in his hand. His Rottweiler – otherwise known as his son, Michael – was also there, which didn't surprise Jackson. He gave Brian a quick look, reminding him of the lecture he'd given him about not upsetting Michael.

'Adrian. I wish I could say I was pleased to see you,' Robert said, 'but considering the circumstances...'

'What's this about some fuck trying to get one over on us?' Michael said, getting straight to the point.

'Brian here told me that somebody conned my assistant, Rita, into believing he was an investor,' said Jackson.

'Where is she now?' Michael asked, his face like thunder, gritting his teeth.

'That's the thing; we don't know. Uber won't tell us where they took her.'

'Won't they now?' Robert said. 'And this person knows who he's fucking with?'

'Apparently not,' Jackson said.

'Indeed, or the thought would never cross his mind.' Robert looked at Michael. 'Have somebody get the information we need. Do whatever hacking it takes to find out where Rita went. Then find this bastard. Teach him a lesson he'll never forget.'

'We just need to obtain some information about him,' Jackson said.

'I'm sure Mrs Mellon will oblige when we see her.'

Just then Brian's phone rang. 'What? Oh fuck, no. Is she alright?' He listened to the voice on the other end. 'We'll be right there.' He hung up and looked at Jackson.

'It's Rita. She was attacked and she's in the Royal.'

'Is she okay?' Jackson said.

'Yes. They're checking her over.'

Robert stood up. 'Michael, get my driver. We're going to the hospital. Then get a team together. I want that fucker hunted down. No expense spared. If he thinks he's going to fuck with the Molloys, I'll have that carved on his face before we put him in the ground.' He looked at Jackson as Michael left the office. 'You got your car?'

'My driver's downstairs.'

'See you at the Royal.'

THIRTY-TWO

Harry McNeil heard a noise and couldn't figure out what it was. Then he realised it was his phone ringing, playing a stupid tune he didn't know the name of. He'd dozed off on the couch watching some show that was being repeated.

He felt groggy, his eyes tired. The phone was doing the fandango on the table, vibrating its way across to the edge. It almost made the leap before he caught it.

'McNeil.'

'Harry, it's Frank Miller. We've got a situation. A woman was attacked.'

Harry paused for a second. 'What's that got to do with us?'

'She was attacked by the cemetery gates down in Warriston Road. He tried to get her to go into the cemetery. Can you come up to the Royal? I think it was our guy.'

'I'll be there as soon as. I'll leave in a few.'

As he got up, he looked at the clock. Well after eleven. He was relieved that Vanessa hadn't called or come round. Then he felt disappointed that she hadn't. *Make up your mind, Harry.*

'You dressed?' Harry asked Alex Maxwell over the phone. 'And before you come out with a smart reply, we have another possible victim. This one survived. I got a call to go to the Royal. I thought you'd like to tag along.'

'I am, and I can leave in two minutes. I'll see you up there. Unless...?'

'I'll be waiting downstairs.' He put his shoes on and brushed his teeth before going downstairs to wait on Alex.

He was glad she didn't honk her car horn again. He looked over to Vanessa's house, halfway up the hill, diagonally across the bowling green, and saw a bedroom light on. He felt a pang of something. Guilt?

The passenger window rolled down. 'This will be a lot quicker if you actually get in the car, sir.'

He opened the BMW's door and got in and had barely buckled his seatbelt before she floored it.

'*Sir* now? I can't see this new you lasting long. Showing me respect and stuff.'

She grinned at him. 'Me neither.'

'I knew it. I should mark it in my diary. We'll call it the "Maxwell showing respect" holiday. People all over Scotland will be celebrating.'

She hit the top of the street and turned up towards Queensferry Road, making it without having to wait for traffic at this time of night. She cut through the city centre and went up Lothian Road to The Meadows.

Harry was lost in his thoughts as Alex turned on a radio station that was playing tunes Harry didn't even know the names of.

THIRTY-THREE

Miller was waiting for Harry in the accident and emergency department. Stan Weaver and Charlie Meekle had also turned up.

'Tell me what this has to do with our case, Frank,' Harry said. He hadn't bothered fiddling with a tie.

'Her name's Rita Mellon. She's been taken up to a ward and we have somebody guarding her room. Come on, I'll tell you on the way.'

They walked through to the lift, Weaver and Meekle following.

'It seems she met the guy, who had told her he was an investor,' said Miller. 'They had dinner, and he drove her to the cemetery in a van, saying they could look around the film set.'

'I'm assuming this guy has nothing to do with financing

the show?' Alex said to Harry as they stepped into the lift and hit the button for the second floor. He was ignoring the other two detectives. If they wanted a fight in the lift, Harry was in the right frame of mind.

'Nobody knows who he is.'

'She's lucky to be alive. How did she get away from him?' Meekle asked.

They stepped out onto the second floor and walked along the hallway to where Rita Mellon's ward was.

'She screamed, and the crematorium manager – who lives on the premises – was out with his German Shepherd and he saw the guy attacking her. He threatened him with the dog, and the attacker fled in the van,' Miller said.

'Did he get the number?' As Weaver asked, Harry could have sworn he smelled drink on the older DCI again.

'No. He drove away with the lights off. But get this: Rita got some of the guy's face.'

Harry stopped. 'What do you mean, *his face?*'

'She tried to scratch him but got some latex instead. The bastard had put a mask on, but not like the kind you would buy in a shop. This was like the kind an actor would put on.'

'Christ, do you think it could have some DNA on it?'

'It's already away to the lab.'

Miller slowed down a bit. 'Adrian Jackson and the Molloys are here. Rita is Jackson's nephew's live-in girlfriend.'

'We don't need them milling about here.' Harry looked at

Adrian Jackson as they approached the private ward that Rita was in.

'Any news, Inspector?' Jackson asked.

'Not yet. We need to ask Mrs Mellon some more questions.' Miller gestured to Harry. 'This is DCI McNeil. He's working with us on this enquiry.'

'We're going to need all the details about how Mrs Mellon came to be going out with this man for dinner,' Harry said.

'Anything you need.'

They went into the room. Brian was sitting with Rita.

'We meet again, Brian, or should I say Mr Wellington?' Miller said, referring to Brian's 'business' name of Carruthers Wellington.

'Inspector Miller.'

'Give us a minute, son,' Harry said to him.

'Please catch the bastard who did this to her.' Brian squeezed Rita's hand before getting up from the chair and leaving.

'I'm fine, really,' Rita said.

'They just want to check you out, Rita,' Miller said. 'There's a lot of people worrying about you.'

'That's nice, but I just got a fright. The bastard put a polythene bag over my head.' Her lip started to tremble a bit. 'He tried to kill me.'

'You're safe now. We'll have officers posted here, outside

your door, but I'm sure Adrian will have people close by too. He's not going to get you.'

'Thank God for that man with his dog. He saved my life.'

Miller sat on the edge of the bed while Harry sat on the chair. Weaver and Meekle stood around like a couple of wallflowers at the local singles' club. Alex stood well away from them.

'Tell us from the beginning how you ended up going to dinner with him.'

She did and they listened.

'What about the van? Anything distinctive about it?' Weaver asked.

'No...well, yes, in a way. It was clean. I mean, spotless. Like he'd been on his hands and knees with a scrubbing brush, cleaning it. He said his car had broken down and he'd borrowed this van from a friend, who was a builder. But that was no builder's van. Not a speck of dust in it. But listen to me; I thought he was some high-flying finance guy, and he had a bloody van. More fool me.'

'From what we know about him, he's very clever and very convincing.'

'Is there anything that sticks out about him?' Alex asked.

'No. He was charming, but he did go on about the first *God Complex*. He said it was a wasted opportunity. I thought that sounded strange, because it was a very famous show. A wasted opportunity for what?'

A knowing look passed between Harry and Miller. *He could have killed more people.*

'You grabbed his face and a piece came off,' Harry said.

'Yes. It was like he had a rubber face. He didn't scream or anything, and there was no blood. It was like he had put on a disguise.'

They asked her a few more questions, but it was clear she didn't know much more.

Outside, Miller looked at the others. 'It's somebody who's working for that production company. He would know how to put a face on.'

'Agreed,' Weaver said. 'We'll get a full list of names tomorrow. By then we should have a positive ID on the second victim. If it is indeed Aileen Rogers, then we know she was a make-up artist on the set.'

'Maybe she was doing make-up on our killer. Maybe she found out and he had to kill her,' Meekle said.

'First thing tomorrow, I want a list of people who work there, and I want them re-interviewed,' Harry said.

'I'll make sure we have it first thing,' Miller told him.

He saw Robert Molloy approaching.

'I'll get off, Frank. See you in the morning.' Harry rapidly caught up with the other two detectives as they walked away to where Alex was standing, close by.

'What's up, McNeil?' Weaver said.

'I'm telling you this to your face: you ever call me up at home and talk to me like that again, I'll break your jaw. And you, Meekle, egging him on. You need him to fight your battles?'

Meekle took a step forward, but Weaver put an arm out to stop him. 'Listen to you; you've got a pair of balls after all.'

'In my time with Standards, I've fought a lot harder men than you. Both of you. Pair of bastards.'

Weaver grinned. 'See what you're getting into, Maxwell? Having a boss like him?'

'Better than having a boss like you.'

The smile fell from Weaver's face. 'You watch your mouth.'

'Or else what?'

He sneered at her. 'I reckon that firefighter boyfriend of yours had a lucky escape.' He and Meekle turned away.

'That cheeky –'

Harry put his hands on her arms. 'Forget him. He's not worth it.'

She sagged and let out a breath. 'When I told you Weaver was alright to work with, I lied. He's made my life hell.'

'I thought as much. Come on, you can drive me home.'

'That's the best offer I'm going to get tonight.' She smiled weakly as they walked in the opposite direction from Weaver.

Robert Molloy reached Miller. 'Well, well, Harry McNeil isn't dead after all. I haven't seen that scrote for ages. Or that other balloon, Weaver.' He watched as Harry disappeared into the lift.

'He's not too bad.'

'Compared to what?' Robert shook his head and made a face. 'Who's the other one?'

'Charlie Meekle. He's up from Newcastle.'

'Anyway, I heard that one of your officers is in here.'

'Yes. Steffi Walker.'

'She's such a nice lassie,' Robert said.

'Somebody gave her a kicking.'

'I hope you got the bastard.'

'We did and we didn't,' Miller said.

'Stop talking in riddles.'

'It was a domestic. Her boyfriend gave her a doing.'

'Jesus. And she's a copper too. I hope you gave him a slap in the cells.'

'Come on now, Molloy. You know we don't operate like that, as much as we'd like to sometimes.'

'So he's going to get what? A slap on the wrist from one of those ponces on the bench?'

'We don't even have him yet. But even if we do get him, Steffi isn't pressing charges.'

'He'll walk, in other words.'

'That's the bottom line.'

Robert looked at him. 'You know, Steffi and that other lassie, Julie, they took on a killer who was hell-bent on killing me and they overpowered him. No hesitation. They saved my life that night. And now some fuck has hit Steffi and he's going to get a tickle from some old wiggy judge? That's a fucking sin, Frank.'

'We have to abide by the law.'

'That's true. You do.'

'Behave yourself, Molloy,' Miller said, but there was no conviction in his tone.

'I have no choice. I don't know his name or where he works.'

Miller had an idea Robert Molloy knew *exactly* who Peter Hanson was and where he worked. He looked over Robert's shoulder and saw Julie Stott further along the white corridor, looking back at them. Then she was gone.

THIRTY-FOUR

Graham Balfour had just settled in for the night when there was a gentle tap on his door. 'Christ, you're late,' he said, roughly pulling the door open.

A masked man pushed him. Balfour fell on his back and the big man towered over him.

'Get up,' the man said.

'What the hell do you think you're doing?' Balfour said, getting to his feet. 'I'm calling the police.' He pulled his phone out of his pocket, but the man slapped it out of Balfour's hand before stepping over the threshold and closing the door behind him.

Balfour tried to fight back, but then a gloved fist punched him in the face. 'Shout and I'll fucking kill you.'

The big man grabbed Balfour by the hair and dragged

him through to the living room and threw him down onto the couch.

'Answer my questions and maybe I won't kill you,' he said.

'What? What the fuck are you talking about?' Balfour was scared now and barely holding on to his sphincter muscle.

'You heard. You're not fucking daft, are you? Although you pretend to be.'

'Listen, I don't know what's going on, but you need to leave.'

'I'm going to as soon as you tell me what I want to know.'

'Which is?'

'Who killed Trisha Cornwall?'

'I don't know. I swear.'

'Oh, I think you do know. And now he's killing other people. But I want him first. Was it you?'

'No, it wasn't me. Of course it wasn't me.'

The big man glowered at him. 'Who was messing with Jill Thompson? Who put his hands on a little girl?'

Balfour sat up straighter. 'I really don't know.'

The man stood chewing the inside of his cheek for a moment, then suddenly, like a cobra striking its victim, he lashed out, punching Balfour again. Then he grabbed his hair.

'People think you're special needs, that you lived with Mummy and Daddy because you're daft and couldn't get a job. So now you sign on, and make money from selling autographs. Utter pish. You don't fool me, Balfour. You're fucking at it. How do you really make money?'

'We sell stuff, honest.'

'Don't talk shite.' He punched Balfour again, then pulled him to his feet by the hair.

'Please don't hurt me.'

'How do you make money?'

'We steal their stuff and sell it on a black website. People will pay a lot of money for some of that stuff, especially... underwear. Not clean underwear.'

'Dirty bastard. Was Trisha Cornwall part of this?' He shoved him roughly into a chair.

'Yes. She would meet with some of them and sleep with them and take photos.'

The man shook his head. 'And blackmail them?'

'Yes.'

'Now we're getting somewhere.'

'This is all her fault. A grown woman, for fuck's sake. She couldn't control herself, though, and she started getting nasty. I wish I'd never met her.'

'Did you kill her?' the man asked again.

'Of course not. I slept with her, but I didn't kill her.'

'She let you touch her?' the man said, his voice full of scepticism.

'I'll show you.' Balfour got up and left the room for a moment, and came back in with a pair of women's knickers.

'Some people will pay a lot of money for these – underwear from a murder victim.'

'You disgust me,' the man said, snatching the flimsy garment and putting it in his pocket.

'Hey, those are mine.'

'Not now.' The man was inches from Balfour. 'What happened back then? To Jill.'

'I have no idea. She seemed obsessed with one of the crew.'

'Which one?'

'I don't know,' Balfour said, 'but she was in love with him.'

'Do you think he killed her?'

'Who knows? But what if he got her pregnant and thought it best to get rid of her? It would have ruined him after all. She was a little slag, by all accounts.' Balfour looked into the eyes of the man and saw nothing. Like he was staring into the past.

'What did you call her?' the man said, his voice barely a whisper.

'A slag,' Balfour said. 'She got what was coming to her.'

'So will you…' The man punched Balfour in the face, bursting his nose. 'Do you know who killed Trisha?'

Balfour couldn't speak; he was rolling about on the floor holding his nose.

'I know you know who killed her. I'll be back.'

Then the man calmly walked out of the living room and quietly closed the front door behind him.

THIRTY-FIVE

'You look tired this morning,' Alex said to Harry McNeil as she pulled the pool car into the car park at the back of the station in the high street.

'The last thing I expected was to get called out to the Royal.' He unclipped his seatbelt and rolled the window up. Even fresh air hadn't got rid of the unpleasant stale smell inside the vehicle.

'I swear to God, those lazy sods in the pool garage better take a vacuum cleaner to this thing tonight.'

'We could always use your wee Honda,' Alex said, smiling at him over the roof. 'Do you have dice hanging from the mirror?'

'Your attempt at humour is falling on deaf ears.'

Upstairs, Frank Miller was standing in front of the whiteboard. 'Morning, sir,' he said.

'How're things, Frank?'

'We got word back from the lab that what Rita Mellon pulled off her attacker was indeed synthetic material used for TV. It's painted on. Easy to apply, if you know what you're doing.'

'Where're Weaver and Meekle?'

'I haven't seen them this morning.'

'Listen up!' Percy Purcell came into the room. 'The family of Aileen Rogers were notified last night about the possible death of their daughter, and her dental records have just been checked, confirming her identity. We have to go and speak with the husband. Also, the lab is trying to see if they can get DNA off the piece of mask that Mrs Mellon pulled off the attacker's face.'

'Any leads on the van, boss?' one of the younger detectives asked.

'Nothing. A white Transit van, that's all we've got. We're checking CCTV in the area.'

Purcell walked over to Miller. 'On Trisha Cornwall's phone were numbers for Graham Balfour and Randy Kline. We also identified another number, Aileen Rogers'. She had spoken to Trish on the night of her death.'

'They all knew each other?' Harry said.

'Well, they're connected. Balfour was a friend of Trisha's. Now we know Trisha was connected to Aileen Rogers, and both women are dead.'

'I don't believe this nonsense that Balfour and his little

gang make money selling autographs and the like,' Harry said. 'I mean, they might do, but I can't see them making much money from them.'

One of the junior detectives answered a ringing phone, then shouted for Purcell. 'Sir, Commander Bridge would like a word in her office. Inspectors Miller and McNeil are to attend too.'

Purcell looked at them. 'Gentlemen, let's not keep the lady waiting.'

Upstairs in her office, Jeni Bridge was holding a piece of paper in her hand. She handed it over to Purcell.

'Remember I said we would have Jill Thompson's DNA checked again from the samples we had from 1999? The results are back in.' She looked at Miller and McNeil, then back to Purcell.

'Go get him.'

THIRTY-SIX

Robert Molloy walked along the corridor, his bodyguard holding two bunches of flowers. He stopped at Rita's door and knocked, taking a bunch.

She was pleased to see him and accepted the flowers. There was a bruise on her face from where the attacker had hit her.

'How are you feeling today, Mrs Mellon?'

'Better, Mr Molloy, thank you. And thank you for the flowers. They're beautiful.'

'Call me Robert. We're all one big family now. We look after each other. And that's what I wanted to talk to you about.'

'Oh yes?'

'Yes. This man who took you to dinner last night; did you tell the police anything that might help them catch him?'

'I told them everything I know. Why? Was that wrong?'

'No, of course not. We need to get him, Rita, and I don't care if it's us or the police. As long as he's caught. But did he tell you anything that might have stuck out?'

'He was very charming. He said he had a classic car and that it had broken down, but I don't believe that now. I was surprised when he said we were getting into a van.'

'It was a white Transit?'

'Yes.'

'Which way did he go when you left the restaurant?'

'We drove past the bars at the shore, then we turned right into Commercial Street and headed up to Ferry Road.'

Robert nodded, then made small talk for a little bit before standing up. 'I have to stop by and see somebody else. Two of my people are outside and will be there in shifts until it's time for you to leave, then Adrian will make sure you're safe.'

'Thank you for coming here, Robert. It means a lot.'

He leant over and kissed her cheek. Then he left and walked along the corridor, his man now carrying one bunch of flowers.

Robert told a nurse he was there to visit a friend of the family. The two policemen stood aside to let him enter Steffi's room with the flowers.

'Hello, DS Walker. I'm here visiting a friend and I thought these might cheer you up.'

'Hello. That's very kind.'

Robert's eyes went to the bruising on Steffi's face as she

sniffed the bouquet. He took them back and put them on a table.

'It seems you've been having a bit of a to-do with your boyfriend.' She started to protest, but he held up a hand.

'Please indulge an old man.'

She settled back on the bed.

'Steffi, let me tell you a little story. My girlfriend, Jean, has been married before. She thought her husband was the love of her life. She even took his little boy as her own, before she and her husband had a little girl, God rest her soul. But although the husband was kind at first, as soon as they got comfortable, he would hit her. Just a little slap at first, then they got harder. And he would apologise and promise her it would never happen again.

'Until the next time. He would hit her again, and harder this time, and the frequency increased. Then she'd had enough. It was hard for her, but she had to leave him. And only then did it stop.'

'Do you have a point, Mr Molloy?'

'It's not going to stop, Steffi. It's going to get worse. Why am I here talking to you like this? Because you and Julie Stott saved my life that night, I have no doubt. You are a very brave young woman and I have a soft spot for you. I like you, and I can't say that about a lot of coppers.'

'I'll be fine.'

'Be honest with me: has he managed to sneak in and see you?'

She was silent for a moment. 'How did you know?'

'It's what they do. They are master manipulators. Did he come dressed as a doctor?'

'Yes.'

'It's the logical thing. Frank Miller would go off his nut if he found out. Not at you, but Hanson.'

'Please don't tell him,' she pleaded.

'I'm not going to. Let me leave you with this, though. He promised you it won't happen again and you can start afresh. He told you he will never hurt you again and he's sorry for what happened.'

She stayed silent.

Robert stood looking down at her. 'They're false promises, Steffi. Just bear that in mind.' He saw tears running down her cheeks.

'I don't want to end up alone,' Steffi said.

'You won't. You can find somebody else, somebody who will love you without resorting to hitting you when things get a little rough.'

'I used to be in the army. I'm a detective. I'm not supposed to feel this scared, Mr Molloy. But I am. I can see something lurking in his eyes. I've seen it there before, in people I've arrested: evil.' She looked Robert right in the eyes. 'This is something I can't tell Frank, but I'm scared. I have nobody else to tell that to.'

Steffi started sobbing and Robert put an arm around her.

'You've got me,' he said.

And when he left her a little while later, he called his son. 'Get somebody up to the Royal. I want some men standing outside a couple of doors. And also, there's one other little thing I want taken care of.'

When he was done, he left the hospital.

THIRTY-SEVEN

'I hope Vanessa didn't give you too much of a hard time last night when she got home and found out you had a Chinese with me,' Alex said as she drove down North Bridge behind the other unmarked cars.

'If this is blackmail, it isn't going to work.'

'Oh dear, what a mind you have. I was just hoping that she's not the jealous type.'

'That's none of your business, Sergeant.'

Alex smiled.

'Let me ask you something,' Harry said. 'Did you drive Weaver out of the department? I mean, with your incessant chatter and birdlike laughter.'

'Birdlike laughter?' She opened her mouth in mock indignation. 'Surely you jest, Harry. Tell me you're just tired and don't mean what you say.'

'There. Just like that. I bet I would have read about Weaver being taken away in a straitjacket.'

Alex laughed. 'He never called my laughter *birdlike*. That's all you.'

'Not to your face, anyway.'

'Oh, away with yourself. Stan often said he had never met anybody quite like me in his entire life.'

'I can pretty much say the same thing.' His phone rang and he took it out of his pocket. It was Weaver. 'McNeil,' Harry said, answering.

'Harry. I hope you don't mind, but I need you to come down to the cemetery. I've found something. I can't say on the phone.'

'Oh yeah? We were just heading out, but I can make it down there.'

'Oh, okay. But listen, there are things about that case that weren't right.'

'Like what?'

'Just some things that were said at the time.'

'Okay, I'll keep that in mind.' Harry paused for a moment. 'You been drinking, Stan?'

'What, are you my mother now? I have to answer to you? I don't think so. And you would do well to remember that. Just get your arse down here, McNeil.'

Harry disconnected the call. 'Uncle Stan isn't too happy with me.'

'You should have put it on speaker and I could have told

him where to go.'

'You'll get to say it to his face; he wants us to go down to Warriston.'

'We were going there anyway.'

'I think he's still hungover. He must have forgotten.'

Alex stared ahead through the windscreen. 'I don't care that he's retiring, Harry; I won't have him slagging me off.' She looked at him. 'Or treating us like crap.'

The trailers had moved further down the site when they got there, closer to the old caretaker's house.

Alex pulled in behind Miller's car as it stopped and they saw the others getting out.

'You ready, sir?' Miller said to Harry. Purcell was standing nearby.

'Let's do it.'

'What's going on, sir?' Alex said.

'Come on. You should see this. And later, when you feel like lecturing me, remember that this was on a need-to-know basis.' Harry looked at Miller. 'Which one is Kline's trailer?'

'The one over the other side of that incline. We can't see it from here.'

'Are you going to arrest Kline?' Alex asked.

'Just come with us.'

Purcell took out his phone. 'You ready over there?' He waited for the answer before hanging up. 'Hazel Carter is there with two of your team, McNeil. In case he makes a run for it.'

'Let's go,' Miller said, heading off round the hill.

Kline's trailer was sitting on its own. It was eerily silent. They approached as though they were just looking to sit down and have a cup of coffee.

Miller opened the door and stepped inside, followed by Harry and Alex.

The two men inside turned round suddenly.

'What are you doing here, Miller?' Stan Weaver said. Charlie Meekle was standing next to him. They were both wearing leather gloves, despite it being warm outside. 'Did you bring them here, McNeil? I trusted you!'

'Shut up,' Harry said.

'Talk to a superior officer like that? I demand that you get out of here, Miller. You're impeding an investigation. And take that silly bitch with you.'

'They're here under my orders, Weaver.' Percy Purcell stepped through the door.

Weaver just stood looking at the other detectives.

'What's in the bag, Stan?' Harry said.

They all looked at the carrier bag Meekle was holding.

'None of your damn business.'

'Sorry, Stan. I can't do this anymore. It's killing me.' Meekle handed the bag to Miller. 'It's a pair of that lassie's knickers. I got them from Graham Balfour. He'd slept with her and she'd left some stuff at his house. We were going to say we caught Kline stashing them.'

'Are you fucking daft?' Weaver said.

'It's over. They know or else they wouldn't be here.' The hard-bitten Glaswegian detective now looked pitiful as he looked at Harry. 'I killed Jill Thompson. She was my stepdaughter.'

'Shut up, ya clown!' Weaver shouted. 'They know nothing.'

'Why do you think we're here, Weaver?' Purcell said. 'We have DNA results from that night. Taken from Jill. Go on, Meekle.'

'I had been drinking the night she died. A lot. We had a fight. She said she was going to the cemetery to meet her boyfriend. I followed her, but by Christ I was staggering all over the place. I don't remember much about that night, but I remember catching up to her here, near the old house. We were arguing. It got heated. I tried to grab her arm, but she scratched me. I remember falling and hitting my head on the gravestone. It must have toppled on top of her.' Meekle looked at them all. 'I didn't mean to kill her. You have to believe me.'

Purcell nodded. 'I do believe you. When I said we have the results from the DNA test, I didn't mean we had skin samples from Jill's fingernails when she scratched you. I mean we have the results from Jill's baby. We know who the father was.' He looked at Weaver.

'It's over for you now, Stan,' Harry said. 'We know you're the father.'

Meekle looked puzzled. 'What do you mean, Stan's the father?'

'You know as well as I do that every serving officer's DNA is on file, in case we have to eliminate them from a crime scene. We put Jill's baby's DNA through the system and we got a match. Stan Weaver was the father.'

'Is this true?' Meekle looked at Stan, and Harry thought he was about to take a swing at Weaver. Harry reached over and guided Meekle away.

All the air seemed to go out of Weaver. 'It's true. You said Jill told you she was meeting her boyfriend that night, and she was: me.'

'Dirty bastard.'

'I was thirty-six back then. Not an old fart like now. I couldn't help it. You know yourself, she dressed and acted like she was twenty, not fifteen. She knew what she was doing, let me tell you. Then, that night, she told me she was pregnant. My life, my career, would have been over.'

'You killed my daughter?' Meekle shook his head.

Weaver nodded. 'Yes. I was hiding. We saw you coming in, shouting and staggering about. I didn't want a confrontation. I watched you fight with her and fall against the gravestone. But you didn't hit it hard enough to topple it. I saw that as my way out. I hit her and put her on the ground. Then I pushed it on top of her.

'Afterwards, I took your mobile out of your pocket and called my number, making it look like you had called me. I waited fifteen minutes, then I slapped you and brought you round. You were begging me not to tell anybody. I convinced you that you had called me.

'I knew CID would get called out from Gayfield Square and I was right. We got the case. I was able to hide some stuff and make things disappear when they thought they were getting close, and I diverted their attention to Graham Balfour. He was obviously never convicted.'

'Sorry,' Weaver said to Meekle.

'Bastard. I trusted you.'

Weaver looked at Harry. 'You're getting the cold case unit to yourself earlier than expected.'

'No, I'm not,' Harry said. 'I'm not working the cold case unit. I was brought in to investigate you. I was never going to be a part of the cold case unit. I'm almost finished with Professional Standards; this was my last case with them.'

Alex turned round and left the trailer without saying a word.

'You were investigating me? You little...'

'Why?' Meekle asked.

'When Trisha was murdered in the same way, we had a feeling that Weaver would somehow get involved in the case, to make sure things weren't going to lead back to him. We didn't know he had killed Jill twenty years ago, but there was certainly enough suspicion that he had been up to something. They drafted me in on the pretext that I was taking over the cold case unit.'

'I didn't kill the Cornwall woman,' Weaver said.

'We know you didn't,' Miller said. 'Why did you try to put evidence in here?'

'To divert attention away from us. To make it look like Kline was the killer.'

'If Weaver didn't kill Trisha Cornwall, then who did?' Meekle asked.

THIRTY-EIGHT

Outside, Harry McNeil found Alex sitting in the shadow of some trees on a gravestone that had been toppled years ago.

'Funny place to catch some rays,' he said to her.

She looked up at him. 'Why didn't you tell me?'

'I couldn't. Frank Miller and I were the only two who knew. It had to stay that way, especially since Commander Bridge asked Meekle to come up and give us some insight into the murders.'

'And you just left the two of them to their own devices.' She stood up and brushed off her jeans.

'We were hoping something would unravel. Weaver was a suspect right from the beginning. We hoped they would get together and try to make sure we didn't connect last week's murder to the one twenty years ago.'

She nodded. 'And they put you in place in such a short time?'

'Yes. As soon as Trisha Cornwall was found, this whole investigation was set up.'

'They don't mess about, do they?'

'Don't look so sad,' Harry said.

'Just when we thought we were getting rid of Old Grumpy and somebody half-decent was taking over. I should have known it was too good to be true.'

'Look on the bright side: you still got rid of Weaver and there's no chance he'll be back. He's going to Saughton for murder.'

'Silver linings, eh?' She gave him a grim smile. 'I'd better get to the office now that we're not needed.'

'I'll see you there. I have to come back later.'

Alex walked away without turning round.

'What's going on in there?' Randy Kline said as he came towards the trailer.

'Mr Kline, nice timing.' Miller turned towards him.

'You didn't answer my question.'

'We're waiting for your son.'

'What do you want with Dustin?' Kline looked over into the distance. Saw his son walking between the gravestones. 'Dustin!'

All heads turned and they watched Dustin Crowd break into a run. Miller and his team started running towards him.

Dustin jumped into the white caterer's van, started it up and took off.

The caterer jumped out of his food trailer shouting. 'Where's he going with my van?'

Miller and Harry were about to jump into their cars when they saw an old Ford Focus pull in front of the van, which collided with the passenger side and came to a halt.

They all ran towards the scene, Miller in the lead. He reached the van to find Dustin Crowd with a bleeding nose. Harry approached the Focus. The airbags in both vehicles had gone off.

Harry reached the Focus and pulled the driver's door open. 'Jesus, Alex, are you okay?'

She smiled at him, blood running down her face. 'No more smelly socks.'

THIRTY-NINE

Purcell watched the interview on a monitor in another room. Harry McNeil and Frank Miller were doing the interview in a room in the high street station. Dustin Crowd had been seen to by the force doctor and his nose had stopped bleeding. It wasn't broken.

Miller pushed the folder across towards Dustin's solicitor. 'The DNA results. From the piece of latex that was pulled from your client's face.'

Dustin seemed to be staring into space for a moment. 'My dad had nothing to do with this. He wasn't involved.'

'You have the floor, Dustin,' Harry said. 'You can tell us in your own words why you killed those women, or you can just disappear into the ether and nobody will know the story of why the great actor Dustin Crowd turned into a killer.'

'It wasn't like I was some nut job.'

'Tell us how it was then,' Miller said.

Dustin paused, as if he was going to deliver some line. 'Trisha Cornwall was blackmailing my dad.'

'For the record, can you say who your father is?' Harry said.

'Randy Kline.'

'Fine. Carry on.'

'Trisha was blackmailing him. I overheard them one night, talking in the cemetery. Trisha was Jill Thompson's best friend, twenty years ago. She said that Jill confided in her and that my dad was the father of her baby. She was fifteen! If it came out now that my dad had slept with a fifteen year old back then, his career would be over. Trisha was telling my dad that people would think he killed Jill because of the baby. She wanted more money. My dad said he would get it to her the following day. He left and that rancid cow was about to go as well. I hit her on the head with a real hammer we use for filming certain angles. Then I pushed the gravestone on top of her.'

'Did Kline, your father, see this?'

'No. He was on his way back to his trailer.'

'What about Aileen Rogers?'

'She was my make-up artist. I put latex on my face, made myself up a bit. Put a beard on. You can actually make them look like they're real nowadays and I'd watched Aileen do it for many hours as she made me up. She didn't even suspect.'

'It's hard to believe she couldn't see right through it.'

'I met her when it was dark. I borrowed the catering van, made sure the lights didn't come on inside when we opened the doors.'

'Why did you choose her?' Harry said.

'She was weak and vulnerable. We would talk when she was doing my make-up. She said she was going to leave her husband. I suggested a chatroom and she thought it was a good idea, so I gave her the web address for one. When I asked her if she'd joined, she told me her online name. I contacted her through the chatroom and gave her some spiel and we agreed to meet up. She didn't know it was me.'

'What happened after you got her into the cemetery?' Miller asked.

'I don't want you to think it was easy for me. I just told myself I was filming a scene, which I was going to do anyway, so this was like a rehearsal. I had to make it look like there was a killer on the loose. Physically, it was easy, as I'd put a little something in the champagne we had.'

'And Rita Mellon?'

'Her boyfriend, that idiot who called himself Carruthers Wellington, had left his phone in the trailer one day. Rita called him. I saw her number and chose her. I sent her a text from a throwaway phone and said we should meet up for dinner so I could invest in the show. I told her Brian had given me the number. She fell for it. And I would have killed her if it wasn't for that guy with the dog.'

'And she clawed your face and got some of your mask. Which had your DNA on it because it was on your skin,' Harry said.

'The wonders of modern science.' Dustin sat back in the chair. 'I know what people are going to think of me, but I want them to know my father didn't harm anybody. He was innocent in all of this.'

'There is one thing,' Harry said. 'You said Trisha was blackmailing your dad, telling him he was the father of Jill's baby, twenty years ago.'

'Yes, I just told you that. Jill told Trisha back then that her boyfriend was my dad.'

'Jill was lying. We got the DNA results back and the father wasn't your dad. Randy Kline wasn't the father of Jill's baby. You killed her for nothing.'

The screams Dustin Crowd let out were better than any acting he had ever done.

'Jesus, he was pretending he was in a scene from his show?' Purcell said after Dustin Crowd had been taken down to the holding cells.

'It would seem that way. He doesn't have much grip on reality,' Miller said.

Harry looked at his watch. 'If you'll excuse me, sir,' he said to Purcell, 'I have to get back to the office at HQ.'

'You did well there, McNeil. You both did.'

'Thank you.' Harry was walking away when Purcell stopped him.

'I'll see you soon.'

FORTY

Simon Gregg was arm-wrestling DI Karen Shiels when Harry walked into the office at HQ.

'Bear in mind, I'll kick you in the balls if you hurt my arm,' she said to him.

Gregg let her win.

'Good job, sir,' he said to Harry.

'Thank you. It was a team effort. But we have an announcement to make.'

'Who's we?' Karen said.

'DCI McNeil and I,' said Jeni Bridge, coming into the room. Alex was behind her, a white clip on her nose.

'It's just to help the air flow,' she said.

'DS Maxwell helped stop a killer. We lost a car in the process, but it needed to be replaced, by all accounts.' Jeni sat down on a chair, indicating for everybody else to sit.

'DS Maxwell knows the story, but the rest of you don't. DCI McNeil wasn't here to take over the department from DCI Weaver; he was here to investigate him.'

A rumble of mutterings started up and Jeni held up a hand. 'Sorry for keeping you in the dark, but it needed to be that way. However, I also have some more news for you. The cold case unit isn't going to exist in its present state as of this week. Next Monday morning, this department will be staffed by civilians. Ex-detectives, under the leadership of George Carr and Willie Young, who are doing a sterling job. The chief constable and the police board decided that the detectives here were wasting their talent. Or we were wasting valuable resources – whatever way you want to look at it. Cutbacks are happening all over Scotland.

'So, here's what we came up with. DCI McNeil is going to head up a third MIT unit. God knows there's enough work for us. However, there are smaller police areas that don't benefit from having the resources or the need for a full-time MIT unit, so this third team will go and assist in certain areas of the country.'

'What's going to happen to us?' Alex asked.

'There's a position for you all in the new team. If you want it. You will work under DCI McNeil, who'll report to me and directly to Superintendent Purcell. Would you like to move to the new unit? It will still be based here in the HQ building.'

Alex, Gregg and Karen all said they would be very happy to move.

'Great. First thing Monday morning, nice and sharp. You are all officially off the cold case unit.'

Jeni got up and left the room.

'You're not getting rid of me that easily,' Harry said.

Alex laughed. 'Jesus, that hurts.'

'Let's just hope they get us better cars,' Harry said. 'Or maybe not. What with the way you drive. Pulling out in front of a van like that...'

FORTY-ONE

Peter Hanson paid the taxi driver and waited for his change. 'I don't get a tip at my work!' he shouted to the back of the cab as it drove away. Then he stumbled up the pathway to his front door. To the flat that Frank Miller didn't know about.

'Tell me I'm not already a better detective than he is,' he said out loud, fumbling with his key. Finally, he got it into the lock and went inside.

Then he stopped. He thought he'd heard a noise inside. Was it Steffi? No. She didn't know about this place, his bachelor pad before he'd met his wife.

Nobody knew about this place.

He gently closed the door and walked along the hallway, staggering a few times. He'd left a lamp on a timer and it was switched on.

There were two people in his living room. Women. What the hell was going on?

'What do you think you're doing?' he said.

One of the women turned to him and smiled. 'We're waiting for you.'

'What?'

'We wanted to have a talk with you,' the other said.

'That will be right. Get the hell out of my house.'

Then he felt a push in his back from somebody behind him and he went flying into the room, landing face down on the carpet. He looked round from the floor and saw a big man framed in the doorway.

'Who are you?' Hanson said.

'Never mind who I am, Peter. It's who I represent you should be worried about. My boss wanted us to give you a wee message.'

One of the women kicked Hanson hard in the stomach while the other pulled his hair and punched him in the face.

'I'm going to kick your spleen out, you bitches,' Hanson yelled, trying to get up.

The man stepped forward. 'These two women know more ways to inflict pain than you've had hot showers. We're going to take you somewhere, to a place where you will be taught a lesson.'

'Did Steffi put you up to this? Are you a bunch of coppers who think this is funny? Well, I'll show her. She won't fuck with me again.'

'Oh, you're right on that count. She will most definitely not fuck with you ever again.'

The man walked over and crouched down by Hanson. 'The police couldn't find you. You made yourself disappear; no mobile phone use, no cash machine use, no nothing. They think you're on the run. They don't know kept this place on without telling anybody about it. In other words, you've already made our job easy. You've disappeared and nobody knows where you are.'

'How did you find me?'

'Simple. When you applied for the police, this was the address you used. They'll check your old addresses further, obviously, but by the time they do and come looking, you'll be long gone.'

The man took out a syringe and stuck it into Hanson's neck, then he stood up.

Anybody who'd seen Hanson coming home drunk would just see him coming back out drunk, only this time with three friends. Like they were celebrating.

Outside, the two women acted like they were having a good time and holding their friend Peter up.

A black van pulled up outside the tenement building. This part of Leith was quiet at this time of night. The side door slid open and Hanson was shoved inside. The women got in after him. The man climbed in beside the driver.

Peter Hanson would never lift his hand to a woman again.

STICKS AND STONES

DCI HARRY MCNEIL BOOK 2

ONE

It was the smell that hit him first. He'd read books where the detective said he smelled blood, but the boy had never smelled blood before. He wasn't even sure it was blood, but it was something strange.

He was aware of the silence next. The house was never this quiet. His sister was usually home from school and his mother would be in the kitchen making something for dinner.

Today there was nothing but silence. No smell of cooking, but something else entirely. Something that scared him.

His father's car was in front of the house. He thought maybe he'd got home early, but that in itself was unusual.

All three things scared him: the smell, the quiet and his father's car. Those were the three things he would focus on in the years to come.

He wanted to call out to his mother but felt foolish. He

was sure his voice would sound panicked, as if he were a little boy instead of a teenager. What if they were out in the back garden? No, he would surely hear voices. All he could hear outside was birds.

He made his way to the stairs and stopped, listening for any sound from upstairs. A movement, somebody talking in hushed tones. A floorboard creaking. Anything. But he heard nothing.

He took the first step, his heart starting to beat faster now. He wouldn't have been so worried if it weren't for the smell. He didn't *want* to go upstairs, but he felt he *had* to. There was no way of getting around this.

He took another step and stopped as the tread creaked under his weight. He knew which stairs made a noise, but he hadn't been thinking about that. Now he did, careful where he placed each foot as he climbed higher.

He turned on the small landing to the next set of stairs, which headed up in the opposite direction to the first set. Stairs he had climbed thousands of times before, but it now seemed like he was climbing them for the first time, not knowing it was going to be the last time.

The house was big and isolated.

As he reached the main landing, the smell got worse.

A short hallway faced the stairs. A door on the left led into the bathroom, the opposite door into his bedroom. The other hallway ran left to right and had three doors: his mum and dad's bedroom, his sister's bedroom and the spare room for Uncle Jack, when he had been out drinking with Dad and was too drunk to drive home.

He took the right turn, leading to his sister's room. There was a window at the end of the hallway throwing some light onto the carpet. There was also light coming from Maggie's room. No light from his parents' room and the spare room; the doors were shut.

He walked towards Maggie's room. Later, he would remember looking down at the pattern of the carpet, a gold colour spun through the deep red.

Deep red. Just like blood.

He tried to call out his sister's name, but his voice was just a croak. His mouth was dry and he couldn't get his tongue to move. His legs felt like solid logs of wood that wouldn't move properly, just like the time he'd dreamed that the house was on fire and he couldn't run out, no matter how hard he tried.

He willed himself to move forward, feeling the icy grip of terror. He didn't know why. Couldn't explain it to himself.

The smell.

It was close.

He stood outside Maggie's room. His mother had told him he always had to knock before entering her room, but the door was wide open. He took a few breaths, in through the nose, out through the mouth.

Then he stepped in front of the doorway.

The room was empty.

Her soft toys were on the bed. Their mother always made

their beds early in the day. She said if she accomplished that simple task, it set her up for the rest of the day.

He turned away and walked towards the other end of the hallway, his legs starting to move faster, like an old engine coughing to life and beginning to run normally.

He almost felt relief after seeing his sister's room empty. It was like there was nothing wrong at all.

Except for the smell, which was getting stronger.

His parents' room was on the left. A window was set in the wall at the far end, just like the one outside Maggie's room. The bedroom door was ajar. The door to the spare room over on his right was closed, but this door was open. Where the smell was thickest.

He always had to knock on this door too, if it was closed.

But it was open.

The hinges creaked ever so slightly as he slowly pushed the door open wider. It was a different carpet in here. Beige with no patterns. He was looking down at it, not wanting to lift his eyes. Then he saw the new pattern on the carpet.

Red circles. Different sizes. Not near the door but closer to the back wall. He lifted his head, slowly looking at the wallpaper. It had the same pattern on it.

Little red circles. Big red circles.

As he opened the door wider, he saw that the big red circles became something else entirely. Big patterns, with something else mixed in.

No matter how many times he thought about what he saw

next, the thing he focused on first was his sister's eyes. Looking at him. Looking *through* him.

She was sitting on the bed, facing him. Behind her lay the cooling corpse of their mother. Where her head had been was now a bloody mess. He looked at Maggie, wordlessly begging for her to give him the answer, but she just sat silently.

He couldn't breathe. He tried drawing a breath, but only little pockets of air hit his lungs.

He was standing rooted to the spot when he felt the hairs on the back of his neck stand up. It was the tiniest of sounds, barely audible; he wouldn't have heard it if there had been any other ambient noise in the house. But he did hear the sound, and he felt a kind of fear he had never before experienced in his young life.

He couldn't move, couldn't turn round to see what the noise was. There was nowhere for him to run to even if he had turned round.

Then he felt the barrels of the shotgun placed against the back of his head.

'Sit on the bed beside your sister,' his father said, but it didn't sound like his father. His voice was rough and dry.

He couldn't move at first, but then the gun was pressed harder against his head and he felt himself step forward on shaky legs. He tried not to look at his sister or what was left of his mother. His sister stirred slightly as he sat down on the mattress.

His father kept the gun pointed at him as he slowly walked into the room.

'Please, Dad, don't do this,' he said, his voice cracked and broken.

His father sat down in a chair in the corner of the room, the one that his mother used to sit in and read.

The boy could feel his body tensing, waiting for the buckshot that would kill him.

The buckshot that would create more little red circles.

He wanted to get up and run, but his legs had stopped working. He just sat and waited to die.

But his father didn't kill him.

'Tell them it wasn't me,' his father said, his voice low, barely above a whisper.

He turned the shotgun, which the boy saw had been shortened, and put it under his chin.

The boy jumped a little as the noise of the gunshot reverberated around the room. Maggie sat staring.

He sat looking at his dead father, now lying slumped in the chair. It would be a full hour before he could find the ability to move.

His father's words echoed through his head. *Tell them it wasn't me*. But it *was* him. Who else could have killed his mother?

Only years later would the true meaning of his father's words sink in.

But by then, it would be too late.

TWO

'You can't hide behind those sunglasses forever,' DS Alex Maxwell said, dropping a gear in her BMW and flooring it.

'For the last time, my eyes are not bloodshot. I'm just tired, that's all.' DCI Harry McNeil reclined the seat a bit more after being thrown back into it. Usually, Sunday morning was for sobering up, not heading north out of Edinburgh with a member of his Major Investigation Team.

'None of my business what you get up to in your own time,' Alex said.

'Correct.' He fidgeted in the seat, trying to get more comfortable. 'We could have taken a pool car, you know.'

'A manky Vauxhall that smells like a dog's been in it? No thanks.'

Alex hit the outside lane on the Queensferry Crossing

bridge and zipped past a long line of cars, trucks and weekend warriors towing caravans.

Harry closed his eyes and recalled snatches of the conversation he'd had with Ness that morning. They'd broken up a week ago, and she had wanted to meet for a talk. First were words of disbelief that Harry was being pulled into his office at HQ, then a suggestion that he might want to tell his boss to send him up north with DC Simon Gregg, and she had refused to listen to the fact that he had to travel with a DS and that meant Alex Maxwell. It wasn't his decision; it came with the job.

Her reply had inferred he should check his own colon later, where he'd find his job residing.

'What did Vanessa say when you told her you were travelling with me and we'd be there for at least an overnight stay?' Alex said, as if reading his mind.

'Never you mind. Just keep your eyes on the road and slow down. I don't want the fire brigade to be called out to something that isn't a drill.'

'You're tetchy today. Are you not enjoying your drive out into the country with your favourite DS?'

'You're my only DS. And no, I'm not. I just wish the high heid yins had given us a little more warning.'

Alex slowed the car down a bit for Grandpa Harry. 'She only went missing last night.'

Harry made a noise. 'Pedants. Saturday night is for having a sociable beer and Sunday morning is for recovering from said sociable beer. Not reining it in just in case there's a phone call on the Sunday morning.'

'Must have been a riot, having a drink with Vanessa at the bowling club.'

'We do okay. The prices are cheap – that's why we go. They practically promote alcoholism.' He reached over and fiddled with the radio. 'Why do they have to make trannies so difficult to use nowadays?'

'Tranny?' Alex grinned at him.

'Short for transistor radio. My dad used the term. It stuck.' He found Radio 2.

'Good Lord, how old are you?' she said, and was about to reach over and change the station when he gently slapped her hand away.

'This might be your car, Sergeant, but I've just commandeered it.'

'Yeah, right. I'll just change it back when you fall asleep. And by the look of you, you're not far off it.'

Harry yawned, reinforcing her opinion. 'Okay, have it your way. But since I have my sunglasses on, you won't know when my eyes are closed.'

'You don't snore then?'

'See? This is why I would have chosen to drive up on my own. Peace and quiet and no lectures.'

'Apart from the fact you're hungover and would fail a breath test?'

'Touché.'

A few minutes later, the snoring and head tilt indicated that Harry's life might be in danger should Alex Maxwell decide that enough was enough, but she did nothing more dangerous than change the radio station.

On reaching Pitlochry, they had a quick pit stop and a pie out of the bakery. Two for Harry.

'I'm a growing boy,' he said, squeezing by a tourist with a backpack on.

'Growing sideways, though, eh?' Alex said with a grin.

They got back in the car and drove to a car park in the north part of town, next to where the buses and coaches parked. The sun was out, bathing them in a welcome heat, and they headed over to a small gazebo on the edge of the car park and sat at a little table.

'You know, another time, another life, this would be quite nice. You and me taking a drive up here. This is God's own country. I used to come up here with my mum and dad when I was wee. And my younger sister. You ever seen the Salmon Ladder?' Alex said, taking a bite out of her pie.

'Aye, a few times. I brought my son, Chance, up here a couple of times. We went camping, pitching a tent in the caravan park just up there, on the edge of town.'

'How did that go?' Alex asked, finishing her pie and wishing she had got a doughnut as well. She washed it down with a bottle of Coke.

'It was great. Just the two of us, sleeping in the tent, doing a little bit of fishing. Some hiking.'

'What about Vanessa? Does she like camping?'

'Unless it's got a bar and an en suite, she doesn't even entertain the idea of camping. *Glamping* she says she would do, but I'm sure that involves an expensive hotel instead of sleeping under the stars.'

'I wouldn't mind camping. I've done it before, when my mate and I went to T in the Park.'

'It's hardly the same thing, lying in a manky old tent, trying not to get trampled on, puking into a carrier bag.'

Alex nodded. 'Aye, it was a load of shite. People get raped. I would have stabbed some bastard before he got his hands on me. That's why I stayed sober, so I could look after my mate. She made drinking like a competition.'

'These things can be a magnet for deviants, right enough,' Harry said. 'Present company excepted.' He took the second pie out of the bag and bit into it.

'The diet starts tomorrow, eh?' Alex said.

'You're not going to make me feel guilty,' he said between mouthfuls. 'And Harry doesn't share.'

'As long as you wipe your greasy fingers before getting back into Betty.'

Harry looked at her, his eyebrows raised.

'My car; Betty the Blue Beemer I call her.'

'Of course you do,' he replied, finishing the pie and scrunching up the paper bag.

Harry made a show of wiping his fingers with the paper napkin before putting his rubbish in the bin.

'With the wipes I keep in Betty, I meant.'

'See? I wouldn't have had to wipe my fingers this much with a pool car.'

'I know. A greasy pie would have improved the interior.'

'I'll give my hands an extra-good wash,' he said, getting up, and went over to the toilets.

With his hands thoroughly cleaned, they set off north again, catching the A9 past the campsite where Harry had taken Chance. It brought back a lot of good memories, and he hoped his son wasn't being misled by his mother and the band of gypsies she called a family.

A tune by U2 came on and Harry felt his foot tapping as Alex expertly guided her car up the road.

'You like eighties music then?' she asked him.

'I do,' he said quietly, his mind slipping to a club he'd been in many moons ago with a woman he had subsequently took back to her place. He remembered this particular U2 song being played, 'With or Without You'. He had gone home in the early hours of the morning to an empty house, Morag already having moved out with Chance by then, and had sat on the couch listening to music and slowly drinking himself into a stupor.

'You okay there, Harry?' Alex said, looking over to him for a moment.

He nodded, feeling far from okay. He had messed up one marriage and now he was about to add a failed relationship to the pot. He closed his eyes and ran little private movies in his mind as the car drove north.

He must have dozed off, because the next thing he knew, they were on the approach to Inverness, about to bypass it and cross over the Kessock Bridge.

'You ever been to Inverness before?' Alex asked.

She was either very good at bluffing or she didn't know much about him.

'I was born here,' he said.

'Really?' she replied, taking her eyes off the road for a moment. 'How did you end up working down the road for the Edinburgh police?'

'My grandmother was born in Fort George, in Ardersier, just over there,' he replied, pointing east of Inverness, 'a couple of years before the war, when the fort still had an infirmary. The family stayed up here until 1991, when I was twelve. We moved down to Kirkcaldy to live when my dad got a transfer from the police up here down to Fife.'

'Your dad was a copper too?'

Harry nodded. 'He was. He's dead now. The drink got to him. It ruined his marriage, and my parents divorced.'

'Were you ever in the Fife police?'

'No. I went to Edinburgh Uni, but I was bored out of my crust. On a whim, I joined Lothian and Borders. And the rest is history.'

'And now you're coming home.' Alex looked at him as they crossed the bridge.

It took them less than an hour to make it the rest of the way to Dornoch, and five minutes from there to the Castle Hotel just outside the small town.

And that's when the view of rolling hills became a sea of police vehicles parked on the road with a uniform standing in the middle with his hand up. Another was walking about with a German Shepherd that looked like it hadn't had a good meal in days and any old arse would do to sink its teeth into.

A man in a suit walked over, smiling. 'Never mind that, son. They're the Edinburgh contingent.'

The uniform walked away with a quick glance back as if he didn't believe that. The man in the suit bent down to look through the window.

'DS Alex Maxwell, meet DCI Jimmy Dunbar. He's from Glasgow. The rougher version of Edinburgh,' Harry said.

'Pleased to meet you, sir.'

'Likewise, Sergeant. Now, if my own sergeant would stop disappearing, I would be able to introduce him.' Dunbar looked at Harry. 'Better watch what I say. Considering there's a lassie missing.'

'Aye, that kind of talk might upset the natives.'

'It's no' them I'm worried about upsetting, Harry; it's her old man. And the groom's father. Although the bride's mother's a bit of a Rottweiler too. Looks like his trophy wife. Come on, I was just getting the team together. I want a briefing before we go any further. Follow me.'

Dunbar walked away and got into a car, and they tailed

him through the gates and down the road towards the castle itself.

'He's the lead investigator?' Alex asked.

'He has seniority.' Harry looked at her. 'Look on the bright side; if the bride finally does decide to come back, they have a spa.'

'Not my style, sir. Not my style at all.'

'I forgot. Boggin' old tents and pishing in a bucket for you.'

'Don't knock it till you've tried it.'

'I've had the tee shirt that long, it's faded.'

As they got closer to the castle, Harry could see more police vehicles parked outside the front door. And he got a bad feeling. This was just too much activity for somebody who was only listed as missing.

Then he saw the bride's father striding over to DCI Dunbar's car and shouting at the detective as he got out.

'What's his problem?' Alex said.

'He's the bride's father. Broderick Gallagher. You'll see why he's got a problem.'

They got out of the car into the cooler north air and the man turned and came towards them.

THREE

'Are you the Edinburgh crowd?' Broderick Gallagher said, now rounding on Harry. The man was in his fifties and he was well built, with a red face that suggested he might be in need of the hotel's defibrillator shortly.

'DCI Harry McNeil, Edinburgh MIT. This is DS –'

'Never mind her,' Gallagher said, dismissing the lower ranks. 'I want to know what the hell you're going to do about my daughter. It's been well over twelve hours since she went missing! On her wedding night, no less!'

'That's why we've been sent up here, to back up Inverness MIT, sir. If you could let us inside, we'll get an update and then talk to you all. We're just as keen to find her as –'

'Bollocks. Just get on with it. Bloody well do something.' Gallagher strode away.

Harry looked over at Dunbar, who was resisting the temptation to add Gallagher to the missing persons' list.

'He's a charmer,' Alex said as they made their way into the hotel with Dunbar.

'He's a very rich charmer,' Harry said.

'We've taken over the library,' Dunbar said, seeing his DS poke his head out for a moment before disappearing back inside.

They went in and saw a whiteboard set up, and people being interviewed at the far end by men in suits.

'That's the Inverness lot,' the young sergeant said, coming over to them. 'The old school.'

'That's enough, Robbie,' Dunbar said. 'We're here to help them, not take the piss.' He looked at Harry and Alex. 'This is DS Robert Evans.'

Harry acknowledged the younger man. Boaby by name, boaby by nature. He'd seen many like him before, and all of them had crashed and burned. No doubt Evans would be the same one day.

'Right, let's get a seat and see what's going on,' Harry said to Dunbar. 'We were told only the basics and that you would fill us in when we got here.' He was about to add *sir* when he remembered that he too was a DCI. The promotion had only kicked in a few weeks earlier and he was still getting used to it.

The four detectives sat at a table. 'Tell me what you know, Harry,' Dunbar said.

'I got a call first thing this morning telling me that a young bride had gone missing up here. Her father is Broderick Gallagher, owner of our local newspapers, the *Caledonian* and the *Edinburgh Evening Post*.'

'Aye, and she just married into the Randall family, from our neck of the woods. Terence Randall, head of the Randall car empire. It's his son who got hitched to Marie Gallagher.'

'Both families are multi-millionaires, I assume,' Alex said, 'or else we wouldn't be here for a missing person.'

'You assume correctly, Sergeant,' Dunbar said. 'That's why there's a lot of squawking, and why the chief constable got a phone call late last night. And pish runs downhill. I was given a quick briefing and sent up here with this young reprobate. And told to pack a suitcase.'

'It was much the same for me. Not that DS Maxwell's a reprobate, you understand,' Harry added when he saw Alex looking at him.

'Well, this clown is.' Dunbar looked at Evans as if expecting an argument but got none.

'What's the latest report?' Harry asked.

'Still the same as earlier. They have uniforms out scouring the grounds, along with dog handlers and the stewards who work here. Butlers with kilts.'

'This is a big place then?'

Dunbar scoffed 'Big? It's twenty thousand acres. There are lodges over the other side of the river that splits this place. They also bought land to the north and an old, rundown estate to the west. The properties all border each other. We've been given a room each to stay in while we're here.'

'At the very least, she'll turn up and we can have a wee sesh and then head back down the road,' Harry said.

'Maybe they had a fight, nobody knew about it and she decided to play silly buggers,' Alex said.

'We asked the guests and staff, but none have said they heard anything like that. We're still working our way through them.'

Harry looked at a man who had approached them. He was one of a few he had seen walking about dressed in a tweed jacket and kilt with a bunnet. He had a well-trimmed bushy beard.

'My name is Angus McPhee, the head steward. Can I get you folks anything? Soft drink perhaps?'

Harry was sweating and nodded that he would indeed like a drink. 'Yes, please. I'd like a water.'

'I'll get one of my men to bring some over. A few of them are being interviewed just now.'

'How about you?' Harry said. 'You been interviewed already?'

'I was the first one, sir.' McPhee's accent was rough Scottish, and there was a hardness in the man's eyes that belied his smile.

'Good. I'll want to talk to you myself, just to be brought up to speed. I'm DCI McNeil from Edinburgh.'

'Well, DCI McNeil from Edinburgh, I'll go and get those

drinks organised.'

They watched the big man walk away.

'I'd like to talk to the parents,' Harry said.

'They're through in the big lounge,' Dunbar said. 'Broderick and Anne Gallagher. They've been spoken to by Inverness, but I told them we'd want to talk to them as well. They weren't happy, but if they want help in finding their daughter, they'd better get the pokers out of their arses. We'll talk to them, and I'll introduce you to the Inverness team leader. A young DI. He looks sound as a pound, but time will tell.'

Harry looked over to the other side of the room where Dunbar indicated and saw a man in his thirties busy talking to what looked like a couple of guests.

One of the stewards came over with glasses of soft drinks. Harry took his water and gulped half of it back.

'You should have got a hair of the dog,' Alex said in a low voice.

'Behave. It's just warm outside.'

'Right, let's go over and set the room on fire,' Dunbar said, and they marched across the wide reception hall. Harry could imagine how this would have looked as a private castle many years ago, the men coming back from fighting whoever it was they fought back then.

The only clans in the big room now were the two families; one from Glasgow, the other from Edinburgh. They sat on chairs and couches in different parts of the large room, as if waiting to go into battle.

By the looks of things, some of them already had.

'Any news?' a woman said, standing up. The bride's mother, Harry assumed after Dunbar's less-than-flattering description of her. She was nothing like a Rottweiler. She was Broderick Gallagher's trophy wife, and had Harry not been told that, he might have thought she was one of his daughters. Her eyes were red but had a shiny look to them as if she were ready for a fight.

'We've only just arrived from Edinburgh,' Harry said, turning to look at Alex briefly. 'I'm DCI Harry McNeil and this is DS Alex Maxwell. We'd like to talk to you and your family, if we could. Perhaps in another room?'

The woman turned to her husband and Gallagher looked at her as if prepared for a stand-off, but then his shoulders slumped and he followed her. Harry watched them until they left the room before speaking to Dunbar.

'Where's the groom?'

'Floating about somewhere. He was out with one of the search parties earlier. He broke down when I told him we'd have to get the underwater team out. There's a small lake and the river to consider.'

'Right. What about the Glasgow side?'

'I'll have a chat with them, then we can compare notes.'

Harry indicated for Alex to follow him. Back outside in the grand hall, he just caught a glimpse of Broderick Gallagher slipping through a doorway. Harry thought the man an ignoramus. He was getting all the help he needed in trying to track his daughter down, yet here he was swanning about with complete disregard for the people who were helping him.

The room was a library. It was stuffy, with the kind of smell that old library books had. Harry wished he'd brought the water in with him.

'How the hell can she just disappear from here?' Gallagher said, rounding on Harry. But Harry had been in a room with far more dangerous people than this man, been threatened been attacked, and this outburst didn't come close to anything like fazing him.

'Sit down, Mr Gallagher,' Harry said, taking a seat. Alex sat close by.

Gallagher wasn't used to being spoken to like that and his jaw moved up and down for a few seconds, before his wife put a hand on his arm and he took a seat.

'I want you to run through the events of last night leading up to your daughter going missing, and then what happened after you discovered she was gone.'

They locked eyes for a moment, but once again Harry knew that Gallagher didn't even come close to any of the people he'd had to deal with when he was with Professional Standards, investigating other police officers.

'The wedding was splendid, of course. It went without a hitch, and then we had the dinner. In the banquet hall. It was superb. Marie was so happy. *We* were both happy.' Gallagher looked at his wife. Anne Gallagher nodded, confirming that although it wasn't on the same level as a Caligula family gathering, they had indeed had a good time.

'Then after Marie and Duncan danced, it was announced that the couple were going upstairs to get changed and would be back down. Nobody thought anything of it. Yes, she was taking her time, but she had a big wedding dress to get out of.'

'Was anybody in the room with her?' Alex asked. 'Helping her to get out of her dress.'

'Yes. Claire, her chief bridesmaid. Duncan was in his own room with his best man, Laurence. He wanted to give him the gift he'd bought. An inscribed silver tankard. They had a couple of whiskies, then they went along to Marie's room and Claire came out. Marie said she would be down shortly after that. The three of them came back down to the reception room, where the dancing was in full swing, leaving Marie alone in the room.'

'Duncan went up with her and came back down without seeing anyone else?'

'Yes. Laurence and Claire were with them all the way and never saw anybody else.'

Harry pictured the scene in his mind. 'Are there cameras in the hotel?'

'Yes. Although it turns out the one in that hallway isn't working. There's a gatehouse that's closed at night and there are always stewards on throughout the night in case a guest wants something. Security was a big reason for having the wedding here.'

Alex looked at him. 'Between the bride and groom going upstairs and somebody going to look for Marie, what time span are we looking at?'

Gallagher looked at his shoes as if the answer lay in the carpet.

His wife answered for him. 'A little over an hour. Close to ninety minutes, maybe.' She sounded more like a poodle than a Rottweiler now, Harry thought.

'Who first realised that Marie hadn't come back down?'

Anne Gallagher's lip trembled. 'Look, she was going to get changed into a simple dress. Something she could dance in. Then later on, she and Duncan were going to head up to the honeymoon suite before the dancing stopped, at around midnight.'

'What time did they go upstairs to get changed?'

'About eight thirty or so. It was around ten when somebody noticed she was taking ages. Duncan was already down here, mingling with the guests, and you know what it's like: time gets away from you when you're having a good time.'

Harry looked at the father for a moment. 'Do you know if Marie was having any problems with anybody?'

'Not to my knowledge she wasn't,' Anne said.

Harry looked at Gallagher, waiting for an answer. 'Mr Gallagher?'

'I'm a businessman. In my game, you don't get to the top without stepping on people. Of course I've had threats, but I didn't take anything seriously.'

'Bodyguards?' Alex asked.

'No bodyguards. Marie lived in her own place in the New Town in Edinburgh. Duncan had moved in with her. Much to his father's chagrin. He had suggested they move through to Bearsden, but Marie was having none of it. She's in line to take over my newspapers and head up other business interests of mine. Duncan's family own dealerships through in Edinburgh as well as Glasgow, and he was already a dealer principal for their Lamborghini dealership, so they were both settled. But to answer your question, I never had a direct threat against my daughter.'

Anne started to cry and Gallagher put his arm around his wife's shoulders.

'We'll want to have a look at the room that Marie was last known to have been in,' Harry said. 'And Duncan's.'

'My head steward will show you,' Gallagher replied.

'Your steward?'

'Well, technically mine and Terry Randall's. Terry and I bought this place six months ago. We own the hotel now.'

'I didn't realise.'

'Aye, it was too good an opportunity to pass up. It came on the market and I remembered the place from when we were making wedding plans. My Marie had talked about having her wedding here, but it was fully booked. The original plan was to have it at some place in Edinburgh, but we bought the castle, and since it was under our ownership, we reserved the right to cancel somebody's wedding plans.'

Harry looked at him.

'What, Inspector? Don't look at me like that, just because I rained on somebody's parade. The lassie who was having her wedding here was well compensated. In fact, I picked up the tab for her wedding.'

'Just so your daughter could have her own wedding here?'

'It's just business. My Marie wanted this place and she got it. Besides, Terry and I saw what a good deal this place was. We're really going to put it on the map.'

'Marie didn't have problems with anybody then?' Harry said. *Except maybe a family who had paid a hefty deposit for a daughter's wedding before the rug was pulled out from under it.*

'Not that I can think of. I want your lot on top of this, McNeil. That's our hometown. I don't want some...Inverness clodhopper missing something.'

'I'll get on to it.' Harry stood up. 'We still have a lot of people to talk to and it's going to be dark in a little while.'

Alex stood up as well. 'We'll do everything humanly possible to find out what happened to Marie.'

The parents just looked at the detectives as they left the room.

Harry turned to Alex. 'What's your gut instinct?'

She stopped and looked at him, waiting for a couple of stewards to walk past before answering: 'Somebody took her and now's she dead.'

FOUR

'Aye, it's a strange one alright,' Jimmy Dunbar said when he came out of one of the other rooms.

'How are the Randall family taking it?' Harry asked.

'The mother is up to high doh, but Old Man Randall seems more pissed off than anything, though he's trying not to show it.'

'What has Duncan Randall got to say for himself?' Alex asked.

'Nothing yet that I know of; he's away out on one of the searches again.'

'I think we should talk to the head steward,' Harry said. 'Any idea where he is?'

Dunbar looked over his shoulder. 'Skarting about somewhere. Probably pissing himself in case his job goes south and him along with it.'

'You heard about Gallagher and Randall being the new owners of this place?'

Dunbar lowered his voice a bit. 'I did. Randall's proud that he kicked some poor lassie's wedding into touch so his son could get married here yesterday.'

'Gallagher told me he took care of that wedding too, though, to make up for it.'

'Maybe, but what if one of the other party got his hackles up about being pushed around? I'll have one of the Inverness boys check it out. The lassie is local. Her family are minted, but even so one of them might have spent all Friday night festering.' He looked at Evans. 'Get onto it, Sergeant Evans.'

Evans walked away and headed into the big ballroom, where the Inverness boys were still conducting interviews.

'I'm hoping this is all a false alarm and we can spend the rest of the night getting pished in the bar,' Dunbar said.

'You and me both. But listen, I told Gallagher that I wanted to have a squint at the room where she was last seen.'

'Do that. I'll see if anybody remembers anything from last night, now that they've all sobered up.'

'Is her wedding dress in there, or did she have it on when she disappeared?'

'I spoke to the head of forensics, and the dress is gone.'

'That seems a bit strange. Her chief bridesmaid was in there with her, helping her get changed. I wonder where it's gone?'

'It might be something or nothing. I'll catch up with you,' Dunbar said, and walked away.

Harry caught the head steward again, Angus McPhee. 'Can you show us the room where the missing woman was going to get changed? We can't find the manager.'

'I certainly can, sir. If you follow me up this staircase...'

The staircase ran up one side of the reception area and was covered in a plush tartan carpet. The walls were adorned with swords and animal heads and paintings of men from a long time ago.

'You mind if I ask you a few questions?' Harry said, walking by the man's side. He was taller than Harry, who was a little over six feet himself. But that's where the similarity ended. McPhee had a big build with broad shoulders and looked like he tossed a few cabers before having his porridge for breakfast.

'Were you a military guy?' Harry asked as they reached the landing, Alex right behind them.

'Aye. How did you know?'

'Just a guess.'

'You an army man?'

Harry shook his head. 'My brother was. He jumped out of planes for a living.'

McPhee smiled. 'Those are tough boys, let me tell you I was infantry myself. Nothing different from having a fight in the pub on a Friday night, except we got paid to do it and wear a uniform.' He smiled again and stopped outside a door.

Another man in a kilt and tweed jacket appeared at the other end of the corridor. Like a smaller version of McPhee. 'Sir, we're about to go on another search.'

'Carry on without me just now. I'm showing people around. My Land Rover's down there. Nobody take it and I'll catch up with you.'

'Aye, sir.' The man disappeared through the door again.

'In here, sir,' McPhee said, opening the door and standing aside to let Harry and Alex in.

'Put your eyes back in your head, Sergeant,' Harry whispered to Alex.

'How dare you.' She gave him the briefest of smiles before McPhee came into the room behind them.

'This is where the brides get changed before going back downstairs. Those who want to, of course. Not all of them do. But for those who do want to change, this is the room. Where Marie was last seen.'

'Her husband confirmed he saw her coming in here. He was with his friend and they've corroborated each other's story,' Harry said, then turned to the big man. 'As well as the bridesmaid, of course. But she left. Could anybody have been waiting in here? Somebody who got in somehow and shouldn't have been in here?'

McPhee's face darkened slightly, as if Harry had made a personal slight on his character. 'Not on my watch.'

'How would the bride access the room?' Alex asked.

'Like everybody gets into the rooms: the key is waiting

behind reception. It isn't locked just now because they had a big dog in here earlier, but there has to be the smell of a thousand guests in here, not to mention the staff. Then, as you can see, they had people with wee brushes going about putting powder everywhere.'

'Crime scene staff,' Harry said, like he was talking to somebody from another planet who had never watched TV before.

'Aye, them. But let me ask you: why all the activity? I mean, the poor woman is missing, but people have gone missing before up here in the Highlands and nobody bothered to lift an arse cheek off a seat. Now there're coppers from all over up here.'

'If you were a millionaire, wouldn't you want everything to be done to find your daughter?'

'I would want that even if I wasn't a millionaire.'

Harry thought the man had a fair point. He walked over to the window and looked down. There was no visible means of escape from the room, should a fire suddenly break out round the doorway, so it was safe to say Marie hadn't slipped out here and shimmied down a drainpipe.

'This whole place is around twenty thousand acres, isn't that right?' Harry said.

'Aye. It's a big estate, but it's a working estate. This estate was joined with two other estates. It's going to be a big complex when they're finished. People come from all over the world to hunt and fish here while the womenfolk head off to the spa. Not all the women, like, but a gid few of them. Some of them like to have a go with the guns and they're pretty damned good.'

'They shoot ducks?' Alex said.

McPhee looked at her for a moment to see if she was playing with him, but then saw she was serious.

'Grouse. And clay pigeons of course.'

'There are lodges in the grounds,' Harry said, throwing Alex a look. *Ducks*. He looked around the room without touching anything.

'Yes. We service the lodges too, myself and the other stewards. We have twenty-five main lodges, which are basically houses, and then there're the rustic lodges, which are cabins, further into the woods.'

'And they're all occupied at the moment?' Alex asked.

'Every one of them except a couple of the cabins, which have been made available to some of the police who have come up here. But rest assured, they were searched and given the all-clear.'

'Not much chance of her hiding in any of them while they're occupied, is there?' Harry said.

'No, sir. And the empty ones were searched more than once and they'll be occupied tonight.' McPhee looked at his watch. 'I really need to go, sir. My men are doing another search in the grounds and in the woods and it's going to be dark soon.'

'That's fine. Off you go. Thanks for your help.'

McPhee left, leaving the door open, like he didn't trust them not to steal the family silver.

Harry looked at Alex. 'Marie comes in here, gets out of her wedding dress, packs it away, then just walks out after getting changed, taking her dress with her.'

'That about sums it up.'

'Why, though? There is zero motive for her to do that. Unless…'

'Unless?'

'First of all, discounting your thoughts about somebody taking her and killing her, what if she had a secret lover and she ran away with him?'

'You mean, after taking her vows and not before?'

'Aye, I do mean that. Stranger things have happened. What if she staged it this way? Made it look like she was happily married to her new husband and then just vanished.'

'She would have to be pretty messed up in the head to do that.'

'Alternatively, somebody was waiting for her to come here to the room. Somebody who was confident of being here without being questioned.'

'Duncan, her husband?'

'He could have been standing outside here naked and nobody would have asked him why he was loitering. They would've just assumed that he was waiting for her.'

Alex looked sceptical. 'His best man was with him.'

'I know they were in Duncan's room, but did the best

man leave at any time before Duncan got changed? They were together, but did either man leave the room alone at any time?'

'Damn. We should have asked McPhee before he left. Maybe he would have known.'

'Let's do one better; let's ask the men themselves, Duncan and his friend. Separately. And let's not give them a heads-up we're going to do it. I'll talk to Dunbar about it.'

FIVE

Harry looked at his watch as they arrived in the main reception area again.

'Have you ever had that feeling that you're so hungry you could eat anything on legs?' Alex said.

'No.'

'Me neither. Although I am a bit peckish. It's past dinnertime.'

'You should have had two pies like me,' Harry said, giving her a look that said having two pies was a no-brainer.

'I'm thinking of eating healthier.'

'Weren't you thinking about it last week too?'

'Thinking and doing are two different things.'

'Clearly.'

Harry walked towards Dunbar, who was talking to a

younger man who had obviously given up the fight with his thinning hair a long time ago and was on the fence about either shaving his head or going for a combover.

'Harry, this is DI Barrett. He's in charge of the Inverness team.'

'Good to meet you, sir,' Barrett said, looking at Alex.

'Likewise. This is DS Alex Maxwell.'

Barrett nodded to her, acting like he'd never spoken to a woman before.

'I'd like to speak to the best man,' Harry said. 'And the head bridesmaid.'

'We have them in the ballroom, waiting for you.'

'Lead the way.'

They walked towards the back of the reception area and through a set of double doors guarded by two uniforms, just in case any of the guests decided to make a run for it.

The tables were still set up from the night before, but the guests' faces looked like they were at a funeral.

'The guests who weren't staying in the hotel itself were staying in the lodges in the grounds,' Barrett volunteered. 'The group you're looking for are over there.' He nodded in a vague direction until Harry looked at him and he backed up the nod with a pointing finger.

'Well, that narrows it down a bit,' Harry said.

'The young woman with the green polo shirt sitting next to the man –'

'Got it.' He walked over with Dunbar and Alex.

'Where's your cohort, Jimmy?' Harry asked, almost saying *sir* again. He knew he would be fucked if he let that slip out even once.

'He's going to get his arse kicked when I get hold of him. He was here a minute ago. Probably got one of the bridesmaids upstairs for a private interrogation. That laddie has a one-track mind that's going to get him in trouble one day.'

'Let's just err on the side of caution and hope he's busy questioning some older guests.'

'I'll go and see what he's up to,' Dunbar said. 'You can come with me and get me up to speed,' he said to Barrett. 'We'll see if anybody remembers seeing anything.' They walked away.

Harry and Alex pulled out a chair without any arguments from the people at the table. Harry made the introductions.

'I'm Claire Blythe, Marie's best friend and chief bridesmaid,' the young woman said, her lip trembling briefly before she regained her composure.

'Laurence Spencer, Duncan's best man. Call me Larry.'

'We need to ask you a few questions. They might seem awkward at first, and you might wonder why we're asking, but when somebody goes missing, we have to establish some sort of background,' Harry said. 'Most times, people get hacked off and leave without saying a word and then come back, though a fair number of people don't come back. But it's very unusual for a bride to go missing on her wedding night.'

Claire looked at him. 'You might want to find that bastard Vince Dubois then,' she spat, spittle flying.

'We were told about her ex-fiancé,' Alex said. 'We'll have somebody go and look for him in Edinburgh.'

'They won't find him,' Claire answered.

'Why not?'

'Because he's not in Edinburgh, he's here.'

'You saw him?' Larry said.

'Yes. I didn't see him at the cathedral because of all the excitement, but I caught a glimpse of him in here last night.'

'Why didn't you tell the police?'

'What do you think I'm doing?'

'Are you two a couple?' Alex asked.

'What? No,' Larry answered, making a face.

'You don't have to look like that,' Claire said. 'You'd be doing well to go out with me.'

Larry made another face as Claire turned away.

'Did Dubois say anything to you?' Harry asked.

'No. I just saw him walking about, all dressed up as if he was part of the wedding party. Nobody questioned him. They were all too busy getting drunk and doing the conga.'

'Have you seen him today at all?'

Claire shook her head. 'No. It was a hectic night. We started off looking for Marie, but then they called the police. They came, but there wasn't much they could do. I think they thought there had been an argument and Marie was hiding somewhere. I didn't see Vince again.'

'Can I ask how well you know Marie?' Alex said.

'We met at college. Glasgow School of Art.' Claire looked at the two detectives. 'I know, right? Art college. She could have gone anywhere, but her dad's a millionaire and she wanted to do something fun, so she studied design, like me. We ended up renting a flat together for our time at college and she was so much fun. Not like some other stuck-up tossers who don't want to get their hands dirty.' She threw a quick glance at Larry.

'What about boyfriends?' Harry said. 'Before Dubois came on the scene.'

'She didn't have many. I mean, yes, we went out drinking and had a few laughs, but she didn't sleep around. Despite what other people thought. But we had a few good times and she went out with a couple of guys – nothing serious, until she met Vince.'

'Who broke it off?' Alex said.

'She did. Vince was gutted. I've never seen a grown man cry so much.'

'He saw the money flying out the window, no doubt,' Larry said.

'What?' Claire said, rounding on him. 'Do you think everybody who goes out with somebody who has a bit of money is only after the cash?'

'There *is* a certain attraction to it,' Harry said. 'I've seen it many times.'

Claire looked at him. 'I don't think Vince was like that. I

mean, he wasn't in the same league financially, but he ended up with a good job at a computer games company as a designer. And Marie obviously wasn't bothered by it.'

'Did she ever say why she spilt up with him?'

Claire looked down at her hands before looking back up and locking eyes with Harry. 'They had a fight over something. She never did say what, but I overheard her one night on the phone with Vince.'

'What did she say?'

'I couldn't make out the words, just the sound of arguing.'

'We'll see if anybody saw Vince.' Harry looked at Larry. 'How about you, Mr Spencer? When did you last see Marie?'

'I already gave a statement.'

'I know. And we ask again in case you remember something that you didn't at the earlier interview.'

'Do I need a lawyer?'

You might need a plastic surgeon if Broderick Gallagher finds out you had something to do with his daughter going missing, Harry thought. 'You've been watching too many re-runs of *The Bill*. We're asking you to talk to us so we can see if there's any way we can locate your friend's new wife. If you don't want to help us, you can walk away. But then you'll automatically be the number-one suspect.'

'Good golly. I was with Duncan the whole time. He can testify to that.'

'Run me through the events leading up to you last seeing Marie.'

Larry took a deep breath and let it out slowly, whether giving himself time to fabricate some lies or to blow out the mental cobwebs, Harry wasn't sure.

'The DJ announced that the happy couple would be going upstairs to get changed. Duncan wanted me to accompany him as he had a gift for me. Marie wanted *her*' – Larry nodded to Claire – 'to help her unzip the dress. So the four of us went upstairs. The women went into Marie's room and Duncan and I went into his. We had a drink, he gave me the engraved tankard and he went into the en suite to get changed. When he came out, we went into the hallway and Claire was there, waiting for us.'

'How long did it take Duncan to get changed?'

Larry shrugged. 'Fifteen, twenty minutes. We had a couple of nips and reminisced about our past. Had a laugh.'

'Does that timeline seem right to you?' Alex asked Claire.

'Yes. It took a little bit of fiddling to get Marie's dress zip down. But I helped her fold it and get it into the box. Then we had a glass of champagne. I left her and she said she would be down in a minute. I waited in the hall and a few minutes later those two came out. The three of us headed downstairs to wait, and later on somebody alerted us that Marie was gone.'

One of Larry's friends came over. 'They're going to feed us now. They've been preparing a buffet and they're going to bring the food out. The search is being called off and the staff and other volunteers are coming in. Too dangerous in the pitch dark.'

'Thanks, Raffles.' Larry stood up next to his friend. 'I hope I helped. But if you ask me, I think Marie saw her ex, they got chatting and she fucked off with him. And Duncan will hit the roof if that happened.'

'Well, thanks for that input,' Harry said. *Don't give up your day job, Inspector.*

Dunbar came into the room as Larry walked away. 'They're calling it off for the night.'

'I know. Inspector Morse there just told us.' Harry stood up and stretched. 'They're putting food out for us all. Well, I'm assuming we're included.'

'Fucking right we are. I'm not spending my weekend off up here without getting free scran.'

'Too right. Come on, Alex, we can get a bite and then decide what's happening tomorrow.'

'How many of the original guests are still here?' Alex asked.

'Around fifty,' Dunbar answered. 'They're staying one more night, then they're off. Nothing to keep them here except for helping us with our enquiries. The rest had to leave to go back to work tomorrow.'

'Right.'

'How many stewards work here?' Harry asked. 'The guys who are dressed in all the kilts and regalia.'

'There are twenty-five of them, including the head steward, Angus McPhee. They're all still out searching.'

They were walking towards the room where the food was being laid out. 'Let me ask you this, Jimmy. How do we know Marie didn't just leave in a car with her ex?'

Dunbar stopped. 'Truth is, we don't.'

SIX

Harry had showered and changed into some casual clothes. They had moved into their respective rooms upstairs, with Broderick Gallagher blustering about how people should be out looking for his little girl. Harry was impressed with his room and soon found the minibar after Alex came in.

'In case of emergencies?' Alex said.

'This is an emergency, Sergeant. I'm up here in the Highlands of Scotland and my bottle of Scotch is back home.'

'Slàinte,' she answered, holding her glass up for Harry to clink.

'I don't know what I'm more impressed with, you using big words or drinking whisky.' He clinked her glass.

'I'm a lady of many talents.'

'Just don't say that in front of Jeni Bridge.'

At which point Jeni answered the FaceTime call on Harry's iPad.

'Good evening, Commander,' Harry said.

Jeni cut to the chase. 'How are things there, McNeil?'

'DS Maxwell and I are just going over things now, and to be honest, there are no signs of foul play and nothing to suggest Marie didn't just up and leave.'

Jeni's face looked surreal on the smaller screen. 'We're forgetting one thing. It was her wedding night. You're married, aren't you, McNeil?'

'Was, ma'am.'

'Well, I'll bet your ex was in love with you on your wedding night. I can't imagine why any woman would leave her new husband.'

'Marie Gallagher's ex-fiancé is here too,' Alex said. 'A witness spotted him sneaking around on the wedding day, but we don't know where he is now.'

'Any chance she left with him?'

'That's something we're considering,' Harry said.

'Are they still looking for her?'

'It's dark now,' Alex said. 'They're calling it off and getting everybody back inside. The property has twenty thousand acres and it's pitch black out there. It's getting dangerous.'

'What about her mobile?'

'There's no sign of it,' Harry said. 'It's not switched on, so it's not pinging. Her wedding dress is also missing. Her purse and handbag and all the other belongings that she brought up here with her are still in her room.'

'How many guests are still there?'

'Some of them. About fifty or so. A lot of them left after being questioned, as technically this isn't a crime scene. A lot of them have to go to work tomorrow, but the family are here. Some friends. We want to talk to a man called Vince Dubois. I'll let you know how that goes.'

'I've been in touch with the chief constable and he's authorised any overtime and expenses. Apparently, he golfs with the good Mr Gallagher. He's keen to be seen to be helping out by supplying officers to help in the search.'

The chief was Jeni Bridge's ex-husband. Harry got the feeling Jeni didn't take any crap off him.

'How long are you wanting us to stay up here?' Harry asked.

'We'll give it another couple of days. Call me every day for an update. We'll go from there.'

'Will do.'

'I'll talk with you tomorrow night.' Jeni hung up.

He finished his whisky. Alex sat holding her glass and Harry looked at her.

'Oh. You want me to leave, don't you?' she said.

'Not at all. But if I FaceTime Vanessa and she sees you in my room, she'll make our deaths look like an accident.'

Alex finished the whisky and stood up. 'As parties go, this

one will go down in the annals of history as being the least exciting one I've ever been to.'

'At least you didn't have to pish in a bucket.'

'It was close, though.' She grinned and left the room.

Harry sent a FaceTime call to his girlfriend. No answer. He would try later. If he remembered. Vanessa wasn't the only one who could play games.

SEVEN

'In the name of fuck, what are we doing out here?' Tom Gunn said. 'You know what I think? I think she got married to him, shat herself because she knew she had made a mistake and then fucked off without him.'

'Shut up, you moron,' Sharon Gallagher said. 'That's my bloody sister you're talking about.'

'That's what *you* told me! That she had doubts.'

'Okay, now you need to rein it in. Somebody will hear you.'

'At this point, I couldn't care less. I mean, look at us: it's pitch black, it's starting to piss down, we can't see anything beyond the light from the torches and I'm knackered. This has been a shite wedding. Next time I get an invite to one of your dad's dos, I'm going to tell him to shove it up his jacksy.'

'Christ, you do nothing but moan.' She looked up at the

canopy of trees as the rain fell harder. 'And I'm sure my father would appreciate hearing you talk like that. Give him time to arrange for somebody to slap you.'

'I've got plenty to moan about, though, haven't I?'

'We're going home tomorrow. Just make the most of it.'

Tom suddenly smiled. 'I'm going to make the most of it tonight when we get back to the room.'

'Like I'm going to be in the mood.'

'Fuck's sake,' Tom said under his breath. 'Another reason to not piss on Gallagher should he ever find himself on fire.'

They were on some sort of old track. The steward who was in charge of their pitiful search party had said there wasn't much chance of Marie being out here, but they had to check.

'She'll get a piece of my fucking mind if we catch her lording it back in Edinburgh,' Tom said. 'Did you hear that somebody saw her ex, that arsehole Vince Dubois?'

'What? Vince, here?' Sharon said. 'I don't believe it.'

'Believe it, sister. I think she caught sight of him and would have jilted Dogface at the altar if she'd seen Vince earlier, but she didn't see him until it was too late, then thought she had married the wrong man. Now Vince will be giving it laldy with her in a nice warm hotel room somewhere while us twats are out in the fucking woods –'

'Hey! Tommy Gunn!' one of the party further up ahead shouted. Eddie Lister, Tom's friend.

'I told that arse not to call me that. It's fucking Tom, not

Tommy,' he said to Sharon. 'What's he bleating about now anyway? Probably got a splinter or something.'

'Tommy!' the man shouted again. Not counting the steward, there were five of them, and Tom's friend was the only other man in the group.

'Are you coming up here or what?' Lister shouted.

'I'm coming!' Tom shouted back. *Fucking knob end.* He strode up the incline. The rain was coming down hard now and the track widened as it opened up into a clearing.

'What is it?' Tom said, but he was looking at what his friend's torch was highlighting: an old lodge. 'What the fuck is that place?'

'That steward bloke told us there are old lodges scattered about here. This is obviously one of them.'

'She wouldn't be in there,' Tom said, his lip turning up in disgust. 'And even if she is, she's fucked. I'm not going in there. What if one of us fell and broke a leg? You know how far back it is to the Land Rover? I'm not carrying any of the women. Not even Sharon. I mean, she's not huge, but I have a dicky leg.'

'Let's hope your leg doesn't give out when you're back in the room then.'

'Look, it's some shitey old building that's probably infested with rats. There's no way she's in there.'

Lister had been shining his torch at the window on the ground floor. He switched it off.

'Fuck me,' Tom said, feeling the hairs on the back of his neck stand up. He was looking at a small light in the window.

'A candle?' Lister asked.

'Fucked if I know, but Soapy Soutar can go in there. He's in charge of this party. Where is he anyway?'

Tom shone his own light towards the back of the three women, who were huddled together now. He thought they might be comparing his and Lister's willy size but couldn't be sure. Then one of them giggled, and he hoped it wasn't Sharon.

'Where the fuck is he? Christ, he's supposed to be leading us.' Tom turned to Lister. 'Did you see him coming up here?'

'No. I thought he was keeping an eye on us from the back.'

'Lazy bastard is probably sitting in the Land Rover eating some porridge or something.'

'He looks a bit of a hard bastard. I wouldn't say that to his face.'

'Fuck 'im. There's two of us. If he starts his pish, I'll stick the bastard.' Tom pulled out a little penknife and struggled with the blade for a second before springing it open.

'What are you going to do with that? Trim his ear hairs?'

'Listen, if I get in close, he'll have fucking tears in his eyes.'

'From laughing, ya daft bastard. Didn't you say these stewards are all ex-army?'

'Aye, but our one looks like Daphne Broon with a beard. A good kick up the kilt and he'll be walking like John Wayne just off a horse.'

'He's not wearing a kilt. He's got waterproofs on, like us.'

'Figure of speech.'

Lister put his torch back on and shone it ~~back~~ towards the women. The canopy of trees wasn't helping keep the rain off them much. They were holding their jackets – supplied by the hotel – above their heads.

'Any of you seen Oor Wullie?' Tom shouted.

'Shut up, for fuck's sake,' Lister said, cringing. 'I don't want to get this battered and bruised.' He put the torchlight on his own face for a split second.

'Again, if push comes to shove, it's two against one. And besides, if he did manage to get the better of us, Old Man Gallagher would sort the bastard out. There would be a new tree planted out here with its own compost underneath.'

Lister shone the flashlight past the group of girls and found nothing but trees. 'It's a moot point now, because it looks like he's fucked off.'

'What?' Lister pointed his own torch in the same direction. 'Jesus.'

'I told you he was a weirdo.' Tom turned his torch back to the old abandoned lodge. 'Maybe he went by us and got into the house and lit a candle.'

'Why would he do that?'

'Who fucking knows? But somebody is in there.'

'We should go and have a look.'

'I told you, I'm not setting foot in there.'

'What if she *is* in there? Think of the brownie points you'll get with Sharon. Or better still, her dad.'

Tom thought about it for a moment. 'Come on then, ya smooth-talking bastard.'

The lodge was a good five hundred yards into the woods, with the driveway covered in weeds and brush.

'I'm not taking the women in there. Just in case,' Lister said.

'Fine. We'll let them know to stay here and not split up. Safety in numbers and all that.'

'This is turning into a minging weekend,' Lister said.

'You're fucking minging. Shut up and go and tell the women we're going to have a wee deek at that old house.'

Lister walked away, mumbling to himself. He reached the women, who protested a bit, but he assured them they would only be a few minutes, before returning to Tom.

'If you're serious about settling down with Sharon, you should know she's a fucking nag.'

'Never mind that. You told them to stay?'

'I did, but they're not happy.'

'Come on then, let's make this quick. If it seems okay, we can get them to join us and we can shelter from the rain. And when we see that bearded twat, we can tear a strip off him.

And since Broderick owns the hotel, we can make sure the bastard gets fired.'

They walked through the long grass covering the drive until they got to the house. There were weeds and overgrown bushes everywhere. The lodge looked like it belonged in the old Wild West. It was made of logs, two storeys high, with a redundant chimney on the side. All around it was pitch black.

'This is the bit where the boy with the chainsaw jumps out and scares the shit out of us,' Lister said.

'Only in the movies,' Tom said, not quite believing his own words.

Lister walked up the steps to the front porch and saw the front door was ajar. The tiniest bit of light was leaking out. He turned back to see Tom climbing the steps behind him. He shone the torch back to the end of the driveway, but the women were sheltering under a tree and he couldn't see them.

Tom stood next to him. 'I swear to Christ, I'm going to boot that fucking jockstrap right in the nuts. Leaving us like this. We should make sure all of those caber-tossers are fired.'

'Just stay focused. And stay alert.' Lister pushed the door and, like in a horror film, it creaked as it opened. He flashed the torch around, the light dancing into every corner.

'Hello?' he shouted.

'Fuck's sake. You never seen a horror film? Why are you shouting? Letting the mad bastard know we're here.'

Lister turned to him. 'First of all, we don't know anybody's here.'

Tom turned to look at the candle sitting on the windowsill. 'Who lit that then, Santa Claus?'

Lister didn't have an answer. 'Just watch our backs.'

He moved forward into the living room. A table was in the middle of the room, with two wooden chairs. Otherwise, the room appeared to have been abandoned years ago.

The walls were made of boards that had been nailed over the logs. The candlelight didn't do much to illuminate the room, but was enough for them to see something on the floor and the walls. Tom shone his torchlight on it.

'Jesus. Does that look like…blood to you?'

Lister shone his own flashlight on it. 'Christ Almighty, it does.'

The two men looked at each other.

'Tell you what, if something happened in here then it might be best if we tell them back at the hotel, and then we can come back when it's light.'

'Agreed. Let's get the fuck out of here.'

They didn't quite run, not until they hit the driveway and then it was every man for himself. Tom turned round once to see if there was a masked lunatic chasing them, but there was nobody.

He was out of breath by the time he reached the main track. Lister caught up. They stood for a few moments, calming themselves.

'Right, we tell the lassies that we checked the place out, but it looks dodgy, and we didn't want anybody getting hurt, so we'll come back when it's light,' Tom said.

'Got it.'

Suitably composed, they stepped further out into the track and shone the flashlight around.

The women were gone.

'Fuckin' magic,' Tom said. 'They can't do a simple thing like stay where they are.'

'I can't blame them. It's pissing down now, pitch dark and they don't want to be here, just like us.'

'Well, fuck this for a game of soldiers. If they've gone back then we're not going to be the pair of dafties who're hanging about.'

The rain eased off as they made their way down the track, their torchlight lighting the way.

'How long has it been now?' Lister said.

'About half an hour.'

'I thought we'd have reached the Land Rover by now.'

'You and me both, Eddie, but you know what? I reckon that kilted freak went back and was sitting in the Land Rover, and he saw the women coming and fucked off with them.'

'The women wouldn't leave us behind. Would they?'

'Look around you,' Tom said. 'Do you see any sign of them?'

'I suppose not.'

Their boots crunched the stones on the drive as it levelled out a bit.

'It must have been a hard decision for them to make: sit around a warm fire, drying off and drinking tea, or wait for us.'

'Maybe Sharon will be extra-nice to you tonight.'

'Eddie, with each step I'm getting more and more knackered. I'll be lucky if I can play a game of dominoes when I get up to the room.' Tom stopped so suddenly that Eddie bumped into him.

'What's wrong?' Lister said. 'You see the women?'

'I see something.' Tom looked at Lister. 'Burning. Look. Away in the distance, over there.'

'Christ, you're right. Do you think some bastard set the Land Rover on fire?'

'Maybe the women got a campfire going and now they're roasting marshmallows.' Tom looked at his friend and shook his head. 'How should I know? But there's one way we can find out.'

He started walking with renewed vigour. The track went beneath another canopy of trees and turned away to the right, towards the flames. They could see the flickering light a bit better through the trees now, but their view was partially blocked by thick bushes on the side of the road. Then they rounded the bend.

'Jesus, Tommy, look at that!' Lister shouted.

They stopped and Tom looked. He couldn't quite make out the shape at first.

'I don't believe it,' Tom said. Then they both started running.

EIGHT

Harry McNeil was lying on his bed sleeping when he heard a banging on his bedroom door. He woke up and felt disoriented for a second, before remembering where he was.

More thumping on the door.

He got out of bed and grabbed a poker from the fireside set next to the unmade fire in the fireplace.

'Who is it?' he said without opening the door.

'Harry, it's me,' he heard Alex say from the hallway. He stood the poker against the wall behind the door before opening it.

'You have to come with me,' Alex said.

'Now look. I'm old enough to be your...brother. You'll find somebody one day. Go back to your room.'

'Oh, you're very funny. But before you get ahead of yourself there, Romeo, we have to go. They found Marie Gallagher.'

'I'm assuming it's not good news.'

'It's much worse than that.'

'Right, give me a minute to' – *dampen my hair down and brush my teeth* – 'get my shoes on.'

'Mind and wet your hair a bit. There's a tuft sticking up at the top. You weren't in bed already, were you?'

Harry ignored her and pushed the door closed. After quickly using the bathroom, he slipped his shoes and a jacket on. He'd fallen asleep fully dressed after trying to watch some Netflix.

'Right, tell me what's going on,' he said to Alex in the hallway.

'The shit's hit the fan big time. I'll tell you on the way. There's a car waiting for us downstairs.'

A Land Rover was outside with the engine running. Jimmy Dunbar and Sergeant Evans were already in the back of the big SUV, and it was obvious that Dunbar hadn't stopped to dampen down his hair.

'This is a right turn-up for the books,' Dunbar said, before addressing the steward who was behind the wheel. 'Get going, son.'

The car headed down towards a road at the back of the hotel, in the direction of the new lodges, but then the driver took a left and they were on a dirt track.

'Somebody going to tell me what's going on?' Harry said.

'They found the lassie.'

'Murdered?'

'Oh, you could say that. She was put in a wheelchair, left by the side of the road and set on fire.'

'Jesus.'

'The castle's fire brigade is up there now,' the driver said. 'We have our own fire engine and the maintenance staff who live onsite are the firefighters.'

The lights bounced through the darkness, illuminating trees, until they saw arc lights in the distance, sticking up from what Harry guessed was the fire engine. More Land Rovers were parked at the side of the road with the hotel's logo on their doors.

'Are we the first officers on the scene?' Harry asked Dunbar.

'Aye,' the driver answered. 'The Inverness crowd have been given a shout. They're staying down the road in a hotel. They've been alerted and the local plod are on their way, but you were given priority. It'll put some bastard's nose out of joint, mind.' He looked in the mirror at Alex. 'Excuse the French.'

'Edinburgh women swear too, you know.' She shook her head and lowered her voice. 'Prick.'

Evans grinned.

The detectives got out of the car and were handed torches by the driver, who also got out and stood at the front of the car, to get a better view of the now-deceased bride.

'Broderick Gallagher is going to go off his nut,' Dunbar said.

'Oh yes.' Harry saw something that looked vaguely human-shaped sitting in what was left of a wheelchair, which was just the metal parts. He had to admit, the castle's fire brigade had done a good job of putting the fire out, but he did wonder how they would cope if somebody torched the hotel.

He walked over to the firefighter with the white helmet, assuming he was in charge. 'DCI McNeil,' he said by way of an introduction.

'Aye, I know who you are,' the man said, then got straight down to business. 'We got a shout fifteen minutes ago from two lads who were out with a search party. That's them over there.' He pointed to Tom Gunn and Eddie Lister.

'They came down with their search party?' Dunbar said.

The man turned to him, obviously displeased at the interuption, before turning back and speaking to Harry.

'They came running down to the hotel. The others in the search party weren't with them. They were shouting in reception about a girl on fire. We got the call and they were driven back up to show us where they were talking about. When we arrived, the damage was done. Some of the grass was burning where petrol had spilled onto it, but it was extinguished. The body was smouldering, but no flames were visible. She was clearly dead.'

'You can tell it was a woman?'

'Those boys said they could see the bottom of a dress. It's burnt now, of course.'

Dunbar's phone rang and he took the call, stepping away from the others.

'What a way to go, eh?' Evans said. 'I mean, burning to death like that.'

The fire officer looked at him. 'She was already dead before she was set on fire,' he said to the young DS.

'How do you know that?' Harry said.

The officer looked at him before answering. 'Because she has no head.'

NINE

Angus McPhee was standing near the firefighters, holding his radio. He spoke into it for a moment, but Harry could hear only McPhee's voice, not the reply. The arc lights from the fire engine made the woods look like a set from a horror film.

Harry walked past him and approached the two young men, who were going to be the prime suspects for the time being. Jimmy Dunbar was at his side.

'Let's get them apart, Harry, and see what they've got to say for themselves.'

'They'd better hope they've got good memories if they've decided to come up with some fairy tale.'

Harry took Tom Gunn aside and introduced himself. 'Tell me what happened tonight.'

Tom took in a deep breath and let it out slowly. 'I'm

fucking shaking, let me tell you.' He shook his head as if he was struggling to get his bearings.

Harry felt the chill wind come at them through the thick trees but concentrated on the man's face, looking for any signs of deception.

'We were in the search party. We started off in the recreation hall, an old building way behind the hotel. We split into groups. Him down there' – he nodded to McPhee – 'he gave us instructions. He went with another party and said he would come round and catch up with us, to make sure we didn't get lost. We were lumbered with some guy who has about as much personality as a sausage roll. He parked the Land Rover, and we got out and started walking up the track. He said there were old lodges, but he didn't want to drive there as Marie might have walked towards them and fallen in a ditch or something.

'Then we got to an old driveway that led to a lodge. Eddie and I told the women to stay behind because Eddie had seen a candle in one of the windows. We thought Marie might be in there.'

'What's the name of the steward who was with you?'

'By the way he disappeared, Lord Lucan, I think.'

Harry looked at him.

'I don't know, alright? But I bet he doesn't get many women off Tinder knocking on his door.'

'Where was he when you saw the candle?'

'That's the thing. He was nowhere to be seen. The

women were behind us, huddling together, but the guy was gone. I thought he'd legged it because he's lazy or something. We went into the lodge – saw the candle and not much else. When we came out and got to this track, the women were gone.'

'Did you look for them?'

'Well, we didn't don bush gear and run through the heather, if that's what you mean.'

'Don't be a smartarse, son. A woman's dead here and you two were the ones to find her. You connect the dots.'

Tom looked aghast for a second. 'We didn't do it.'

'Tell me how you found her.'

'We couldn't find the women, so we thought they had just left. Then, when we walked down, the Land Rover was gone, so we thought the steward had maybe driven them down to the hotel since it was raining. We didn't hang around but started walking back. That's when we saw her in the wheelchair. On fire.'

Harry turned briefly, his eye catching the blackened corpse, before turning back to Tom.

'How do you know it was a woman?' He knew what the firefighter had told him, but he wanted to hear it from Tom's mouth.

'We could see a dress. It was, like, above her knees, but the top was on fire.'

'Did you stop to look closer?'

Tom looked disgusted. 'It was a corpse. She wasn't

moving or making a noise. We didn't stop, we ran. Then when we got to the hotel, we told the receptionist.'

'Didn't you think of calling nine-nine-nine when you were up here?'

'Have you tried getting reception up here?'

Harry nodded. The signal was fine in the hotel, but out here in the middle of nowhere might be a challenge. 'Then what?'

'We were asked to show them where it was. The fire engine came up behind us and then they took care of it. Then that big guffy down there came in a Land Rover and started shouting. Well, we'll see how loud he fucking shouts when Broderick finds out.'

Harry looked back at Angus McPhee and saw the man having a heated conversation with the driver who had brought them up.

'Is that the man who drove you up there the first time?'

'No. That guy's bigger. Our driver was a wee short-arse.'

Jimmy Dunbar walked up to Harry and he stepped aside so they could compare notes.

'Sounds about right,' Dunbar said, 'unless they're pretty good at sticking to their concocted story. And mine didn't smell of petrol. Did yours?'

Harry shook his head. 'Did Lister mention the candle in the lodge?'

Dunbar nodded. 'Sounds a bit farfetched to me. You fancy taking your sergeant and young Evans there with those two miscreants? Check it out? I'm sure that steward will be glad to get away from Shuggy McNasty.' He nodded to the steward who was getting a dressing-down from his boss.

'Aye. Marie had to have been kept somewhere before she was set on fire. And it's a bit suspicious that the steward who drove them there disappeared and then they saw the corpse on fire.'

'I want him found, Harry. He might have taken the women. And it's looking like he might have taken Marie.'

'I'll take them up there now.' Harry motioned to Alex. 'Go and tell Evans and our driver that we're going for a wee jaunt in the woods.'

Alex looked at him. 'Any particular reason?'

'Those two witnesses are coming with us. Mine gave me some spiel about a candle in a window in an old lodge.'

'Right. But before we go, I'm going to have a uniform frisk them.'

'Good idea.'

While Tom and Lister were being frisked, Harry walked up to McPhee. 'The women who were in this group are unaccounted for. Have you been in touch with the driver who was with them earlier?'

'Andy?'

Harry glowered at him. 'I haven't personally been introduced to him, but if that's his name, then yes, I mean Andy.'

'I haven't been able to reach him on the radio.'

'What about the car he was driving?'

'It's missing.'

Harry thought about this for a moment. 'What sector were you in?'

'I was going between sectors, getting updates and making sure everybody was alright. I only heard about this from one of my men.'

'Tell me about this guy Andy. Like, what's his last name, for a kick-off.'

'Andy Buchan. Good guy. Bit quiet, but he was a hell of a soldier.'

'You guys know how to look after yourselves out here, don't you?'

'We do. We've trained for it. Especially since Mr Gallagher bought this estate. It never used to belong to the hotel, or the castle as it was years ago. But they bought two other estates, quadrupling the size of the place. There're big plans for here, with shooting lodges and all sorts of things. The tracks are going to be repaired and all the lodges are going to be pulled down and rebuilt. It's going to be a massive estate when we're finished.'

'And I'm assuming this Buchan knows his way around?' Harry said.

'As we all do. It's our job to look after the guests. There are already new lodges built, and we not only look after the rooms, but we escort them on shooting trips into the hunting areas.'

Harry nodded, wishing he'd put on a heavier jacket. He'd forgotten how cold it got up in the Highlands.

They snagged a couple of uniforms too and had them ride with them in the Land Rover. If the two witnesses turned out to be psychos then they'd be outnumbered and could be overpowered. In theory. Harry had seen the best-laid plans go awry before.

The two uniforms sat on the bench seats way in the back of the big car, with Lister sitting opposite. Tom was in the second row between Alex and Evans, while Harry was sitting up front, hoping that Alex was on the ball should Tom Gunn decide to reveal himself as a nut job who wanted to kill them all.

'Tell the driver where to go, son,' Harry said to Tom.

'It doesn't seem that far when you're driving, but it was a hoor of a trek down here. And it was pissing down at first. God knows why we allowed ourselves to be persuaded to come up here.'

'You know Andy Buchan well?' Harry asked the driver as the four-by-four handled the track with ease, the headlights picking out nothing but trees and bushes.

'We all know each other, but Andy was one of the least talkative guys.'

'He hardly said a word to us,' Lister said from the back. 'I didn't want to start talking to him in case I couldn't get away.' He made a face. 'But listen, pal, if your mate's touched our girlfriends, he'll be getting his bollocks booted, no matter how many of you bastards there are. There are a lot more of us bastards down in Edinburgh.'

'Shut up,' Tom said, turning to his mate.

'Good idea, Mr Lister,' Harry said. 'Just concentrate on showing us where this lodge is.'

'There!' Tom shouted.

The headlights picked out the overgrown driveway and the driver turned left into it. The canopy of tall trees showered them with raindrops from the leaves as the wind shook the branches above.

'Stop,' Harry ordered.

The driver jumped on the brake like somebody had just run out in front of them.

'Kill your headlights.'

The man did and darkness came at them from all sides. There was no light to be seen anywhere.

Harry turned to Gunn. 'Where's the candlelight?'

Tom moved forward in his seat and squinted. 'I can't see it now.'

'You're sure this is the place?'

'Yes. We didn't see any other driveways.'

Harry looked forward again. 'Drive on.'

The steward put the headlights back on, continued up the drive and stopped right in front of the old lodge.

Harry once again turned to the others. 'You two, come with us. The driver can stay here.'

They got out into the dark and took out their torches. The car was still running and lit up the front of the house.

They climbed the old rickety steps up to the porch and Harry looked at the two young men. 'If you're yanking my chain, you know what will happen, right?'

'We're not yanking your chain,' Tom said, his lip curling up, as if he was insulted the detective should even consider such a thing.

'I'm going in. I want you, Evans, right behind me, and Alex, you follow those two. Ready?' He nodded to the two uniforms at the back.

They all nodded. Harry opened the door and the smell hit him. Not of decay, but the smell that a body made when it voided its contents.

'Jesus Christ, this is worse than before,' Lister said. 'It's boggin' in here.'

Harry shone the torch around and they turned to the right and went into the living room. The beams cut through the gloom. He found a light switch, but nothing happened when he flicked it. A staircase was in front of them.

'You two check upstairs,' Harry said and watched as the two sergeants went up to the next level.

'It looked like blood on the walls over there.' Tom stopped and pointed. Harry went over, shining his torch about.

'It could be blood,' he said, looking at the spatter on the wall. Blood with little bits mixed in. *She doesn't have a head.*

Harry knew where the corpse had been before she was put in a wheelchair and burned.

He straightened up. 'Jesus.' His voice was barely above a whisper for a moment, before he turned to Alex and Evans. 'Cuff them both!'

The uniforms grabbed hold of Tom Gunn and Eddie Lister and handcuffed them.

'What's going on?' Tom said.

'Keep them there,' Harry said by way of an answer. 'Don't let them come round here.'

He walked closer to the small, square table and looked at the bloody corpse sitting on a chair. What was left of...him? He couldn't be sure. The head was gone, just like the woman in the wheelchair.

He ignored the two handcuffed men as he shone the light around the dining area. More blood on the walls. And what was left of the victim's head.

Rain started lashing down on the roof. He thought he heard a noise coming from upstairs, but it could have been the rain.

The light jabbed into the darkness, bouncing off the kitchen cabinets. There was nothing else here. He walked back to the corpse. It was dressed in wet weather gear, just like the people in the search parties were wearing.

He went through the pockets and found a wallet, opened it up and found a driving licence: Andrew Buchan. The team leader of the search party who had come here. His radio was gone as well as his head.

'Upstairs is clear,' Alex said.

'We have another victim. Let's get back to the car.'

'Who is it?' Alex asked.

'According to his ID, it's the steward who was driving this lot about.'

'He wasn't here a little while ago, I swear,' Lister said.

'Take them out to the car.'

They were taken out. Harry pulled up the hood on his weatherproof jacket and approached the driver's side of the Land Rover.

'Is there another way to this lodge?'

The man nodded. 'Aye. There're always two roads that lead to them. The main one like this, and a service road to each one that we can use to stock up supplies. All these old lodges have a road running behind them so we won't get in the way of the guests.'

Harry nodded. 'Alex? With me.'

'What's up?' she said when Tom and Lister were safely in the back of the big car.

'We're just going to have a little look round the back. I want you to watch my back.'

'Not Evans?' she said. 'Or are you just being PC?'

'He's a clown. I want somebody I trust watching my back.'

Alex didn't know what to say for a moment. 'Lead the way.'

The rain was getting heavier by the minute. It fell through the trees as if being thrown at them. Harry stopped and put a hand up.

'There's the garage there,' he said in a low voice. The grass and bushes were even more overgrown round here. The forest was slowly reclaiming the ground.

Alex took out her extendable baton and flexed it open.

Harry looked at it. 'You do realise that the two corpses had their heads blown off?'

'You got any better ideas?'

'Apart from going back and returning with armed response, no.'

He walked forward and grabbed hold of the handle at the bottom of the garage door. He pulled up on it and it creaked and squeaked as he lifted.

He pointed for Alex to stand to one side and then got a hand underneath and gave it a shove. The door shot up and then: silence. Nothing but the sound of the rain battering the branches and thunder exploding overhead.

Harry swung his flashlight around, then looked, ducking down and putting his head inside. He prayed the killer wasn't standing there with a gun.

He wasn't.

The lights picked out one of the hotel's Land Rovers sitting in the dark. Harry stepped forward and shone the torch inside the vehicle. He cupped one hand against the glass, but there was nothing inside.

'Empty,' he said. 'Let's get back to the hotel. Don't take your eyes off those two guys. This could be a game to them.'

They went back to the Land Rover and Harry told the driver to take them back.

Then, suddenly, headlights lit up the back of the car. Harry and Evans got out as Angus McPhee walked up to them.

'Mr McNeil, you're wanted back at the hotel. There's been a development.'

TEN

Harry felt tired, but the adrenaline was keeping him going.

'You look knackered,' Alex said to him as they got out of the big car.

'I feel it.'

'You need to get some rest.' She looked at him. 'When did Vanessa call it quits?'

He stopped, the rain pelting off his weatherproofs. 'What are you talking about?'

Alex shrugged. 'I'm just curious. I can see it's taking its toll. In the office this past week, you've looked knackered every day.'

'What makes you think Vanessa dumped me?'

'I'm a woman, Harry.'

Harry looked at her for a moment. 'A week ago. She wants time to "get her head straight". Quote unquote. I was going to FaceTime her, but she might think I'm begging. Now can we go inside?'

'We can indeed. I'm here if you want to talk.'

'About what?'

'Oh, you know, the price of cheese, stuff like that.'

They shook off the water as they made their way into the hotel entrance. People were rushing about like they were doing a fire drill but without the alarm sounding.

'Reminds me of the dark old days on the south side,' Dunbar said, shaking the water off his jacket. 'Pissing down, cold and full of nut jobs.'

They took their wet gear off in a side room and then Harry found McPhee in reception. 'Have the family been told?'

McPhee turned to look at him. 'They were told to wait in the library, that there's some news.'

'Right. I have some things to do, then we'll be in to see them. Can you make sure they stay there?'

'Will do. I was just arranging for hot drinks to be taken in.'

Harry nodded and turned to Dunbar. 'We'll have to get the forensics crew up to the lodge after they've finished with the woman's body.'

'Aye. They said they had finished photographing the poor lassie before the rain came on, so they're going to head up there now. A couple of the stewards are going to take them, including the guy who drove you. Busy night for him, I think.'

'Sitting on his arse driving a Land Rover about is hardly taxing his abilities,' Harry said.

'True. Lazy bastard.'

'Did you find out what the development is?'

The head of the forensics team came across to them. 'We're going up to that lodge. We were doing a search of the rooms again and we discovered something. Duncan Randall's tux had blood on the front. We've taken it away for examination.'

'Where is Randall now?'

'I have no idea.'

'Thank you.' Harry described to her what the lodge was like and where the corpse was.

'Let's go and talk to the family, Jimmy.'

Dunbar took a deep breath and let it out. 'I wonder what they've got to say for themselves about the boy's suit having blood on it?'

'Just remember, money talks. Whatever it is, it will be swept under the carpet.'

'Or Randall will pull some strings for his son. They all walk on water in Glasgow.'

'And since Gallagher owns newspapers, he'll only allow his own people to talk to the guests, at least on the property. And they'll put a spin on it.'

In the library, Broderick Gallagher was a mess. Tears were running down his face and his eyes were red. Anne Gallagher was shedding some crocodile tears while she bounced her little boy on her knee. Harry wondered how well she'd got on with her stepdaughter.

The members of both families were sitting in various chairs and they all looked up as the detectives entered.

'Is it my Marie?' Gallagher asked.

'We're not sure yet,' Dunbar said.

'How can you not be fucking sure? It's either her or it's not.' Gallagher's face twisted with rage.

'It's not been possible to identify her,' Harry said.

Anne let a mask of fury rush over her face. 'What do you mean? We want to see her.'

'That won't be possible just yet.' *Not now, not ever.* 'She's been transported to Golspie hospital up the road before she gets taken for a formal post-mortem in Inverness.'

'But I'll still get to see my little girl, won't I?' Gallagher looked pleadingly at Harry.

'This is going to sound very clichéd, but you need to remember her the way she was. She isn't in a very good state.'

'What do you mean?' Gallagher stood up now.

'He means she was burnt, Mr Gallagher,' Dunbar said. Neither detective thought it prudent to tell him that there was no head on the corpse.

'Oh God, I can't believe it.'

'I have to ask,' Harry said, 'did she have any broken bones when she was younger?'

Gallagher looked into space for a moment. 'I...I can't think. Why?'

Anne looked up at him, while her little boy looked confused. 'She has the pin in her arm above the elbow. Remember, she fell off the horse when she was taking riding lessons a few years back and broke her arm?'

'Yes. Of course.' Gallagher looked at his wife and then back at Harry. 'You need that information to identify her?'

'Yes.' Harry watched as Gallagher sat back down. 'Did you know Marie's ex-fiancé was here?'

'What? Of course he isn't here.'

Claire was sitting behind them on a chair. 'He is here, Broderick. I saw him.'

Harry turned to Alex. 'Did you have the manager go through the CCTV?'

'He said he would check. I left a photo of Dubois with a uniform.'

'Can you go and see if there are any results?'

She walked away.

'Where's Sharon?' Gallagher said. 'My other daughter. Somebody said they got separated from the two men they were with. One of them is Sharon's boyfriend.'

'The two men went into a lodge looking for Marie. When they came back out, the women were gone.'

'Gone? What do you mean, *gone*?'

'Right now we're trying to locate them, but this is a big area to search.'

'Where the bloody hell did they go? Call in as many people as you need. Money is no object.'

'We're doing everything we can. We'll have more volunteers tomorrow.' It was a lie, but Harry hoped the father wouldn't see through it. There was no way that any more volunteers were going out searching, not with a nutter on the loose, ready to shoot anybody.

Angus McPhee came in with a tray, followed by two female staff members. 'I thought you might like a cup of sweet tea,' he said, then left the room again.

'Tea. I want my bloody daughter, more like,' Gallagher said.

'The search has been called off for the night,' Dunbar said. 'It's getting too dangerous out there.'

Gallagher looked at him. 'Called off? Didn't you just hear me? I'll pay whatever it takes to have men out looking for my little girl!'

'Not while there's a possibility that somebody will pay with their life,' Harry said, and walked away.

ELEVEN

Monday morning started out with a coffee and toast for Harry. The detectives were down in the dining room, and a sense of foreboding lingered over the hotel like a plague.

Alex came in, poured some coffee and chose a cereal. Rain battered the windows, giving them a not-quite-so-warm Highlands welcome.

'Not got your sunglasses on this morning, I see,' Alex said, standing next to Harry at his table.

'That seat's taken,' Harry said, indicating the other three seats round the table.

'You lie. And don't think you can get rid of me that easily.' She put her cereal down.

'There's going to be a report written when we get back, and I have to tell you, it's not looking too good for you. I mean, you could redeem yourself by filling my coffee cup. Just saying.'

'Just so you know, I'm not running after you.'

'That's it, put a positive spin on it.'

She left and came back with a coffee and sat down.

'Next time I'll go for them,' Harry said.

'Aye, you'd better. I'm marking it in my diary anyway, just to blackmail you with later.' She grinned and ate some cereal. 'Is this what you usually do? Get Vanessa to run after you, fetching coffee, then she polishes your shoes for you?'

'She butters my toast for me between the coffee and shoe thing,' he said, sipping his coffee. 'I've been up for ages. While you were pruning your eyebrows, I was down here. And guess what?'

'You didn't know how to spell muesli, so you wrote down cornflakes on your breakfast order?'

'As much as you'd like that to be true, no. Broderick Gallagher sent his family home this morning. They left a little while ago to drive down to Inverness and board his private jet.'

'Really? What about all that talk last night about how money was no object and he'd hire Robin Hood and his Merry Men to go traipsing through the woods looking for his daughter?'

'It was all piss and wind. His wife has gone back home with their little boy. Something about overseeing the business while Gallagher stays up here. Randall's family too, but they're not sharing a jet. They each have their own. Randall himself is still here.'

'I was sitting in bed reading last night when I started thinking.' Harry gave her a look and was about to make some disparaging remark, but Alex held up a hand. 'Just remember who's driving you home. But anyway, I got to thinking about Duncan Randall.'

'What about him?'

'Don't you think it's funny how we never see him? I mean, where is he now?'

Harry looked at his watch; eight thirty a.m. 'I'm sure he's grieving the loss of his wife.'

'He wasn't with the family last night. I checked. When they found out, he was nowhere to be seen. He still isn't.'

Harry looked up as Terry Randall walked in, looking ten years older than he had the day before. Harry stood up. 'Mr Randall. Can you spare us a minute?'

The older man walked over, looking more like a worn-out car salesman than the king of the empire.

'What is it? Do you have any news?'

'Not as such, no, but I have a question. How long did Duncan know Marie before they decided to get engaged?'

'Why?'

'Just curious.'

'They met a couple of years ago. They got engaged after a year, and...well, you know the rest.'

'Okay. Where is Duncan now?'

'Up in his room, I suppose. Do you need to talk to him?'

'Yes. We'd like to ask him some background questions. Nothing to be worried about. We want to catch Marie's killer as soon as, and sometimes just a snippet of information can break a case.'

'When I see him, I'll tell him to come and find you.' Randall walked away.

'He's probably wondering what's going to happen to his little empire,' Jimmy Dunbar said, coming up to the table.

'You heard what he said?' Harry asked.

'I overheard because I was listening in. Nosy nebber, my wee lassie used to say.'

'Get some breakfast, then grab a pew, sir,' Alex said.

'Don't mind if I do, Sergeant.'

Dunbar walked over to the buffet table and took some toast and coffee before joining them. 'I had a hoor of a sleep last night and now my old joints are creaking.' He looked at Harry. 'How about yours?'

'Never been fitter.'

'Delusional or liar, your choice,' Dunbar said to Alex.

'I'll toss a coin.'

'When you two are finished slagging me off, I'd like to get some plan of action going for today.'

'Relax, Harry. Time for coffee first.' Dunbar looked around. 'Where's that heid-banger got to? I told Evans to be down here at eight thirty. He's done hee-haw since we got here. He's doin' my bloody tits in.'

Just then, DS Evans strolled in and smiled when he saw Alex.

'Good morning. I'm surprised to see you sitting with the old coffin-dodgers.'

'Shut up. Grab a pot of coffee and bring it over here,' Dunbar said. Then: 'That laddie's doolally. If he spent more time thinking about this case than posting shite on Instagram, then maybe he'd get more work done.'

'I heard that,' Evans said.

'You were meant to. And don't get any of that bloody hair gel on the coffee pot.'

Evan sat down. 'Five hours' sleep and I'm raring to go. *And* without the added benefits of medication.'

'Good for you,' Harry said. 'Just wait another twenty years and you'll have some young Jock pulling *your* pisser.'

'Better to die young. Go out in a blaze of glory.'

'Considering a young lassie was burnt to death, maybe keep that opinion to yourself,' Harry said.

'Anyway,' Dunbar said, pouring more coffee for everybody, 'they're going to start the search for those girls shortly. I spoke to Angus McPhee and he says his men want to go out searching and they've suggested they take some of the hunting guns with them, but I told him there's more chance of Scotland winning the World Cup than a bunch of gung-ho ex-soldiers going out there with guns. I mean, for God's sake, it's not grouse they're after.'

'Or ducks,' Harry said, looking at Alex. She pretended not to hear him.

'And now that a lot of the guests have gone home, we don't have that many suspects,' Evans said.

'Have a word with yourself,' Dunbar said. 'Do you think it's Marie Gallagher's granny who shot her? Or one of her old cronies? We can go through the wedding list and start narrowing it down.'

A man in a suit walked over to Harry. 'We were finally able to track down a timeframe on the CCTV for the man you were asking about.'

'I'll come and look.' Harry got up from the table and followed the man through a door behind the reception area and into an office.

The footage on the TV screen was paused. The man played it, rewound it a little and then hit play again. Vince Dubois was clearly visible walking out of the hotel and getting into one of the hotel's Land Rovers.

'Can you see who's driving it?'

The man shook his head. 'It's impossible to tell, but we can see the time stamp, so I can ask McPhee who would have been driving around that time, see if he knows.'

'Okay, thanks. Let me know when you get something.'

Harry left the office and saw McPhee going into the dining room. He called him over.

'I'd like you to take a look at a CCTV picture and the

time stamp and see if you can hazard a guess as to who's behind the wheel of one of your Land Rovers.'

'Sure.' They walked back into the office and McPhee had a look. 'That's me driving.'

Harry looked at him for a moment. 'You drove this man?'

'Yes. Is there a problem?'

'Where did you take him?'

'We were at the stables, breaking into groups. He asked me where he could go and join the others to help search for Marie. I told him I was going there and I would take him. I dropped him off when I got to the stables and there were quite a few people hovering about.'

'Did you see him after that?'

'I can't tell, to be honest. I was focused on getting my men into groups with the guests. He was just another face.'

Harry nodded. 'Thank you.'

He started walking away, but just then McPhee's radio crackled and he put a hand on Harry's arm. 'That was a call coming through on the radio. It's rough, but Sharon Gallagher is one of the lassies who's missing, yes?'

'Yes. What about her? Has somebody found her?'

'I'm not sure. I just heard the name and the words "Clover House".'

'What does that mean?'

'All the old hunting lodges were given names of flowers by the previous owner. I know that because we have them marked on the maps so we know where we're going and what we're searching.'

'Get some four-by-fours round the front. I'll get my team. You know where this place is, right?'

'Aye.'

'Then move, man!'

Harry ran back into the dining room and Alex was up in a flash. 'What's happening, sir?'

'McPhee just got a call on the radio. Somebody told him where Sharon can be found.'

'Whereabouts?' Jimmy Dunbar said as he and Evans stood up.

'One of the old lodges. He's getting some cars round the front so we can go and look.'

'Let's go. Move it, Boaby!' Dunbar shouted when Evans stopped for a quick chug of his coffee.

Randall rushed over. 'What's happening?'

'Go and get Gallagher and wait in the library for us,' Dunbar said and they left the room.

TWELVE

The big Land Rover bumped its way down the rough road, followed by two others. The lead car had four armed-response officers and the detectives were wearing stab-proof vests.

'I don't think this will stop a shotgun, somehow,' Dunbar said. 'We can always shove young Boaby in front of us, though, use him as a shield.'

'You're not funny, sir,' Evans said. He had a worried look on his face.

Harry smiled, but he felt the adrenaline rushing through him.

Crackling came through on the radio, and the Land Rover stopped. The lead car was being driven by a police officer and it turned right into an overgrown driveway.

The house had to be checked by the armed officers before they could go in. Harry looked through the rear window of the Land Rover and saw the ambulance holding back at a distance.

'I hope to Christ she's alive,' Harry said. 'But if we're going by what's already happened, it's not looking good.'

'Who called over the radio?' Alex asked.

'Nobody knows. They're thinking the killer took Andrew Buchan's radio and he's now using it.'

Alex looked puzzled and mouthed, *Buchan?*

'The driver who took Tom Gunn and the women up to the lodge. The one we found dead last night.'

They sat and waited, the drone of the diesel engine the only sound in the car. Everybody sat waiting for the radio to kick in, or the sound of gunfire to erupt through the woods.

Nothing happened.

A few minutes later, an officer with a machine gun approached their Land Rover.

'There are two young women in there. They're being brought out now, sir.'

Harry nodded, and then they all filed out and walked up to the lodge, which was in worse shape than the one they'd been in the previous night.

The ambulance crew made it past the parked cars and escorted the women out of the house and into the back of the ambulance.

'Where's Sharon?' Harry asked.

Both women were sobbing and it took a moment for them to calm down.

'She's gone,' one of them said. 'He took her.'

'Who did?'

The woman stopped crying for a moment. 'We didn't see his face. He was dressed in waterproofs, just like everybody else, but he had a mask and a hood on. He brought us here and tied us up, then he took Sharon.'

'How long ago did he take her?'

'Last night, right after we were taken at gunpoint. I'm not sure of the time.' The woman started crying again.

'Thank you. You're going to be taken to the hospital for a check-over, then I'll have somebody take a statement.'

Harry walked away and spoke to Dunbar. 'He took Sharon.'

'I think those two laddies who took us to the other lodge are in deeper than they're saying.'

'Could be. It fits in with the timeline. Have them taken to the station for more questioning.'

Dunbar turned to Evans. 'You heard the man. Get on it. You might get a Boy Scout badge if you get this right.'

Evans nodded. 'Sir.'

'I'd like us to get back and have a talk with Angus McPhee, see if he has any idea where the killer could have taken Sharon,' Harry said.

'There's not much else we can do until forensics go over the place,' Dunbar agreed, and they returned to the Land Rover to head back to the hotel.

'Broderick Gallagher is already on the edge,' Harry said, 'and this is going to be the shove that puts him over.'

'You can have the pleasure of dealing with him,' said Dunbar. 'I have enough on my plate with Randall.'

'Talking of which,' Alex said, 'where's Duncan Randall?'

Nobody had any idea.

When the detectives walked into the hotel, Terry Randall was standing in the reception area having a full-blown argument with Broderick Gallagher.

'I told my son not to marry that fuckin hoor!' he said, then deftly sidestepped the swing that came towards his face.

'Whoa, whoa,' Harry said, as Angus McPhee approached the two men. 'What's going on here?'

'This fuckin loudmouth, bleating on about his boy,' said Gallagher. 'Arsehole. I wish my Marie had never clapped eyes on that dim-witted fuck of a son.'

'Now we'll never have to see each other again,' Randall said. He was looking round McPhee. 'Don't worry, son, I won't sully my fucking hands with him.'

'Where's your son?' Dunbar said.

'I don't know. Out with a search party probably.'

Dunbar looked at Harry before answering the man. 'There are no search parties out. Are you sure he isn't in the hotel?'

'I don't know where the hell he is. My wife has gone home. Like Gallagher's has. We didn't want them to be here while their lives could be in danger. I'll go and have a look around, see if I can find him.'

Harry took Broderick Gallagher aside. 'Look, sir, I'm sorry to have to tell you this. We got the women back –'

'Thank God!'

Harry held up a hand. 'I'm sorry to say, he took Sharon. We only found the other two.'

'What? For fuck's sake! Why is he doing this to me?'

'We need to find out why you're being targeted. Now, do you have anybody here who can be with you?'

Gallagher shook his head. 'They all went back to Edinburgh.'

'What about Marie's friend, Claire?'

'She's been a rock. But she went back home. She's one of the best designers on the team at my newspaper, not to mention my Marie's best friend.'

'Did she go home on the jet?'

'Yes. She went with Anne.'

Harry's phone rang. He listened to the caller before hanging up.

'The doctor wants me to go along to Golspie, to the hospital.'

'What's wrong?' Alex asked.

'They just want to talk to me about something.' Harry turned his attention to Dunbar. 'How do you want to play this? We have another woman missing and we know for a fact that there's a nutter loose with a shotgun. I don't want to put any civilians at risk.'

'Agreed. But the problem we have is, this place is so fucking big. What with all of those lodges scattered around, he could have taken her anywhere.'

'If you want my opinion,' Alex said, 'he's not going to shoot anybody other than his target, unless he maybe gets cornered. But he's on a mission.'

'And what would that be?' Dunbar asked.

'He's trying to get back at Broderick Gallagher. Now, our main suspect is Vince Dubois, who we know for a fact was here. He has means, motive and opportunity.'

Harry waved McPhee over. 'Where would somebody get hold of a shotgun?'

'We have an armoury, where we keep the guns for the guests who haven't brought their own.'

'Which is where?'

'Down in the basement.'

'How many people have access to it?'

'All of the stewards. We receive the requests for the shotguns and we go down to the armourer – who is a trained firearms expert – and the guns are logged out.'

'Do you know if any are missing?' Alex asked.

'I can send a text and find out. But if one of our shotguns is being used, then it could be missing from one of the guests who logged it out.'

Harry gritted his teeth for a moment. 'Look, son, you already told us that this hotel has been closed for normal bookings this whole weekend because of the wedding, so you must have a rough idea of how many guests logged out a shotgun.'

'My apologies for the confusion, sir. I should have said that there are several families who are up here for a week. They wanted to stay after the wedding and do some clay pigeon shooting. The guns have already been logged out and were transported to the lodges and locked away in the gun cabinet that is in each lodge. I'll get a list of those who requested a gun.'

'Thank you.'

McPhee walked away.

'I have to call my team in Edinburgh, then we'll get over to the hospital,' Harry said.

'Do that,' Dunbar said. 'We'll hold the fort here.'

Harry left the hotel with Alex. 'I'm going to requisition a patrol car to take us to Golspie.'

'Betty will be most upset.'

'I couldn't care less if Thomas the Tank Engine is upset; we're going in a patrol car.'

'Fine, but you're sitting in the back of Betty on the way home.'

'You know they're going to think you're special if you keep on talking like this?'

'That's fine because I used to be a Special Constable.'

'And now you're a Special Detective,' he said in a slow voice.

Alex made a face as they got in the car.

THIRTEEN

They got a uniform to drive them to Golspie, which took no time at all. From the A9, the small hospital looked like a mansion house, but as they got closer, they could see the addition on the left-hand side with the Accident and Emergency sign above the door.

'Wait here for us,' Harry instructed as the driver pulled up to the main entrance past A&E.

They walked up the steps to the front door and inside saw a woman sitting at a reception desk.

'We're looking for the mortuary,' Harry said, showing his warrant card.

She pointed them to the lift and told them it was one level down.

'I thought this place would be a lot smaller,' Alex said as the lift doors closed.

'It's small enough. At least you won't get lost in here, unlike the old Royal Infirmary in Edinburgh.'

'That place used to give me the creeps. My granddad died in there.'

'And now it's flats. I wonder if your grandfather moved on or if he's still wandering about.'

'That's not very nice, is it? All the happy memories I have of him, then seeing him lying there in that bed. You've ruined them all.'

'If it's any consolation, my own grandfather died in the Western.'

'It's not. And didn't you say you were going to call the team back in Edinburgh?'

'I'll call DI Shiels after this.'

'You forgot. See? I am an asset to this team,' Alex said as the doors slid open.

'That's one way of describing it,' he said as they walked along a brightly lit corridor towards a sign that told them they were indeed going in the right direction.

After passing through a set of rubber doors, they were in the mortuary itself. A small office was over on one side. Two plate-glass windows looked out into the main area. A woman was sitting at a desk, staring down at paperwork.

Harry knocked on the door.

'Fuck me,' the woman said, jumping back in her chair.

'DCI Harry McNeil, DS Maxwell. I'm assuming that's Gaelic for "Welcome"?'

'No, it means, "Fuck me, you nearly gave me a heart attack."'

Harry looked at the woman, who might have been in her early thirties. She was slim with dark hair and eyebrows that looked like they had been drawn on with a Magic Marker. The white coat she was wearing billowed out as she stood up. He thought she could have been a Goth in her early years, with the right hairdo and black lipstick.

'You get many patients coming back to life then?' he said with a quiet smile.

'That would have been a first. Angie Patterson.' She held out her hand for him to shake.

He gently gripped it, and he could feel a strength in her hand that her looks belied.

She let go and nodded to Alex.

'You'll be here to look at the burn victim,' Angie said matter-of-factly.

'We are.'

'This way.'

She turned right out of the office and Harry couldn't help himself; he looked down to see if she was wearing Doc Martens. She wasn't. She stopped at a row of fridges. She looked at the names for a second, as if they were all full and she couldn't remember where the body she was looking for was stored.

'Ah, here she is.' She turned to look at the two detectives.

'They're coming for her later today to do the PM in Raigmore.'

'I understand that. We just want a look.'

Angie gripped the handle and pulled out the drawer. 'I put her at waist level so it would be easy to look at her. The other headless body is in the next drawer. You want to see him too?'

'No, we know who he is.'

'There're only two more and they're further down. Poor old sods whose time on earth was over. But they've nothing to do with your case.'

'Why so many drawers here?' Alex said, counting fifteen.

'It goes back to the war. Bodies were housed here, and I think they expected there to be a lot more. There weren't that many, so I'm led to believe. My predecessor was a history buff.'

'What's your official title?' Harry asked.

'Mortuary attendant. Although I help out in records when we're quiet down here. Which is not that often, because we have the geriatric ward.'

Harry steeled himself to look at what was left of the young female. He'd been to many fatalities, but it was always the burn victims that got to him.

Marie looked exactly like she had in the wheelchair. She was lying curled on her side, having been fused by the fire. She had no head and most of her body was burnt. Except the bottom of her legs. A little piece of dress material clung on to the charred skin.

'I was told there was a pin in one arm,' Angie said, 'but I can't see anything like that. Then again, I didn't go to medical school and they don't pay me the big bucks. But there're no pins in either arm. It would show, the way her skin is.'

'It was a long shot,' Harry said, 'but I thought maybe somebody could tell.'

'Hang fire there. Are you always in such a hurry with a lady?' Angie looked at him with raised eyebrows.

'Only if I have a bus to catch.'

'Because his car is getting fixed,' Alex added.

Angie looked at him. 'See at this.' He looked at the corpse, but instead she had pulled up her trouser leg. 'See it?'

'You didn't shave your legs in the shower this morning?' Harry said.

Alex rolled her eyes. 'Other side,' she said.

'Oh. Nice.' *I suppose.* He was looking at a small tattoo of a Scottish thistle behind a heart that had been filled with the Scottish Saltire.

Angie put her trouser leg back down. 'My point is, sometimes a woman will have a discreet tat. Not all women, but some, like me. It's not obvious at first.'

Please God, don't let her show me any piercings. 'And?'

Angie went around to the other side of the drawer and moved the headless corpse onto her other side. 'The legs didn't burn all the way down. They were covered in soot, but the bottom of the legs and feet weren't burnt. And you did say that your victim had no tattoos.'

Harry looked at her for a moment. 'Hold that thought.'

He walked away, back through to the office, and made a call to the hotel. Jimmy Dunbar promised to get right back to him. He sat on the edge of the desk while he waited. The small room had an old smell about it, like his granny's house. Like old furniture. Or his old primary school.

He could hear the two women chatting around the corner. As far as he was aware, Alex didn't have any tattoos, or at least none that were visible. He didn't want to ask.

There was a calendar on the wall showing classic motorbikes. He wondered if Angie was a biker chick, or whatever else they were called. *Biker hoor* didn't have the same ring to it, and he thought she might kick his head in if he asked if that was what they were known as.

His phone rang, drawing his attention away from a Triumph. 'Hello?'

'I asked Old Man Gallagher. He about blew his fucking stack, Harry. He said Sharon has a tattoo like that. Why do you ask?'

'Because the woman we found burning last night isn't Marie – it must be Sharon.'

FOURTEEN

'Look at you, acting all innocent,' Alex said as the patrol officer dropped them off back at the hotel.

'The Highland air has obviously gone to your head.'

'Young Miss Angie has her sights on old Uncle Harry.'

'Were you dropped on your head when you were a baby or something?'

'Oh, come on, Harry. She gave you her number. *And* she showed you her unshaved leg.'

'No, she gave me the hospital's number and said I should call if I needed any more information. Weren't you listening? You *were* in the room.'

'Secret messages. There was an edge to her voice that would have sounded like purring if she were a cat.'

'I'm not listening to you anymore.'

They walked into the reception area to find chaos ruling.

'Jesus,' Jimmy Dunbar said, coming over to them. 'Gallagher's running about alternating between wanting to murder his daughter's killer with his bare hands, hire a team of hitmen or burn the hotel down with, and I quote, "all of you useless bastards in it".'

'He's upset then?'

'Rightly so, but he's off the fucking scale, Harry.'

'I can understand why. Somebody made us believe that Marie was murdered, but it was his other daughter. I think it would drive me mad too.'

'Let's get into the library where we can gather our thoughts.' Dunbar clapped a hand on Harry's shoulder and they moved away.

Some of the junior detectives from Inverness were in the library, along with Robbie Evans.

'We're going through CCTV right now, or at least we have some of the Highland Coo Brigade doing it,' Evans said. 'We want to see if Marie can be spotted anywhere. And how in God's name is that her sister, Sharon?'

Harry poured himself a quick coffee. 'I'm thinking Marie was taken, or killed. Then he was watching the search party with Sharon in it. Then he took the steward and the women, killed the steward and took Sharon away with him. He dressed her in Marie's dress, then killed her. He wanted us to think Marie was dead.'

'Why?' Alex said.

'To put us off the trail, as it were,' Dunbar answered.

'We don't know the *why* yet,' Harry answered. 'Why wouldn't he kill Marie? Unless Sharon was the real target.'

'You!' a voice shouted from the doorway. Broderick Gallagher. He was standing looking at Harry.

'Mr Gallagher, I'm sorry for your loss.'

'Fuck you. What the hell is going on?'

Harry walked over to him. 'It seems that somebody took Marie, then took Sharon and dressed her in Marie's clothes to put us off the scent.'

'Not to mention blowing her head off! You forgot that little nugget!' Gallagher was starting to shout and getting more hysterical by the minute.

'I'm going to have somebody take you aside so you can relax a bit.'

'I don't want to –'

'Mr Gallagher!' a voice shouted from behind them. 'Kenny David from the *Morning Star*. Can you confirm it was your other daughter, Sharon, who was murdered?'

Gallagher turned to him as the room went quiet. 'You snivelling little fuck. Who the fuck let you in here?'

'Is it true then?' David said, smiling.

For an older bloke, Gallagher could move. Or maybe it was just the adrenaline coursing through his veins that made him shift, but it was enough to wipe the smirk off the reporter's face.

Gallagher got a punch in, connecting with the man's jaw and knocking him sideways. David's face changed, and before

Harry could get to him, he snarled at the older man and took a swing at Gallagher.

Gallagher ducked and the reporter's fist connected with Harry's nose, knocking him off his feet.

Harry saw a blur of movement as Alex blocked another punch and body-slammed the man to the floor. Then Robbie Evans was also on top of him, followed by uniforms.

Harry felt himself being dragged away from the hustle and looked up to see Dunbar standing over him. Harry had tears coming from his eyes and blood from his nose.

Stewards came running to help and the reporter was taken away by uniforms. Alex rushed over to Harry and knelt down beside him.

'You okay?' she said.

Harry could only nod his head for a second.

'This laddie's been in worse fights, I'm sure,' Dunbar said. He turned to one of the stewards. 'Get a first-aid kit, man! And towels. And get a fucking medic in here.'

Angus McPhee rushed across with a first-aid kit from behind reception and knelt down. 'I was an army medic,' he said.

Harry groaned as the big man checked him over and stemmed the blood flow.

'You're going to be fine. You might have a shiner, but your nose isn't broken. I'll have paramedics check you over.'

'It's fine. I've had worse.'

Ten minutes went by and Harry started to feel better.

'I'll have that wee bastard arrested and charged with assaulting a police officer.'

'It's fine, Jimmy. It just got out of hand, that's all.'

'If this was fucking Govan...'

'You okay, sir?' Alex said.

'I'm fine. Good work. Your reflexes are okay, that's for sure.'

'Not bad for a wee lassie, eh?' She smiled at him.

'Thanks. But I have to call the team. I won't be long, Jimmy.'

'Take your time.'

'Come on, Alex, you can help me, in case my eyes start watering.'

'It wouldn't be the first time I made a man's eyes water.'

They walked upstairs to Harry's room. 'Maybe you should have a wee something from the minibar,' she said as he closed the door behind them.

'A Milky Way?'

'Yeah, if that's what you want to call it.'

He got his iPad and FaceTimed Jeni Bridge. 'Start at the top and work our way down, I reckon.'

FIFTEEN

DC Simon Gregg got out of the car and grabbed his jacket from the back seat. 'Would it kill them to get cars with air conditioning?'

'They have air conditioning,' DI Karen Shiels said. 'It's called *rolling the window down*.'

At six feet six, Gregg was a big man, dwarfing Karen, but what she didn't have in stature, she made up for in attitude.

'How can it be this hot in Edinburgh? I read that it's going to be hotter here than in Rio. Can you believe that?' he said.

'You'll soon be complaining about the snow when it comes.'

'You've been working with me for too long.'

'You're stuck with me now, Simon. Now that we're part of Harry McNeil's team, I'm not going anywhere.'

'Did I ever show you how to thwart somebody if they go

in for one of those crushing handshakes?' he asked as they walked up to the front door of the house in Dovecot Road in Corstorphine.

'That's why I don't shake hands,' she answered.

'I thought it was because you had hands like shovels.'

'Like you? You know what they say about a man with big hands, don't you?'

'They have a big heart?'

'Something like that.'

She knocked on the front door, a bright-yellow affair, and took in the details of the detached house. It was old, a solid stone-built property that looked like it had attic conversions in the roof to create more rooms.

Finally, a young woman answered and both detectives held out their warrant cards for her to read.

'Mrs Dubois?'

'Miss Dubois. Sheila. Is there something wrong?'

'Can we step inside?'

She stood to one side to let them in and showed them into a room on the right. It was light and airy. Wood panels surrounded the bay window while a large-screen TV was opposite a comfortable-looking couch.

'Please, sit down,' Sheila said. 'It's not Vince, is it? Nothing's happened to him?'

Karen shot Gregg a quick look before they took their seats on the couch, and waited until Sheila sat on a chair.

'Can I ask your relationship to Vince?'

'I'm his sister.'

'It *is* about Vince, but we just need to ask you a few questions.' Karen looked at the young woman; unkempt hair, no make-up, wearing a baggy sweater. She didn't judge people, but she always took note of the way they were dressed.

'Is it about that damned wedding? I told him he shouldn't go. I saw it on the news this morning; that lassie's missing, isn't she?'

'If you mean Marie, then yes. We're still looking for her.'

'Not you personally of course, I take it,' Sheila said.

'Our colleagues. But we'd like to know why Vince travelled up there.'

Sheila looked at them as if they were crazy. 'He was invited, that's why.'

Karen looked puzzled. 'Invited? By whom?'

Sheila shook her head. 'That bloody trollop.'

'Marie Gallagher?'

'Yes, Marie bloody Gallagher. You would think it was bad enough that she dumped him for that other man, but to then invite him to attend the wedding? That was rubbing his nose in it.'

'Did he say why he wanted to go?' Gregg asked.

'He said, "At least it's a free meal."'

'Have you heard from Vince at all?' Karen asked.

'Not since Friday. He let me know he had got there safely. Why? Is there something wrong?' Sheila asked again.

'Not that we know of, but my colleagues want to interview him and they keep missing him. He's been joining search teams.'

'That's my brother; generous to a fault. I would leave the lassie to rot.'

'You didn't get on with her?' Gregg asked.

'Oh, don't get me wrong, I got on well with her. Her family were nice, no complaints there. It was the way she dumped him. She accused him of having an affair and ended the engagement overnight.'

'*Was* he having an affair?' Karen asked.

The young woman sat back in her chair like she was expecting an electric current to start shooting through it at any moment.

'He said no. That she was just being jealous, but she had already struck up a friendship with Duncan Randall. Vince said he thought Marie was just looking for an excuse to get out of marrying him. That she had found somebody better. Turns out, Duncan Randall was that somebody.'

'Does Vince have a girlfriend now?'

'He doesn't have a steady girlfriend. He's not ready to settle down after what happened with Marie.'

'Do you know if he went to the wedding with anybody?' Gregg said.

'Oh no, he went on his own.'

'It must have stung, being treated like that and then being invited to watch his ex-girlfriend marry somebody else.'

Sheila shrugged. 'It was water under the bridge.'

'Can I ask what Vince does for a living?' Karen said.

'He's a video game designer.'

'That must pay well,' Gregg said.

'It does. This is his house. Bought and paid for. I live with him.'

Karen looked at the ornate fireplace, which appeared original and housed a gas fire. On top was a row of photos, all of them portraying a young man, along with different women. One had been taken on a ski slope somewhere with the sun shining. In it, Vince was smiling and the blonde woman next to him was showing off a set of perfect teeth. There were another couple of photos of Vince and his sister.

Sheila saw Karen looking at the pictures. 'That was in better times. That's Marie with him on a trip to France. It's hard to believe that she turned out that way. He loved her. I still can't believe she married somebody else.'

'Do you have Vince's mobile number?' Karen asked.

'I do.' Sheila fished her phone out of her pocket and read the number off.

Karen wrote it down, then stood up. 'Thank you. You've been very helpful.'

Sheila let them out into the sunshine.

'It seems that Vince was up there legitimately. I'm going to give him a call. Why don't you get the car running and put the air conditioning on?' Karen made a *roll down the window* motion with her hand and took her phone out. She dialled Vince Dubois' mobile number.

After a few seconds, it went to voicemail and she left a message telling him to contact her.

When she got in the car, Gregg had the air conditioning going and Karen stuck her arm on the window edge.

'See? Now you're getting the hang of it.'

Sheila smirked as she looked through the net curtains and watched the two detectives get back in the car, the mobile phone held up to her ear.

'It's me,' she said. 'There was a little problem at this end, but I took care of it.'

'What sort of problem?'

'Two detectives showed up when I was in the house. Don't worry, I took care of them.'

'They weren't suspicious?'

She laughed. 'Not at all.'

'Be careful, for God's sake. We can't afford to blow it now. It's almost done.'

'I know. I'll be careful. The next part will be easy, and I'll have my little helper with me, so it should look convincing.'

'See you soon.'

'Yes, you will.' She disconnected the call and watched the police officers drive away.

SIXTEEN

'Tell me some good news, Harry,' Commander Jeni Bridge said. She was in her office, sitting on one of the lounge chairs near a coffee table.

'I wish I could, ma'am. It's not very good news at all.'

'Broderick Gallagher was on the phone to the chief constable this morning. And since the chief is my ex-husband, he felt the need to call me up and have a chat. He also knows what side his bread is buttered, so he said it in a nice tone. Apparently, Gallagher is being a Grade-A pain in the arse. He's going to let the chief have it the next time they're at the golf club together. Somehow, Gallagher thinks that we can wave a magic wand and solve the case.'

'That would be nice.'

'Since we both know that it's going to be good old-fashioned police work that will solve it and not a little boy wearing a gown, tell me what's going on.'

'We thought we had found the burning corpse of Marie Gallagher last night. I checked at the mortuary this morning, and it turns out that it was the corpse of Gallagher's other daughter, Sharon.'

Jeni all but blew her coffee over her screen. 'What in the name of Christ do you mean?'

Alex leaned forward. 'Ma'am, we thought he had killed Marie and was playing games. He'd blown the head off the body with what we think was a shotgun. There is no visual identity. We had been told Marie has pins in her arm after it was broken years ago, but the burned corpse doesn't have any pins. That's when the mortuary technician showed us the tattoo. That's how we identified Sharon Gallagher.'

'Any sign of Marie?'

'No,' said Harry. 'We found the guide who had taken the group searching for Marie. Somebody had taken him and the three women, killed the guide, tied up the other two women and then taken Sharon.'

'You told me that you want to talk to a man called Vince Dubois in connection with Marie's disappearance. How has that gone so far?'

'He was spotted on CCTV here at the hotel, and he was last seen being dropped off at a gathering point for a search party. He hasn't been seen since. I asked DI Shiels to go and talk with his mother in Corstorphine. I'm still waiting for her to call me back.'

'Here's what I'm thinking, from what you've told me,' said Jeni. 'Dubois was upset that he had been dumped. He attended the wedding, pretending to be a guest, then waited for an opportunity and killed Sharon.' She sat back for a moment. 'Nah, that sounds all wrong. Why wouldn't he kill Marie? Why would he kill her sister?'

'Maybe he wanted to hurt Marie,' Alex said. 'There's been no sign of her.'

'The problem is, we don't know where he would keep her,' Harry said.

'Couldn't he have just driven off with her? Put her in the boot of a car and driven out?'

'Ma'am, the press has been camping out for days, waiting to take a photo of Marie in her wedding dress. All the editors want to stick it to Broderick Gallagher because he banned the press from his daughter's wedding. It turns out that he did a deal with a magazine, one of those society jobs, and they did the wedding photos. Outside the gates, it's a circus. There's no way Dubois would have been able to drive out without them getting a photo of him. Besides, one of the stewards dropped him off when they were gathering people to make up search parties, and that's the last they saw of him.'

'The magazine crowd didn't stick around to get a photo of her mutilated sister, I hope?'

'Apparently, they've already left. They were going to do a

follow-up with the honeymoon and take photos of the couple in their first marital home. But the red tops are still out in force.'

'What's Marie's new husband got to say about all of this?'

Harry gave Alex a quick sideways glance before answering. 'That's just the thing; we haven't spoken to him. DCI Dunbar has, but only briefly. Nobody's seen Duncan since. He's been distraught and out looking for his wife.'

Suddenly, they heard shouting from outside the hotel room door. 'Ma'am, there's a ruckus going on again. I think we should go and see what's happening.'

'You haven't been fighting, have you, DCI McNeil?'

'There was a to-do with a reporter and I got in the way of his swing as he tried to hit somebody else.'

'You should learn to duck faster. It worked for my ex-husband.'

Jeni Bridge disconnected the call and Harry put his iPad away before they left the room.

He called Karen Shiels. 'How did things go at your end, Karen? I need to hear something positive.'

'Greggs have their Scotch pies on sale,' she said. 'If that helps.'

'It doesn't. But it's something to look forward to when I get home. Anything else?'

'We spoke to Vince Dubois' sister. He was up at the wedding because he was invited.'

Harry was quiet for a moment. 'Invited?' He looked

across at Alex. 'Hold on, Karen, I'm going to put you on speaker here. I have DS Maxwell with me.'

'Hello, Alex.'

'Hi, Karen.'

'Right, so now we're all sitting round the campfire. Why would Marie invite her ex to the wedding? I mean, is that the done thing?'

'I'm not sure about that,' Karen said. 'I wouldn't invite my ex to my wedding if I was getting married.'

'Me neither,' Alex said. 'I can't even imagine. Unless Marie's ego was so big that this was her chance to rub Vince Dubois' nose in it. Like, "Look at me, loser. I'm marrying somebody else."'

'To be honest, I didn't get that impression from his sister.'

Raised voices were coming from downstairs. They rushed down the grand staircase and saw Terence Randall standing shouting at Broderick Gallagher again.

'Clean your fucking ears out! I said, this is all your fault! Nobody's seen my son and I don't know where the hell he's gone!'

'You should have been keeping an eye on him!' Gallagher spat back at Randall.

'If you had been keeping an eye on that hoor of a daughter of yours, my son wouldn't have got entangled with her. You and that toerag wife of yours. Barely older than your own daughter, you mucky old cunt!'

'Fucking jealous! I couldn't even get it up for that old

washed-up boot you call a wife. At least I still have it in me to produce offspring!'

'If he really is yours! I bet he looks like the fucking milkman!'

It seemed that Gallagher had had enough of the word slinging and decided to make it physical. He threw a punch that landed on Randall's left cheek. The man fell down and skidded across the polished marble floor.

Several women screamed as stewards came running, Angus McPhee in the lead.

'Gentlemen! I know you own the hotel, but you employ me and my men to dispel any unruly behaviour. How about I start with both of you?'

He was glaring at Gallagher, who was standing there out of breath and rubbing his hand. Some of the kilted stewards lifted Randall to his feet. They escorted him through to the back office and one of them mentioned he was going to get a first-aid kit.

'I've not seen a right hook like that for a long time,' Harry said to Gallagher.

'Bastard deserved it.'

'That's not for me to judge, but why don't we go into the bar and relax a bit.'

Alex walked through with Gallagher as Jimmy Dunbar came running in ~~through~~ the front door. 'Evans told me there was a pagger,' he said, stopping and trying not to have a coronary in the hotel lobby.

'Hardly a pagger, Jimmy,' said Harry. 'Terence Randall got skelped by Gallagher, and now they're away to their corners, as it were.'

Dunbar's breath was still coming thick and fast. 'Jesus, that wee arsehole has a lot to answer for. I thought it was the razor wars starting up again. I'm going to kick him in the fucking goolies.'

'You would make a great phone perv with that breathing, Jimmy. Maybe you should make use of the hotel gym while we're here.'

'I'm going to make more use of the bar, let me tell you. *And* it will not be put on our bill, if Randall knows what's good for him. He still has to go back to Glasgow.'

'We should at least go through and get you a glass of water.' Harry clapped Dunbar on the shoulder as they headed to the bar, where Alex had gone with Gallagher. 'See? This is why I don't exercise.'

'My wife is always telling me I should go to the gym back home, but unless there's a bar called The Gym, I'm fine going to my local.' Dunbar looked at Harry. 'Don't let that woman of yours tell you otherwise, m'man.'

'Preaching to the choir, Jimmy.'

They saw Gallagher sitting at a table with an ice-filled bar towel wrapped around his hand. Alex sat down close by as the barman brought over a whisky for Gallagher. Harry asked him for another two waters.

'What in the name of Christ is going on here, Gallagher?' Dunbar said.

Gallagher looked at the policeman like he had lost his marbles. 'Excuse me?'

'You have one daughter who's been confirmed deceased and one missing, and now the new bridegroom is also missing. You might not have noticed, but we've got a lot on our plates here without you two acting like a pair of daft wee laddies.'

Harry waited for the fireworks, but none came.

'You're right. I'm sorry. I should be mourning Sharon and trying to find Marie, but instead I'm bickering with that twat.' Gallagher looked at Harry. 'I never liked him. I grew up in Niddrie and made my own money. Randall's father bankrolled him, and granted, he's made a bob or two, but he would be cleaning toilets now if it weren't for his old man propping him up.'

'Let's try to keep calm about everything,' Harry said. 'It's not doing Marie any good, everybody in here going boxing when we should be focusing our energy on getting your daughter back.'

Gallagher couldn't argue with that.

SEVENTEEN

'How do I look?' Kerry Hamilton said, standing in front of the mirror in her office. It was always important to look good, no matter what you were doing.

'You might want to lose the cigarette,' said Rose, her assistant. 'A ciggie bobbing up and down with ash flicking all over the place might not give the right impression.'

Kerry took the cigarette out of her mouth and stubbed it out. 'Clucking like a mother hen. Why *do* I put up with you?'

'Because you love me, you little toerag.'

Kerry turned and smiled. 'I do. I haven't heard from my own mother in years, so you'd better have aspirations of staying here for a long time.'

Rose saw the worry lines on Kerry's face and went over to give her one of what she called her 'gentle hugs', which was basically putting her arms around her without creasing the business suit.

'I'm not going anywhere.'

Kerry stood back and looked at Rose; the older woman was dressed in a business skirt and jacket, with a white blouse. 'You look perfect.'

'I look like an old dinner lady who's just won the pools.'

'*Lottery*, Rose, *lottery*. Who does the pools nowadays?'

'You know what I mean. Some daft old boot with money in the bank and no idea how to spend it.'

'You're earning good money now because you've worked bloody hard for it. Don't you ever forget that, lady. And yes, there is a lot more where that came from. You're my right-hand woman now.'

Rose smiled. 'One thing is concerning me.'

'What's that?'

'This business with Marie Gallagher.'

Kerry smiled. 'It's all in hand. You said her mother called this morning and it's all a storm in a teacup.'

'That's not what the papers are saying. They're reporting that she's still missing.'

'You know what the tabloids are like. Besides, Broderick Gallagher owns the *Caledonian*. I heard he didn't allow any of the hacks to get into the hotel.'

'He did a deal with *Here Today* magazine,' Rose said. 'They wanted exclusive access to the wedding, which they got.'

'And that's why the red tops are saying she's still missing! They want sensationalism. They'll write anything to make Gallagher look like a clown.'

'He is a clown.'

'A *rich* clown. Who do you think bought the honeymooners this new apartment along the road?'

Rose looked at her watch. 'Is that woman still coming?'

'If by "that woman" you mean Anne Gallagher, then yes, she's meeting us there. Gallagher himself wanted her to be there, to represent Marie and her new husband. To oversee everything. He has trust issues, that man. We could have handled everything perfectly for his spoilt little princess.'

They left the offices in the West End and climbed into Kerry's little Porsche Macan.

'See? I got rid of the Nine-eleven. Two low indeed. Is this better for you?'

'It is, but let's see if you can do the two-minute drive without me reaching for a sick bag.'

Kerry made it down to Haymarket Terrace and drove along to The Rhind, a fabulous complex of apartments that had once been a school for children. The development was named after famous Edinburgh architect David Rhind.

'You said the finishing touches were being put on the houses built round the back of the school,' Rose said as the German car swept through the gates and up the driveway.

'Yes, they are. It's all interior work now. We're all going to make a bloody fortune out of this, Rose. You included.' Kerry smiled as she turned the engine off.

They walked into the entrance hall of the building.

'You must be Kerry Hamilton,' a young woman said, approaching. She had a little boy with her.

'I am.'

'Anne Gallagher. This is my son, Rory. And my daughter's friend, Claire.'

Kerry smiled at the child, who was beginning to tug at his mother's arm. 'I'm so sorry to hear about your daughter. Has there been any news?'

'No. We're hoping it was just some kind of spat. Marie has always been very highly strung.'

They got to the top floor and Kerry led them along to an apartment door. 'This is the one you and your husband bought. I know you haven't seen it yet, but I'm sure you'll be just as impressed as he was.' She took out a key and let them in.

'He raved about it. And since it's for our daughter, he wanted the best.'

It was a two-bedroom apartment with a small terrace. After looking around, Anne seemed to be satisfied.

'It looks good. My husband would have been here in person, but he's still up north, waiting for any news. However, he instructed me to get the keys. Our daughter and her husband should be doing this, but I'm sure everything will work out. It's our gift to them and I can't wait to hand over the keys.' There were tears in Anne's eyes and Claire stepped forward and put an arm around the woman for a moment.

'I was shocked when I heard the news. I'm praying for the safe return of your daughter, Mrs Gallagher,' Kerry said.

'Thank you. Let's just hope she was overwhelmed by the wedding and is on a spending spree in London or something.'

They went back downstairs, Rory running ahead.

'Don't go too far, darling!' Anne shouted, but Claire got hold of the little boy.

'Looks like somebody could do with a nanny,' Kerry said.

'You're telling me,' said Rose. 'But he's not our problem.'

'And to the Lord we are thankful.'

They stepped out into the sunshine and watched as Anne Gallagher struggled to get her little boy into the big Range Rover while Claire got in behind the wheel. Claire didn't look in their direction as she sped away.

EIGHTEEN

Terence Randall came into the bar and had a quick look around. He didn't see Broderick Gallagher anywhere, so he stepped up to the bar.

'Have you talked to your son?' Harry asked him.

Randall looked like a very old man now. He looked at Harry and slowly shook his head. 'I don't know where the hell he is.'

Dunbar looked at the man. 'What do you mean? Isn't he in his room?'

'I'd have said so, wouldn't I?'

'Have you tried calling him on his mobile?' Harry said.

'I did. When I went into his room. I heard it ringing and it was in a drawer in the nightstand.'

'Nobody goes anywhere without their phone nowadays,

especially the younger crowd,' Harry said, which made him feel ancient.

'Aye, well, my son has. God knows where he is.'

Dunbar put a hand on Randall's shoulder. 'Get yourself a brandy, Terry. A stiff one.' He indicated for the barman to supply the drink. 'Is the room open?'

Randall nodded. 'Aye. I'm telling you, if he hurt that lassie, I'll give him a fucking good belting, ~~let me tell you~~. Then you can throw the book at him.'

'Let's hope there's some reasonable explanation for why there's blood on his suit jacket,' Harry said.

'It looked like the bed had been made, then slept in a bit. Go up and have a look for yourself.'

Harry nodded to Dunbar, and they left the bar and headed upstairs to the bridal suite, where the bride and groom's rooms were, as well as the room where they would have been staying after they were married.

Harry gripped the door handle as if he were expecting an axeman to jump out at them, but it was all quiet. The bed was just as Randall had said: made, but it looked like somebody had had a romp on it. Albeit a very quick romp.

'Pull the covers back, Harry,' Dunbar said.

Harry didn't argue and gingerly approached the bed as though there was a horse's head in it, although the lack of a bump in the covers indicated otherwise. He pulled the quilt towards himself and looked down at the blood on the sheets.

'Jesus, what's that laddie got himself into?' Dunbar said.

'Are you thinking what I'm thinking?' Harry said.

'That he's a murdering bastard who's topped his wife and now he's hiding?'

'More or less.'

'Jesus, Harry, have we been looking in the wrong place all this time?'

'I'm beginning to wonder. I thought Duncan Randall was just grieving for his wife and out helping to look for her, but all this time he's possibly murdered her.'

NINETEEN

Claire Blythe sat in the driver's seat of the Range Rover and floored it towards Roseburn, heading back to the house at Barnton.

'Thank you for coming with me, and for staying with us,' Anne Gallagher said.

'That's what friends are for, Anne. You and I were friends before you met Broderick.'

'I know that.' Anne took in a breath and let it out slowly. 'My husband wanted security guards round the clock, but that's no way to live. I do feel safer with you here.'

'Safety in numbers. But I don't think we have to worry about Vince. To be honest, I didn't figure him for the jealous type, far less a murderer.'

Anne reached over and squeezed Claire's hand. 'Marie thought a lot of you. I mean, she loved Sharon, of course, but sometimes you bond with friends more than siblings. You know what I mean?'

'I do.'

It didn't take them long to reach the big house. Claire clicked the button in the car that would open the electric gate and waited for it to open before driving through. She parked at the house and waited until the wood-covered steel gate slid closed behind her. Then she unlocked the car and walked round to the back to extricate the little boy from his car seat. It was hot outside, a big difference from the cooled interior of the car.

'You want to get some ice cream?' she said, smiling.

'Yes, please,' the boy said as she took him by the hand and they walked up to the front door.

TWENTY

Harry felt a headache coming on. The thought of a millionaire's son topping his wife on their wedding night was the stuff of fiction, but there they were, the forensics crew fiddling about with their tools of the trade.

One of them had come over to him and confirmed it was human blood.

'Now we just need to find out who it belongs to, but that's not going to happen very quickly,' Dunbar said.

'We should see if the Inverness team have come up with anything.'

'Let's get back downstairs before Evans manages to burn the hotel down or something.'

'The laddie's doing well.'

'Compared to what, Harry? He's destined for traffic, so he is.'

By the time they got back down to the bar, Evans was sitting talking to Alex.

'There you are,' Dunbar said.

'Did you manage to calm the situation down, sir?' Evans said, not quite smirking.

'It was hardly the Highland Uprising, Evans. And I'm glad you find that funny. Your sense of humour will come in handy when you're seeing old women across the road with your lollipop.'

Just then, Tom Gunn and Eddie Lister came in. They saw the group of police officers and were about to turn round, but then decided a pint was in order.

'I'm telling you, we're the victims here,' Tom said as he approached Harry. 'But oh no, let's get them down to the station and give them a going-over.'

'It was hardly a going-over now, was it?' Harry said.

'Might as well have been. And you know those twats with their cameras were waiting outside the police station. Did somebody tip them off?'

'None of us did,' Dunbar said.

'Aye, well, somebody did,' Lister said. He ordered two pints.

Harry turned his back to the two men, who were now standing further along the bar. 'Two of my officers visited Vince Dubois' house today.'

'They find anything?'

'They spoke to his sister.'

'What did she have to say about things?'

'She said that Vince was invited up here.'

Tom walked up and stood between the two detectives. 'I heard you talking about Vince Dubois' sister. We've known him for years and there's one thing you should know about him.'

'What's that then?' Harry said.

'He doesn't have a sister.'

TWENTY-ONE

He drove the car down the long-disused track before coming to a halt in front of the property. Grass and weeds had sprung up, taking back what was rightfully theirs. Nobody tended the place now. It was only a memory, and a distant one at that.

The weeds had grown through the gravel parking area in front of the house and now the grass was knee high all around the abandoned place. He stood still, listening to the birds. He thought he could hear children's laughter if he concentrated hard enough. A dog barking too. A black Lab. He expected to see it running round from the back of the house, but no dog appeared.

The window frames had been painted green a long time ago, as if the owner had wanted to camouflage the property, so the house would blend into the forest.

He stepped round the right-hand side of the house, his boots trampling the tall grass down. He had to push aside some thick branches from a small tree that had grown sideways as it had sought out sunlight.

He was carrying a large holdall, but it was light.

The back door hadn't been touched, he was glad to see. But if it had then he would have heard about it. He took out his key and unlocked the padlock.

The door opened silently. He'd oiled it well before all this started. He closed it quietly behind him and walked through the gloom. The windows had been boarded up years ago and only slivers of light made it through the wooden slats. The little torch was ample to guide him through the debris inside, and he had already cleared a path for himself a long time ago.

He climbed the stairs and made his way along to one of the bedrooms, the floor creaking, announcing his arrival.

'There you are!' he said.

The man struggled in the chair, the gag muffling his voice.

'Relax there. Why are you so antsy today?' He strode across to the man, took a knife out of the holdall and reached round to the back of the chair to cut the plastic cable ties. 'Same rules apply: you try anything stupid and I'll kill you without breaking a sweat. Don't be a hero. Understand?'

The man's head nodded. His hair was bathed in sweat. It was hot in the house, especially upstairs, with no breeze filtering through any of the boarded-up windows.

'Right, we'll get you through to the bathroom so you can

do what you need to do, but I'll be right here. If you run, I'll cut your tendons so you'll never run anywhere again. If you try to hit me, I'll cut your thumbs off. You do believe me, don't you?'

The man nodded. He had to be helped to stand up straight. His muscles were stiffening. There was no way he was going to be running anywhere.

He tore the duct tape off the man's face. 'P-please let me go. I won't say anything. I don't even know who you are. I… can't identify you.'

'Go to the bathroom.' He didn't look down at the front of the man's trousers, knowing he had already soiled himself.

They shuffled out of the room and across the hallway to the toilet. He helped the man sit down. The smell was bad, but it was fighting with the odour of decay. The house was dying on its feet, just like the man who was sitting on the toilet.

'Take a shower. The water's still running, but it's only the cold, obviously. Clean up and get dressed in the clothes I brought you.' He fetched some soap and shampoo from the holdall.

He stood outside the bathroom door listening to the water running, before heading along to the other end of the hallway.

He opened the door and saw the woman sitting on the chair where he'd left her. Her head was slumped on her chest and he stopped to study her for a moment, watching her chest rise and fall.

'See what I have for you? You're going to be wearing it soon.'

He took the wedding dress out of the holdall and laid it on the bed. The dress was large and he'd struggled getting it in.

The drugs would be wearing off soon, so he knew he would have to get the other one out of the shower and dressed.

He walked back along to the other bedroom and laid out clothes on the bed. He'd already made sure the sheets and covers were fresh.

He heard the shower stop running, and strode over and gave the man a towel. 'Dry quickly and get back to the bedroom.'

The man stood shivering and gratefully accepted the towel and started drying himself. His captor didn't leave the bathroom, instead positioning himself in the doorway. He didn't think his prisoner would try to escape. He had been told what would happen if he tried anything. He wasn't in a position to fight his captor, but even if he did, the man was big and would easily beat the weakened man in a fight.

'Right. Get back to the room.' He watched as the man walked carefully in his bare feet; getting a splinter was the least of his worries. He had the towel wrapped round his waist and held on to it with one hand.

'Good. Now get dressed. And drink this. It's a protein

drink. I don't want you getting dehydrated. If you do as you're told, you'll be out of here as soon as possible.'

The man drank the first cup, a thick, milkshake type of drink, then the second and third. The added ingredients would keep his senses dulled and make him feel a little tired.

'Now, I'm going to tie you to the chair –'

'No, please don't.'

He looked at the victim. 'As I was saying, I'm going to tie you to the chair. Just for a little while. Then they'll be coming for you.'

'Then I can go home?' The man's voice was raspy, failing now as the drugs kicked in.

'Yes, you can go home.'

The prisoner dressed in the clean clothes. He went to sit back down on the chair but was led to a clean one. Once he was sitting, the man started to put cable ties round the supports but sensed movement behind him.

The bedroom door slammed shut, and before he could get to the handle, the key was turned in the lock.

'Open this door!' he shouted, but there was no reply. He threw his shoulder against it, but it didn't budge. He himself had reinforced the door jambs, both round the lock and the hinges on the other side, to stop his prisoner kicking the door down if he should somehow wake up and start battering the door.

It didn't stop him trying.

The holdall! He knew he had something in there that would take care of the door.

He turned round in the now-darkened room, took the small torch out of his pocket and turned it on. He opened up the bag and took out what he needed.

TWENTY-TWO

They were in the library, a uniform guarding the door, all sitting round Harry's iPad.

'This is what it must have been like when they did the first moon walk,' Jimmy Dunbar said.

'Michael Jackson?' Robbie Evans said.

Dunbar turned to look at him. 'Boaby, if I hear another bloody word out of you while this tablet is open, I swear to Christ...'

Evans waited until Dunbar had turned away before looking at Alex, who was sitting next to him. He made a face behind Dunbar's back.

'Right, Harry, when you're ready, give the order.' Dunbar was sitting next to Harry, while DI Barrett from Inverness was sitting on the other side. All eyes were glued to the small screen.

'I thought you watched the first moon walk?' Evans said. 'You were old enough to see it.'

'For fuck's sake, Evans, shut your pie hole.' Dunbar looked at Harry. 'His Native American name is Running with Scissors.'

Harry nodded. Looked at the screen, at Karen Shiels' face. 'DI Shiels, breach!'

She turned the view so that the team up in the Highlands could watch a uniformed entry team smash the lock on the front door of the house. The door crashed back against the hallway wall and an armed response team was the first in. When the house was clear, a swarm of uniforms entered, followed by the detectives.

'Nobody upstairs, ma'am.'

'Right, I'll leave a copy of the search warrant. Everybody listen up: tear the fucking place apart.'

The detectives in the Highlands watched as if looking through Karen's eyes. She turned right into the living room, moving her phone around, then walked up to the mantelpiece.

'Christ, they're gone,' she said. 'The photos of Dubois and his sister. They're gone.'

'A young blonde woman, you said.' Harry looked closer.

'There are other photos too, with other women in them, but the ones that had his sister in them are gone. Just those. The others are still there, as you can see.'

'There must have been something incriminating in them.

But why would she have kept them on display when you were in there?' Dunbar asked.

'She wasn't expecting us. Whoever she is.'

'Describe her to us again,' Harry said.

'She was dressed casually, and she was about thirty-ish, give or take. Blonde hair, slim build, medium size up top. She had the makings of a good-looking woman, with a bit lippy and clean hair.'

'Thanks, DI Shiels. Have a good look around. Call me when you're done.'

Harry disconnected the FaceTime call and looked at Dunbar. 'This woman pretends to be Vince Dubois' sister when my officers turn up. If she knew he didn't have a sister, why would she pretend to be his sister? I mean, she was taking a hell of a risk, knowing we would find out.'

'I don't think she cares, whoever she is. For some reason, she thought that would throw us off the scent.'

'Unless she panicked,' Alex said. 'I mean, there she is, in Vince's house for whatever reason, and then the police turn up. Maybe she just panicked and said the first thing that came into her head.'

'Or maybe she was stalling,' Evans said. 'She knew the story wouldn't check out, but she didn't care. By the time we found out, she was away.'

'Good point,' Dunbar said. 'The question is, why is this woman protecting Dubois?'

'Maybe a girlfriend?' Harry said. But something told him it went deeper than that and they were being played.

TWENTY-THREE

Marie ran as fast as she could downstairs, hearing the maniac banging on the bedroom door. She didn't know he had reinforced it, didn't know it was designed to keep somebody in the room. All she knew was, there had been a key in the lock and she had closed the door and turned it.

He had been giving them stuff to drink, and she'd had no choice but to drink it because she had been so thirsty, but she'd woken up feeling disoriented. It had to be a date rape drug.

Her feet thundered on the stairs as she went down, first to the small landing where the stairs turned, then down to the ground floor and across to the front door. There was no key in this lock, no windows to break, no loose panels to kick out.

She turned and ran down a little hallway that led to the back of the house. It was dark but not pitch black. She heard the banging intensifying upstairs, getting louder and louder. She ran, staggering against a wall and through an old doorway that hadn't seen a door in many years.

Into the kitchen. It was dirty and mouldy and smelled awful. But it was lighter in here. She ran to the back door, grabbed the handle and turned it.

And the door opened.

Her heart was beating like a drum, but she didn't hesitate for one second. She was out of the door and into…where? She realised she didn't know where she was, but anywhere was better than being stuck in here with…him.

It wasn't full dark, but the darkness would come down with a vengeance soon and she didn't have her phone with the little light in it.

She ran out into the overgrown garden, the noise from upstairs diminishing. The house was in the middle of a forest, tall trees closing in, blocking the sunlight so that everything was in shade.

She turned and had a look at the house. It was big and dirty, with the windows boarded over, including the window in the kitchen door that she'd just run through. Nobody was coming just now, but she guessed it wouldn't be long before he smashed the door down and came after her.

She kept on running, battering her way through the weeds and tall grass with her thighs. She had been dressed in dirty old jeans and a grubby tee shirt. Prickly bushes grabbed at her clothes, but she shrugged them off, fuelled by adrenaline.

Then, suddenly, she was on an old path. It was rough going, but not as bad as the garden had been. Which way? Left or right? Either way took her beneath canopies of trees. She couldn't see far into the woods.

She chose left and ran as fast as she could, but she was weak and soon started tiring. She slowed, trying to conserve her energy.

She turned to look back again.

There was nobody there.

She didn't see the prying eyes looking out at her from the top window of the house.

TWENTY-FOUR

'Any news?' Broderick Gallagher asked. He was back in the bar, resorting to drinking whisky.

'Nothing yet,' Harry said, keeping the information about Vince Dubois' phantom sister to himself.

Gallagher shook his head as if he was about to say something derogatory, but then thought better of it.

He hadn't wanted any dinner. Time for eating later, when he was in his room. Alone. Where he could think about what he would do to Duncan Randall if it turned out he had killed Marie and Sharon. Terence first, though. He was the man who had brought Duncan into this world, so he was ultimately responsible.

The thought pleased Gallagher.

He watched as Harry walked away, then moved over to a corner of the bar, one with big windows overlooking the grounds. Lights were on now, starting to light up the area surrounding the hotel. How could things have turned out like this?

He had decided to sell his share in this place. How could he ever enjoy it after what had just happened?

He put his glass on the table and took his mobile phone out and dialled his wife's number. Hopefully, speaking with her would cheer him up.

TWENTY-FIVE

It was dinnertime and Alex had a little side salad sitting next to a dish that smelled good but looked awful. 'This case is getting twisted, Harry,' she said, poking at something green that looked like it may or may not be alive.

'It has to be related to Gallagher somehow. Sharon dead, his other daughter missing. Maybe a business deal gone wrong?'

'You don't get to his position without stepping on a few toes.'

'What's that you're eating anyway?' He put a piece of beef into his mouth and chewed, pointing at her dinner with his fork.

'Beef Bolognese.'

'Really? I thought you were more a mince and tatties kind of girl.'

'You saying I'm chunky?'

'Not at all. Just…built for fun.'

She looked at him for a moment, not sure how to take his comment. 'You do see the salad there, don't you?'

'Camouflage, that's what that is.'

'Listen to Johnny Two Pies.'

'I can handle it. My mother always said I burn fat off like nothing on earth.'

'Ah, a mother's love. Looking at her wee boy through her love goggles.'

Harry's phone buzzed about on the table. He saw Vanessa's name pop up and wondered if he should answer it. Then it stopped and a message came up saying he had a voicemail.

'I would think before you answer it, sir,' Alex said. 'You don't want to show her you're too keen.'

'How did you know it was Vanessa?'

'Duh. I can read upside down.'

'Is there no end to your talents? Don't answer that.' He picked the phone up and listened to the message. Then he put the phone back down.

'If you want a woman's opinion –'

'I don't.'

'Let me finish. If you want a woman's opinion, you'd be better off letting her stew. It doesn't matter why she called you; just the fact she did means she wants to communicate. If you call her, the next thing you know, you'll be running back to her, and then she'll have won. And then it's game over, Harry, I'm telling you.'

'She just wanted to let me know that all my stuff is in boxes now and she's leaving them outside my door.'

Alex poked at some salad. 'Okay. That was my second choice.'

'Your female intuition is needing a little tune-up.'

'No, no, that's not it at all. I stand by what I just said. Now, if she really wanted to end it, she wouldn't have done anything with your stuff. Trust me, Harry. This is her attention seeking. If you want her, call her. Explain things. Tell her you'll be round to pick the boxes up and then she'll talk to you. But if you think it's over then don't call her.'

He ate some more beef. 'I already sent a text to my next-door neighbour. She'll look out for the boxes.'

'Good man. I'm proud of you.' They ate in silence for a moment. 'Where's Jimmy?'

'DCI Dunbar to you.'

'Really? We're doing this again? I can't call a senior officer by his first name?'

'No, you bloody well can't.' Harry's voice had got higher and the other guests looked across for a moment. 'Sorry. My blood pressure got up a bit there.'

'Duly noted, DCI McNeil. I will never call you Harry again.'

'You're kidding, right?'

'Yes, Harry.'

'I knew it was too good to be true.'

Alex washed down her salad with some water. 'Seriously, where did Jimmy get to?'

'I haven't a clue. Evans is doing his nut in. I'm glad I don't have an annoying sergeant with me.'

'That would be tragic.' She looked at him. 'Oh, I see; that was sarcasm.'

Harry finished off his plate. 'I don't think there's going to be anything more we can do tonight. Vince Dubois is still giving us the runaround.'

'And let's not forget Duncan Randall. Do you suppose Randall caught Marie and her ex in an embrace and he let them both have it?'

'I'm not ruling anything out. But these damn forests go on forever.'

'You should mention that to management. I'm sure they can use that in their next brochure.'

Despite himself, Harry grinned. 'I want a commission.' He sat back. One of the waiters came over and took their plates away, then returned with a coffee carafe.

'Thank you,' Harry said after the coffees were poured. Then he caught the waiter's attention again. 'I have a question.'

'Go ahead, sir.'

'The stewards who work here. Who hired them?'

'The management.'

Harry nodded.

'Oh, and Angus McPhee had a say too, since he was the one who recommended some of them.'

'How long have they worked here?'

'Since the hotel was bought by Mr Gallagher and Mr Randall, sir. About six or seven months, like a lot of us here.'

'Do you have much interaction with them? Meaning, do you know them well?'

'We work with them, but I don't know anybody who socialises with them. They live in the barracks that were built for them on the property so they don't have to travel to work, and they do shifts so somebody is available twenty-four hours.'

'Okay, thank you.'

Alex waited until the waiter was away before speaking. 'What was that all about?'

'I'm just wondering how a trained soldier let himself be taken like that steward Andy was.'

'Look at the surroundings: woods, overgrown bushes and long grass. Anybody could get lost there. Just because he was a soldier, doesn't mean he couldn't be taken by surprise.'

'I know, but by somebody like Vince Dubois? A desk jockey? The only gun he's fired is a virtual one, as far as we know.'

'He's crafty, Harry, and very cunning. Plus, he's got one of the shotguns and plenty of ammo.'

They finished their coffees, then Harry threw his napkin onto the table and stood up. 'Come on, Sergeant, let's go and talk to somebody.'

TWENTY-SIX

The track seemed to go on forever, meandering through the woods. She thought she should have come to a road by now, but there was nothing. Where the hell was she? Maybe she should have gone the other way, but it was too late now.

She felt the cramp in her stomach kick in. It had been there when she woke up earlier, but it had subsided. Now it was back again. She stopped running for a moment, thinking it was maybe this that was causing her discomfort. But cramps were nothing compared to what the lunatic might do to her if he came after her.

She started running again. Marie thought about Duncan, and how they should have been going on their honeymoon and coming back to their new apartment that her dad had bought them. Now, here she was in the woods, trying to escape the clutches of a crazed killer.

She didn't know how long she had been running, but the sun was slowly going down and she had to find something before nightfall. Which looked like it was just round the corner.

She kept on going, and then she saw it in the distance: a road. The trees thinned out here and it was like a clearing or something. It wasn't a paved road, but it was a proper track, leading to...where? It had to be to civilisation.

The path she was on stopped at the road, which seemed to be going east to west, if the lowering sun was anything to go by. It was tucking in behind hills in the distance, so that meant that the house was on her left, way back.

Then she saw it: headlights coming! Jesus, she couldn't believe it. She ran into the middle of the road and jumped up and down, waving her arms. It was a Land Rover, and she thought it could be one belonging to the hotel. Why would anybody else be out here?

That was it, they were out looking for her. And one of them had found her. She was blinded by the full-beam headlights for a moment and put her hands up to shield her eyes.

Then the Land Rover was pulling up alongside her and the passenger window was wound down.

'I'm Marie Gallagher! The woman you've been looking for!' As her eyes adjusted a little, she could make out the hotel's logo on the door. She felt such relief as the driver unlocked the door and she climbed in.

'You're in safe hands now, ma'am,' the bearded steward

said. 'I'll get you back.' He continued driving in the direction he had been going.

'Aren't you going to turn back?' she said.

'The main road's this way.'

'I think that's where the house is where I was being kept.'

The big car drove along the track with ease.

'The lodge house or the gatehouse?'

'It was big.'

'That'll be the lodge house. Great big dirty thing?'

'Yes. Looks like a haunted mansion. You know it?'

'Aye. I'm pretty sure it was checked out already, but maybe they thought nobody was in there because it was boarded up.'

Marie was excited, relieved, but she also felt the anger kicking in. Why the hell hadn't somebody gone into the house to check? To damn well make sure?

They rounded a corner and the house came into view.

'There it is!' Marie shouted. 'My husband is in there! Can you call the police? I locked the guy in a room.'

The Land Rover stopped right at the door.

'I can do better than that,' the steward said. He reached round the back of the seat and pulled out a shotgun. Marie was hesitant to step out, but she didn't want to let the man out of her sight.

He had switched the headlights off and now the darkness enveloped them, but her eyes started to adjust to the gloom.

'Where is your husband?'

'Upstairs. Turn left. There's a door on the left with a key in the lock. Please be careful.'

The man smiled, his white teeth showing through his beard. She'd never thought she would be so happy to see a man in her life. She knew the stewards were all ex-army, so her captor was going to be up against a former soldier.

He walked up to the front door and turned the handle, and the door opened silently. The steward lifted the shotgun up to his face, then he turned round to Marie.

'You need to wait here. But tell me what he's wearing.'

'He always had a ski mask on. Wearing waterproofs. Jacket and trousers, with a hood.'

'Even inside?'

'Yes.'

'Right. Leave him to me. Scaring a wee lassie like that, the bastard.'

'Oh God. Please be careful,' Marie said, ignoring the remark about her being a wee lassie.

'I will. If he tackles me, he'll know all about it.'

She watched as he walked into the hallway, then climbed the stairs to the first landing, before continuing to the foot of the second staircase and disappearing from sight.

Marie looked all around her, but everything was dark. *Please let Duncan be alright,* she prayed.

Then she heard the shotgun go off.

TWENTY-SEVEN

Jimmy Dunbar had appeared after dinner and sat with Harry at a table, while Evans was up at the bar with Alex.

'He's as good as a man short,' Dunbar complained.

'At least he's putting his hand in his pocket.'

'That's his one redeeming feature. What about that lassie you're here with?'

'She's proving to be a good detective, to be honest.'

'Don't let her go anywhere then. They're hard to come by.'

The two sergeants came back from the bar with the drinks.

'Cheers,' Harry said, and took a sip from his pint. The bar was quiet and there was no sign of either Gallagher or Randall.

'It's nice to relax a little bit,' Alex said. 'I felt guilty standing up at the bar when there's a woman and her husband still missing. I know one of them might be a killer, but I wish we had more of a lead.'

'Sometimes leads can come in thick and fast; other times things go dry very quickly.'

'I told her not to be daft,' Evans said. 'We can't be on duty all of the time.'

'Jesus, that's twice you've made sense since we came here,' Dunbar said. 'I'll need to mark it on the calendar.'

Evans gave his boss a look that could have meant either *thanks, sir* or *cheeky sod*.

'Oh, heads-up, here's Harry's new fancy-piece,' Alex said with a grin.

They all looked at the doorway to the bar.

'What's this? Playing away from home?' Dunbar said with a grin.

'Give it a rest.' Harry shot Alex a look as Angie Patterson looked around the bar and saw them all. She walked across to them.

Harry stood up. 'Hello again. I didn't recognise you at first.'

'Didn't recognise me with my clothes on? My work clothes, that is.' She smiled. 'It's a joke.'

Jimmy stood up. 'I'm DCI Jimmy Dunbar and the young man who is about to get you a drink is DS Evans.'

She nodded. Then smiled at Alex. 'Hello again.'

Evans got up and took her order, and Angie sat down, putting her handbag at her feet.

'So, Miss Patterson, I take it this isn't a social call?' Harry said.

'Correct. I came looking for you.'

Alex raised an eyebrow at Harry, but he ignored her. Evans came back with the Coke.

'I'm driving,' Angie said by way of an explanation.

'We're just comparing notes,' Dunbar said, as if he was worried she'd think they were well on their way to getting blootered.

'I was almost given a hard time by one of the uniforms guarding the gate. Those newspaper reporters were shouting at me, asking questions. I felt like royalty or something.'

'It was worth the barrage of questions just to have a drink with your favourite copper,' Alex said.

'Indeed it was. But I'm actually glad I can talk to you all.' Angie took a sip of her drink first. 'I got to thinking about Sharon Gallagher, as they came for her and the other victim today. I mean, they will have to go the extra mile to get an identification of the steward, considering his head was taken off with what we believe to be a shotgun.'

'They can match DNA from his family,' Dunbar said.

'It just sent a shiver down my back, considering what happened all those years ago. It brought back a lot of memories.'

The detectives looked at her, waiting for her to go on. 'You know, the other shootings?'

'What shootings?' Harry asked.

'Fifteen years ago. When the man shot his wife dead and blew his own head off in front of his kids.'

'We don't know anything about that.' Harry looked at the others and they all shook their heads. 'Tell us about it.'

'I was fourteen at the time. I was friends with the family. And Maggie in particular, of course. She went home from school one day and found her mother dead in the bedroom, shot by their father. Her brother, Michael, came home, and when he went upstairs, they were all in the parents' room. Maggie sat petrified on the bed and their father put the gun under his chin and pulled the trigger. Apparently, it was a sawn-off shotgun.'

'That happened here?' Dunbar said.

'Yes, here in town.'

'Do they know why he did it?' Alex asked.

'Because Edward, their father, was accused of abusing and killing two little boys. He was persecuted by the press. Maggie was hounded and they were bullied at school. Finally, they were taken out of school and they left.'

'So he thought he would kill himself instead of going to prison?' Evans said. 'I don't blame him.'

'It couldn't have been easy for them,' Harry said.

'That's not all,' Angie said. 'It was a month later...'

TWENTY-EIGHT

Michael sat on the settee in the living room, watching the woman's TV. He didn't think of it as *his* TV; it belonged to the woman they were forced to live with now. She wasn't bad, despite all the horror stories they'd been told: *They'll kick your head in,* and, *You'll be given the belt for not eating your greens.*

But the woman was okay with them. She didn't take any shit, but she was fair, and the husband liked football, so they went to the match sometimes. Maggie was having a harder time than he was, but he reassured her he would look after her.

It was a Saturday afternoon that he found out his father hadn't been a child molester. Michael was sitting watching TV when it was announced that police had arrested a man in connection with the abuse of several boys. He'd admitted to murdering the boys that Michael's father had been accused of killing.

Michael cried that evening. His father killing his mother and then taking his own life had all been for nothing.

The woman they lived with spoke to the police, who told her that it was early days and they would have to investigate further, but it was looking likely the man was telling the truth. He knew too many details that had been kept out of the press.

Michael's sorrow turned to anger as he looked at the face of the man on the TV. He hated him with every fibre of his being. The man was a schoolteacher! He even knew Michael's dad, and he was also was a football coach in his spare time; the two murdered boys had been on the team he coached.

Then Michael read the report in the papers.

The teacher said he had abused the boys, who were then going to tell their parents, but the teacher couldn't have that. He'd be ruined! He was a pillar of the community. He was a father to two little boys. What would people think? That he had touched his own two boys? No, he couldn't have that. It was an illness he had. He wasn't really a bad person.

At first, the teacher had spoken to the boys, told them he was a Scout leader. They were going camping and he was coming along as a leader. They were at school, and they seemed daunted by the teacher talking to them about going on the camping trip, but when they saw him in his Scout uniform, he was just another one of the boys.

They had a good time that weekend. They seemed pleased to see the teacher at school, and they were more excited about the second trip they were going on.

On that trip, he invited them round to his tent. He exposed himself and began touching them. He said they were frozen with fear. Afterwards, he told them not to say anything and he would give them a drink round at his house.

He invited them over the following weekend, when he knew his wife was going to be out with his own boys. They said they weren't coming round. In fact, one of them said he was going to tell his mother. The teacher promised them a lot of money. They just needed to meet him to collect it and then they would never talk of it again.

He drove in his car to the waste ground. The boys arrived on their bikes.

He killed the first one with a hammer behind some bushes. The other boy didn't know his friend had been killed.

The teacher came out and shouted for him to come over and help his friend. He was ill.

As the second boy got closer, he saw the teacher holding the hammer and he ran. He was fast, but not fast enough to outrun the man.

He'd just made it to his bike when the hammer caught him on the shoulder. He screamed and fell down. The teacher stood over him, looking down. He apologised, then he brought the hammer down again, this time on the boy's head.

The teacher had hired a van, and he put the boys' bodies

in the back of it. He drove it onto the estate after dark and along the track, then dumped the boys where they would be easily found.

He then took a blood-covered sweater and put it into the Land Rover that the coach drove for his work around the estate.

The following day, after the boys had been reported missing, he went to a phone box and made an anonymous tip. Unbelievably, ncither of the boys had told their parents where they were going. It would have been only a matter of time, the teacher thought, so he felt relieved to have taken care of the problem when he had.

The police went to the estate and asked Michael's father, Edward, if they could search his Land Rover. He agreed, thinking it strange they should be looking at his car. They came back with the sweater.

Edward was arrested, but he employed a lawyer, who argued anybody could have put it there, since the coach didn't drive the Land Rover exclusively and it wasn't kept locked at night.

Edward walked, but the police kept him as suspect number one and they came back with sniffer dogs.

The following day, they found the two boys.

Edward knew they would crucify him, that he would be found guilty by the court of public opinion. He drove to the house, waited for the kids to come home and then shot himself after shooting his wife.

The teacher thought he'd got away with it. And he would have if his *illness* hadn't taken over. He touched another little boy at Scout camp, but this boy told his dad, who went looking for the teacher and caught him in the showers in the park pavilion after a football training session, touching another little boy. Although tempted to batter the man, he called the police instead. The teacher confessed to touching the boys and to murdering the other two lads.

Michael watched the reporter on TV telling the world that his father had been innocent after all.

A week later, the teacher hanged himself in prison while he was awaiting trial.

'And this happened locally, you said, Angie?' Harry said.

'Yes, it did.'

'Near here?' Dunbar asked.

'Not *near* here – *here*. On the estate that Gallagher and his friend bought. They're adding it to this estate to make this place vast. The old estate fell into disrepair after the murders; the old man who owned it abandoned it. The mansion house was set on fire. The police think it was some vengeful locals, but nobody was ever caught, and the place fell apart. Until Gallagher bought it.'

'Show us,' Harry said.

TWENTY-NINE

Marie was shaking. It wasn't from the cold that had descended from the night sky, but fear. Total and utter fear. The steward hadn't come back to say he had taken care of the crazed killer and rescued her husband.

Shouldn't he have been back by now?

She knew the sensible thing to do was to go and get help, so that was what she would do. She ran round to the driver's side of the Land Rover and got in.

The driver had taken the key.

Of course he had! Why think this would be easy?

She got back out, adrenaline coursing through her now. She wasn't armed, but the steward was. She walked into the hallway, her eyes adjusting to the gloom. It was dark, but she could see the stairs. She didn't shout out to the man. What if she took him by surprise and he shot her? He had obviously shot at something.

Maybe he was trying to free Duncan. Yes, that had to be it. He was ex-army and probably knew how to do this fighting in houses stuff.

She took the first step and started walking upstairs. She couldn't believe she was actually here, back in the house she had escaped from only a little while ago.

She reached the first landing, turned and took each step slowly until she reached the next landing. God, she wished she had her phone right now, just for the little light.

Marie turned left and walked along the hallway. The bedroom door, the one she had locked, was open. The wall next to the door jamb was smashed, as if somebody had taken a hammer to it.

She inched along, expecting the man to jump out, but nobody did.

Then she saw Duncan on the bed, his wrists tied to the bed frame with cable ties. He was looking at her, fully awake, but the tape over his mouth prevented him from speaking.

Marie couldn't move. Not at first, but she steeled herself. *Just go in, cut the plastic ties somehow and get Duncan free.* Then she saw the shoes, and then the socks. On somebody lying on the floor.

Oh God, no, please.

She inched further into the room and looked round the

door. A steward was lying face down, his kilt up above his knees.

She was about to turn and run when the steward who had driven her here appeared behind her.

'Marie,' he said.

She gasped, her heart hammering. 'Oh, thank God!' She looked at the man on the floor. 'Is that...the man who kept us here?'

He grinned at her, the shotgun pointing towards her midriff. 'I'm afraid not. You see, when you got out, I smashed my way out and drove round the other track and came out ahead of you, so it would look like I was coming from the hotel. I took off my waterproof gear so you would think I was one of the stewards. Now, get back in the room, put your wedding dress on and get on the bed with your husband.'

Marie's breath left her body as she froze. This couldn't be happening. But it was. This was very real.

'Who's that lying on the floor?' she asked.

'One of the other stewards I brought here a little while ago. He was in the other room, unconscious. He's part of the plan. He just didn't know it.'

THIRTY

They went in two Land Rovers, the armed officers in the front. They had decided to drive through the estate. If the press saw them leaving, it was inevitable that somebody would follow them, and then they would have civilians in the way and none of them wanted that.

'I don't understand what all of this has to do with Broderick Gallagher,' Evans said to Angie.

She was sitting in the back with strict instructions not to move from the car. She was to show them where the house was and that was it.

'I haven't a clue,' she said. 'But I'm sure a young detective like you will be able to figure it out.' She smiled at him in the dark of the vehicle.

Harry looked at Alex, sitting next to him in the middle seats. 'Don't get all jealous now,' she said in a low voice.

'Just when I thought Angie and I could make a go of it,' he said.

A uniform was following behind the lead car, both vehicles driving with just their sidelights on. 'I hope he knows where he's going,' Dunbar said.

'You can't miss it,' Angie said. 'This track leads right into the parking area for the house, then a few hundred yards further on you come to the main road. There's a small gatehouse there, but that's been abandoned for years too.'

The lead car slowed down and so did theirs.

'We're here, sir,' the driver said, keeping well back.

'The Reynolds' house,' Angie had told them, *'where Reynolds shot his wife and then himself.'*

There were nine men in the front car, all of them armed to the teeth. They got out and pointed their guns at the windows, some men holding back to cover the men who were going in.

Harry glanced at his watch, before looking out of the windscreen. They could only see part of the house from where they were, but their driver was ready to swing the car round and drive away at speed.

After ten minutes, an officer with a torch walked towards them and waved the driver forward. He drove up and they piled out.

'We've checked the house out, sir,' the officer said to Dunbar.

'And?'

'And it's not a pretty sight.'

The officer led them forward into the house. They all switched their torches on, the multiple beams cutting through the darkness of the house.

He led them upstairs, and they saw the body lying on the hallway floor, his head completely blown off. He was one of the stewards from the hotel, dressed in the kilted uniform.

'Who's that?' Evans asked.

Harry went through one of the pockets and pulled out a wallet. 'Angus McPhee,' he said. 'The head steward.'

'Christ, Dubois must have gone mental with a shotgun to blow his head completely off,' Dunbar said. 'I don't think he's going to go down without a fight.'

'Maybe he was searching this place and the killer got him. Jesus.'

'You'd better have a look in there, sir,' the officer said, pointing with his torch. The other marksmen were in the hallway, but two of them were in the room.

They don't want to contaminate the crime scene, Harry thought. He stepped forward along with Dunbar and they looked into the bedroom.

Marie Randall, née Gallagher, and her husband, Duncan, were dressed in their wedding outfits and lying on the bed, side by side. Each of them had massive a gunshot wound to the front. They were both clearly dead, but the officer confirmed it.

'I'm not a pathologist, but the wounds are clearly from a

shotgun aimed at the heart. Death would probably have been instant.'

Harry nodded. 'We'll have to tell Gallagher and Randall that their children are dead.'

'I wonder why he didn't blow their heads off like the others?' Dunbar said.

'Simple, Jimmy. He wanted to make sure we identified them right away.'

'We thought it might be Duncan Randall, but it was Vince Dubois all along,' Evans said.

'Don't say that to Terence Randall. We need to clear out and get forensics in here right away,' Harry said. 'Officer, stay here with your men, just to make sure. Post a couple outside and a couple round the back. Make sure they're safe. We're going back to the hotel to break the news.'

'Yes, sir.'

Harry opened the back door of the car and looked in at Angie.

'You were very helpful.'

She smiled at him. 'Glad I could be of help.'

Harry was about to get into the front of the Land Rover when he stopped.

'What is it?' Alex asked.

'Look around you. What *don't* you see?'

Alex had a look around the area in front of the house. 'Angus McPhee would have driven here. There's no car.'

'Vince Dubois shoots everybody in the house and then

takes the keys to McPhee's Land Rover. Then where does he go to hide?'

'McPhee's apartment. It's on its own, above one of the garages where the golf carts are kept.'

Harry issued orders to the firearms team and then they headed back to the estate.

There were several buildings in a clearing not too far from where the brand-new lodges had been built. The garages held the golf carts that the guests could use, which was recommended, as cars weren't normally allowed on the tracks through the woods.

Angus McPhee, being the lead steward, had his own apartment above one of the garages. There were stairs on the outside, on the left-hand side of the building.

A Land Rover was parked at the foot of the steps. Nobody else would park there except McPhee.

Two firearms officers led the team up the steps. The door was open. They went inside, followed by the rest of the team.

Less than a minute later, one of the officers came back out and waved for the detectives to join him.

'He's here.'

'Alive and in handcuffs?'

The officer shook his head. 'Come and have a look for yourself.'

The lights had been switched on and they walked into the apartment to see Vince Dubois sitting on the floor in the bedroom, hands tied behind his back and with a ligature round his neck that was tied to a door handle. He was obviously dead.

'I wonder why he chose to come here and kill himself, instead of just doing it in the house where he had killed the others?' Alex said.

'We'll never know. At least we don't have to worry about a manhunt now.' Harry looked at her. 'Let's go and break the news to the families.'

THIRTY-ONE

Terence Randall and Broderick Gallagher were in the same room together and no fists had been flying.

'Is it Marie?' Gallagher said. He had been sleeping and his eyes were puffy.

'Yes, it is. And Duncan. I'm sorry to tell you that we found them both. Deceased,' Harry said. He waited for the outburst, but none came.

Randall started crying and Gallagher sat with his mouth open, saying nothing. There were family liaison officers from Inverness in the room and they went to sit beside both men. More uniforms were in the room, and DI Barrett from Inverness was standing back.

'How?' Gallagher suddenly said, brushing the FLO aside. 'How did she die?'

'That will be up to the pathologist to determine, sir,' Harry said.

'Don't mess me around, McNeil. You saw her. I want to know.'

'Me too,' Randall said, sniffing and wiping his eyes.

'It looks like they were both shot dead with a shotgun,' Harry said.

Gallagher stared into space for a moment before looking up at Harry. 'Both my girls were killed with a shotgun? Have you any idea who did this?'

'All we can say is, there was another person found at the scene, also deceased. Also shot dead by the killer.'

Gallagher stood up. 'Do you know who's responsible? If you do, just tell us. We're going to find out anyway, for God's sake.'

Harry looked across at Dunbar, who nodded his head. 'It was Vince Dubois. He'd also killed one of the stewards up at the house before going elsewhere to commit suicide.'

'Vince? The one who was engaged to my Marie?'

'Yes, the same one.'

'Christ. The little bastard. He couldn't have her, so nobody could, is that it?'

Dunbar stepped forward. 'It's not like he gatecrashed. He had an invitation. We were told he was invited and my sergeant found his name on the guest list. We saw him on CCTV, so he was definitely here at the hotel.'

'Maybe he approached Marie when she was upstairs getting changed,' Randall said. 'I mean, nobody would have questioned him if he was walking about and he didn't look out of place.'

'Bastard. Who knew he was such a maniac?' Gallagher shook his head. 'I don't suppose I can see my Marie?'

'Not yet. Forensics are making their way to the scene and they'll be there all night. Then she'll be taken to Inverness for the PM. Then she'll be released, but I think you'll be able to see her at the mortuary.'

Gallagher sighed deeply. 'You know, I think I'll wait. I'll have my Anne with me. We will have to arrange the funerals for both girls. Randall can do what he likes, but I don't want to look at Marie in a smelly mortuary. I'm going to fly home in the morning when my jet gets back up here.'

He walked away, out of the bar.

Randall stood up. 'I agree with him. I don't want to see my boy lying on some trolley, covered in a sheet. I'll see him back in Glasgow.' He also walked out of the room.

'It must be tough, being a detective at times,' Angie said to Alex.

'We both deal with dead bodies. Just in different forms. We get to see them first, then you deal with them.'

'Well, not me so much, but the pathologists.'

'This is the end of it then, Harry?' Dunbar said.

'You would think so.'

'You got some doubts there, my friend?'

'Oh, it's nothing, Jimmy. Maybe I'm just overthinking things.'

'I'm going upstairs to write my report. We'll be leaving tomorrow after breakfast, but I'll call my super tonight.'

'Me too. I'll catch you tomorrow, Jimmy.'

'I don't know about you, but this feels anticlimactic,' Angie said after Dunbar and Evans had gone. 'I mean, I know I'm not part of your team, but –'

'You acted like you were a part of the team. You told us about the house, Angie,' Harry said.

'I wish I was coming down to Edinburgh. I'm bored out of my skull working at that tiny hospital.'

'I'll keep my eyes and ears open. If a position opens up at the mortuary in Edinburgh, would you consider it?'

'I certainly would.'

'Give me your mobile number and I'll put you in my contacts.'

Angie gave it to him. 'Thanks, Harry. I'll head off home now. Hopefully, you won't forget me.'

He smiled at her. 'After tonight? I won't forget you.' He watched her walk out of the room.

'Smooth-talker. That was almost like the ending of a Humphrey Bogart film.'

'*Of all the murder enquiries...*'

'Don't give up your day job.'

'You're not jealous, are you? That old Uncle Harry still has it in him to attract a younger woman?'

'I'm not the one you have to worry about, Harry. And you damn well know that Gus Weaver has retired from the Edinburgh city mortuary. *If a position comes up.* Are you going to put in a good word for her?'

'Of course not. I'll just let her know. Time we headed up as well.'

As they reached his room, he said, 'Goodnight, Alex.'

He watched her walk along the hallway to her room before going into his own, then sat down on the edge of his bed. Instead of feeling tired, he felt wired. He knew he should maybe call Vanessa. Truth be told, he missed her. He took his phone out and was about to dial her number when there was a knock at his door.

He debated whether to pick up the poker, but decided not to bother as he opened the door.

Alex was standing there looking at him.

'You really need a boyfriend,' he said.

'Why? I have you, don't I? But let me in. I want to talk to you about something.'

He stood by and let her in.

'If this is about you drinking on duty, I'll put in a good word for you,' he said to her.

'I think I'm the more sober one, don't you?'

'Not really, and I don't want to rush you, but can you say what you've come to say? I need to make a phone call.'

'Sounds like rushing to me. I'm just having a hard time getting my head round this. Obviously, it looks wrapped up. Ex-lover of bride turns up at the wedding, and kills the bride and her new husband in a jealous rage. That's how the papers will see it. But there's something wrong.'

'Like?'

'Like, why did he pick that old lodge house to kill them in? More to the point, how did he know about it? And why was Angus McPhee there without anybody knowing about it?'

'Maybe he was just checking it out and was in the wrong place at the wrong time.'

She sat on a chair while he sat on the bed. 'I just got to thinking…We were told that the camera up in the bridal suite wasn't working. That was convenient. But if Vince Dubois was up there and was seen, somebody might have said something, despite what Randall thinks. But there is one person who could have floated about up there and nobody would have questioned him.'

'A steward.'

'Correct.'

'We've both dealt with murder cases before and we've seen plenty of people try to cover up their crime, but not Vince. He accepted the invite, he was seen on CCTV, he got McPhee to take him to a group who were going out on a search.'

'Maybe he didn't care anymore. The love of his life was

getting married to another man and he was at the end of the road.'

'Maybe. It just stinks, that's all.'

'We'd better get some rest,' Harry said. 'We have to drive back tomorrow and I still have those calls to make.'

'See you in the morning,' she said as she left the room.

Harry waited until he was sure she was really away. Then he called Vanessa. It went to voicemail.

He called Angie Patterson. 'I wanted to thank you again for your help tonight. And I have another question, if you don't mind.'

'Sure, Harry. Hold on, though. I'm just giving my cat some food. He's always hungry before bed.'

'What's his name?' *Please don't be called Harry.*

'Alice Cooper.'

Harry was silent for a moment. 'Great. I just wanted you to remind me of the names of the kids who were left behind when their father shot himself.'

'Michael Reynolds. And his sister, Dee. Well, Maggie was her name, but everybody called her Dee. They were moved into foster care and the social work department changed their names and their whole identities. I didn't see Dee again for a long time.'

'You met her?'

'Yes. I was down in Edinburgh for the festival years ago and a woman came up to me and introduced herself. It was Dee. She recognised me right away. She said she'd missed me for all those years, but the social workers had taken her away. She had started a new life and was even engaged.'

'Do you know what her fiancé's name was?'

'I can't remember his last name, but his first name was Vince.'

THIRTY-TWO

Rain fell hard throughout the night and Harry tossed and turned, thinking about Vince Dubois. He'd told DI Barrett from Inverness that he needed to post uniforms throughout the hotel, just to make sure everybody felt safe, even though the threat was over. People were still shaken.

'Why did he shoot the steward?' Alex had asked him. She'd called him when she got back to her room.

'Collateral damage. He got in the way. It's why he left the other two women alive; he just wanted Sharon Gallagher, and he got her. Making her up to look like Marie was just him playing for time. He was showing us he was in control.'

'Love's a strange thing.'

Harry slept fitfully and was glad to see the sun coming in through his bedroom window. He got up, showered and dressed. He tried calling Vanessa again, and hung up when he got the voicemail. He didn't want to sound desperate. Maybe he'd just leave it until he got back home. He doubted she wanted to hear from him, but maybe Alex was right and the whole 'putting all your stuff in boxes' thing was the ice-breaker Vanessa was looking for.

He put on the TV while he got his shoes on and saw a report on BBC Scotland about the killer who had savagely murdered a newly-wed couple in the Highlands, as well as several other people.

Then he put his jacket on and walked along to Alex's door, but there was no answer. He found her downstairs, having a coffee and talking to DS Evans.

'Where's your boss?' Harry asked Evans.

'He'll be down shortly,' he said.

'What's the hurry, sir?' Alex said.

'We want to get down the road, that's all.'

Dunbar appeared. 'Good result, Harry.'

'I just wish we had caught him rather than found him after he'd taken his own life.'

'Aye, well, at least he's no longer a threat.' Dunbar shook Harry's hand. 'I hope to see you again, pal. Safe journey home.'

'You too.'

Harry and Alex were grabbing coffee when Gallagher came into the room, looking haggard.

'I appreciate all you did for us, McNeil,' he said. 'That bastard fooled us all. It's just as well he took his own life.'

Harry took a sip of his coffee. 'You didn't tell us you had family up here, Mr Gallagher.'

The older man didn't say anything for a moment. '*Had* being the operative word. None of them live round here anymore.'

'Were they at the wedding?'

Gallagher shook his head. 'They were invited, but they didn't come.'

'I can imagine how hard it would have been for them,' said Harry.

Alex looked at Harry, puzzlement on her face.

'People have long memories round here. I don't think they would have been welcomed,' Gallagher said.

'We know all about the case,' Alex said.

Harry sipped more coffee. 'I stayed up late, playing around on the internet. Doing some research. And you know how one link leads to another. I found out that the teacher we've been told about, the one who murdered the two boys, was your brother. Edwin Gallagher.'

'Who told you about that?' Gallagher said, his face going red.

'It doesn't matter who told me; it's public knowledge. And Mr Reynolds, the man who was accused, might have gone down in history as a child killer if your brother had said or done nothing more. Edwin was going to get away with it, but he couldn't help himself and he got caught. Then he decided to hang himself.'

'He was ill,' Gallagher said. 'He couldn't help himself.'

'A man killed his wife and took his own life because he couldn't stand the shame. They lived in the lodge house on the estate next to this one. Did you know that when you bought the place?'

'Of course I did. I was going to have the place razed to the ground.'

'Eradicate the memories? Here's what I think,' said Harry. 'I think that Vince Dubois used to be Michael Reynolds. He wanted to get back at your family, so he killed your daughters and he killed Marie's new husband.

'I think Vince took a chance and started dating Marie. It was a risk, but he knew everything there was to know about her. He worked in computers after all. He got lucky when she went out with him, but she dumped him for Duncan Randall. That was just over a year ago, wasn't it? Despite you telling us otherwise. I think Marie saw thirty coming and she didn't want to be left on the shelf, and let's face it, Duncan was a good catch. Then somehow Vince got invited to the wedding. Do you know how he got invited?'

Gallagher tried to look bored. 'No, I don't.'

'Did you know he used to date your wife, before he dated your daughter?'

Gallagher looked at Harry like he wanted to smack him. The cockiness had left him now. 'How the hell did you find that out?'

'I overheard Claire Blyth talking to your wife about Vince. Not nosing, you understand, but I'm not deaf either.'

'Obviously, Anne had a life before she met me.'

'She's only a couple of years older than Marie and you're what, sixty?'

'Fifty-five. Plenty of men have younger wives.'

'Did she tell you about Vince Dubois before you married her?' Alex asked.

'She didn't go into specifics.'

'It must have hacked you off to see him come to the wedding. Knowing he had been with both your wife and your daughter.'

'Just what is it exactly that you're getting at here, McNeil?'

Harry drank more coffee. 'After young Michael Reynolds witnessed his father shooting himself after killing his mother, he and his sister were taken away into foster care. They were then given new names. I think that Michael Reynolds became Vince Dubois and that he targeted your family. He was just waiting for the day when he could kill your daughters. Make you feel the pain that he'd felt all those years ago. I think you arranged for Angus McPhee, the lead steward, to keep his eyes and ears peeled, and then somehow McPhee saw Vince and took him to the apartment. Where you killed him or had him killed. Not knowing he had already killed Marie and Duncan.'

Gallagher suddenly looked a lot more than his fifty-five years. 'This is just a story, isn't it?'

'I prefer to call it a working theory.'

'You couldn't be more wrong. Vince wasn't Michael Reynolds. He was just some jealous lowlife who got mad at my daughter because he thought it should be him getting married up here. But anyway, I'm heading off home now. The funeral director will take care of my daughters.'

'How can you be so sure Vince isn't Michael Reynolds?'

Gallagher turned briefly before leaving the room. 'I just am.'

Harry grabbed some toast.

'You really believe that Michael was Vince, don't you?' Alex said, pouring more coffee.

'It was just an idea I bounced about inside my head last night.'

DI Burnett came in and found Harry. 'It was good working with you, sir.'

'We're going home now things are at an end. I'll make sure I send your super a copy of my report and so will DS Maxwell.'

'Thank you, sir. Good working with you both.'

Harry watched as Gallagher's car drove away from the hotel.

'Must be nice, having a private jet take you home,' Alex said.

'Him and Terence Randall. Jesus, they must both be worth a fortune.'

Just then Randall came in, looking for coffee.

'I thought they had lackeys to do that?' Alex said.

'Probably back home, but this started out as a wedding, remember?'

'True.'

Harry stood up and walked over to the man. 'I'm not going to ask you how you're feeling this morning, sir, because I can't imagine what you've gone through. I just wanted to say, if you ever need me for anything, give me a shout. I know we're from Edinburgh, but all the same.'

'That's very decent of you. Harry, isn't it?'

'It is, sir.'

'Call me Terry. I appreciate your words, Harry. My wife is going to be devastated.'

'I know. Are you going back home soon?'

'My jet just landed, so I'm going to get packed, then I'll be flying home in a little while. I appreciate everything you did to try to find my son.'

The men shook hands and Harry sat back down. 'Poor bastard. I don't know how he's still standing.'

Harry was back up in his room, getting the last of his stuff together, when he had a thought. He walked along to Alex's room.

'Now who's desperate?' she said.

'I want to run something by you,' he said, walking past her into the room.

'Well, my door's always open,' she said, closing it behind them. 'Not always, you understand, but most –'

'Where's the shotgun?'

'What?'

'The shotgun that Vince used to kill everybody?'

'He obviously dumped it,' Alex said, all humour gone now.

'It doesn't make sense, Alex. What if he had encountered one of the other stewards? He'd already proven that he wouldn't hesitate to kill. He shot the steward who was with the girls. He wouldn't want to be stopped, not before he got to that apartment to kill himself. He was too much in control. That wouldn't have gone down well with him.'

'Maybe he dumped it close by,' she said.

'No. Something's not right here. I don't think this is over. Get your bags ready quickly. I'm going to speak to somebody.'

THIRTY-THREE

'I called my wife,' Terence Randall said as stood up in the private jet. They had touched down at Edinburgh Airport a few minutes ago and taxied to an apron reserved for the private jets. 'She's beside herself just now, but says if there's any chance that there's some other bastard out there who killed our little boy, then you have everything at your disposal.'

'You've done more than enough by flying us down to Edinburgh, Terry,' Harry said.

'Gallagher didn't want to listen, did he?'

'I think he thinks people will blame him for all of this. Better to have it that a jealous ex-lover killed them all.'

'Are you going to tell me what the result of the phone call is that you made on the plane?'

'I can't go into too much detail. Members of my team

reached out to social services and the chief constable himself gave them a kick up the arse, but all they would confirm was that Michael Reynolds did *not* become Vince Dubois.'

'Somebody set him up. Bastard. Do you know who?'

'I have an idea. If I'm wrong, then it's back to the beginning.'

'Good luck, son.'

They left the plane and saw the waiting unmarked car. Karen Shiels got out and came to greet them.

'Good to see you again, sir.'

'You too, Karen. Let's put the bags in the car and we can get going.'

'I hear you did some good work up there, Alex,' Karen said.

'I was just Mr Laurel to his Mr Hardy.'

DC Simon Gregg was sitting in the back. 'Welcome back. How was that wee hooly compared to a weekend break in Blackpool?' he said, grinning.

'Definitely Blackpool next time,' Alex said as Karen sped off.

'You know where you're going?' Harry asked.

'We've already driven past it, sir.' Karen looked at him. 'I wish we could have backup there as well. Considering there's a firearm involved.'

'Our careers are on the line here. In fact, I'm quite happy for you to drop me off and you lot leave. I'll take the can for this.'

The other three detectives looked at him.

'Are you daft?' Alex said. 'If I get the boot for doing this, I'm going backpacking round the world. Screw them putting me in some other crappy department. What say you, Simon?'

'We're a team here, boss,' said Gregg. 'We're all going.'

'I appreciate that,' said Harry. 'But I won't put any of you in danger.'

'Is he a big bastard?'

'He is.'

Gregg grinned. 'Magic. The bigger, the better. Just point the way.'

Fifteen minutes later, they were at their destination, driving slowly along the street.

'You sure he touched down already?' Harry asked.

'Half an hour before you did,' Karen said.

'They had to change our flight plans or something,' Alex said. 'Plus Randall's jet had to be refuelled. That's why he had a head start.'

They looked at the house that was their target. It had a big wooden gate across the driveway.

Harry turned to look at them all. 'This is the last chance. I'm working on a hunch here, and if I'm wrong then we'll all be mopping floors somewhere.'

'Then let's get the buckets ready,' Alex said, opening the car door. The others got out.

'Simon, walk past the gate and look over it. You're six foot six, so it should be easy for you.'

Gregg walked over to the gate and peered over. He turned round and gave the thumbs-up: the Range Rover was parked inside.

'Okay, round the back,' Harry ordered. Gregg and Karen took off running.

'I'm going to climb –' Harry started to say, but Alex was up and over the gate before he could say another word and the wooden door beside the gate opened.

'You going to stand there all day?' she said.

He quickly entered and they sprinted to the front door. It was ajar. They both took out their extendable batons.

'Seems a bit ineffective against a sawn-off,' Alex said.

They pushed the door gently and it swung in on well-oiled hinges.

The house was a modern design. Big windows in the living room, and the same in the kitchen, which was an open-plan extension of the living room.

Simon Gregg was standing outside with Karen, trying the door handle, so Alex unlocked the door and opened it.

'This is Broderick Gallagher's place?' Karen said. 'Must be nice, being able to live here.'

'He's already spoken for,' Alex said. They kept their voices low.

The ground floor was empty. No signs of life.

'I'm counting on them not wanting to go out gallivanting after what's happened to his kids,' Harry said in a whisper, feeling his pension get flushed down the toilet.

'I know I wouldn't be,' Karen said.

They climbed the white marble stairs to the upper level and they could all smell it when they got to the top.

The master bedroom had double doors and they were both wide open. Broderick Gallagher lay on his back on the huge bed, his front a dark red from the shotgun blast.

There was nobody else in the house.

'Jesus,' Karen said.

'That's nothing compared to what the killer did to some of the others,' Alex said.

'Where's the wife and the little boy?' Gregg said.

'I'm not sure.' A thought struck Harry. 'Karen, can you and Simon take care of this? Call it in?'

'Yes, of course, sir.'

'I can think of one more place, but we're going to need backup this time. If I'm right, we're going to have to go in stealthily, not gung-ho. There's a wee boy in the middle of this.'

'I know. Let's go now,' Alex said.

Before they left, Harry told Karen and Gregg where they were going, and that he needed somebody to make a phone call. He thought he knew where the killer was.

THIRTY-FOUR

The entrance was grand, Harry had to admit. It was somewhere he could get used to living, the old Donaldson's children's school.

'They housed prisoners of war here during the Second World War, I think,' Harry said to Alex as they climbed the wide stone steps.

'I'll keep that in the back of my mind the next time I'm at a pub quiz.'

'You're sure she told you there's nobody else in the other apartments?'

'Yes. I spoke to Kerry Hamilton herself and she said that's the only one. The others are sold, but the keys haven't been handed over yet.'

The two members of the firearms team were right behind them.

'What's the plan, Harry? Blow the door off its hinges? Have the entry team blast their way in?' Alex asked.

He shook his head. 'I'm just going to knock on the door. If they don't answer, the negotiator will call. No answer and the entry team go in. Hard.'

They walked along to the front door of the apartment and an armed officer stood on either side. Harry raised his hand to knock, but Alex put up a hand to stop him.

'Nobody else here,' she whispered, then gently reached down for the door handle and pushed down. 'So why lock the door?'

'You were obviously brought up in the country.'

The door opened.

Harry had told the armed team that a toddler could be in here and to be extra careful. They both looked so wired up at that moment, Harry was surprised they didn't just go in guns blazing anyway.

He pushed the door open further and walked into the luxury apartment. The carpets were thick and they didn't hear anything at first, but then they heard a little boy's voice. He was crying.

'You were right,' Alex said.

They made it along to the living room. The door was ajar. Harry gently pushed it.

'Come in, Harry,' Claire Blythe said.

'Hello again, Dee,' he said, keeping his hands in sight. 'It *is* Dee Reynolds, isn't it?'

She smiled. 'Not for a long time.'

The further he got into the room, the more he could see they had walked into a trap.

There was a man sitting at a dining table with a woman opposite him. He was pointing a shotgun at her. Anne Gallagher. The wall was made up of glass doors that led out onto a terrace, with the peaked rooftops behind it, giving it a secluded feel.

'We meet again, Gus,' Alex said.

Angus McPhee smiled at them. 'Sit down on those chairs across there. If you do something stupid, I'll blow her away.'

The two detectives sat down.

'Good job faking your own death,' Harry said. 'Since you all dress the same, it was easy to leave your wallet behind. Were you going to go back to using your old name, Michael?'

'I left Michael Reynolds behind a long time ago. Time for a wee change.' McPhee kept the shotgun steady on Anne.

Rory was sitting on the front of the large settee, with Claire behind him and a cushion in between them.

'I have one of those,' she said, nodding to her brother's shotgun. 'I don't need to tell you how unhappy I'll be if you do something silly like try to rush either of us.'

'It doesn't have to be like this, Claire,' Alex said. 'I mean, you wouldn't want to harm a little boy, would you? You punished Broderick Gallagher already, so why don't you just let Rory go?'

'I don't think so. This is the final phase.'

Harry looked at McPhee. 'You should have left the shotgun with Vince Dubois' corpse. The gun not being there made me question everything. Up until that point, I thought Dubois was actually Michael Reynolds, that he had killed the Gallagher girls because of what Broderick's brother had done fifteen years ago. I almost got it right.'

McPhee smiled. 'Almost. Yes, we did that because of what that scumbag did to our parents. He knew his brother was guilty, but he had to have the finger pointed at my dad, just because my dad was one of the other football coaches. Gallagher had his reporters hound my dad, until he couldn't take it anymore. My dad knew he was being framed and would end up in prison. You of all people should know what they do to child killers inside.'

'I'm sorry your dad had to endure that, but killing Gallagher's wife and son won't bring your father back.'

McPhee laughed. 'No, it won't, but it will give us satisfaction.'

Alex looked at Claire. 'That was you in Vince's house when our colleagues came round, wasn't it?'

'Yes. I just made up the first thing that came into my mind.'

'Instead of saying you were his girlfriend, which might have raised more questions. This way, we'd be chasing our tails looking for a phantom sister.'

Harry looked at McPhee. 'Why don't you just walk out of

here and leave Claire, Mrs Gallagher and Rory with us? You can still get away. We came here alone.'

'Enough!' McPhee roared.

Young Rory started crying and slipped off the settee and started running towards his mother. McPhee jumped up from the table.

And swung the shotgun at the little boy.

THIRTY-FIVE

Later on, Harry would replay this event over and over. In some of the replays the shotgun blast killed him instantly, and the thought gave him nightmares.

In his twenty years as a police officer, he'd been threatened and assaulted, and had walked away from every one of those attacks. As he jumped up off the chair, he didn't think he was going to walk away from this one, but instinct propelled him across the few feet to grab Rory.

It seemed that several things happened at once. Alex was also on her feet, and she threw herself at the young woman, and then they were both flying over the settee, which was tipping backwards. Her hand reached for the shotgun and pushed it upwards and it was discharged into the ceiling. As they crashed to the floor, the shotgun slipped from Claire's hand and Alex punched the woman on the jaw, knocking her out.

Meanwhile, Harry grabbed Rory and shielded him with his body, hoping the shotgun blast would hit his back and not the little boy. He didn't have time to think about dying, but he held on to the toddler, and for a split second it reminded him of the days when he would hug his own son, Chance. Harry tensed in that moment, waiting for the pain.

As he threw himself down, still covering Rory, the first marksman's bullet cracked through the double-glazed door at the terrace. Deviating from its course slightly, the bullet hit Angus McPhee in the back of the head. With the glass now shattering into a million pieces, the second bullet hit the target, behind McPhee's left ear, entering his brain and switching everything off. His trigger finger didn't get the message to pull the trigger and the shotgun fell silently with McPhee to the floor.

Anne Gallagher jumped up and screamed as more marksmen rushed into the living room.

Harry rolled over and Anne grabbed her now-hysterical little boy.

Now it was over.

THIRTY-SIX

'You still haven't moved those boxes,' Alex said, coming in with the Chinese food. She put the bags on the little dining table by the window overlooking the bowling club.

'I've been busy,' Harry said, putting some plates down.

Alex smiled. She knew Harry was delaying emptying the boxes as that would mean this business with Vanessa calling it a day was final. If she took him back, the boxes were already packed. It had been a week since they had been up in the Highlands and she still hadn't called Harry.

Harry brought two bottles of beer from the kitchen and sat down opposite Alex.

'Now we've got matching commendations, we should put them in a frame,' she said.

'Mine will go in a drawer with all the other commendations.'

'Oh, look at you. How many do you have?'

'A few. To me, they're bits of paper, waiting to spring into action should I ever run out of toilet roll. To you, it means that somebody noticed your dedication and bravery.'

'I didn't think about it. I just saw that wee boy and that bitch had a gun.'

'Not everybody would have made that call.'

He looked down at the bowlers on the bowling green having fun. It was a nice, warm evening, a time to enjoy being alive. He looked over to Vanessa's house, across the road and up the hill a bit. He wondered what she was doing, but then stopped himself. It wasn't healthy. She had made the choice and now he would have to work his life around it.

'I'm meeting Angie Patterson for a drink tomorrow,' Alex said. 'She got the job at the mortuary. She called me a little while ago.' She looked at Harry. 'Did you put in a good word for her?'

Harry made a face. 'I just told Angie there was an opening after Gus Weaver retired. I didn't make a call.'

'Liar. But it was very nice of you. I'm sure she'll appreciate it.'

'I deny all knowledge.' In fact, he had spoken to Jeni Bridge about the woman helping to crack the case and it was Jeni who had put in a good word with Leo Chester, head pathologist.

'You should come along and have a drink with us.'

'Nah. You don't want me there.'

'You're right; I don't. But she does. "Bring Harry along," she said. "Please." She doesn't feel confident to ask you out herself, so she's doing it through me.'

'I'm not interested, Sergeant Maxwell.'

She laughed. 'You're so cute. Pretending you're not interested in women.'

'I never said that,' Harry said, and washed some sweet-and-sour chicken down with the beer. 'I said I'm not interested in *that* woman.'

'Just one drink, Harry. A quick beer. She just wants to thank you.'

Harry shook his head and made a noise. 'Okay, but just one. I mean it. On a professional level too.'

'Of course. Just one.' Alex clinked bottles with Harry and smiled. 'Just the one.'

BACK TO LIFE

DCI HARRY MCNEIL BOOK 3

ONE

She saw him running down the tight, one-way street and wondered if she should just punch it and run him over. The engine revved harder as she dropped a gear and floored it, the headlights cutting through the cold, dark night, picking him out as he ran down the middle of the road.

The road was slick since the rainfall had thrown leaves onto it, but she didn't care. She didn't take her eyes off him – time was running out.

The road ended down here. They both knew it. That was why he was running harder and she was driving faster.

Then he was on it. The Leamington Lift Bridge, which did exactly as its name suggested; it lifted the small bridge that spanned the Union Canal so the houseboats could get along to Lochrin Basin.

The man actually stopped in the middle of the bridge for a moment, his breath coming out in plumes like a dragon that couldn't get its fire to work.

There were bollards at either side of the bridge. She didn't know if traffic had crossed here before, or what the deal was; she just knew her car wasn't going across it.

She swung it left and pulled onto the pavement and parked in front of a *Private Parking* sign.

He looked at her and started running again.

She jumped out. 'Stop!' she shouted, and slammed the car door when it was obvious he had hearing problems. She took off after him, having the advantage of not being out of breath.

Good shoes, that was the key to running, and actually running on the treadmill and not using it as a clothes horse. She did three miles on it every day before breakfast.

She ran down Gilmore Park to Fountainbridge, gaining on him as she got into her stride. She wished she had thrown her overcoat into the car, but it was too late now. She could open it and look like Batman fleeing down the road without a mask on, but she kept it buttoned.

She turned right and saw him. He looked back at her. She was about to cross when a double-decker bus came barrelling along, its tyres hissing on the wet road. The pedestrian crossing light came on and she sprinted over it, her breath coming faster now.

Then she saw him run into the new hotel.

'Gotcha, you bastard,' she said to herself, running along the pavement, almost knocking down somebody who was walking towards her, looking down at his phone.

She ran into the reception, but she couldn't see the man anywhere.

'Did you see a man come in here?' she asked the receptionist, her breathing heavy.

'Yes,' the young woman answered.

Sarcastic remarks played through her mind for a moment. 'Where is he?' she asked instead.

'He's a guest.'

She brought out her warrant card and showed it to the woman. 'Where did he go?'

'Room two-oh-five.'

She walked over to the lift and stood behind an old couple. They all got in and she hit 2 after they'd hit their floor button.

She got off, saw a sign telling her which way the room numbers ran, then walked along to her right. Counted off the door numbers until she got to 205.

She stood, controlling her breathing. She knocked on the door and waited. A few moments later, she could sense somebody on the other side.

'Who is it?' a man's voice asked.

'It's me. Open up.'

The door opened and the man she had been chasing

stood there looking at her before stepping aside. 'Come in,' he said. His own breathing was slowing down.

She stepped into the room and walked towards the bed.

'Can I get you anything?' he asked.

'Water.'

He got two small bottles from the minibar and drank some himself.

'Why did you run?' she asked him after she'd drunk some of the cold liquid herself. Just a sip; she knew the human body could go into shock when overheated then plied with a cold drink.

'I got scared.' His eyes wouldn't settle and he looked around the room.

'Nobody knows about this. You didn't have to run.'

His eyes were wide and his lips trembled for a little bit. He walked slowly towards her. Leant in to whisper something as he pressed a flash drive into her hand.

'Go now. They're waiting.'

'What do you mean?'

'Run!' he shouted, then the bathroom door exploded inwards. A large man in black made to grab her, but the first man threw himself at the intruder, knocking him aside.

She was opening the door as the two men fell to the floor, then she was in the corridor, the bottle of water dropped. She took the stairs and flew down to the ground floor and out through reception into the cold night air.

The lane she'd just run down was across the road. It was

uphill this time and she dug deep, her thighs starting to burn. She knew she shouldn't, but she turned around to look.

Nobody was there.

She got to the top of the road. Her car was just across the way. Across the lift bridge. Safety. Should she just walk and get the car in the morning?

'You look exhausted,' a man said, stepping into view from the canal path. He smiled at her. 'Bit late for jogging, isn't it?'

'Not exactly jogging,' she said, her breath coming in rasps.

'Well, you be careful now. You don't know who's hanging about here at night.'

'I will.'

'People like me,' he said, and he smacked her in the head with something, then grabbed her from behind.

Before she could fight back, she felt a cold, stinging sensation in her side. She tried to scream, but she couldn't breathe. Her lungs wouldn't work.

Blind panic set in.

She thought he would drop her to the ground, but he held her up and walked her along the canal path like a drunk, still behind her, with his hand over her mouth. He was bigger and stronger, and all the fight had left her.

She walked before him, her brain screaming for air. Her hand went to her throat, but nothing was there. No power, no sensation, nothing. Just fear.

He kept hold of her as he spun her round and then she

felt the cold steel enter her again, over and over, and she saw the stars as she fell backwards.

She didn't feel the cold canal wrap itself around her. She looked up once, but the man wasn't there.

And then there was nothing.

TWO

'Bit nippy for June,' DCI Harry McNeil said, rubbing his hands together.

'You should try flipping your calendar over at the start of each month like me,' DS Alex Maxwell said. 'That way, you'd know it was November the first.'

'Christmas is just around the corner, and I'm in denial.'

They were standing on the edge of the Union Canal along from the end of the ride at Lochrin Basin. A grey houseboat was moored along from the Leamington Lift Bridge; it had been turned into a floating coffee house a while back.

DI Karen Shiels walked up to them. Uniformed officers had secured the footpath, while forensics were scouring the area. A grey mortuary van sat at the end, a harbinger of death.

'Good morning, sir,' Karen said.

'Morning, DI Shiels. What do we have?'

Karen took a quick look back at the scene: a fire brigade rescue team standing by a forensics tent that had been hastily erected over a body.

'A female was seen floating in the canal. By the owner of the coffee house there, and he's not best pleased at having his business impacted.'

'I dunno; there're a lot of uniforms here. He might score in the long run.'

'Seems a bit tacky to be selling his stuff to the emergency personnel here, don't you think?' Alex said, shrugging inside her overcoat.

'Well, if he's giving freebies, make mine black with no sugar.' Harry looked at Karen again.

'The body was between the coffee house and a visiting boat. He called treble nine and a uniform patrol saw her. They thought it might have been a dummy at first, since it was Halloween last night, but on further inspection, they saw it was human.'

'And I'm guessing we're here because it isn't a simple drowning?'

'You guess correctly. The pathologists are over there.'

Harry looked past the firefighters who were hovering around and saw one of the mortuary assistants, Angie Patterson, whom he had met a few months ago up north. She turned to him and smiled. He smiled back.

'Any ID on her?' Alex asked.

'Yes, her warrant card.'

Harry snapped his attention to Karen. 'She's a police officer? From round here?'

'Yes. Control are getting onto it right now and they'll get back to me.'

'What's her name?'

'Linda Smith.'

'Let me know as soon as you hear something.'

As Harry and Alex walked over to the forensics tent, one of the pathologists came out. Dr Kate Murphy, from the city mortuary.

'Good morning, DCI McNeil,' she said with her clipped English accent.

'Morning, Doctor. What are we looking at here?'

'Come on, I'll give you the tour.' She walked back into the tent and Harry followed.

Harry nodded and smiled at Marie, who had recently transferred down to Edinburgh. He had put in a good word with the commander of Edinburgh Division, Jeni Bridge, and she had pulled strings for Marie because of her input in solving a case up north.

Jake Dagger, one of the other pathologists, was also in the tent. 'Morning, Harry,' he said.

'Morning, Jake.'

The only other person in the tent was the officer called Linda Smith, lying motionless on a plastic sheet.

'She was found with her overcoat buttoned up, but it has puncture holes in it. They went right through.'

Harry looked down at her. The face looking back at him wasn't familiar. 'Rough idea how long she's been deceased?'

'We're estimating twelve to fourteen hours,' Dagger said.

'Between ten and midnight last night,' Harry said, looking at his watch.

'Around that. We'll know more when we get her back to our place and have her dried off properly.'

'Would either of you like to hazard a guess as to what sort of instrument was used to kill her?'

'Something slim,' Kate said. 'Probably a knife, but a long one.'

Harry stepped out into the cold morning air. There was still a light frost on the ground. When he'd left his flat this morning, the bowling green opposite had looked like somebody had tried to turn it into a skating rink.

'Uniforms are going door-to-door,' Alex said, coming up to him.

'What about the boats?' he replied, nodding along towards the basin, where more houseboats were moored.

'Simon's along there now with the uniforms.' DC Simon Gregg was another member of Harry's team. Alex turned and looked at the bridge. 'Speak of the devil.'

'You two talking about me?' Gregg said, striding across to them. At six foot six, he towered over them. 'My ears are burning.' He grinned at Alex.

'If your feet move as fast as your mouth, maybe we'll have

this solved by lunchtime,' Harry said. 'Tell me what you've got.'

'There're three boats over on the other side, all occupied. One resident, Jane Biggs, told me that she's just retired and decided to have a go at living on a boat for a while, but it's getting colder so she's going to leave and go home.' Gregg looked at his notebook. 'Glasgow. And by the look of the boat, she's making the right choice. It looks like a pile of kindling waiting for a box of matches, and it's only a few days till Guy Fawkes Night.'

'Apart from casting an expert nautical eye over her vessel, anything else stand out? Like, did she hear anything?'

'She did. It was after midnight when she heard a scream. She looked out one of her wee windows, but she thought it was coming from the bar just across the way. She thought nothing of it.'

'That was a bit of a build-up just for nothing,' Harry said, shoving his hands into his pockets.

'Not for nothing, boss. Her little dog, Trixie, goes for a pee before bed so she doesn't get up in the middle of the night. She was granted shore leave, then spent that time sniffing about. Jane doesn't like the cold, she told me, and was ushering the wee dog along when a man walking from the bar stopped and stared across at her.'

'Maybe he knew her?' Alex said.

'Jane said she didn't recognise *him*, so she was doubtful he recognised *her*. It spooked her, anyway. So as soon as the dog dropped troo, they were back on the boat, where she locked the door and kept the frying pan by her side. If the guy somehow got on board, she could either fry him up a couple of eggs in the morning or batter him over the napper with it, depending on what his likely intentions were. Her words, not mine.'

'Anything else?' Alex asked, hoping the coffee houseboat owner had the kettle on, or whatever else it was he used to brew coffee.

'There was nobody on the boat in front of Jane's. This is where it gets interesting. A young woman lives on the boat in front of that one, on her own. Annie. She heard the scream. She went up on the...whatever the top of a boat is called.'

Harry looked to Alex to see if she had the answer, but she was as clueless as he was.

'Anyway,' Gregg continued, 'she had already been heading up there for a smoke. Around midnight, the last one before she went to bed. She heard the scream and looked over here and saw a man and woman struggling.'

'Did she call us?'

'She did. And a patrol car turned out. Their report says when they got here, there was nothing.'

'If he was attacking her, then he could have stabbed her to death and shoved her over the side by the time the car got here. Nothing to do with their response times, but I'm assuming he wouldn't want to hang about,' Alex said. 'Make sure we get the report from last night, and we'll want to talk to the responding officers.'

'I already got their names. They're back on duty this afternoon.'

'And they saw nobody running away, covered in blood, waving a knife?' Harry said.

'Correct. DI Shiels has been organising the door-to-door at those flats, and the other ones over there, which are serviced apartments. And the boats moored outside those apartments on the other side of the Leamington Bridge.'

'Get uniforms looking for any place that might have CCTV.'

'Will do.' Gregg walked away to join a group of uniforms.

Angie Patterson and a young Polish woman – whose name Harry had forgotten but who went by the moniker *Sticks* because she played drums in a band – were loading the deceased woman into the back of their van.

'Could you stare any harder?' Alex said.

Harry turned his head towards her. 'You do realise I'm thinking of putting your name forward for retraining at Tulliallan, don't you? I mean, I can open up my email when I get to the office and hit *send*, or you can get me a coffee. That might take my mind off it.' He nodded to the houseboat coffee shop. 'Hurry up, there's a queue forming.'

'This is blackmail.'

'Black email. I like the sound of that. No milk and no sugar, if you insist on buying.'

'Only if it's your round in the pub tonight.'

'I can't make it tonight.'

'You're otherwise engaged with Angie.'

'First of all, please don't use the word *engaged*, and secondly, I'm having dinner with Vanessa.'

The smile dropped from Alex's face. 'What? Harry, no, tell me you're winding me up.'

'Her idea, not mine.'

'After the way she's treated you these past few months?'

'There are two more people in line. If you don't hurry, the queue will be snaking back to the old bingo hall on Fountainbridge.'

Alex walked away, taking change out of her pocket.

'Make mine...' Gregg started to say as she passed him, but he stopped when she gave him the kind of hand signal that she hadn't been taught in the Girl Guides. 'Never mind, I wasn't thirsty anyway.'

Karen Shiels walked quickly up to Harry. 'Control got back with the information on our victim. Linda Smith is dead.'

'I know, I just saw her in the forensics tent.'

'No, I mean she was already dead.'

THREE

'A BMW isn't my first choice,' Harry admitted, 'but I do like these bum warmers.'

'Your poor wee CR-V not got heated seats then?' Alex said, driving along Slateford Road.

'First of all, like I even need to remind you, the car is my ex-wife's.'

'Still going with that story, eh?'

He held up a hand. 'And my car is in the garage waiting for parts.'

She threw him a quick look. 'What sort of garage keeps your car for six months waiting for parts?'

'One that has dedicated craftsmen working in it, not like the robots that clearly service your overpriced jalopy.'

Alex laughed. 'Tell that to Angie. She drove it down from Dornoch for me and loved every minute.'

'Does she have her own car now?'

'Why? So she can chauffeur you about on your date?'

'We sometimes have a drink. As colleagues.'

'For your information, she doesn't have a car but uses Uber when she goes out with her older colleagues for drinks. Otherwise, she has a bus pass.'

'Good to know.'

'You'll have to dust off your Honda if you want to be a gentleman when you go out for a date. It wouldn't be the same trying to bag off with her on the back seat of a bus.'

'Your attempts at trying to get a rise out of me are sad and pathetic.' He lowered the seat heating level.

'To be honest, I'm more worried about you going out with Vanessa.'

'Why? It's a Friday night. Plenty of people go out for a meal on a Friday night.'

'*Couples*, Harry. You haven't been a couple for months now.' She turned up Craiglockhart Avenue and turned right. The address they were looking for was along on the right-hand side. A detached bungalow with a red-tiled roof.

The BMW fit right into the neighbourhood.

A man answered the door and Harry played the *guess what age he is* game. Around sixty, fifty-eight if he was being kind and the man had been clean shaven. He was leaning on a walking stick with a fancy duck's head, Harry noticed.

'Brian Smith?' Harry said as they showed their warrant cards.

'Yes.'

'Can we come in and have a word?'

'What about?'

'Linda.'

Smith looked unsure for a moment, as if wondering if he'd locked up the family silver, then he stepped to one side.

The house had been well kept at one time, but the discarded newspapers, the dirty mugs on the coffee table, and the general air of uncleanliness told them that housework wasn't at the top of Smith's to-do list.

'Grab a seat,' he said, walking over to the little mantelpiece, where he picked up a pack of cigarettes and lit one. 'I'd offer you a coffee, but I'm a lazy bastard and there's nobody else to do it, so this might not be your lucky day if you were expecting one.'

'It's fine,' Alex said, moving some magazines to sit on the couch. There was a little leather pouch on top and Smith moved to take it from her and put it on the mantelpiece. Harry looked at the only chair that didn't have its surface covered and Smith moved to it as if he'd seen Harry eying it up. Harry remained standing.

'What do you want to know about Linda?' Smith said, blowing out smoke and putting his walking stick to one side, where it promptly fell onto the floor. 'I take it you know she's dead?'

'Yes, we do,' Harry said, 'and we're sorry for your loss.'

'Why? Did you know her?'

'No, we didn't.'

'Then why are you sorry?'

Alex sat up straighter. 'It's what people say, Mr Smith, out of respect.'

Smith shrugged like he couldn't care less. 'Carry on then.'

'When did she die?' Harry said.

'Three months ago. But you don't need me to tell you that. And since she was a copper, you'll know that fucker ran her down and he was never caught. I'd have hanged the bastard if I could. But he was never caught. You shower of bastards couldn't tie your fucking shoelaces without watching a YouTube video on how to do it.'

'We found a woman this morning, deceased, and she was carrying Linda's warrant card. Can you tell us how that came about?'

'How should I know?'

Harry gritted his teeth for a second. 'Listen, we have a dead woman who we're trying to identify, and she was carrying your daughter's warrant card, and if you could stop being a smartarse for a second and explain, then maybe we can go to the family and tell them they've just lost a daughter, much like the respect you were afforded.'

Smith looked at him for a second, as if he was about to come back with something, but then his shoulders slumped and all the wind left his sails. His lip trembled. 'I miss her. Every single day. Every single fucking day, and that scumbag is still walking God's earth. Tell me how that's fair.'

'It's not fair, Mr Smith. But it's not going to bring Linda back. She was a police officer, and a good one from what I've heard. We just need to know the circumstances which led up to her warrant card being on a civilian.'

Smith hung his head for a moment and his eyes were red when he looked up. 'Linda left her uniform in a holdall in her car one day. She met a friend for lunch, and when she came back, the window had been smashed and the uniform was gone.'

'Where did this happen?'

'In the Ocean Terminal car park.'

'The fact that a uniform was stolen is a big deal. What did my colleagues do about it?'

'They checked the CCTV and saw a man wearing a hoodie breaking in. He took her bag and walked out. They tracked him all the way out into the street and then he was lost. They think he got into a car that was waiting for him.' He took a deep breath and blew it out. 'I told her not to leave stuff in sight. Especially her bloody uniform in a bag. As soon as those dirtbags see something in a car, they'll break in and steal it.'

'How long before she was killed did this happen?' Alex said.

Smith looked at her for a moment and she could almost see the wheels in his head going round.

'Only a couple of months.'

'I'll have a look at the report later.' Harry looked at Alex, about to give her the nod to start taking some notes, but she was ahead of him.

'You'll have to excuse us, Mr Smith, but my colleague and I were seconded to another force area when Linda died, so we only briefly heard about it later. Can you tell us what you were told about her death?'

'She told me she was on duty, some overtime thing. She didn't call anything in, but witnesses said they saw her lying in the road and a van driving away up the street without its lights on. Maybe he'd been drinking or something and she was trying to stop him. We'll never know. The guy mowed her down and took off. They found the van abandoned. It had been stolen.'

'Did she live here at home?'

'She did, but she spent a lot of time at her friend's flat down by the canal.'

Harry didn't take his eyes off the man. 'Can you tell us her name?'

'Fiona Carlton. Nice girl. I met her once, briefly, but I don't know much about her.'

'You wouldn't have an address for her, would you?'

'It was one of those new places at Lochrin Basin. Some of the flats are serviced apartments. Fountain Court they call it. I have it on my phone. Linda spent a lot of time there, so I wanted the address – you know, just for emergencies.'

Smith fished his phone out of his pocket and took some

time to find the details. 'Lower Gilmore Bank.' He gave them the number.

'Thank you, Mr Smith,' Harry said, and Alex stood up.

Outside, the wind had picked up. 'Does that thing have remote start?' Harry said, pulling his collar up.

'*Thing?* No, Betty does not have remote start. Do you want me to ruin the environment by running the car unnecessarily?'

'I hardly think you'd be doing it single-handedly.'

They got in and there was a semblance of warmth from before.

'What do you make of Smith?' Harry asked as Alex pulled away.

'Poor sod. I can't even imagine losing a child. What about you?'

'I can't blame him for still grieving. I'd be a basket case if something happened to my son.' Chance was Harry's only child, and he only got to see his son every so often.

She took a right and headed up towards Colinton Road, making her way back down to Viewforth. There was still a hive of activity down by the basin as Alex parked her car on Lower Gilmore Place.

Harry called Karen Shiels. Asked her if the address they were looking for had been included in the door-to-door. Uniforms were there, but hadn't reached that number yet.

They walked along the path on the canal's edge and

through a communal garden to the entrance. They buzzed the number they were looking for.

'There's no guarantee she'll be in,' Alex said, just before the little metal box crackled and a voice said, 'Hello?'

'Police. We're looking for Fiona Carlton.'

Hesitation for a moment before the lock on the door clicked. They walked into the communal hallway and saw a young woman standing at an open door.

'Fiona?' Alex said.

'No, I'm her flatmate, Bea.' The woman stepped aside to let them in, then closed the door and showed them through to the living room. It was a modern apartment and with contemporary architecture came contemporary room sizes. It didn't appear that Bea had a cat, but if she did, Harry wouldn't have attempted to swing it.

A kitchen was off to one side, in a nook.

'Coffee?' she asked. She looked like a student, dressed in old jeans and a big comfortable cardigan, and she had tucked her hands up into the sleeves.

'No, thanks,' he replied and Bea indicated for them to sit down.

A TV hung on what looked like a slab of wood nailed to the wall but was probably a design feature. Three windows looked out onto the courtyard at the front, the bottom panes made of frosted glass. Handy if a pervert was on his hands and knees trying to peek in, but if he was feeling adventurous, he could always stand up and look through the top half of the windows.

'What's this about?' Bea asked, pulling the cardigan tighter. She yawned. 'Sorry. I was up late working last night. Sometimes I do some work from home.'

'The body of a young female was found in the canal this morning, just along from here, and she had a warrant card on her that didn't belong to her. No other identification, just the warrant card, so we're trying to find out who she was.'

'Oh God, no.'

Bea jumped up out of her seat and left the living room. Harry stood up, not wanting to be caught out if Bea turned out to be an axe murderer. Alex sat on the edge of the settee, quite happy for Harry to be the cannon fodder should things take a downswing. Harry picked up a photo in a frame that had been sitting on a shelf.

Bea came rushing back in. 'Fiona's bed's not been slept in.'

'Is that Fiona?' he asked, turning back to look at Bea and gesturing to the photo.

'Please don't tell me that's who you found in the canal.'

'It's somebody fitting that description. Is there any way you could try to call her?' He put the photo back.

Bea took her mobile phone out of her cardigan pocket. Harry was amazed that the phone was in there. He was old enough to remember an age without mobile phones, when the world had revolved quite happily without everybody taking photos of themselves and feeling the need to take medication when a total stranger didn't like them. It would have been like him walking through a mall with a packet of photos and showing them to every Tom, Dick and Harry and then having to check himself into rehab when young women told him to fuck off.

You sound like your own father, Harry, he thought, glad he hadn't voiced that opinion to Alex, who probably posted photos of her cat to Instagram every day. If she had a cat.

Bea paced the room, her mobile pressed to her left ear. 'Fee? It's Bea. Call me as soon as you get this.'

Fee and Bea, Harry thought. There had to be a punchline there somewhere.

She hung up and looked at him. 'Voicemail,' she said unnecessarily.

'Can I take one of the photos?' Alex asked.

Bea put her phone away and took one of the photos of Fiona out of a frame and handed it over.

'When did you last see Fiona?' Harry asked. They were all standing in the middle of the living room now, all signs of bonhomie gone.

'Last night. She was going out for a drink or something.'

'Do you know who with?'

Bea shook her head. 'No, sorry.'

'Where does she work?'

'McCallum Technology. It's a research and development company near Bilston. I work for them too.'

'What does she do there?'

'She's a software engineer.'

'Obviously, the young woman we pulled out of the canal bears a resemblance to your friend, but it's not a certainty that it's her, so we would ask you to say nothing at the moment. In case we get an identification, would you know if Fiona has a next of kin?'

Bea lowered her head for a moment, either racking her brains or noticing a spot on the carpet that would need taking care of with the hoover.

'She has a sister,' she said finally, making eye contact again. 'Maggie.'

'Same last name?'

'Yes.' The phone came out again and a finger moved across the screen with deft precision. Then she held it out for Harry to see. He put the number in his own phone, with accuracy if not the same speed.

'Thank you. I'd also ask you to not make contact with her at the moment.'

Bea nodded. 'I understand.'

'I don't suppose you heard anything last night? Late, around midnight,' Alex asked.

Bea shook her head. 'No, sorry. I had headphones in, listening to music. I was in my room working. I'm a software engineer too. Fee and I met at uni. I wouldn't have heard Fee coming in because she knows not to disturb me when I'm working from home. She does it too at times, so she knows what it's like.'

'Thanks anyway.'

Harry led the way out and Bea closed the door softly behind them.

'It's Fiona, isn't it?' Alex said.

'Pound to a penny.'

FOUR

Alex drove through Bruntsfield, heading south, past Hillend and continuing on the A702.

'You ever been on the ski slope?' she asked Harry as they drove past it.

'I can think of easier ways to break my neck. And they all involve alcohol.'

'Fair dos.'

'How about you?'

'I know I'm a lean fighting machine, but like you, I prefer to keep all my limbs intact.'

Harry laughed. 'You know where you're going?'

'Do I look like I know where I'm going? That's why I bring you along.'

'No, you bring me along because I'm your boss.'

'That as well.'

Harry was holding his phone and he looked down at the map on the screen. 'Turn left up ahead. Bush Loan Road.'

She saw the green-and-white sign pointing the way to Roslin and turned left at a junction by two terraced cottages. Further along the road, they turned right into the Bush Estate. A large gatehouse sat just inside the property and some new-looking low buildings were on their right. They drove past and stopped at a road on the left to read the sign. They took the left and followed the road round until the magnificence that was Bush House appeared on their right.

'Can you imagine having all of this as your own property, way back when?' Alex said, impressed with the sand-coloured building. They parked beside some expensive cars out the front in the little parking area.

Harry glanced around at the grounds as he stretched. The land in front of him looked like a park, and if he had just opened his eyes without seeing where they had driven in, he would have sworn that was what it was. The sun was out, weak and watery, and the openness let a wind blow through.

A magnificent portico entrance protruded from the front of the building. Inside was a stark contrast to the outside. It was every bit as modern as the name suggested; McCallum Technology.

Inside the entrance hall, they were faced with a wall of wood and glass. A man sat behind one of the glass panels.

'Can I help you?' he asked, his voice coming through a loudspeaker.

'Police. We're looking for somebody who works here.' Harry and Alex showed their warrant cards.

The man looked at them like a teller waiting for a guy with sunglasses to produce a shotgun.

'Pass me your IDs, please.'

A metal drawer came out and he looked at them. They put their cards in and the drawer snapped shut. The security officer took the cards and copied them before making them reappear in the drawer like he was a magician.

'Who are you looking for?'

'Maggie Carlton.'

The man typed something on a keyboard. 'Come through the door on your left. You'll be escorted to talk to somebody through there.'

A door in the wall clicked and opened by itself. A robot was waiting for them. Above its base, its body was skinny, and it was taller than Harry. It had a dark-glass screen for a face.

'Follow me, please,' it said. The skinny part turned three-sixty on the base and off it went.

'There's no obvious way it's moving,' Harry said.

'Wheels?' Alex said. 'Like a hovercraft? Tracks?'

'Black magic?'

They came to another door along a short corridor and the robot stood looking at a scanner. The door opened and the robot moved through, the detectives following.

'Wait here,' it said to them. Its top half moved round again and it went back the way it had come, the door closing behind it.

The door in front of Harry and Alex opened, and they walked through and were greeted by a smiling woman behind a desk.

'Hello. I believe you're looking for Maggie Carlton?'

'Yes, we are,' Harry said.

The walls were white, like a hospital. Another glass wall was blocking their entrance into the building proper, and he watched people walking about with papers in their hands. *Working or skiving?* he thought.

'I'll have to call her supervisor and see if she can be taken from her workstation.'

'We're not here with good news. We have to talk to her.'

'You heard the man!' said a voice from their right. A man in an electric wheelchair came around the corner, followed by another man.

'Yes, sir,' the woman said, her cheeks going slightly red despite the man's beaming smile.

'James McCallum,' he said, holding out a hand.

'DCI Harry McNeil. DS Maxwell.' They both shook McCallum's hand.

'I got a notice through the intranet about the police being here and I was worried you'd had a tipoff about my stash of weed.'

'No, we'll leave that for the drug squad,' Harry said.

McCallum looked to be no older than his late thirties. He

laughed, showing a good set of teeth. 'This is my assistant, Max Blue.' He smiled up at the man who was standing next to him.

'Pleased to meet you,' the man said, revealing his American accent.

McCallum laughed. 'Max has been my assistant ever since, well, you know...' He patted one of his legs. 'But let's go and find the young Miss Carlton.' He turned and they went through another glass door.

'What do you know about my company, Detective?' McCallum asked as he moved his wheelchair along a pristine corridor.

'Not a lot.'

'We were featured in *Techno Science* magazine last year.'

'I'm more of a *Top Gear* man myself.'

McCallum laughed. 'I do like my cars, I must say, but that's how I ended up in this contraption; too fast and over-confident.'

Blue stopped at a panel next to a sliding steel door. A reader scanned his right eye and the door slid open.

'I can talk about some of the things we do here, as they were mentioned in the magazine, but there are other things that I'm not at liberty to discuss. I hope you understand?' McCallum said as the door slid closed behind them.

'Of course.' Harry gave Alex a couldn't-care-less look.

'Primarily, we work on AI here, and our main focus at the moment is self-driving cars. We're developing not only software but the hardware to go with it. I like to think we're ahead of the Americans at this game. They've had some disasters.'

'It can't be easy.'

They went into a lift and took it up to the next level.

'You're right, it's not. But we have some brilliant minds working for us. And since I bought Bush House, we've had some extensive work done. Did you see the new lab out front?'

Harry shook his head. 'I only saw grass and trees.'

'That's because we opened the grounds up and built an underground lab. We're doing a lot of construction here in the grounds. A lot of it has been completed and it's ongoing. We've just completed a test track for the final phase of our car testing. The world is moving along fast, Chief Inspector, and we're going to be at the forefront.'

'When I was a boy, I thought we'd be flying in cars by now.'

McCallum stopped outside an office door and smiled. 'Autonomous cars are the future, and the future is already here. Miss Carlton is waiting for you in there. If we don't get to meet again, it was nice having a brief chat. My security team will see you out.'

He moved his wheelchair along and Max Blue smiled at Alex as he walked alongside his boss.

Harry and Alex entered the room and found a young woman sitting on the other side of a table.

'Miss Carlton?' Harry said.

'Yes. What's wrong?'

Harry did the introductions again. 'You have a sister called Fiona?' he said as they sat down.

'Yes. Why? Has something happened?'

Harry took out his phone. 'I'm sorry to say it, but a woman's body was found this morning and we have reason to believe she may be your sister. Would you mind taking a look at a photo?'

Maggie's lips trembled, but she shook her head to indicate that she wouldn't mind.

'Oh God. That looks like her,' she said, putting a hand to her mouth.

'We're sorry to do this, but could you come with us to the mortuary for an identification?' Alex asked.

Maggie started crying. Alex got up and went round to her, putting a hand on her shoulder.

'I know this must be hard, but we'll make it as quick as possible.'

After a few minutes, Maggie brought her head up. 'I'll go and get my things together.'

'We can drive you if you don't feel up to it.'

'No, I'll take my car.'

She left the room and the two detectives followed to wait in the corridor.

They waited five minutes. Then ten. When fifteen had minutes passed, Harry started getting antsy.

'Where has she got to?'

A door opened in the wall facing them, the one that Maggie Carlton had gone through. A woman appeared and let the door close behind her.

'We're waiting for Miss Carlton,' Harry said as she looked at them.

'She's not here.'

'What do you mean? She was here a few minutes ago.'

'I mean she just left. Maggie Carlton is no longer on the premises.'

FIVE

'I've never had that before,' Alex said as she backed her car out of the parking space. 'I imagine you have, though – having a woman leave without any explanation.'

'I've had some rough dates, I admit. But they all soldiered on to dessert.'

As Alex drove through the south of the city heading for Maggie Carlton's address, Harry made use of the time to call DI Karen Shiels.

'Tell me you've found the culprit, preferably covered in blood with some sort of sharp object on his person.'

'We're still working on that, sir. We've called the dive team in to search the canal, in case he threw the weapon in there.'

'How are we on the witnesses?'

'Nothing else reported.'

He explained where they were heading and hung up.

The address they had been given was in Baberton Mains on the west side of the city, just off the city bypass. Alex drove round the main road until they found the side street they were looking for.

'Down on the right,' Harry said.

They had been told what kind of car Maggie drove as well as her address and Harry spotted it in a little cul-de-sac off the road. A green Volkswagen Beetle. The house was detached with a garage way in the back of the garden.

Harry saw a plume of smoke coming from the back garden as he walked up the driveway, Alex just behind him. It was damp and cold, though the property was shielded by trees on one side.

They looked over the small wrought-iron gate and saw Maggie Carlton throwing papers into a box that had flames licking out of it.

'Mind if we come in and warm our hands?' he said.

'Not at all,' Maggie replied. 'I was expecting you.'

Harry opened the gate and they walked through and across to her. 'Early bonfire?'

She looked at him. 'It's not illegal to do this.'

'I didn't say it was.' He could feel the heat from the fire as the wind blew the flames around. There was a small bottle of white spirit and a watering can nearby. One to kick-start it, the other to put it out, but the watering can wouldn't do much good if some embers flew onto the house and set it on fire.

'If you were expecting us, then you'll know what my first question is going to be.'

She looked at him, took one of the papers from the top of the pile, scrunched it up and threw it into the flames. 'It's not as if I don't want to go to the mortuary with you.'

'But...?' Alex said.

More papers into the fire. Harry noticed a box at Maggie's feet with more in it.

'But I needed to come home and do this. Besides, if you weren't aware, they were listening to us.'

'How do you know that?' Alex asked.

'After I said I would get my coat, there were two security guards waiting in the lift, weren't there?'

'They could have been waiting there before we went into that room.'

'And the moon is made of cheese.' More papers, more flames.

'We'd still like you to come to the mortuary with us, if you don't mind. Unless your parents are alive and we could ask either one of them?'

Her head snapped up. 'No. They're both dead.' Another few sheets went to meet their maker. 'Fiona left a lot of stuff behind when she moved into the apartment. It's no use to me now.'

Harry looked down and saw a newspaper clipping before Maggie grabbed it, balled it up and threw it into the fire.

It was a story about a helicopter crash.

SIX

They stood around in the little waiting room across from the viewing area like they were actors in a horror movie. Harry had spent four years investigating other police officers and was a little out of the loop, despite having been back on regular duties for a few months. Alex, on the other hand, looked like this was second nature to her. Which it wasn't, as she had spent a lot of time working in the cold case unit.

'I'll be right here with you, Maggie,' she said, putting a hand on the other woman's arm.

'Thank you, Alex.'

Harry turned round when Angie Patterson, one of the mortuary assistants, approached the entrance. He started a little bit but shrugged as if he was only adjusting his overcoat without using his hands.

'They're ready for you, sir,' she said.

He nodded and turned back to Maggie. 'If you could approach the glass now, Miss Carlton. Take your time.'

She walked out of the little room, followed by Alex, and walked up to the window. Harry stood back, watching. When Maggie was ready, Angie gently knocked on the glass and the curtains behind it rolled to the sides, revealing the body with a sheet covering it.

One of the other attendants, Sticks – real name Natalie, Harry now remembered – was standing to one side. Maggie stepped closer to the glass and looked down at the woman's face, freshly cleaned, her hair in a style that wasn't how the woman would have worn it in life.

'That's my sister, Fiona,' Maggie said, and then the tears came. She stepped away from the glass and Angie nodded to Sticks, who closed the curtains.

'Thank you,' Harry said to Angie, who merely nodded, then she stopped as she was about to walk away.

'Sorry, I forgot to say that Kate Murphy wants a word, sir.'

He turned to Alex. 'I'll be out in a minute, if you want to wait in the car with Maggie.'

'Okay.'

'You're enjoying all this *sir* stuff, aren't you?' Angie said as they walked down the corridor to the offices.

'I am indeed.'

They walked through a set of rubber doors. 'I haven't seen you in the pub for a little while,' she said.

'I haven't been to be honest. We'll have to do a catch-up sesh soon. Just the four of us.'

'I'll look forward to it.'

'How's the flat hunting going?'

'It's steady. I haven't found anywhere I want to settle down yet. The rented place is okay.'

'I'll keep my ears open.'

Dr Kate Murphy was in her office. A detective from one of the other Major Investigation Teams was there, a man whom Harry had worked a case with just a few months ago.

'Sorry to disturb,' Harry said, knocking on the door.

DS Andy Watt was sitting on the edge of the desk and stood up when Harry came in. 'I was just leaving, sir,' Watt said.

'No need, Andy. Kate said she wanted a word.'

Watt stood to one side while Kate picked up a clear plastic bag that was sitting on her desk. 'This was in Fiona Carlton's shoe.'

Harry took the bag and looked inside. 'A flash drive. Funny place to keep it. Do you know what's on it?'

'We just bagged it. That's for your computer geeks to figure out.'

'Oh, I'm sure they would appreciate being called that,' Watt said.

'I'm sure they've been called worse, Andy,' Harry said. 'Besides, it gives them validation; otherwise we'd be thinking of them as amateurs. I'll pass it on to them.'

'Okay,' said Kate. 'DI Shiels was here for the preliminary exam, but we'll do the full autopsy tomorrow. I've been run off my feet.'

'Okay. Talk to you soon. Good seeing you again, Andy.'

'You too, sir.'

Outside, the late-afternoon cold was starting to grip the city.

'I'm sorry for your loss,' Harry said to Maggie. 'It's never an easy thing, coming to the mortuary.'

'I appreciate that. Would you mind driving me to my sister's flat before taking me home? She had borrowed a laptop from me. I'd like it back.'

'Not at all.'

Alex drove them up to Lochrin and parked in the underground car park. They rang the buzzer on the front door, but there was no answer.

'I have a key,' Maggie said. She let them in.

They walked into the living room, but Bea wasn't there. 'Maybe she's in bed. I just wanted to look at my sister's stuff.'

Maggie walked into Fiona's bedroom and stopped.

'What's wrong?' Harry said.

'This room. It's spotless.'

'Is there a problem?' Alex asked, looking around the room, at the bed that was made, at the dresser that was tidy and the small desk that was neat.

Maggie turned to her. 'Yes, yes, there is. My sister wasn't a slob, but she would have clothes lying about. She would catch up with laundry at the weekend. But look.' She stepped forward to the small dresser. Ran a finger across the top. 'There's not a speck of dust on here. Like it's brand new and not even had time to collect dust yet.'

She walked over to the laptop sitting on the desk. It was open. She pressed the on button and the computer came to life moments later.

Maggie stepped back like she'd just stood on a Lego brick.

'Somebody's touched this.'

'How do you know?' Harry said, stepping forward and looking at the screen. It had one of Apple's wallpapers on it.

'First of all, she had a photo of me and her on here as the background. And secondly, she wouldn't have put a default photo up.' She leaned over and started clicking the keys.

'Christ, there are no documents on here.' She straightened up and looked at Harry and Alex. 'I mean, we don't leave important stuff on these machines, in case they get stolen, but we do generic work that we can email to the supervisors. Then it's all deleted. There's nothing here.'

She went back and clicked again. 'Jesus, there aren't even any of my photos here.' She straightened again.

'What's going on?' a voice said from the doorway.

They all turned to see Bea standing there.

'We're just looking at Fiona's laptop.'

'Oh, okay.' Bea looked at Harry. 'This is a secure serviced apartment for employees of McCallum Technology only.

They don't allow non-staff in here, for confidentiality reasons.'

'I am a police officer,' he said, not appreciating her tone. 'And we're here for personal belongings. I'm sure Mr McCallum wouldn't mind, and if he does, then he can call me directly.'

Bea shrugged. 'No, it's fine. I just know how strict they are about having people in here.'

'We'll take it away and have it examined,' Alex said. 'In case there's any deleted stuff we can get into.'

'I can look, if you like.'

Harry held up a hand. 'We're taking it in for our tech people to have a look at it.'

'Okay, no problem.' Bea walked away and into the kitchen.

'Anything seem to be missing?' Alex said in a low voice.

Maggie scoured the room. 'Nothing jumps out at me.'

'Have you got an evidence bag on you?' Alex asked Harry. 'I'll take this home and have the tech guys look at it first thing Monday morning.'

Harry pulled one out of his pocket. Just like the nitrile gloves, you never knew when you were going to need one.

'I'm going to stay here for a little while,' said Maggie. 'I want to look through some of Fiona's things. I want to still feel connected to her. Even though…' Her voice trailed off.

'I can't let you do that,' Harry said. 'I'm going to call

forensics to come round here and look through her things. I hope you understand.'

Maggie nodded, while Alex went to tell Bea not to enter the bedroom.

Half an hour later, the crew turned up and went to work.

SEVEN

It was dark and cold. Just what Harry's ex-girlfriend had accused him of being not that long ago.

'How does my tie look?' he asked Alex. He was FaceTiming her.

'It won't win any competitions, but I think it's perfect for tonight.'

'You mean it'll do just for seeing Vanessa?'

'Exactly.' She smiled and took a sip of the wine she was drinking. She too was at home. 'Chin-chin.'

'She just wants to have a quiet chat,' he said in his own defence.

'Harry, she lives just across the road from you.'

'Along the road and round the corner, to be precise.'

'You can see her house from your window if you look right across the bowling green.'

'Okay, now we've established where Vanessa lives, can we move on?'

He carried the phone in front of him, moving from the bathroom mirror into the living room.

'My point is, she could have walked round to your flat, or vice versa. Just be careful you're not walking into a trap.'

'It's hardly the gunfight at the OK Corral.' Although he'd seen many a fight in Edinburgh that wasn't far off it.

'I'm just saying. I know I've only ever met her the one time, when we were all in the pub and she waltzed in with some of her staff, but I sized her up right away. I could see she took an instant dislike to me.'

'I think you're imagining it, Alex.'

'You're not a woman. You wouldn't understand.'

'It's just a meal and a drink. As friends.'

'Okay. If you say so.'

'I do. And thanks for your help.'

'Catch you tomorrow. Oh, look at the time. Angie Patterson and I are having a couple tonight in Diamonds bar.'

'Have fun.'

'You too.'

He signed off, feeling a knot in his guts. Why wouldn't Vanessa like Alex? He knew you couldn't make somebody like you, but Alex was likeable. He put his jacket on just as he heard the car horn downstairs.

'Have you ever been here before?' Vanessa asked as the taxi dropped them off outside Gusto's, an Italian restaurant in George Street.

He had thought they knew everything there was to know about each other when they had been dating, but maybe in the few months they'd been apart, she had wiped her mental hard drive clean.

'No. You?'

She gave him a sly look, one his mother used to use when he'd got caught taking a biscuit from the tin when he was a boy. *You should know that, Harry,* she was saying, and didn't bother replying.

Harry paid the taxi driver and dodged through a small group of women who looked like they were bar-hopping. Friday night in the centre of Edinburgh. It had been a long time. He remembered the shifts he'd done here when he had been in uniform. It went like a fair until the wee hours.

'You coming or what?' Vanessa said, the smile on her face belying the aggravation in her voice.

He strode forward and they went into the warmth of the place. Harry liked Italian and had suggested Gusto's to Vanessa like he knew the place. Truth was, Alex had given him the tip about it.

They made chit-chat while they ordered their food, a pizza for Harry and salmon fillet with saffron potatoes for Vanessa.

'How are you liking being the boss of an MIT?' she said after ordering some wine.

'It's good. It's what I was used to in CID before I went to Professional Standards.'

'Alex seems nice.' She looked at him over the rim of her glass as she tipped it up to her mouth.

'She is. She's a good detective and she'll go far. She'll be my boss one day, no doubt.'

'Among other things.'

'What's that supposed to mean?' He took a sip from his bottle of beer.

Vanessa grinned. 'She fancies you.'

'What? Behave.'

'She does, Harry. I'm a woman. We see things that men can't.'

'Listen, when you're a cop, you become close to other cops you work with. I'm close to Karen Shiels too.'

'No, you're not. Not like Alex.'

'You're being ridiculous.'

'Am I?' There was something in her eyes now as the waiter brought their order.

Harry felt a heat inside, fuelled by anger. 'We're colleagues, nothing more. You know how it was with me in Standards; all my old friends wanted nothing more to do with me. It's hard trying to work with people who don't trust you, but luckily I'm working with people now who do trust me. Yes, Alex and I get on better than I'd hoped, and we have a bit of a laugh, and we go out for a drink with some of our other colleagues. But that's where I draw the line.'

He could feel his face flush as he cut into his pizza. Christ, it was like being in an interview room back at the station.

'Don't get all defensive on me now.' She smiled at him. She had gone into a battle of wits with him and won. He mentally kicked himself.

'I'm not getting defensive, I'm just telling you how it is. Why should you worry now?'

'I'm not worried. In fact, I couldn't be less worried. I just asked you to dinner so we could have a civilised chat. So I could tell you my news.'

He finished his bottle of beer and asked the waiter for another one.

'Go on then, I'll take the bait; what news?'

'I've moved on, Harry. These past few months have been hell. I've lost weight...'

He looked at her, struggling to see the difference, an opinion he would keep to himself for the moment.

'I've not been sleeping well. I even contemplated doing something stupid at one time.'

'Something stupid' probably meant prank-calling him in the middle of the night. There were people out there who really did contemplate doing something stupid and she was comparing herself to them. He couldn't have been more disgusted.

'Let's not forget something here, Vanessa; you chose this. You made the choice to call it a day.'

'Only because you backed me into a corner.'

'By not giving up the lease on my flat? Christ, we were doing fine. Everything was ticking along nicely, until you wanted me to' – *step into your lair* – 'move in with you.'

'People do that sort of thing. Move in with each other.'

'I'm sorry, I didn't feel comfortable doing that. Not last summer.'

'And now?'

The waiter brought the bottle and Harry drank from it, all thoughts of his pizza now gone.

'You called it a day. What else do you want me to say?'

'I've met somebody, Harry. One of the fathers who has a little boy in my nursery. His wife left him, we got talking and he asked me out. I said yes.'

'Why are you here with me then and not him?'

'I'm meeting him later. I just wanted to tell you about him here.'

'In a public place, in case I had a meltdown? You don't have to worry about that.'

She was looking down at her phone, her thumbs dancing across the screen. 'Work,' she said, looking back at him and smiling. 'Listen, I don't want this to end awkwardly. I want us to stop in the street and say hi if we bump into each other. Especially since we live around the corner from each other.'

'Fine. We can stop and talk about the weather. How does that sound?'

Her phone buzzed just then. She picked it up and again her thumbs danced. 'Harry, I'm so sorry. I have to go.'

There it was, the get-out-of-Dodge routine. He called the waiter over and explained they had an emergency and he paid the bill.

Outside, it was cold and damp. *Never mind, only a few days before Edinburgh sets fire to itself,* he thought.

'This is it, Harry. We go our separate ways.' She pecked him on the cheek before starting to walk away. Then she stopped and turned around. 'Thanks for dinner.'

The last supper. He stood at the kerb, waiting for a taxi, which wouldn't take long. He watched a man move away from the wall further along, and Vanessa walked up to him and kissed him on the cheek. Harry guessed the man had been responsible for the *Get me the hell out of here* text Vanessa had been sent.

He shook his head and put out a hand for the taxi driving towards him.

EIGHT

Vanessa could have called Harry and told him the news about her new boyfriend, but she had chosen to make a display of it, making sure he saw the new man in her life. He tried to brush it off, but the feeling wasn't going away anytime soon.

The taxi took him down to the St Bernard's Bar in Raeburn Place, within walking distance of his flat, further along in Comely Bank. It was busy, mostly with older clients, but a few younger ones were getting fuelled up on cheaper prices before parting with their hard-earned cash up town.

Harry was settling in, chatting with a couple of the older blokes he knew just from coming in here, when the front door opened. He idly looked round and did a double take. It was Alex. She hadn't seen him and she squeezed her way through to the bar to order a drink. He excused himself and sidled up to her.

'Can I buy a lady a drink?'

'No, thanks...' she started to say but then saw who it was and smiled. 'I was about to add some derogatory comment if you didn't go away,' she said.

'That's the effect I normally have on women,' he said, getting the barman to give him a half to add to his pint.

'Glass half empty or half full?' Alex said, nodding to his glass.

'Vanessa always said I'm the half-empty type. Me? Depends on what the weather is like.'

They moved away from the bar and found a corner to stand in; then a couple vacated a table, heading for more exciting climes, and they grabbed it.

'Talking of the great Vanessa, how did your date go?'

'First of all, it was not a date, as you fine well know.'

'I'm a detective, so let's examine the evidence: Friday night, both unattached, going to dinner and having a few drinks. Where I come from, that constitutes a date.'

'Where you come from, they eat their young.'

'Don't be cheeky. You know I'm right. That's why you're flushed and sweating. Or is that just because you saw me?'

'Okay, I'm bowing to your pressure here. Your interrogation skills are second to none.'

'And yet here I am, still waiting for the juicy gossip. Will they get back together? Has Vanessa finally seen through Harry's devious ways? What does Harry say that will bring them both crashing down? Tune in to next week's episode...'

'Oh, for God's sake. She wanted to have dinner to tell me she's found somebody else. Satisfied?'

'She wanted to publicly humiliate you.'

'She also sent a text, then got one back, feigning some work emergency. Then her boyfriend met her along the road.'

'The old "This date is shite, get me out of here" text. Yeah, I've used that one before.' She took her phone out of her pocket and looked at it. 'Sorry, Harry, I have to go.'

'Really. Everything okay?'

She laughed. 'See how easy it is?'

'Christ, you were convincing.'

'Like she was, I'll bet. But why not just call you and let you know? That would have been easier, but no, she wanted to flaunt it in your face. It was all staged.'

She saw him looking into his pint for a second and put a hand on his arm. 'She was just playing a game with you. She's trying to get in your head now.'

Harry looked up at her. 'It's not working. Yes, I was pissed off, but I knew she was trying to get a rise out of me and it didn't work.'

'You're the bigger person here.'

'I know.' He drank some of his pint. 'What about you? I thought you were meeting Angie Patterson tonight?'

'We did meet up, but she's on call and was only drinking some fancy French fizzy water. And try saying that fast three times.'

'It's not even ten yet on a Friday night, and here we are in a little boozer that's not even in the city centre. I feel old.'

'You and me both, and you're a lot older than me.'

'Ten years is hardly classed as *a lot older*.'

'I'm only thirty and I feel like I should be in a nightclub somewhere, being swept off my feet.'

'Why aren't you?' Harry looked at her face, watching her closely.

'I could call up a couple of friends and go dancing with them, but I just don't feel like it anymore. My fiancé gave me trust issues. I hate to admit that, but him cheating on me has made me put my guard up.'

'You're too young to be feeling like this. There's a lonely man out there, standing with his back to the wall, looking out on the dance floor, wishing he had somebody like you to dance with. Waiting to go home to his mother if he doesn't get a pull. He won't meet you if you don't go out.'

'Ha bloody ha.'

'Seriously, there's somebody out there waiting for you.'

'That's very philosophical. Too much for a Friday night. You want a chaser?'

'Sounds good. A wee nip.'

He watched her go to the bar and couldn't understand why men weren't falling over her, but then men did have a sixth sense for women who were putting up a barrier. A few minutes' conversation would give them the message. He didn't blame her. He hadn't been cheated on in his own marriage – that he knew of – but he could imagine how hard it would be to find out the person you loved didn't want to give you that love and trust back.

She sat back down with the two glasses.

'Cheers,' he said and they clinked glasses.

'Don't look round, but I think there's somebody following me,' she said.

Harry suddenly went into protection mode. He was sitting with his back to the door.

'What's he look like?'

'Around fifty. Close-cropped hair. Big guy. Black jacket. Standing at the bar, nursing a pint but not drinking much of it.'

Harry turned slightly as the door opened and an older man entered. He smiled and waved to the man; he didn't know him, but it afforded him the opportunity to look at the man at the bar. He was clean shaven and had the look of somebody who had been round the block.

'I see him. But why do you think he's following you?'

'He was in Diamonds up the road too.'

'Call Angie, just to make sure she's okay.'

Alex took her phone out and called their friend, and Angie assured her she was already home.

'She's fine. Tucked up on the couch with her cat watching Netflix.'

Then Harry saw the man stand up straight and nod to the barman. He left without looking in their direction.

'Maybe I was wrong,' Alex said.

'Probably just a guy out for a few pints.'

'Norrie nae mates.'

But neither of them completely dismissed the idea that the man had been following Alex.

Harry got up, ordered a couple of drinks and waited patiently. Then he sat back at the table. At least they could breathe. He remembered the days when this place would be like it was on fire with the cigarette smoke.

'Do you think this murder was a mugging gone wrong?' Alex asked him.

'No. It was too vicious.'

'We have a nutter on the loose then.'

'No. I think he was looking for something. The something that was hidden in her shoe.'

'The flash drive. Why would she have a flash drive in her shoe?'

'And what's on it?'

'We won't know until the tech boys have had a look, Harry.'

'I wonder if it's any good after being in the water.'

'We'll soon find out.'

After finishing her drink, Alex looked at him. 'I'm going to hit the hay.'

'I'll walk you home,' Harry said. 'If you like.'

'Okay. But listen…'

He put a hand up. 'Just to your front door. I'm going back to my place. Just walking you to your door.'

'Let's go.'

Her flat was literally a five-minute walk from the pub, round the corner, down a narrow lane and into the first street of the Stockbridge colonies.

'Reid Terrace,' Alex said, 'named after one of the men who originally invested in the building of the colonies.'

'Funny last name for a bloke, *Terrace*.'

'You're too bloody funny at times.'

It was well lit, with a small green in front, bordering the Water of Leith. Alex lived halfway down. The doors here were all up a small set of steps, these flats being the upper ones.

'Thanks, Harry. I would invite you up for a drink, but... you know...'

'I said to your front door. I'll stay here until you get in.'

'I would have walked round myself if I hadn't met you in the pub, you know.' She laughed. 'You're very chivalrous.'

'I've been called worse.'

Two things happened then almost at once: the headlight on a motorbike parked further along sprang into life as the engine kicked over, and Alex's front door burst open and a man wearing a helmet roughly pushed past her and started running down the steps.

'Hey!' she screamed.

Harry tried to grab the man but was pushed aside.

The motorbike came speeding along the street and the man jumped on the back. Harry saw a wheelie bin just inside the small garden next to the steps, picked it up and fired it at the bike. It caught the pillion passenger and knocked him off. The bike carried on and the passenger got up like he had just bounced off the road.

Then, as the bike turned the corner and roared away, headlights emerged from around the corner and a car raced into the street and stopped. Harry started running after the passenger from the bike, but he was fast. The car was a big black Range Rover. The driver's window rolled down and Harry thought he saw the man from the pub, but he couldn't be sure. The running man opened the back door and the big car shot backwards.

Harry stopped, and turned and ran back towards Alex's flat. She wasn't at the front door, so he ran up the steps. Then he looked over the Water of Leith and saw the motorbike and Range Rover speeding along the road opposite.

Alex was standing outside her front door at the top of the steps. As Harry approached, he noticed the wheels on her car and pointed them out to her.

'Bastards. They've slashed my tyres!' Alex said, coming down to have a look.

'I don't see any slash marks. It looks like they just let all the air out of them.'

'Crap. That's not so bad, but it's going to take some time to blow them up.'

'They're run flats. You could drive round to a petrol station later. We can have a patrol car drive behind you, just so you get there in one piece.'

'Later. Not tonight. I might be over the limit.'

'Fair enough.'

They went back up to the flat.

'Did he take anything?' Harry asked as she looked around.

She turned to him. 'He took what he came for.'

'You mean...?'

'Yes. The MacBook Pro. Fortunately, he took the wrong one.'

'What do you mean?'

'I mean, I keep one sitting next to the stereo over there. It's knackered, an old one. I bought a new one, but instead of throwing the old one out, I keep it out as a decoy. As you well know, thieves want to be in and out, and they look for laptops and iPads and the like.'

'That makes sense.'

'The one I took from Fiona Carlton's house is in the tech lab in Fettes. I told you I was going to drop it off on Monday, but you and I know it's open seven days. Two other people thought I was going to bring it home and keep it here until Monday, Maggie Carlton and Bea Anderson.'

'That bloke we saw in the pub who we thought was following you? The guy who broke in here jumped into the back of a Range Rover and Baldy was driving it.'

She looked at him. 'See? I thought the bastard was following me.'

'I think whoever wanted that laptop was keeping an eye on you and reporting to the reprobates on the bike. This was no ordinary break-in and they're not amateurs.'

'At least he didn't get my new laptop. That would have been a pain.'

'I'll call this in, then we'll get forensics here.'

Alex nodded and went through to the kitchen to switch the kettle on.

Thank God Harry was there.

Within five minutes, the small street was bathed in flashing blue lights. Within half an hour, the other members of Harry's team were there.

'Boss,' Simon Gregg said as he entered the living room ahead of DI Karen Shiels. There was another woman behind them.

Karen turned to look at her before addressing Harry. 'Sir, this is the newest recruit to our team, DC Evelyn Bell. She was going to join us on Monday morning, but she's a friend of mine and she was at my place when I got the call.'

Harry smiled and shook her hand. 'Welcome aboard, Evelyn,' he said. 'I've heard good things about you.'

'Thank you, sir, but you can call me Eve.'

'Eve it is.'

'What's going on here, sir?' Gregg said. The smallish room made him look like a giant.

'Somebody broke in here looking for something. They didn't get it.' Harry explained about the computer and the people who had come looking for it.

'If they took the wrong one, they might come back for round two,' Gregg said. 'I'd like to meet the little bastard you knocked off the motorbike. I'd make sure he couldn't sit down for a week.'

'You do know I was in Professional Standards, don't you?' Harry said.

Gregg had the good grace to look embarrassed. 'Just words, sir. I wouldn't really kick him up the arse, much as I'd like to.'

'I understand, but somebody else took over my position, investigating cops like us. Just one word out of turn and somebody reports it, and they'll be all over you. You just won't know it.'

'Sorry, sir. I was just venting. Maybe the guy will come back. Maybe he'll come at me with a knife. Then I can arrest him.'

'Trust me, son, these boys don't come at people unprepared. If they want to fuck us over, I'm sure they're well versed in it. These guys are professionals all the way.'

'You think they could be behind Fiona Carlton's murder?' Karen asked.

'It's what I was thinking. The bald guy I saw tonight made no attempt to hide himself. He was following Alex and we saw him in the pub.'

'You both saw him in the pub?'

'We bumped into each other round the corner.' Harry looked at Eve. 'I live along the road in Comely Bank, so the pub is one of my regular haunts.'

'You don't have to explain, sir,' Gregg said.

'I know I don't. Just breaking down the dynamics of how this went down tonight.' Harry looked up at Gregg, waiting for more questions to field, but none came.

'We also got a flash drive that had been stuck in the dead woman's shoe. I passed that on to the tech team at Fettes and they said they would start working on it. I don't know how far they got, but I'll call in the morning.' He looked at Eve. 'They work seven days, in case you didn't know that. But they'll be closed just now.'

'I knew that, sir.'

'I don't think Alex should be here by herself,' said Harry. 'Things could turn out way differently next time.'

'You're right,' Karen said. 'She could crash at my place.'

Alex came into the room. 'I appreciate it, ma'am, but I won't be pushed out of my own home. If they come back, they'll have to deal with me.'

'There was a team of them,' Harry said. 'They could have more with them next time.'

A white-suited forensics man came up to them. 'We have a lot of prints, but round the door, nothing. And by that, I mean it looks like before he came in, he wiped the area round the lock and the door jamb. These were professionals who knew what they were doing. I doubt we'll get anything useful. Sorry to be the bearer of bad news.'

'It's nothing we weren't expecting,' Harry said.

'I'm not happy about you staying here by yourself, Alex,' Karen said.

Alex relented. 'Okay. Then I'll go and stay with a friend. Maybe you're right. We don't know how dangerous they are.' She grabbed a bag from her room and came out with it.

'That was quick,' Harry said.

'It's my bug-out bag. In case the zombie apocalypse happens.'

'Good God,' Harry said, shaking his head. 'Did you remember to pack your Spiderman pyjamas?'

'It's a real thing, boss,' Gregg said. 'Millions of people all over the world are ready for it.'

'I might have guessed you'd have roped him in to it.'

Alex laughed. 'Let's just call it my weekend-away bag then. In case you get scared of the big, bad monsters.'

'I'd be more worried about a bloody nutter in a Range Rover than the undead.'

After the forensics crew had left, they went their separate ways.

Harry accepted a lift from Karen, with Eve sitting in the back. Gregg took Alex.

'See you first thing Monday,' Harry said, getting out of Karen's car back at his place. He watched her drive away and looked up the hill towards Vanessa's house. The outside light was on, waiting for her to come home with her new boyfriend.

Things had been ticking along nicely, and they had only gone pear-shaped because he didn't want to give up his rental flat.

Upstairs, he switched the TV on and watched some mindless crap. He should have been out with Vanessa instead.

He took his phone out and thought about calling his son, Chance, but then thought better of it as it was so late.

Then his buzzer rang from downstairs at the front door.

He picked up the intercom.

'Hello?'

'It's Alex.'

He was silent for a moment. Should he tell her to come back in the morning? Was Gregg with her? He didn't want this to turn into some sort of sesh. He'd feel obligated to crack open a bottle of Bells, just to be sociable, although Gregg was driving, so maybe he wouldn't have to. Maybe a quick coffee…

'Thank you,' he heard Alex say, her voice sounding distant now.

'Alex?' he said, but he was speaking to himself now. No reply, and he could hear feet thumping on the stone steps. Christ, she was coming up.

He opened the door just as she got there, out of breath, holding her bag.

'I hope you don't mind. I told Simon just to drop me off at

HQ. I told him I wanted to speak to somebody and I'd get an Uber.'

'You'd better come in,' he said, stepping back. 'You didn't get an Uber, did you?'

'No, I just walked.'

She came in and walked through to the living room, where she dropped her bag next to the settee.

'You want something to drink?' he said.

'What you got?'

'Horlicks. Cocoa.'

'I'm fine.'

'So what happened?' He indicated for her to take a seat.

'Nothing. I went to the lab to see if they'd done anything with the computer yet. They're closed for the day. It's got me wound up, somebody being in my home.' She stood up. 'Right, I'm going home. I'll call you tomorrow.'

'What do you mean, going home? I thought you were going to stay with a friend?'

'Yeah, well, I thought she was a friend. Turns out, not quite so much. It was a definite *no* to my sleeping on her couch.'

'Jesus.'

'It's the uniform for some people. They think it changes us personally. I mean, I was out having a drink with her just a couple of months ago. It doesn't matter, though; I'll jam a chair behind the front door.'

Harry had a feeling that a chair would be nowhere near enough to keep the men out.

He stood up. 'I'll make up the spare bed.'

'Oh God, no. I couldn't do that.'

'Why not? There's a lock on the inside of the door. Jam a chair up against it too, if it makes you feel any better.'

'Look, boss, I don't want the others to think I'm trying to get a leg-up by…staying overnight with the boss.'

'Nobody has to know. And FYI, you're not getting a leg-up.'

She smiled. 'If you're sure we can just keep this to ourselves?'

'Trust me on that. And close the curtains, will you? No point in advertising the fact.'

As Harry walked through to the linen cupboard to grab some sheets and a couple of blankets, a thought occurred to him: *What if they know where I live too?*

NINE

Harry thought he'd get up early and have a shower before Alex got up, but she was already in the kitchen making coffee when he eventually got dressed.

'I didn't disturb you, did I?' she said, pouring him a coffee.

'No, no, not at all.' *I always get up at seven thirty on a Saturday morning.* 'You sleep okay?'

'Eventually. I kept thinking about those guys and what's so important about that damn computer.'

'Let's go across the road and find out,' he said. 'You had breakfast?'

'No. I thought we could grab a roll in the canteen.'

'Sounds good to me.'

They made their way downstairs. It was overcast with a little wind throwing the fallen leaves about.

'You want me to drive?' she said, grinning, when Harry unlocked the CR-V.

'I do still have my faculties about me,' he said, getting in behind the wheel and starting it up.

'That's not what I meant.'

'I know what you meant, and I'm not rising up to the debate on whether or not men drive these cars.'

'There's nothing wrong with them.'

'I know,' he said, stopping at the end of the road. He took a little longer than was necessary looking up to his left. Where Vanessa's house was. Her Lexus was parked in the street.

Alex's face took on a serious look. 'She set out to play games with you and it looks like it worked,' she said. 'If Vanessa's moved on, then it's fine for you to move on too.'

'I know. I thought that van was coming right down the hill.'

'He turned two minutes ago.'

He pulled away. Alex was right; Vanessa had drawn a line under their relationship, so he had to as well. He felt like a teenager who had been dating the most popular girl in school before she moved on.

He parked in the car park at the side of the police headquarters. Their office was located here, though there was talk of relocating them, but the big yins upstairs hadn't decided where to yet.

'Ah, it's the heid honcho,' a young technician said as they walked into the lab down on the basement level.

'You got anything yet, Ricky?' Harry said.

Ricky Morrison: young, eager, and what he didn't know about computers could be written on an ant's arse.

'I've been up since the crack of dawn.' Morrison looked at his watch. 'Well, not the crack, you understand, but not far off it. But I digress.'

'Yes, you do,' Harry said, grabbing a tall bar stool at the side of a workbench. On the bench sat a MacBook Pro, presumably the one that the thieves were after. Alex sat on the other side of Morrison.

'Whoa, whoa, what's this? I haven't had anybody sit so close to me since fourth year when I had to stay behind and show my teacher a thing or two. But that's a story for another day.'

Morrison grinned at them. 'I had a look at the computer when I came in first thing. I looked in the files, and in the sub-files. I was able to find a lot of technical drawings and the like. Nothing out of the ordinary, I'm afraid.'

'What sort of drawings are they?' Alex asked.

'Schematics, mostly. Electronic things. Blueprints for electrical paraphernalia.'

'Just random gobbledegook?' Harry said.

'To the untrained eye,' Morrison said. 'But to young Ricky, it's just another day at the office. These, my friend, are schematics for battery-powered vehicles. Nothing too science fiction, but then I loaded the flash drive into one of our computers here and it all made sense.'

There was silence for a second, a pause for dramatic effect.

'Come on, Ricky, don't keep us in suspense for God's sake,' Harry said, beginning to think the coffee in the canteen was the best thing he'd ever looked forward to, and why hadn't they gone there before coming here to see the young geek?

'There are technical drawings and code on the flash drive. They're like two pieces of a puzzle. If you take the information from the flash drive and put it together with the schematics on the computer, the two pieces fit together. It's like if you were to draw three small squares and you needed to add another small square to make a big square, then the fourth square is on the flash drive. Now, that's it in the simplest terms. However, there is one problem.'

'What's that?' Alex asked.

'I could tell what was missing from the schematics on the computer, and there was another schematic on the flash drive that should have worked, should have fit in to make the square. If we're still using the square analogy. But the fourth bit that's needed isn't quite a little square. It's more like an oval.'

Harry tried not to look blank but missed the mark.

'Sorry. Let me try again. It's like drawing a car and leaving a space for the engine. You haven't drawn the engine bay big enough. Your engine just won't go in. So you saw the corners off and shoehorn it in. It's there, it's connected and you even get it running, but it's not as silky smooth as if it would have been had you designed it the right size.'

'You're saying there are two projects that are supposed to link up, but one of them doesn't work with the other?' Harry said.

'Bingo. By all accounts, both designs should click together, but they don't.'

Harry stood up. 'Thanks, Ricky.'

'No problem. Might see you in the police club one night. We'll get a game of darts.'

'As long as you don't want to play cards for money.'

TEN

The drive up to Baberton Mains didn't take too long. The Saturday rush hadn't started yet. The traffic would intensify after lunch when people had sobered up and were wondering what to do with themselves only a month and a half before Christmas.

'When's your ex-wife coming back for her car?' Alex said from the passenger seat.

'Who knows? Meantime, I'll keep using it.'

Harry drove along Queensferry Road, skirting the city centre altogether. 'I wonder what all of this puzzle stuff means?'

'I haven't a clue. I can't even do Sudoku.'

He laughed. 'I bet you can't.'

'I'm serious; all those numbers, trying to get them in order one way, then another. Jesus, it should be listed as an instrument of torture.'

'You're not into figures then?'

'I am not! Bloody figures. I hated maths at school. I was lucky to get through the police exam. I mean, I passed, but my numerical skills aren't going to set the world on fire.'

After coming off the bypass, he drove along Calder Road, then up Wester Hailes Road, entering Baberton from the bottom.

A few minutes later, he turned into Maggie Carlton's street. And was blocked by fire engines.

'Jesus,' Harry said, looking over at the smouldering wreck of what had been Maggie Carlton's house.

They got out and walked over to the commander in charge of the scene. They showed their warrant cards.

'What happened here?'

'Don't you know? I thought your colleagues had called you out.' The commander indicated a uniform patrol parked across the street.

'No, we came here looking for the occupant.'

'Well, you might be out of luck. We found a body. Not burnt; she probably died from smoke inhalation.'

The roof was burnt off and the walls were a blackened shell.

'Is there ID on the body?' Alex asked.

'She was already outside being attended to by a doctor, but it was too late.'

'What sort of fire would do that?' Harry said.

'An accelerated one. Some liquid, not petrol, but maybe lighter fluid, or white spirit. Something got it going well and good, though.'

'Has the body been removed yet?'

'Yes. She was taken away a little while ago.'

'What time did the call come in for this?'

'A little after five thirty.'

Harry thanked the man and they walked over to one of the uniforms, who recognised Harry before he could show his ID.

'Since this fire is suspicious, do you have any witnesses?' Harry doubted anybody would have been walking around on a cold, dark Saturday morning in Baberton Mains, unless they were a ne'er-do-well.

'One man across the road...' The officer turned and pointed out onto the main road, across from the cul-de-sac. 'He got up for a pee around five-thirty. His daughter was staying over with a friend, and he noticed headlights through his curtains. Nothing unusual in that, but he thought maybe his daughter had changed her mind and decided to come home. She's in her twenties and was in the town on a night out.

'Anyway, he peeked through the curtains and saw a black Range Rover parked with its lights on in the cul-de-sac. The flames were already licking through the roof and the car backed out at high speed.'

'I don't suppose he got a number plate?' Alex asked.

'No, ma'am. And when we got the call to come here, the duty doc was already here and he had pronounced the victim. Then the mortuary crew turned up and took her away.'

'Which house?' Harry said. The uniform pointed again.

Harry and Alex made their way to the house and rang the doorbell. The sun was out, but it was teasing them, offering them no warmth as a wind blasted across the road.

A woman answered and looked out at them with a hint of suspicion, as if they were the fireraisers come to do her house next.

'We're police officers. Could we have a word?'

'Oh, yes, come in.' She let them in and closed the door to keep the heat in.

'Would you like a coffee?' she said as she led them into the living room. It was spotless. Nothing was lying around and Harry had seen dirtier show homes.

'No, thank you. Can we take a note of your name?'

'Carol Mathers. You can sit down, if you like.'

They sat down on the pristine couch, Harry looking for any dirt he might have tracked into the woman's house, sure she would be right out with the hoover after they'd left.

'I believe your husband may have seen something in the early hours of this morning in regard to the fire across the road,' Harry said.

'He said he did. He'd been round at the golf club. It's just through the trees next to the house that was on fire, but you can't walk through that way of course. Anyway, he and his pals have a good drink there on a Friday night, which means he has to get up for a pee through the night.'

'Have either of you seen a car like that at the house before?'

'I'm not nosy, son, so I wouldn't know. My husband is, though, and he said he hadn't seen anything like that around here before. But we saw a taxi leave the street. Maybe the driver saw something.'

'A black cab?' Harry asked.

Carol nodded. 'There are a few cab drivers living around here, but who knows?'

'What about the woman who lives in the burnt-out house? Do you know her to talk to?'

'Only in passing. There used to be the two of them living there, sisters I think, but I've only seen the one recently.' She took a deep breath and blew it out again. 'I saw them take the body away in that van. God bless her.'

'Have you seen anybody suspicious lurking about recently?' Alex asked.

'Not that I can think of. It's a very quiet place. We don't get much trouble here at all.'

Harry stood up and took a business card out of his wallet and handed it to Carol. 'If you can think of anything else, please don't hesitate to call.'

Outside, the cold hit them after the warmth of the house. 'That bloody Range Rover gets about,' Harry said.

'It might have been that taxi. Big black car. The husband was probably still drunk. It was dark. Who knows?'

'If I see that baldy bastard again, I'll be having a wee chat with him.'

'Make sure you have Simon Gregg with you,' Alex said.

'Meaning what?'

'That you're of a smaller stature and not as young.'

'The bigger they are and all that.'

'That's bollocks, Harry. The bigger they are, the more chance you have of getting a ride in the back of an ambulance.'

'Still. I owe Baldy a wee talking-to, and if he's not with his motorcycle chum, we'll be having that talk.' His phone rang and he answered it. 'Hello?'

'DCI McNeil? It's Maggie Carlton. We really need to talk.'

ELEVEN

'I should go back to my own flat tonight,' Alex said as Harry drove along Slateford, following the shopping centre brigade.

'Okay.'

'No, no, Alex, I insist you stay at my place,' she said.

'I didn't want to sound like I was desperate for you to stay.'

'Like you were some kind of perv trying to take advantage of a younger colleague?'

'Something like that.'

'Or are you worried that Vanessa might see me and wonder what's going on?'

'I couldn't care bloody less what she thinks. She took herself out of my life, so she can sod off. Of course you can stay tonight. Stay as long as you want until we get those bastards.'

Harry felt himself getting revved up, now more than anything wanting to have a word with the little bastard he had knocked off the motorbike.

'I was just joking. About staying. I should just go back.' She looked sideways at him for a moment as he navigated round a bus that was pulling into a stop.

'It's your call. There's nobody else using the spare bedroom, and I don't want to be one of those condescending men who think that women can't look after themselves, but there's a team of them, and if they come at us, I think we'd have a better chance if there was the two of us.'

'You have a good point. You've talked me into it.'

'There was no *talking you into it* bollocks. The decision is yours.'

'Okay, Harry, I'll stay, if you insist.'

'You know, sometimes I pray for God to take me in my sleep. Just so I won't have to listen to your gums flapping.'

'That's the nicest thing a man has ever said to me.'

'You never give up, do you?'

'Nope. It's one of my best qualities.' She grinned at him.

He found a parking space in the underground car park of the flats and they got to the door just in time for Maggie Carlton to answer it.

'I have to say, I was surprised when you called me,' Harry said as they went through into the living room. 'You know about your house?'

She looked blankly at him. 'What about it?'

'I'm sorry to have to tell you this, but your house was set on fire overnight. They found somebody inside. We thought it was you.'

'What?' Maggie stopped for a second. 'Was it deliberate?'

'That's what they're thinking.'

'Where's Bea?' Alex said.

'I'm not sure. I just woke up a little while ago. Last night I was in Fiona's room. Bea made me a cuppa, and the next thing I know, I'm waking up on top of Fiona's bed.'

'Go and check on her,' Harry said to Alex.

She walked through to the hallway and knocked on Bea's bedroom door, then opened it when there was no answer.

Harry stood looking at the photographs on the shelf again. There were none of Bea, but there were two of Fiona Carlton with a young man. Harry took photos of them with his phone.

Alex came right back. 'She's not in,' she said. 'Maybe she went to work?'

'Maybe,' said Maggie. 'We didn't have much of a conversation.'

'How long have you known her?' Harry asked.

'Just a couple of months. Although I wouldn't say I *know* her. Just to say hi to. I don't come over here a lot.'

'Does she have a car?'

'No, she said she didn't want to drive in the city.'

'Then how does she get out to the Bush Estate to work?'

'The bus. She doesn't have to go out there often. The company promotes *artistic independence*. McCallum doesn't want his staff to feel stifled by working in their offices. We have to go in every couple of weeks for a conference to discuss what we're working on, but as long as we do the work at home and sent it in every night, he's happy.'

'Have you ever heard anything about Bea at work?'

'No. I work in a different department. Although we technically do the same job, we're working on different projects. And we're not allowed to talk to people in other projects.'

'Does Bea have a boyfriend?'

'I wouldn't know. But I did see her out with an older man in the pub one night.'

'Can you describe him?' Harry said.

'Fifties, maybe. Bald. Heavily built.'

'Do you have anywhere you can stay?' he asked. 'If your clothes were upstairs in your house, then they're all gone.'

'I could call HR and see if they'll let me stay here. I'm sure it will be fine. I'll have to go shopping.'

'Bea won't mind you staying?' Alex asked.

'She doesn't have a choice.'

'Does anybody else know you're here?' Harry asked.

'Not that I'm aware of.'

'Just be aware of your surroundings, and don't go near your house. The fire investigators are all over it.'

His phone rang. He spoke to the caller before hanging up.

'We have to go. If you need me at short notice, please don't hesitate to call me.' He handed Maggie a card.

'Thank you.'

Back down in the car park, Harry started up the Honda. 'That was Kate Murphy at the mortuary. There's something she wants to show us.'

TWELVE

The mortuary had a distinct quiet air about it as Harry and Alex entered through the back door. They were met by Angie Patterson, who smiled when she saw Harry.

'Dr Murphy is waiting for you upstairs in the PM suite.'

'Thanks, Angie.'

'When I'm not on call, maybe we could all go out for a Chinese and something to drink?' she said, smiling.

'Of course. You up for that?' he said to Alex.

'I suppose.'

'Her enthusiasm knows no bounds. But yes, I'm up for it.'

They went upstairs in the lift and Kate Murphy was waiting for them. 'Hello, Harry.'

'Morning, Doc,' he replied, looking at his watch and seeing it was well after lunchtime. 'Well, it was morning when I got up.'

'There's something very odd going on,' Kate said, cutting to the chase.

'What's wrong?'

'You'd better come into our small conference room. I have something to show you.'

Inside, the room was functional, with a rectangular table and chairs round it, and a TV sitting on a cabinet at one end.

'God knows how we're going to explain this one away, but here we go. Take a seat. You're going to need it.'

They all sat, Kate near the front with the remote control. She pointed it at the screen and it came to life.

'Before I start the show, let me fill you in. Angie was on call, and she got the call to go to a house fire in Baberton early this morning. When she got there, the force doctor on duty was there and he said he had pronounced the death. The woman was life extinct. The strange thing was, he had already put her in the body bag. He helped lift her into the van. Then Angie brought her here and put her right into the fridge. The other assistants would have taken her out first thing Monday morning and prepared her for the post-mortem. But then this happened. Angie went out on another call. Just watch.'

There were cameras inside the loading area and all around the lower level of the mortuary. They saw the Judas door open and two men walk in. Kate pressed *pause* and the image froze.

'The one on the right is the force doctor who pronounced

our victim at the scene. He was there when Angie turned up. Do either of you recognise him?'

'No. It's old Doc Wilson who's one of the duty doctors. That man isn't one of ours that I know of,' Harry said.

'I haven't seen him either,' Alex said.

'He wasn't worried about hiding his identity,' Kate said. 'The CCTV cameras had been put out of action before these men came to the mortuary. All the council ones. They're all on a circuit. They were knocked out. However, last year, at Halloween, somebody broke in to steal a body, though they abandoned the idea after gaining entry. The council put up an independent CCTV system that doesn't run on Wi-Fi or Bluetooth or whatever. We have cameras all over the place now. The feed goes right into a recorder. I'm assuming they thought they'd knocked out all the cameras, but they hadn't, obviously.'

She started playing the tape again. The men walked through to the refrigeration area and switched the lights on. Then one of them pulled open the drawer that the fire victim was in. He unzipped the bag and opened it up. They all clearly saw the face of the victim. The men had a look inside before zipping it back up again. Then they took an end each and carried the bag outside and put it into the back of a black van.

'We know the victim,' Harry said. 'Her name is Bea Anderson.'

'That's strange,' said Kate. 'That's not what her ID says.'

'What ID?'

'Her warrant card. And this is where it gets weird and it's why I called you personally. The first officer on the scene of the fire got a look at the warrant card before putting it back in her pocket. He thought you knew about it when you turned up at the fire. But when Angie logged her in, there was no ID on her.'

'What? What did the warrant card say?'

Kate looked at Alex. 'DS Alexis Maxwell.'

THIRTEEN

'And you've no idea why she would have your ID on her?' Harry said, pulling the car into the spot outside the front door of McCallum Technology.

'For the ninety-ninth time, I do not know why Bea had a warrant card in my name. I still have mine on me.'

'What happens when I ask for the hundredth time?'

'Go ahead and pull the trigger on that one, find out for yourself.'

'I'll wait till there's some distance between us. Maybe I'll call and ask you.'

'Considering I'm going to be staying at your place again tonight, that would be very wise.'

He locked the car and shrugged into his overcoat as the wind whipped across the open parkland. 'Seriously though, somebody seems to know a lot about you. They know where you live. They know your name and rank.'

'I thought there was something dodgy about Bea. Then when Maggie Carlton told us this morning that she'd fallen asleep and was out for the count until this morning, it crossed my mind that Bea had slipped Maggie something.'

'So Maggie wouldn't see or hear anything.' Harry shook his head. He'd known men who had done that on a night out with the roofies, but this was different.

Inside, they went through the rigmarole of getting into the building to speak with somebody. And once again James McCallum appeared in his wheelchair, as if by magic, Max Blue by his side.

'You must like this place,' McCallum said with a smile.

'I've been to worse places,' Harry said.

'My front-end staff tell me you're looking for information on a certain member of staff. Unfortunately, HR don't work at the weekend.'

'You don't seem to mind putting the hours in,' Alex said to him.

'I live on the premises. In a house just along from here. With my staff. Max lives here too, but in his own place.'

'And who do we have here?' a blonde woman said, approaching them.

'Chief Inspector McNeil, may I introduce my wife, Melissa McCallum.'

Harry shook hands with her and introduced Alex.

'What can we help you with today?' Melissa asked. 'Are we in trouble?'

'Have you done something wrong?'

Melissa grinned. 'I don't believe we have.'

'Then I won't be slapping the cuffs on today. But we need some information about an employee of yours.'

'What's the name?'

'Bea Anderson.'

'The name doesn't ring a bell, but I can certainly find out what you need. We have plenty of staff working today. Not HR, but I'm sure we can find somebody. Max? Why don't you help me while my husband entertains Police Scotland's finest?'

'Jolly good idea!' McCallum said. 'I was going over to the track. You can come and watch.' He manoeuvred his wheelchair round a series of corners, Harry and Alex following him while Melissa and Max made their way upstairs.

'Have you done any research on self-driving cars, Harry?' McCallum said. 'You don't mind me calling you Harry, do you?'

'That's fine. And no, I haven't done any research.'

'It's a fascinating subject. May I ask, do either of you have children?'

'I have a son.'

'I don't have any yet,' Alex said, and Harry thought he detected a hint of regret in her voice. He wondered if she was thinking about her fiancé and what could have been if he had kept it in his pants instead of messing about on her. Maybe she would have had children by now.

They reached a back door and went through a security area with guards. Then they could see the disability-adapted van waiting for McCallum. He drove his wheelchair in through the side door and motioned for them to follow him. There were smaller seats, which they sat on, and the driver climbed in behind the wheel.

'Harry, how old is your son?' McCallum asked.

'Just turned sixteen.'

'And keen to get behind the wheel of a car, no doubt?'

'He can't wait.'

The van took off slowly, left the private car park round the back of the house and drove along a one-way road with hedges bordering it. There were new buildings peeking up above the hedges.

'I was like that. All gung-ho, couldn't wait to go speeding around with my friends, showing off. And I did. But that's not how I ended up in a wheelchair. Oh no, that one wasn't my fault at all.'

They drove into an open area with a lot more vehicles around. The mention of McCallum in his wheelchair had killed the conversation for a moment.

'You would want your son to be as safe as possible, Harry, yes?' McCallum said as the van stopped.

'Of course.'

'And one day he will be. Along with the rest of humanity.

Oh, don't get me wrong, it's not going to happen tomorrow, but it is coming. Look at the technology from ten years ago. It was utter garbage. Yes, we put men on the moon fifty years ago, but even a luxury car has more computing power than those rockets. It's just a matter of harnessing the new technology in the right way, and we here at McCallum Technology have harnessed that power. And it's not a case of Icarus flying too close to the sun, I can assure you. But come, let me show you rather than tell you.'

The driver had lowered the ramp and McCallum drove himself down, expertly guiding the wheelchair. Harry and Alex followed as McCallum crossed to a small hangar. The driver stuck with him and Harry suspected the man was more than just a driver – probably an expert in taking out somebody's eyeball with a thumb should anybody get close to the boss.

'What do you see there, Harry?' McCallum asked, gesturing to several people carriers parked outside the hangar.

'Some cars.'

'Exactly. Some ordinary-looking cars, would you say?'

'I would.'

McCallum pulled up the collar on his coat. 'Come on, let's step into the office.'

The office was a modern building with a ramp at the front. Inside, it was warm and clean, just how Harry expected it would be.

McCallum turned to them. 'You see those new offices we

just passed? That's where the real brains of the operation are. We have a new building behind Bush House where a lot of our computer engineering goes on, but then their work is sent into those offices and more nerds work on the ideas. Then it goes to the underground lab that I told you about yesterday. Then that work is forwarded to here. The next step? Out on the road. But watch.'

He led them through to a suite where banks of monitors were attached to a wall.

'Larry! Let's get this show on the road,' McCallum shouted to a man in a lab coat.

'Yes, sir.'

McCallum nudged Harry in the leg. 'Keep your eye on the eighty-five-inch screen in the middle.'

The image showed a view out of one of the people carriers.

'Have you seen those American cars on YouTube, Harry?' McCallum asked. 'The self-driving ones, I mean.'

'Can't say I have.'

'They have these stupid things sitting on the roof of the cars. The brains of the operation. What we've done here is scaled things down a bit. No added modifications like that, no big boxes on the roof. No, we've gone a step ahead of that.'

'Several steps ahead,' said Larry, the lab man, looking at the boss like he thought McCallum was going to argue with him.

'Several steps. I stand corrected. You wouldn't think I was

the one who was responsible for giving them a job. See how they treat me? Contradict me at every turn, show me little respect.'

'No respect,' Larry interrupted.

'See? If Larry wasn't so good at his job, I'd...'

Harry stared at McCallum, waiting to see what was going to come out of his mouth next.

'...fire his arse out the door.' McCallum pointed to the screen. 'Now watch.'

There was a camera inside the car, facing out, as though a GoPro was attached to the driver's head.

'This is a demonstration we did a few months ago. To compare with what we have now.'

The people carrier was driving on a road leading through trees.

'That's a private test track. It's not a public road, so don't worry.' McCallum sat back in his chair, a smile on his face as he anticipated what was going to happen next.

The car was getting up to speed, the canopy of trees overhead putting the road into shadow. The speed increased to fifty miles per hour. The road disappeared into a right-hand turn and the car was slowing down when a big four-by-four came around on the people carrier's side of the road. At high speed.

Suddenly, it was right in front of the vehicle and it hit it head on. There was an explosion of glass, the airbags erupted and there was a sensation of the back of the car being lifted up into the air while pieces of the interior flew about unhindered.

'The big SUV was going at seventy miles an hour. The driver didn't have his seatbelt on and he died at the scene. The driver of the people carrier was doing less than the speed limit, but despite the driver having his belt on, he was severely injured.'

Harry looked at McCallum and saw a tear running out of one eye and realised he had been describing his own crash.

'The driver of the people carrier was left handicapped for the rest of his life, while his young son and wife were both killed.'

'This is a recreation of that crash?' Alex said.

'It is. When we created the tracks, both the open ones and the forest ones, I wanted the part of that road recreated down to the last detail, and the engineers made it happen. My own accident happened down in England. The man who died had fought with his girlfriend and had been drinking. He was five times over the limit. Later on, his girlfriend said that he'd left saying he was going to kill somebody. That somebody was himself, and my family.'

'I'm sorry to hear that,' Alex said.

McCallum wiped the tear away and smiled at her. 'Don't be. A lot of good has come out of it. I put my heart and soul into working on this new technology and now I have a lot of good, clever people working for me. Except Larry. He's a cheeky bugger.'

Larry turned and gave McCallum a thumbs-up.

'But let me show you the difference now.' He nodded to Larry, who tapped a man on the shoulder, somebody who was sitting down at the consoles. There were other people next to him and it was like being privy to a space launch. Harry hoped it wouldn't be a case of, *Houston, we have a problem.*

The view was now out of the windscreen of one of the people carriers that had been sitting outside the hangar. It moved slowly along the track and then it got up to speed just as it entered the forest section. It was obeying the speed limit and keeping on its own side of the road. After a few minutes, it approached the spot where the accident had happened. Then they saw the lights of an oncoming people carrier and Harry thought they were going to crash again, but the vehicle sailed on by without any hint of a problem.

'Both of those cars are driving themselves. There's nobody behind the wheel. There are people in them, checking diagnostics and the like, but the cars are thinking for themselves. If it had been a self-driving vehicle that had come round the corner that night, my wife and son would still be here.'

'It's impressive,' Harry said without much conviction.

'I'm sure you've seen the news stories where those self-driving cars have crashed and people have died?'

'I have indeed.'

'People wonder why self-driving cars are involved in crashes. The answer is simple: people don't obey the rules of the road, but the self-driving cars do. For example, you might have a self-driving car stop at a stop sign, but the person behind wasn't intending to, and he's expecting the car in front to slide on through, but it doesn't, and the car in front ends up getting back-ended.

'That won't happen with our technology. You see, not only are we building the technology to be fitted into every new car, but we're building units that will be retrofitted to any car that has a computer in it. I'll be lobbying the government to have all cars fitted as a matter of law. Nobody else has to die on the roads. Of course, they will, until our technology hits every car.'

'That's powerful stuff,' Alex said. 'Can you imagine all the accidents that wouldn't happen every year?'

'Yes, I can. No accidents on the roads means that we're also freeing up time for the ambulance services and the hospitals. The government will be saving a fortune on the NHS if they adopt our technology.'

'You just have to convince them to use it, right?' Harry said.

'Yes, we do. We've had representatives come here and see it for themselves, and so far they've been impressed.'

'Not everybody's going to be convinced,' Alex said.

'People are sceptical about everything. Think back fifty years. Well, I know we can't because I'm sure you're not even thirty, but once upon a time, VHS was thrust upon us, then the CD and then digital music. Computers used to cost a fortune, but now every child has one in his or her hand every day. The mobile phone. And laptops, and iPads. The list goes on. Artificial intelligence is coming for us, and those of us who aren't at the front trying to harness it will be left on the floor. By the time young kids today grow up, they will be used to the new technology, so self-driving cars won't be so far-fetched for them.'

'What other kind of AI do you research?' Alex asked.

'Sorry, I can't talk about that. It's for the government, so it's classified.'

'Fair enough.'

On the screen, two people carriers were driving at high speed towards each other, but before they even got close, both vehicles slowed down and stopped.

'That's a scenario where there's traffic following the other car and they're both talking to each other. The one on the wrong side of the road is an older vehicle that's been retro-fitted with the new computers. It was still able to talk to the new vehicle, and both vehicles knew what was going on in a matter of seconds and did something to prevent a crash.'

McCallum was smiling again, then the smile slipped a little bit as his mind transported him back to the night his family were killed.

'How long before we actually see these vehicles on the roads?' Harry asked.

'Five years. Legislation moves at a snail's pace, but we're heading in the right direction, and the technology is getting tweaked every day. In another five years, the cars you see today will be the VHS of cars and the CDs will be taking over.'

'What about digital?' Alex said, smiling.

'The world won't be ready for digital in five years. Maybe ten, but by then we'll be so far advanced.'

They all turned to see McCallum's wife walking towards them. 'He's been showing you his toys, I take it?' Melissa said, smiling at them.

'He has indeed,' Harry said.

'Anyway, I asked somebody to do some checking, and it turns out that nobody called Bea Anderson works here.'

'She said she worked from home but was employed by the company.'

'Sorry. Nobody by that name has *ever* worked here.'

FOURTEEN

The four-piece band were the typical private club quartet, doing numbers that would appeal to everybody, except maybe those of the younger generation who were into acid house, or whatever it was called.

'Same again?' he said to Alex.

'I'll get them, Harry. We don't want the regulars to think you've brought some floozy here to show her off.'

'That ship already sailed. I saw one of the committee members giving you the eye earlier.'

'He was astounded to see you with such a beautiful woman.' She smiled at him.

'He's got cataracts, but whatever keeps you off the bridge.'

She nudged him and went up to the bar.

'Harry! How lovely to see you!' a female voice said from

behind him. 'Bowling season might be over, but socialising on a Saturday night certainly isn't.'

He turned to see one of the bowling club's committee members, a woman in her late fifties who was still struggling to come to terms with turning forty, if her short dress was anything to go by.

'Rena. I haven't seen you for ages.'

'Not so much since you and Vanessa split. In fact, we've seen more of her now that she has a new…friend.'

'Boyfriend, Rena. I know all about him.'

Rena laughed and sat down beside him. 'Is that what she told you?'

'I saw him for myself just last night.'

'Well, unless they've accelerated their relationship, I was led to believe that he's just a friend of hers. And I should know, being the gossipy old cow that I am.'

Harry couldn't help but laugh. 'Hardly old, Rena.'

She guffawed and gently slapped his arm. 'Trust me, if she's pretending to have a boyfriend, then she's playing games with you. But sticking with the nosy cow theme, I haven't seen that young lady with you before.'

'She's my colleague, nothing more. DS Alex Maxwell.'

'She seems nice.'

'She is, but I don't want you talking to her and spoiling the illusion about me.'

'She's not your next conquest then?' Rena said with a grin.

'We're just friends.'

'Friends with benefits. You can tell old Rena, Harry. Go on, make my day, spill the juicy gossip.'

'Well, I heard that Waitrose round the corner is going to put the price of beans up, but I can't confirm it.'

'Oh, you're such a wicked boy. Wait till I see your mother next.'

'Seriously, Alex and I are just colleagues.'

'That's why you're in the bowling club with her on a Saturday night? You've got a long way to go before you can pull the wool over Rena's eyes. But enjoy yourself. Life's too short. Look at me: my Stu's been gone two years now and do you think I've had a bite?'

'The dating game can be dangerous, Rena.'

'Not if you go out with a copper.'

'If I didn't know you better, I'd think you were hitting on me.'

'Oh, you damn well know I'm hitting on you, Harry McNeil. If I was twenty years younger, we could get tangled up in your duvet, but at my age, I'd settle for wrinkling the sheets a bit.' She laughed again. 'But here's some advice from an old bint who's been round the block a few times: don't let any woman get under your skin. Especially Vanessa. And by God, if I hear her badmouthing you in here, then her arse will be barred before the door bangs it on her way out.'

He squeezed her hand. 'I'm glad I have you in my corner.'

'Hello,' Alex said, coming back with the drinks.

Harry made the introductions.

Rena stood up. 'Don't worry, honey, we weren't about to start snogging. Me and Harry go way back.'

Alex smiled. 'Don't let me stop you. Harry and I just work with each other.'

'Keep an eye on him, doll. His last one was into playing mind games, and that's not something I find acceptable.' Rena stood taller than Alex, and when she wasn't smiling, she presented a formidable force.

'I'll certainly look out for him.'

'Just remember, Vanessa has some friends in here too, people who will smile at your face and stab you in the back, Harry. I'll bet one of them has already been on the phone to her about you being in here.'

'Thanks, Rena. I'll bear that in mind.'

'Good. Now where's old Bill? He promised me a dance and I think he's avoiding me.' Rena looked around. 'No, there he is. Another few Bells and I'm sure he'll be up for buying me a fish supper. Catch you later, Harry. Good meeting you, Alex.'

'Likewise.'

They watched Rena make her way over to an older man who was smiling as she approached.

'I hope he doesn't care if his duvet gets shredded tonight,' Harry said.

Alex looked puzzled.

'Never mind. What was it you were saying before you

went to the bar?' He raised his glass in a salute and they clinked glasses.

'I think Bea Anderson was connected to the break-in at my house somehow. I mean, she was there when I said I was taking the computer home, she had a warrant card on her with my name on it and now she's turned up dead.'

'She lived with Fiona Carlton, who had a flash drive in her shoe with information on it that could have been connected to the schematics on the computer they wanted. It's like they were living in the same flat and Bea wanted what Fiona had, but she didn't know exactly where it was or how to get it.'

'I want a background check done first thing on Monday morning. Give the new lassie something to do. What's her name again?'

'Eve Bell,' Harry said.

'Aye. Eve Bell. Let's see what she's made of.'

'I'd like Simon Gregg to check out the CCTV near the canal basin.'

Alex was looking at the front door of the club. 'Isn't that what's-her-name?' she said.

'Who?'

'Her nibs.'

'Again, who are you talking about?' He didn't turn his head in the direction that Alex was looking, but his heart started beating a little faster. He knew damn well who she was talking about. He lifted the pint glass to his lips and turned his head slowly. *Shite.* Vanessa, Queen of the Darkness, was walking in with a friend of hers. Not her boyfriend, or fake boyfriend, whoever the hell he was, but some busty blonde with a laugh that would strip wallpaper.

'Christ. Drink up, we're leaving,' he said and started to chug his pint.

'Will you calm down? She's already playing head games with you, so why don't you play her at her own game?'

'How do I do that? Dance with you on a table?'

'No, but you could sit here and smile and show her that it's none of her business, you being here with a colleague. Fuck her, Harry, I'm not being intimidated.'

'You know what? I'm doing nothing wrong. Let her look.'

Suddenly, Rena was at his shoulder again. 'Just give the signal, Harry, and I'll rip her a new arsehole. People like you in here, but nobody would be lining up to urinate on Vanessa if she spontaneously combusted.' She smiled at Alex. 'You look after him, honey. Don't let Miss Butter-Wouldn't-Melt-in-My-Mouth there play with him.'

'Way ahead of you there, Rena.'

Rena smiled and patted Harry on the shoulder. 'She's a keeper, Harry.'

'She's just…' he started to say, but Rena was walking away.

'Just what?' Alex said, smiling.

'You're enjoying this, aren't you?'

'Immensely.'

Harry watched as Vanessa and her friend got a drink and squeezed in at a table on the other side of the room. *Fuck it,* he thought and held out his hand to Alex.

'You want to dance?'

'I thought you'd never ask.'

FIFTEEN

'Never again,' Harry said, standing at the kitchen sink and washing down a couple of pills he'd found in the cupboard, hoping they were aspirin and not some leftover birth control pills. He'd put his dressing gown on and was leaning on the kitchen counter when Alex appeared.

'Good morning.' She smiled at him as she put the kettle on.

'What in the name of God happened last night?'

'First of all, you were adding a chaser to every pint you had. I mildly suggested you might want to slow down, but your reply went along the lines of, *Vanessa can go fuck herself*. Then you put your arm around my shoulders to steady yourself just before you puked your load onto a neighbour's hedge.'

'No. Tell me you're yanking my chain.'

She laughed again. 'There's no chain-yanking going on, I can assure you. But let me finish. You came upstairs and wanted to crack open a bottle of wine, but I talked you out of it. My dad always warned against mixing the grapes with the hops. Or something like that. But you get the idea: no wine. Then you started falling about the place and yes, I did take your trousers off to get you into bed.'

He started to say something, but she held up a hand. 'I'm not finished. I meant 'getting you into bed' in the literal sense, and don't worry, I've seen a grown man in his skids before.'

'Christ. Is my face red? It feels like it's on fire.'

'Then I put your covers on you, and just so there's no ambiguity, no, we did not do anything we shouldn't have done last night. Your reputation remains intact. Mine, however, might be in tatters. Vanessa was standing looking at you as we crossed the road.'

'How come my skids were on backwards when I woke up then?' He finished the glass of water.

'Harry, what you do in the privacy of your own room is your business.'

'Seriously, thanks for seeing me home. God knows what I was thinking.'

'You were trying to metaphorically poke Vanessa in the eye.'

'I need a shower.'

'I'll do you a coffee when you get out. I know how you like it. You want some breakfast?'

He waved as he left the kitchen. When he came back, showered and dressed, she made his coffee and made herself another one.

'I hope my snoring didn't interrupt your sleep,' he said.

'It didn't. The man outside with the chainsaw running all night woke me up once or twice.'

'I've been known to snore on the odd occasion.'

She laughed. 'I'm just kidding. Those G&Ts put me out like a light. Of course, I drank within my limitations and I feel fine this morning.'

Harry's mobile phone rang and he thought it might be 'that woman from across the road', as Alex described Vanessa now. It wasn't. He listened to the caller before hanging up.

'As if my head isn't hurting enough.'

'What's wrong?'

'That was control. We're needed down at the mortuary. Somebody broke in again.'

Alex pulled in behind the patrol cars and the forensics van. There were other cars in the small car park.

'This is probably the busiest Sunday they've seen in a long time,' Harry said as they made their way inside.

'You weren't here a couple of Christmases ago,' Kate Murphy said, leading them through to the refrigeration room.

'We were full to overflowing. We had to wrap them up and stack them on the floor.'

'Typhoid Mary in town that year?' Harry said.

'It was bitterly cold and a lot of homeless people died.'

'Gotcha.'

He excused himself for a moment and found the drinking fountain outside the bathroom door. The door opened and DC Simon Gregg came out. Harry jumped.

'Christ, I thought it was one of them come back from the dead.'

'Sorry, boss,' Gregg said, grinning. 'Were you out on the lash last night? Your eyes are all red.'

'No, I was just crying at the thought of seeing you on a Sunday.'

'They say the hair of the dog is good for when you've been "crying".' He ended the sentence with air quotes.

'Just show me what's been happening here, Gregg.'

'This way.' He led Harry back to the fridges, where Kate Murphy was standing with Alex and Angie Patterson.

'Kate was just saying how they had to be professionals,' Alex said. 'The people who broke in here. They left no marks on the door. The CCTV system was disabled again.'

'And no doubt they were driving a big black car.' Harry turned to Gregg. 'See what businesses near here have CCTV cameras outside. Take what help you need. The hotel at the foot of St Mary's Street will probably have some.'

'What timeframe are we looking at?' Gregg asked.

Harry looked at Kate.

'Well, Angie was on call and there were two deaths through the night. One person was stabbed and there was a man who was a sudden death. Heart attack, more than likely. Then nothing else. He was logged in here at six thirty a.m. That's when Angie noticed the Judas door was open. She didn't want to come in on her own and she did the right thing, calling treble nine.' Kate looked at Angie. 'That sounds about right, doesn't it?'

'Yes, that's right. The stabbing victim was brought here because he was pronounced dead at the scene, and he was logged in at one-thirty this morning.'

Harry turned to Gregg. 'There you have your five-hour window. Get at it.'

'Sir.'

Harry watched as Gregg walked away, taking one of the uniforms with him.

'That's not all,' Kate said. 'The worst is still to come.'

Harry looked puzzled.

'Both of you come upstairs to the conference room. I'll show you there.'

Once they were settled in the room, Kate started playing the footage. 'The council's CCTV cameras had been fixed, but they cut them off again. Thank goodness we have the extra coverage from the secure system.'

They watched as two men came in. One had a bigger build than the other.

'Looks like a different man this time.'

'Looks like it,' Kate said, 'but watch what they do next.'

All eyes were on the large screen as the two men put on scrubs, then they opened another drawer and pulled out a corpse. The sheet was pulled down to reveal Fiona Carlton's lifeless body. They loaded her onto a trolley and wheeled her to the lift.

Kate played around with the buttons on the remote and then they saw the view from inside the post-mortem room, with the stainless-steel tables sitting in a row. Fiona Carlton was wheeled in and her body was moved on to one of the tables. The sheet was removed entirely. Then one of the men wheeled over a stainless-steel stand that had surgical tools on it. He lifted a scalpel and, while the bigger man watched, he expertly cut into the corpse. The man reached his hands into the stomach and rummaged around, like a medical student who hadn't been paying attention.

'Jesus,' Alex said.

After a few minutes, he was finished and he walked over to a sink to wash his hands before taking his gloves off. Then they walked out and the cameras followed them downstairs. They took off their scrubs, left them on the floor and walked out.

The outside view showed them getting into a black Range Rover.

'Good God,' Harry said.

'I know. It's horrific,' Kate said. 'They just left Fiona where she was, on the table.'

'That man. We've seen him before, driving that big car.' He looked at Alex. 'And at the pub.'

'You're right, that *is* him. One of the men who attacked us Friday night at my house.'

'They steal a corpse first, then come back for a DIY post-mortem. What the hell are they doing?' Kate asked.

'And where have they hidden the corpse they stole?'

SIXTEEN

'Your head feeling any better?' Alex asked as she drove them up to Fountainbridge.

'It's starting to feel like it's attached to my neck now.'

'I hadn't realised what a drinking machine you are,' she said, pulling into the underground car park at Lower Gilmore Place. 'And you're sure you actually spoke to Maggie Carlton on the phone and hadn't dialled Santa's hotline by mistake?'

He looked at her. 'I have used a mobile phone before, you know.'

'Well, at least we know what list you'll be on when you finally do get around to calling Santa.'

Upstairs, Maggie Carlton opened the door. She looked like she hadn't slept much, and Harry wondered if the young woman now kept a cricket bat beside her bed.

'Have you found Fiona's killer?' she asked.

'No, we haven't. We were hoping you might have some more information on Bea.'

They sat down, Harry glad to get the weight off his feet. Normally, he'd still be in bed, ready to go out for a quick pint with Vanessa at lunchtime. He mentally kicked himself for even thinking her name.

'I'm not sure I have anything to add.' Maggie was sitting on a chair with her legs pulled up and she put her arms round her knees.

'How long had Bea lived here?' Alex asked.

'I already told you, I'm not sure. Fiona lived with me in my house. A couple of months ago, she came to live here.'

Harry nodded. '*Why* did Fiona move here?'

Maggie looked at the floor. Said nothing.

'Was that her stuff you were burning in your back garden?'

Maggie looked at him. 'Not exactly. It was just some rubbish she'd left behind. But we'd had an argument before she left.'

'That must have been hard for you, Fiona being your sister,' Alex said.

'It was. We were arguing over this guy she insisted was just a friend, but I didn't believe her. I wanted her to stay with me. I thought it would be safer. But she insisted on moving out. She was here first, then Bea moved in. Which could have happened at any time. These flats are like dorm rooms; you can have somebody come stay with you at any time. Of the same sex, of course. That's when Bea showed up.'

'What about Fiona's boyfriend?' Harry said. 'Didn't she want to move in with him?'

'She told me she didn't have a boyfriend, that he was just a guy from work.'

'Did you know this guy?'

Maggie nodded. 'Dave Pierce. He's nice. He works as a technician at McCallum and he was just another guy at the office, until Fiona started spending more time with him.'

'You didn't know Bea all that well, but you did meet her,' Alex said. 'What was she like to talk to? Did she give you any background about herself?'

'No. It was just general chit-chat. She was new to McCallum Technology. She just started hanging out with Fiona a few months ago, and she worked in a different department from mine.'

'Was there anybody there who Bea was particularly friendly with?' Harry asked.

'I don't really know. I never actually saw her in the building, but I didn't like her much. You know how you take an instant dislike to somebody?'

'Yes,' Alex said. Harry knew she was thinking of Vanessa.

'It was like that. She was sort of cold towards me. I didn't care. It wasn't as if we were going to hang out in the pub together.'

'Has this friend of Fiona's got an address we can have?'

'I don't know where he lives. I don't know much about him at all.'

'Did he ever come round here when you were here?'

'Once, I think. Months ago.'

'Was Bea here at the time?'

'Not that I remember.'

Harry looked at the woman. He had sat across from police officers he had been investigating and he could tell when they were lying. He'd seen it so many times that he knew exactly how to read their body language and facial expressions.

And he knew Maggie Carlton was lying to them right now. About what, he didn't know.

But he would find out.

In the car park, Harry put a finger to his lips briefly.

Alex was still on driving duty. Not that he trusted her driving more than his own, but he didn't want an awkward conversation with a traffic cop in which he told him to bog off and refused to give his licence or take a breathalyser. He wasn't one for drinking and driving, and he wasn't about to start now, so he let Alex drive him home.

'Maggie Carlton is up to something,' he said. 'She knows something, but she isn't sharing it with us.'

'We'll have to go and talk to Dave Pierce tomorrow. I'll call McCallum Technology and see about getting his address.'

They got back to Harry's flat, and when he got inside, he had a strange feeling. Something wasn't quite right.

And then he realised what was wrong when he walked into the living room.

Alex's MacBook Pro was sitting on his dining table.

SEVENTEEN

Monday morning, Harry made sure he was up before Alex. He hadn't been able to sleep much for wondering how they'd got into his flat. Then again, he'd known sneaky little bastards who could circumvent the most capable of security systems, never mind a front door lock.

Nevertheless, he'd jammed a chair under the front door handle.

'I thought I'd do some research on my iPad last night,' he said to Alex as she poured some cereal.

'Really? And what were you researching? What wood makes the best chair for shoving under a door handle?'

'You might mock, but it kept us safe, didn't it?'

'I concede your point. But seriously, they have some damn gall coming in here with my old computer. They're just trying to show us that they know where you live and they can get in any time.'

'What we need to know is, *why*? Yes, we know there's something on the flash drive they want, but why break in here to return the computer? Why not just dump it?'

'As I said, it's a message. They're showing their superiority and no doubt trying to scare us into the bargain. Maybe I should go round to my place and see if they've been in there again.'

'If we do go there, we go in force. I'll have a couple of patrols with us.'

She sat down at the table opposite him. 'What were you researching?'

'Now that you've got it out of your system, I'll tell you. Artificial intelligence is scary. I have to ask myself, why would we want to build things that will be more intelligent than us? To build machines that will have the power to think independently of us, and then one day take over? The people who do this stuff need to be stopped. It's all ego, like with James McCallum. Clearly, he wants to build a self-driving car that won't allow accidents to happen.'

'Did you google him?'

'I did, and what I read scares me.'

'Okay. Is he part of some mafia group?'

'You could say that,' Harry said, 'the AI mafia. The power they're going to wield is tremendous. The Americans want to get self-driving cars on the road so badly. When you think about it, all the new technology in new cars is leading up to this. Like lane-keep assist, cars that will brake for you, read speed signs, spot pedestrians. I personally don't think they will perfect it any time soon, but they're close. And what McCallum is doing is going one step further.'

'What do you mean?'

'Right now, the problem is mixing old cars with the new self-driving ones. Everything will be fine when we take driving out of the hands of the humans. And McCallum saw this; that's why he's making units that can be retrofitted to older cars. Once he corners that market, he'll be laughing all the way to the bank.'

'I think you're right,' Alex said. 'It's all a pissing contest with these rich people. But I agree, we're still a long way off having self-driving cars and proper electric cars. The battery technology just isn't up to speed yet. If it was, we'd all be driving about in electric cars, and we'd go into a station to charge up and it would take no longer than it does to fill a petrol tank just now. And then get a thousand-mile range.'

'I think they have the technology already, but the big oil companies have been suppressing it for years. They buy up the patents and file them away, just to line their own pockets. And let's face it, when fossil fuels run out, it won't matter, because they'll slowly be phasing in the new technology and it will be in place when the oil runs dry.'

'I think the car manufacturers are in cahoots with the oil companies. Everybody's scared to take them on. Except for people like James McCallum, but even he knows he can't take them on entirely.' Alex felt herself getting fired up. 'The whole oil game was just to screw the public. It had been going on for a very long time, but nobody stood up to them.'

'It still doesn't explain why Bea Anderson was taken out of the mortuary.'

'They're cleaning up behind them?' Alex said.

'I agree.'

Now it was gone ten and the whole team was gathered in the office.

Harry was on his third cup of coffee, despite knowing he'd be visiting the big boys' room more frequently later on.

'Just a recap,' he said, sitting on the corner of a desk. He'd taken his jacket off as the old building was pumping out a fair bit of heat. 'Fiona Carlton was taken out of the Union Canal. She'd been hit over the head with something and stabbed repeatedly. Her sister, Maggie Carlton, had her house set on fire. The woman who Fiona shared a flat with was found dead in Maggie's house. Somebody went to the mortuary and stole her corpse. The following day, they broke in again and did a rough post-mortem on Fiona. They opened her up. And I have no doubt they were looking for the flash drive that was in her shoe. Maybe they thought she'd swallowed it before she died. Now, what have we got? Eve?'

'We went out yesterday and got some CCTV footage from around the time the woman on the houseboat heard screams. Two hours before and after. And we got lucky with the hotel on Fountainbridge. I'll show you.'

She was sitting at her desk in front of a monitor and they crowded round. They watched as a man ran down the lane from the canal, crossed over the road and went into the hotel. Fiona Carlton was right behind him and she too went into the hotel. Fifteen minutes later, she came back out.

'We lose her going up the lane again,' Eve said. 'Looking at the timeframe, this wouldn't be long before she was murdered.'

'What about the man?' asked Harry. 'Did you get any images from him in the hotel?'

'Yes. More than that, though, we got him coming back out. He had booked a room for one night but didn't stay in it. As soon as Fiona left, he checked out. But you'll see him coming out in a minute.'

Harry looked at the face and thought he recognised it. He went through the photos on his phone and looked at the ones he'd taken of the framed photographs in Fiona Carlton's living room. The CCTV had got a clear shot of the man's face.

'Print it off. His name's Dave Pierce. He worked with Fiona Carlton. I don't know why they were meeting in a hotel, but I'm willing to bet it wasn't to do the nasty, considering she was only in there for fifteen minutes. Unless he's a quick worker.'

Harry's phone rang and he stepped into his office to take the call.

'Harry, it's Kate from the mortuary. We were going over Fiona Carlton's body, since they violated it, and we took photos of the mark on her head where she was struck. It looks like an eye.'

EIGHTEEN

'What do you think of the new sergeant?' Harry said as Alex drove them back to the Bush Estate. It was damp and miserable, a grey sky threatening to dump its contents on them as they pulled into the car park.

Harry heard a buzzing above them and looked up to the sky. He saw little flashing lights.

'Look, there's a drone,' he said.

Alex turned to look up at it. 'Nothing unusual about those nowadays. Arseholes are always flying them about.'

'It's like it's watching us. Probably McCallum got a bit bored playing with his toy cars and he's moved on to his wee aeroplanes,' Harry said.

Inside, they were shown into a waiting area. And then James McCallum appeared, followed by a woman the detectives hadn't seen before.

'Good morning! And how can I be of help today?' McCallum smiled at them, and Harry couldn't be sure if this was the man's normal personality or whether he'd had too much caffeine that morning.

'We'd like to talk with Dave Pierce, one of your employees.'

'Dave Pierce? I don't know him personally, but we do have a lot of employees. I'll have somebody find him for you. May I ask what it's in connection with?'

'I'm sorry, I can't discuss that. It's a question of privacy.'

'No problem.' The smile stayed fixed. 'Give me five minutes and I'll see what I can do. Let's go and have a coffee while we see if this Mr Pierce is indeed a member of my staff.'

They got in the lift and stepped off at the basement level. The young woman stayed in the lift and it took her away again.

'Denise will do the searching. She has plenty of people working under her. Come on, I want to show you some other stuff. How did you like the cars?'

They were going along a white corridor, approaching a security station.

'They were impressive,' Harry said.

'And you, DS Maxwell?'

'Cars are a means of getting from Point A to Point B.'

'Exactly!' McCallum said, beaming at her. 'And don't we all want to get there safely?'

'Of course we do. I think we need to educate young drivers, though, not rely on computers.'

Harry looked at her like she had just insulted the Queen.

McCallum merely laughed. 'I can sense some scepticism.' They approached the security guards. 'These are police officers. Let us through, please.'

'Yes, sir.'

Two glass doors ahead of them slid open and McCallum wheeled his chair through, followed by the detectives. They made their way down another corridor before turning left, then they were in a lab of sorts, with giant screens and consoles and a crowd of people working.

'This is the lab where we work on large vehicles. It's not just cars that will be self-driving. You may have seen the YouTube video of Mercedes-Benz putting their articulated truck through its paces on a private track? Very impressive. We have our own version. Fitted with computers that interact with not just other cars and vans but with the surroundings. And yes, nowadays cars are fitted with pedestrian detection software and that is the next step in automation, but we take that several steps further.'

He rolled over to a set of large windows and Harry stood beside him. They looked into an arena that must have been the size of ten football fields.

'That's massive,' he said.

'There're train tunnels at both ends. See them?'

'Yes.'

'Two adjacent at either end. The train runs in a loop. We can watch it from here and there are also screens that provide an alternative view.'

McCallum looked over to one of the techs. 'Bring the train in.' Then he turned back to the window and he and Harry looked down.

Alex stood beside Harry. 'Who are those people down there?' she asked.

McCallum was sitting in front of a console and he typed some instructions. The window in front of him became a TV screen and he used a joystick to zoom in.

'Jesus,' Alex said.

'Not quite. They're automatons. More commonly known as robots. We're ninety-nine per cent sure that they're in a safe environment, but it's that one per cent that could make the difference, so we're not using humans just now.'

He zoomed out a bit and they saw the lights of a train coming out of the tunnel. Harry looked over and saw a man sitting in what looked like a gaming chair, a huge console in front of him. The train driver. The screen in front of the man showed a simulated view out of the train window. On another console, a man sat inside a tipper truck.

'Let me switch on the audio, so we can hear things better.' McCallum looked at Alex. 'So you can hear the robots screaming.'

Alex looked at him like he was insane.

'I'm kidding,' he said. 'Listen to the silence.'

They couldn't hear anything but a low hum.

'We have to artificially dial some noise in, just so people can hear the traffic. You wouldn't believe how quiet we've made these electric engines.'

He played around with a few sliders on the console and they started to hear engine noises.

McCallum smiled, obviously enjoying himself. 'People are used to hearing diesel engines, so we fit the trucks with a diesel engine sound. Thankfully, not the emissions, just the noise.'

A tipper truck came into view. Harry turned to look over at the train cab and saw it was in the tunnel. A large speedometer in the top right-hand corner indicated that the train was travelling at forty miles an hour.

The tipper approached a level crossing, drove onto the tracks and stopped.

'We do real-world scenarios here. I've watched trucks getting stuck on level crossings. What if suddenly the tipper lost power for some reason? Now he's on the crossing and the barriers are coming down. The train is going to collide with the truck. Only it isn't.'

They could see a red beacon flashing on the roof of the truck.

'That's it just pointing out its position and letting us know which vehicle is in play. It's more a visual thing for any guests we have watching. The truck is already communicating with the train, through its own Wi-Fi. A box at the side of the barriers is sending out the signal that a train is approaching and the truck has picked up the signal. The truck is talking with the box, telling it that it has a problem and is now blocking the tracks. The box is talking to the train and an emergency procedure has been put in place. The train is now braking. By the time the gates come down, a sweep by the trains onboard sensors is made of the track, it's been calculated that the train will have enough time to stop because of the speed limit on the approach to the crossing. The train knows what the speed limit is, so there's no human input. If a driver is distracted on a normal train, the train can speed up and go way over the speed limit. This system takes the need for humans out of the equation.'

'What if some idiot drives round the barrier?' Alex said.

'As you can see, the barriers cover the whole road. And we're talking about a time when all the idiots will, in effect, be just passengers. The vehicles are making all of the decisions.'

Harry watched the train come out of the tunnel and slow down and stop before it got to the truck.

'One day, nobody will be killed in a vehicle on a level crossing,' said McCallum.

'I can only imagine how much money this will cost,' Alex said.

'The savings will be made by not having to buy fuel. The engines on the train and truck are self-generating electric engines. They don't need recharging stations. They're highly advanced and very expensive, but the cost will come down.

Right now, we obviously have more affordable electric vehicles that need charging, but what you see there is the future.'

'Way in the future, I would imagine,' Harry said.

'Think back twenty years, Chief Inspector; mobile phones were in their infancy. New technology just becoming more widespread. Now think back thirty, forty years. What were mobile phones like back then? Big bricks with a handset on top. Only people with money could have one. Today, how many young people do you know who don't have a phone? And it fits in their pocket! In thirty years, we'll be travelling around in electric cars that will be powering themselves and the greedy oil company execs will be crying into their soup. They've had it their own way for too long, poisoning the planet with their fuels and plastics. The planet can be saved, Harry, but we all need to be on board. And my company will be leading the way.'

'Zero emissions,' Alex said.

'Exactly. But we need the AI to go along with this. Human interaction will need to be at a minimum. Not taken out of the picture entirely, but at a minimum. At McCallum Technology we're staying two steps ahead. The world isn't ready for this technology at the moment, but when they are, we will be at the forefront. Meantime, our self-driving cars are almost ready to be unleashed onto the world, and when we've finished testing the retrofit units, there'll be nothing stopping us. The world will be a safer and cleaner place! And you never know, maybe somebody will invent a plastic bottle that degrades in weeks, not centuries.'

'We can hope,' Harry said, feeling that Alex was about to go on a rant.

'Come on then, let's find that coffee. We have a nice lounge upstairs.' McCallum led them back out.

When they got to the lounge, which was really a canteen with comfortable seats, the assistant came over to them.

'We do have a Dave Pierce who works for us. He was due to be at work right now, but there's no sign of him. He's a no-call, no-show.'

'Really?' McCallum said, clearly annoyed. 'What department does he work in?'

'He's a programmer, sir.'

'That's not good enough. Does he have a habit of doing this?'

'No, sir. First time.'

'Can we have his address?' Harry asked.

'Of course.' McCallum nodded to the woman, who brought out a piece of paper with Pierce's address on it.

'Thank you,' said Harry, and he and Alex stood up. 'Is your wife not around today?'

The question threw McCallum for a second, but he smiled quickly. 'She's in a meeting with some shareholders. Why? Did you want to have a talk with her?'

'Oh, no, I was just wondering. Thank you for your time, Mr McCallum.'

'Please come around any time.'

Outside, the drone was nowhere to be seen.

But Max Blue was standing at a window on the top level of the house. Watching them. He smiled, then turned away.

'That was an eye-opener,' Harry said as Alex drove away in the Honda.

'Boys and their toys, eh? I could see you starting to foam at the mouth.'

'I have to admit, if that stuff becomes reality, it could save a lot of lives. How many times have we read about vehicles being stuck on a level crossing? Not just here but in America. All over the world. And that's not taking into account the environment.'

'I didn't see you as being an environmentalist.'

'It's not that, Alex; it just pisses me off that people with money are ruining the planet that belongs to us all while they're getting even richer. We all need to be more proactive, and I haven't seen a rich man be more proactive when it comes to the environment than McCallum.'

'His business is AI, and if you want my honest opinion, his first consideration isn't the environment. But his machines will be good for the future, which is a good thing.'

'I don't disagree. But let's not lose focus on why we're here in the first place.'

'I know. Dave Pierce might be a killer.'

Alex drove Harry's car onto Bush Loan Road, turning left, and then the car accelerated.

'Whoa there, Stirling Moss.'

'Fuck, Harry, it's not me!' Alex screamed. The car took off faster and she wrestled with the controls. 'My foot's on the fucking brake, but it's not stopping!'

They were on a straight part of the road, but a slight curve to the left was coming up and the car was already doing sixty and getting faster. She guided the car, and then there was a slight curve to the right, and then the A702 main road into Edinburgh was only a few hundred yards ahead.

'Turn the ignition key!' Harry shouted. 'Put it in neutral!'

Alex did both things, and then the car started to slow down and came to a stop right at the T-junction.

'Jesus Christ, what the hell just happened?' Harry said, looking at Alex, who was visibly shaken.

Then they saw the tendril of smoke creeping out from under the bonnet of the car. They both jumped out just as flames started licking out from under it.

They got out of the way, and as Harry took out his phone and made the call, Alex looked up into the air.

And saw the drone watching them before it flew away.

NINETEEN

Dave Pierce was exhausted. Every night now, sleep eluded him. He couldn't concentrate at work.

Especially after what had happened to Fiona.

Two women he knew, both dying in the space of a few months. He didn't like that at all, and it gave him a bad feeling. He was thinking of moving on, starting afresh.

Besides, what was left here for him? Nothing. His girlfriend was dead, he'd started to hate his job and there was no prospect of advancement with McCallum. Things couldn't get any worse, he thought – then the doorbell rang. Things were about to get a *lot* worse.

'Oh, it's you,' he said to the visitor. 'What brings you here?'

'Are you going to leave me standing on your doorstep?'

Pierce stood for a moment, not wanting to let the man in. 'I'm busy.'

'This won't take long.'

'Famous last words.'

'I have something for you.'

'What?'

The man grinned. 'You want to discuss it with me at your front door?'

'I don't know what you're talking about.'

'I think you do.' He held up a flash drive.

'What's on that?'

'Again, walls have ears. Do you really expect me to stand out on your landing and talk about what's been going on?'

Pierce ran his tongue over his lips, which were starting to dry out. 'You'd better come in.'

'That's more like it.'

Pierce closed the door behind them as the man walked up the hall. He'd been here before. Knew the layout of the flat.

'How about a cup of tea?' he said.

'I'm not a café,' Pierce answered, brushing past the man. He went into his little office. It was a box room, which was a fancy way of saying it was a large cupboard with a window.

'Can I have a drink of water? I'm parched.'

'Help yourself. You know where the kitchen is.'

He heard the man go through and then the tap was run for a few seconds. He pressed the on button and waited for his computer to come to life.

The man came back.

Pierce sat down at his computer. 'I'm assuming you want me to plug the flash drive in?'

'That would be helpful. You can see for yourself what's on it.'

Pierce let out a sigh, not making any effort to disguise it. He took the flash drive and plugged it into the tower that sat next to the monitor.

He opened it up and looked at the images. 'What the fuck is this?' he said, and had just started turning round when he felt a blinding pain in his head. Then again on the top of his head. The man tried for a third time, but Pierce dodged it. Then the man grabbed his hair and pulled him off the chair and dragged him kicking and yelling across to his bedroom.

The man threw Pierce roughly onto his bed, then pulled a kitchen knife out of his pocket. It was a steak knife, Pierce realised, just before it was plunged into his chest, over and over.

The man walked back to the box room and retrieved his flash drive.

And calmly walked out.

TWENTY

'You were lucky you could stop the car in time,' the fire commander said as the last of the smoke fizzled out. The day had got colder, but they'd warmed up a little from the flames of the car on fire.

'Bloody thing wouldn't stop,' Harry said.

'It could be an electrical fault. Something burns through and then the brakes don't get the message.'

DI Karen Shiels turned up with Simon Gregg shortly afterwards.

'Jesus, boss, is everything okay?' she asked.

Harry told them what had happened.

She looked shocked. 'I read a news article about something like this happening to a car somewhere in America. Some computer geek was able to hack into a car's computer system and he took it over. He could steer it, do anything he wanted, because he'd hijacked the car's computer system.'

'I don't think my wife's old Honda would have a sophisticated computer system. Nobody could hack into it, I don't think.'

'Unless they put in a retrofit box that brought the car's brain bang up to date,' Alex said.

'Why would anybody do that?'

'Why would somebody kill Fiona Carlton?'

He didn't have that answer. 'Where's the new girl?'

'Back in the office,' said Karen. 'She's looking over the schematics that were on the flash drive and the computer to see if she can see anything that we missed.'

'Ricky, the tech guy, said he couldn't see anything that sticks out. They both have schematics on them, but if you were to try to fit one thing in with the other, they wouldn't join up.'

Harry pulled up his collar against the chill wind that was coming off the Pentlands. He and Alex went to sit in Karen's car, along with Karen and Gregg, until the breakdown truck came for what was left of Harry's car.

'I hope you didn't have a sentimental attachment to her,' Alex said as they watched the truck and the fire engines pull away.

'It wasn't mine. So no, I don't have any attachment to it.'

'This is just the perfect excuse to get a Beemer like me.'

'I have to admit, I've never had so many beamers since I met you.'

'Now you're just being ridiculous. In front of the DI as well.'

Karen smiled. 'Just wait till he has a sesh with us. I'm sure there will be more than a few beamers that night.'

'And that's just watching me dance.'

Harry sat in the front passenger seat as Karen drove them back into town. Down to Harrison Road, Dave Pierce's address. It was a flat in a tenement, one of the older buildings.

'He was a no-call, no-show at work this morning,' Harry said as they went up one flight to the number they had been given at McCallum Technology.

'This is the man who was running from our victim, so keep your eyes peeled. He might be a fighter with a knife.'

The others took out their extendable batons, like they were part of a circus act.

Harry rang the bell and banged on the door. 'Police! Open up!'

A neighbour across the way opened her door. 'Is everything alright?'

'Have you seen Mr Pierce?' Alex asked her.

'No, I'm sorry. Not since last night, when he was going out. I was coming in. Is there anything I can help you with?'

'Just stand back, ma'am,' Karen said.

Harry nodded to Gregg. 'Get that door in, son. I smell something funny.'

Gregg lifted a leg, but the woman stopped him. 'I have a key, if that helps?'

Gregg stopped with his leg up, and they looked at the woman.

'That would be great,' Harry said, and they watched her scuttle away.

'Nice yoga move,' Alex said.

'It's a kung fu move,' Gregg replied.

'From a cartoon?' Harry said. 'Put your leg down, silly sod.'

The woman came back with the key, and whilst not quite asking if she could stay and watch, she pulled her cardigan tighter round herself, implying that she was in this for the long haul.

'You want me to go in first?' Gregg said.

Harry handed him the key. 'No point in having a dog and barking yourself, is there?'

DC Simon Gregg had never backed down from a fight in his life, but he wasn't stupid. He knew how to fight with his baton and would not hesitate for a moment to use it. Harry let Karen and Alex follow him in while he guarded their backs.

They cleared each room, leaving the bedroom until last.

Gregg didn't hesitate and went in first.

Dave Pierce was waiting for them, or rather his lifeless corpse was. His eyes were looking at them, pleading for help, but it had arrived too late. A kitchen knife was sticking out of his chest, his shirt stained a dark red. His face had marks on it from being beaten with a blunt object.

Each of the detectives had smelled death before, but it was never something they got used to.

Karen Shiels backed out, getting on her radio without being asked to.

'Jesus, that's fuckin boggin',' Gregg said. 'This reminds me of the time I was in uniform and we found an old boy in his house. Been dead for weeks and his two dugs had started eating him. That was fuckin' minging.'

'Well, thanks for that trip down memory lane. Not that I wanted any dinner tonight,' Harry said. 'Two dugs indeed.'

'You should have been there.'

'Why? We have you to tell us all about it in great detail.' He shook his head and turned to Alex. 'This is the third person connected to McCallum Technology who's died.'

'Who's the third one?'

'Bea Anderson.'

'I thought they said she *didn't* work there.'

'They did. I think whoever killed her made a mistake. He was after Maggie Carlton, and he thought he'd killed her, but he'd killed Bea because she was in Maggie's house looking for something.'

'She just happened to be in there while there was a lunatic killer waiting?' She sounded sceptical.

'No, I think the killer turned up to do in Maggie, and Bea

was creeping about in the dark and he *thought* she was Maggie, because Maggie was his target.'

'That means she's still in danger,' Alex said. 'I wonder if there are other people on his list? And why target this small group of friends?'

They left the bedroom to wait on the cavalry turning up. They pulled on nitrile gloves and started looking around the flat. Nothing remarkable stood out. Pierce had kept the place clean. The décor was fresh.

Harry walked into the little box room where the computer desk sat. There was a window high up on the wall giving plenty of light. The computer tower had its power light on, and when Harry nudged the desk with his thigh, the monitor sprang into life.

He sat on the chair, not sure if forensics would have been able to pull anything from the vinyl covering. He rolled the mouse around on its mat and clicked on the icon that showed something was minimised.

Up came an article about James McCallum and his quest to be one of the first companies in the world to run fully autonomous electric vehicles. Harry started reading, scrolling down the article, which wasn't akin to watching paint dry as he had thought it would be. He was familiar with a lot of the stuff mentioned in the article thanks to the demonstrations he'd seen at the Bush facility. But it was mention of something else that caught his eye.

McCallum was working on a military contract. The

article didn't go into exact details, but it said it was widely known that McCallum Technology was working with the British government.

Harry minimised the page and was about to roll the chair back when he noticed the wallpaper Pierce had put on his desktop; it was a photo of Pierce, his face close to a young woman.

Linda Smith.

'Hey, Alex,' he shouted.

She came through to him. 'What you got?'

'Doesn't that look like Linda Smith?' he said, pointing to the screen.

Alex bent a little closer. 'From what I remember of her. There was a similar photo on a sideboard in her dad's house.'

Harry took his phone out and snapped a photo of the screen.

'Let's go for a drive.'

'We don't have a car, remember? Honey the Happy Honda went to that great scrapyard in the sky.'

'I won't dignify that with an answer.'

Karen Shiels came back in.

'Karen, can you and Gregg hold the fort here while Alex and I go and visit somebody? I'll need the car keys. Have Eve Bell come up with another pool car.'

'Sure, no bother.' She handed him the car keys.

'If Gregg asks if you want to hear a story about two wee dugs, taser him.'

TWENTY-ONE

'That was a fucking stupid idea of yours,' Melissa McCallum said, pacing around the hotel room. 'They're police officers for God's sake.'

'Don't wet your panties,' Max Blue said, then immediately regretted it when she flew at him.

'Don't you ever fucking talk to me like that!' she yelled.

'Okay, I'm sorry. I'm just on edge.' He looked into her eyes and saw two deep pits that were a conduit to hell itself.

Her breathing was fast, her body going into *fight* mode without the slightest thought of whether it should go into *flight* mode. Blue knew she had a temper, but lately he'd been seeing it in action.

'Just relax. Everything is going smoothly.'

'That's just the thing. I can't relax. The contract is

coming up for final revision, so the timing is crucial, you know that.'

'Everything's in place.' Blue was starting to feel edgy. 'What about the other sister?' he asked, putting ice into a glass.

'Hopefully, she'll give up the witch hunt soon. Or else we might have to scare her.'

Her mobile phone rang and she fished it out of her pocket. 'Yes?'

'Where are you?'

'I'm shopping. Why?' She knew her voice sounded sharp, but her husband was used to it.

'We have a problem. One of our programmers was found dead. Dave Pierce.'

'How is that our problem?'

'Don't you think they're going to wonder why two of our employees are dead?'

'I couldn't care less.'

'He was the one who was working with Fiona Carlton, Melissa.'

'I don't see what that's got to do with us.'

James McCallum hung up.

'Who was that?' Blue said, not liking the look on her face.

'Dave Pierce was found dead.'

'Jesus. How the hell did that happen?'

She ran a hand through her hair. The hotel room was

starting to feel stifling. 'I don't fucking know. He was a careless bastard. And now he's dead.'

'We just have to keep it together for a little while longer, then everything will fall into place.'

She looked up at him. 'Then we can be together. Just you and me.'

'It's going to work out,' he assured her.

'Just call your people. And make sure they don't get the jitters if they find out about the dead man.'

He would call them alright. And everything he'd said was the truth: it *was* going to be alright.

For him.

TWENTY-TWO

'Look on the bright side, the garage who are doing up your car might get the job done more quickly now that you're carless,' Alex said as she drove the manky old Vauxhall up Harrison Road towards Colinton Road.

'Classic cars take time. They can't be rushed.'

'I said that to see if you would tell me the truth or maintain the fairy tale you have going.'

'I may have to get myself a newer runabout while I'm waiting for the classic to be finished.'

'Daft *and* delusional. Qualities that can only be attributed to senior officers.'

'Which you will not get to be if you keep this pish up.'

'You could always buy an old pool car like this when they sell them.'

'I was thinking about a quality piece of engineering.'

'Like Betty?' she said, grinning.

'Not quite.'

'Tiny the Toyota, more like, eh?' She shook her head in disgust as she turned into the street they were looking for in Glenlockhart.

'Now, try to turn your attention to the murder case we're working instead of some children's show where all the vehicles have names.'

'Aye-aye, Captain.' She parked in front of the bungalow and they walked up to the front door, Harry looking around.

Brian Smith answered the door and scowled when he saw who it was. 'Help you?' he said, leaning heavily on his walking stick. It was one of the metal, NHS-issue kind. Loved by benefits cheats everywhere, Harry thought.

'We'd like a word, Mr Smith, if you don't mind.'

'Unless you've come to tell me you've caught my daughter's killer, I do mind.'

'I don't have any news on that front,' Harry said.

Smith stepped back slightly, as if he were about to shut the front door.

'I wanted to ask you about Dave Pierce.'

Smith stopped. 'What about him?'

'He *was* your daughter's boyfriend, wasn't he?'

He looked between Harry and Alex before answering. 'Yes, he was. He was her boyfriend at the time of her death. Useless bastard if ever I met one.'

'Why do you say that?' Alex said, shrugging her coat up

further. It was clear that Smith wasn't going to invite them in for tea and crumpets.

'He should have been protecting my daughter, that's why!' Smith stopped short of adding 'you silly cow' to the end of his sentence, but the implication was there.

'She was a trained police officer; why would she need protecting?' Harry said, starting to get irritated.

'He was her boyfriend. He was supposed to look after her. I mean, it's not as if I could!' Smith shook his walking stick. 'I could when she was little, but not now. Not after the accident. That's where a father steps aside and lets the boyfriend take over. But that useless sod had his head in a computer all the time. Linda was the fighter, not him.'

'He's dead,' Harry said.

Smith stopped talking and looked at Harry. 'What? How?'

'We're still determining the cause.'

'Oh. I wonder what's happened?'

'Did you keep in touch with him after Linda's death?' Alex asked.

'No. I didn't see him after the funeral. I asked him for some of her stuff, but he kept what was at her house. He wanted to keep it himself.'

'Do you know if he had any problems with anybody?' Harry said.

'Not that I know of, but he was an obnoxious prick.'

Smith looked at his watch. 'As much as I'd like to stay and chat...'

'We'll leave you to it—'

But Smith had already closed the door. They walked back to the car and Harry turned to look at the bungalow.

'I've seen some people mourning, but he takes the biscuit.'

'He's certainly a strange one.'

They drove down the road. 'I'll have to go along and have my tyres blown up,' Alex said.

Harry looked at his watch. As usual, the day had got away from them and darkness was slowly covering the city with its blanket.

'Take that big lump of wood with you.'

Alex raised her eyebrows at him.

'You know I mean Gregg. Just don't go alone.'

'Lump of wood? I thought you would have called him *that lanky streak of piss*.'

'I'm graduating up to that.'

He called Karen Shiels. There wasn't anything more they could do at the crime scene as forensics had turned up and kicked everybody out.

'The mortuary crowd are here and they're waiting to take him away,' Karen added, making it sound like the mortuary crowd were some sort of rabble.

'Get Gregg to go back with Alex to her house. She needs her tyres blown up and he's full of air.'

Silence for a moment.

'No, really, Karen, I need him to go with her, just to watch her back.'

'Okay, sir. I'm at the office. I'll get Gregg to get a pool car.'

'No need, Karen. Alex is going to drop me off, then she'll pick up Gregg.'

'I'll get him to wait outside.'

He hung up and Alex reached his house a few minutes later.

'Don't go talking to any strangers,' he said. 'See you back home.'

'Whatever you say, boss.'

He hated to admit it, but it was good having Alex stay with him for a little while. Not that he got bored, but it was another human to talk to. He had thought about getting a cat, but that meant remembering to feed it. And clean up after it. At least Alex cleaned up after herself.

He watched her pull away and then stood at the door to his stairs, contemplating whether to go round to Vanessa's. He walked to the end of the street, pulling his collar up. He felt much colder after the heat of the car.

He stood by the hedge that bordered the bowling club and looked up Learmonth Place, towards Vanessa's house. He thought about the first time he'd been in there, how warm and inviting it had been. Christ, that was almost two years ago now.

He knew she was playing games with him, but he couldn't completely let go of the good times they'd had. *And still could have had, Harry,* he thought. Why couldn't she have just wanted things to go on the way they were? He started walking up the hill a bit, then stopped. What was he doing? Making things worse for himself. She would think he was weak, and then the games really would start.

He turned back and walked back to his door. Inside, he climbed to the top floor and was about to turn the key in the lock when his neighbour across the way opened her door.

'There you are, Harry,' she said, smiling at him. She was a young woman, not long moved in. 'Your girlfriend asked me to give you this.'

'What is it?'

'A big brown envelope. What does it look like to you?' She laughed as she handed it over to him and stepped back inside her own flat.

'Thanks, Mia.'

She gave a little wave before closing the door all the way. He looked at the envelope; it was sealed and had his name written on the front.

What was Vanessa doing now? Maybe he had been right not to go up to her house.

He let himself in and put some lights on and switched the kettle on, then thought better of it and took a bottle of beer from the fridge. He took his jacket off and hung it up, then sat down on the settee in the living room and tore the envelope open.

Inside was a newspaper article.

He scanned it, looking at the photos. It was about a helicopter that had crashed a few months earlier in the Highlands. It had been foggy, and the helicopter had crashed into some woods, killing everybody on board.

He put the article and envelope down on the coffee table and went out and across to his neighbour. She answered after a few minutes.

'Hey, Mia, did you ever see my girlfriend Vanessa up here?'

She looked at him, her smile fading a bit. 'I don't think so. I'm not sure. If I did, you never introduced me to her.'

'You said my girlfriend dropped that envelope off. What did she look like? Got a few spare pounds on her, brown hair.' *Lies a lot.*

She giggled. 'Who says that about a woman? A few extra pounds. I hope you don't say that about me!'

Mia was the exact opposite of Vanessa. If she turned sideways beside a lamppost, she'd disappear. 'Of course not.'

'Well, she was young, blonde, about my height and not skinny, but not heavy either.'

'Sounds like my dream woman, but unfortunately she isn't my girlfriend. I don't suppose she left a name?'

'No. She just said, could you please give this to Harry?'

'Thank you.'

Mia was about to close her front door when Harry stopped her. 'Just one more thing; I don't suppose you saw her get into a car?'

'Well, Harry, you know I'm not a nosy cow or anything, but I did think it was a bit strange, her asking me to give you this when she could have put it through your letterbox, so I did look out and I saw her standing at the side of the road. Then a big black car came along and picked her up.'

'Do you know what kind of car it was?'

'One of those big things. The kind you see rich country folk and snobby mothers dropping their kids off at school in.'

'A Range Rover?'

'Yes!' she exclaimed, pointing her finger at him, like he had just won first prize in a competition only she knew about.

Harry thanked her and went back into his own flat. He drank some of the beer and started reading through the article again.

And one name jumped out at him.

TWENTY-THREE

'Nice street,' DC Simon Gregg said, stopping the car at the entrance. It was narrow and there didn't appear to be any parking spaces further down.

'I like it.'

'Look, I'll park on the main street around the corner, then I'll walk round.'

'You don't have to, Simon. I'll be fine. Harry was just exaggerating. You can go home.'

'Like hell I will. Just sit tight and we'll have you up and running soon.' He backed out and found a space outside what used to be little shops but had long ago been converted into flats.

They started walking round, darkness enveloping the city now.

'What do you think of McNeil?' Gregg asked.

'I like him. I really do. He's fair and he's not worried about getting his hands dirty. He'll roll his sleeves up and get in about somebody.' They turned the corner into her street. 'Why? What do you think of him?'

He grinned. 'He busts my balls all the time, but I like him a lot. Better than that wanker Stan Weaver. I get the feeling that when the shit goes down, McNeil will have our backs.'

They walked down towards Alex's BMW and she stopped.

'What's wrong?' Gregg asked.

'Look. The tyres. They're inflated.'

'What? I thought you said they were all flat?'

'They were.'

'Are you sure, Alex? It was dark that night.'

She turned to look at him. 'I'm not dumb, Simon. Ask Harry. About the tyres, I mean.'

'If you say so.'

'I do say so. What the hell?' She shook her head.

'Maybe they self-inflate.'

She looked at him. 'I am at a total loss for words right now. Self-inflate? Does that come with the self-cleaning package? And the self-hoovering package?'

Gregg shrugged. 'I don't know.'

'For God's sake.'

'I don't know much about cars, you know that.'

'I know that, but you can have an intelligent guess sometimes.'

'I don't know what to tell you. Maybe a neighbour who thinks he's in with a chance with you?'

'Shut up. They're all older and married. I think I'm the youngest on the street.'

'Don't look a gift horse and all that.' He smiled at her. 'You going to be okay?'

'Of course. I just need to go in and get my car keys. Thanks for driving me.'

'No problem. I might be as dumb as an ox, but if somebody lifted his hand to you, I'd break him into little pieces.'

'I know you would.' She patted his arm.

He insisted he go into the house to make sure it was clear, but she was right behind him. It was empty.

'See you at work tomorrow.'

'See you, big guy.'

She watched him walk down the stairs and walk up the road heading back to the car, and wondered if he got lonely and still mourned the loss of his wife and baby girl.

She grabbed her car keys and went down to the little BMW. It felt good to get in behind the wheel after driving the pool car. She felt good going back to Harry's flat. He was her boss, but she also regarded him as a friend now. She had lost a lot of her friends after becoming a copper and now she only hung out occasionally with some other female coppers.

She was glad Angie Patterson had decided to come down from the Highlands to live in Edinburgh. Angie liked Harry a lot, but Alex didn't know if the two of them would hit it off enough to start going out.

She started the car and drove it slowly out of her street, turning right. She would have to go round by Inverleith Park since the council had decided, in their wisdom, to close St Bernard's Row to through traffic. Sometimes she wondered about the sense in blocking off rat runs, just so the traffic could sit in other streets, spewing fumes into the air.

She turned up Arboretum Avenue and followed the road round, her bright headlight beams cutting through the darkness. She started to slow down at the top of the road as she approached the T-junction with Inverleith Terrace – and then the car started speeding up.

She jammed her foot on the brakes, but nothing. She tried to steer the car to the side of the road, but her input did nothing.

The car flew across the traffic island, knocking down an illuminated traffic sign, and careened across the road onto the opposite side and smashed into the front of a parked car, throwing her against the steering wheel.

The airbags exploded and she felt herself being held back by the seatbelt as her face smashed into the airbag.

The car crumpled at the front with a loud explosion. As she settled back into her seat, she saw the first wisps of smoke snaking up from the front of the car in the dark.

She was aware of other vehicles stopping. She felt the first tendrils of panic as she grabbed the handle to open the door and it wouldn't open. She pulled and pulled, but nothing happened.

That was when all her training went out the window. She tried undoing her seatbelt, but it was stuck. And that was when her panic went into overdrive.

There were lights outside, vehicles stopping, people shouting. Then she saw a shadow at her door. She couldn't see for the smoke in front of her windscreen.

Then he was banging on the glass. He was screaming at her. *Duck!*

She leant sideways, further into the car, and he banged on the glass with the red extinguisher until the glass shattered. He threw the extinguisher aside and then reached in with a knife and cut her belt. She sat up and scrambled to get out, and the man's hands grabbed her and pulled her free.

She fell on the pavement, gasping and crying. Then she looked up into the dark night sky and saw little green and red lights.

And heard the buzzing as the drone flew away.

TWENTY-FOUR

Harry parked the pool car in the car park at the Royal Infirmary in Little France. Inside, he was taken right to the bay where Alex was. She smiled when he came in.

'Thank God you're alright,' he said. He held her hand for a second.

'I'm more shook up than anything else. A few cuts and scrapes and I jarred my shoulder, but I'll be fine.'

The doctor came in. 'She was lucky,' he said after Harry identified himself. 'A few days' rest and painkillers and she'll be right as rain. She can go home now.' He turned to Alex. 'Follow up with your doctor,' he said, then left.

'Jesus, I nearly crapped myself when I got the call from control. What happened?'

'I couldn't control the car, Harry. Just like your car when I was driving today. I had no input. Some bastard took it over.'

'How? How could they do that?'

'I don't know how, but when Simon and I got to the car, the tyres had been inflated. I thought it strange, but then I thought maybe one of my neighbours had done it for me. I got in and drove away, and when I got near Inverleith Park, the car got away from me.'

'It was hijacked,' Harry said, gritting his teeth.

She nodded. 'Thank God that guy pulled me out.'

'Did you get his name? As a witness.'

'No. I was busy lying on the ground watching the little drone fly away.'

'What? A fucking drone? Well, guess who we'll be talking to tomorrow. I'll kick his fucking arse, trying that on with us. And you, twice in one day. That's attempted murder.'

'They'll cover their backs, and you know it. We have to find out why they want to harm us.'

A nurse came in with the discharge papers. 'You can go home. Take more painkillers before bed. Is this your husband?'

Harry didn't say anything for a second.

'No, he's my boss,' Alex said, trying to keep a straight face. 'We're both police officers.'

'Oh, right. Do you have anybody at home to look after you, if you feel you need to come back here?' the older woman asked.

'Yes. I'm staying with a good friend of mine.'

'Good. You can leave when you're ready.'

Alex had blood down the front of her shirt from her busted nose. 'It isn't broken, thank God, but it's going to hurt for a week or more.'

'We'll get you cleaned up. You hungry? I have the car outside. I've called Jeni Bridge and updated her on the situation. She's livid. We can—'

'Ease up there, Harry. My face will be sore, but Betty protected me like she should have. I can't fault the BMW. But somebody tampered with her and she's ruined now.'

'She was burnt out. Just like my...I mean, my ex's Honda.'

She laughed. 'Christ, don't make me laugh. My ribs feel like they've been kicked. And yes, I feel hungry. Maybe hit the chippie on the way home? You can drop me off at my place. I think I'll be safe.'

'Safe? You've been involved in two accidents in one day. There's no way you're going to stay at your place. I mean, if that's okay with you.'

'It is. And thanks for caring.'

'I would do it for any of my officers.'

'I know you would. But thank you anyway.'

They started walking out together. 'I've had your car taken to the impound yard. They'll have some techs look it over. Or what's left of it.'

'They won't find anything. Just like they won't find anything on your car. Whatever it was they put in there, the fire will have taken care of it.'

'Let's just get you back to my place and get you into something more comfortable.'

'Is that your best pick-up line?'

'Nope. My best pick-up line is, *I'm Harry. You're welcome.*' He grinned at her.

'It would work on me.'

'Of course it would. You're vulnerable. You let somebody sell you a BMW.'

'My new car has to be a Honda CR-V.'

'Or a manky old Vauxhall. One of which I just happen to have out here.'

She shivered in the cold until they got across to the car.

'There is something I want to mention,' Alex said as they got into the Vauxhall.

'What's that?'

'The bloke who pulled me out of the car and probably saved my life.'

'What about him?'

'He was driving a Range Rover. It was the guy we saw in the pub the other night.'

TWENTY-FIVE

'You did what? You stupid bastard. What are you trying to do? Bring us all down?' Melissa McCallum paced back and forward in her office.

Max Blue stood in front of her, smiling. Like he was enjoying this.

'You need to relax more. You're too tense. Here, let Maxi take care of you.' He stepped towards her.

'Fuck off. Get away from me. Playing with fucking drones. God almighty, what if you'd killed her? What if you'd killed them both earlier today?'

Blue was still smiling, like he couldn't help himself. 'That was our technology working perfectly. The car accelerated because I made it, then I switched it into auto mode and it stopped perfectly. Then tonight, with the other one, it went exactly where I told it to go. You have to believe in your own products, Melissa.'

She stopped and looked at him. 'They're police officers. You might have a complete disregard for the law where you come from, but here they'll hunt you down and rip you a new arsehole. Oh yes, the courts are about as useful as a chocolate fireguard, but the police tend to look after their own. You would die in custody after falling down some stairs accidentally.'

'God, look at you. I don't think I could be turned on any more than I am now.'

'Jesus Christ. Will you listen to yourself? Get a fucking grip. Tomorrow is when the world sees what McCallum Technology is all about and we don't need any unwanted attention.'

Blue was still smiling like a schoolboy who didn't know he was in trouble.

'I just wanted that McNeil guy to be occupied with something other than bugging us.'

Melissa lowered her head and shook it. Then she locked eyes with him. 'Don't you see? By doing what you did with that bloody drone, you've done just the opposite. Now they're going to be all over us.'

'Somebody pulled her from the car. That wasn't supposed to happen.'

'Oh my God. You were actually trying to kill her?'

'I assumed she would be able to get out of the car on her own without any help.'

'Oh, don't fucking lie.'

Blue wasn't fazed. 'Don't get all sanctimonious on me now. This is just a means to an end. Besides, if I'd wanted to kill her, I would have waited until she was on that long street and taken the car up to a hundred. But I didn't.'

'Oh, I should feel grateful for that?'

Blue laughed. 'Yes.'

'This is not funny, Max. The investors' reps are coming tomorrow and everything has to go according to plan. We cannot afford to have anything come back at us.'

He walked over and held her. 'Don't worry, it won't.'

'I hope not, Max. We've come this far.'

'Listen, I was with the engineers all day today, going over last-minute calibrations. I was working on the software. It's going perfectly.'

'Good. By this time tomorrow, we'll be on our way. And nothing will stop us.'

TWENTY-SIX

Harry walked round to the passenger side to grab the fish suppers.

'How're you feeling now?' he asked.

'Harry, between the chippie and here, I haven't deteriorated. I'm fine. You don't have to act like a mother hen.' She looked at his face and smiled. 'But thanks for asking.'

He locked the car and they were walking to the stair entry door when it opened and Mia, Harry's next-door neighbour, came out with her little dog.

'Hi, Harry. Hey, Alex.' She looked puzzled. 'You look like you've been in the wars.'

'I was in a car accident,' Alex said.

'Oh dear. I'm glad it wasn't too serious. I hope you feel better soon.'

'Thank you.'

'Hopefully, your girlfriend will be able to help out, Harry.'

Harry and Alex both looked at Mia.

'Vanessa?' said Harry.

'Is that her name?'

'The one I described to you earlier.'

'Oh no, not her. The young blonde one.'

'She was here again?' he said, feeling his heart beat faster.

'Not *was*. Still is. She just opened the door to your flat a minute ago.'

'You wait here,' he said to Alex.

'Like hell I will.'

'I mean it, Alex.' He fished out the car keys and pressed them into her hand. 'Mia, please stay down here for a moment.' He turned back to Alex. 'If you hear a commotion, call treble nine, then call Karen Shiels.'

'I can't let you go up there alone.'

'You can and you will.'

'Jesus. I don't like this at all.'

'Please. Just stay here. There's somebody in my flat and she's going to damn well tell me what's going on.'

He handed her the fish and chips and went towards the stairs. The stairwell was well-lit and he climbed the stone steps as quietly as he could, knowing that the woman could lean out from above and open fire on him, if she was armed.

Why would she be armed? he thought, climbing higher.

He reached the next landing and started making his way

up to his own landing on the top floor. Step by step. If the woman who was in here was responsible for hurting Alex, she was going to bloody prison.

Staying alert, he reached the landing and approached his front door. He took the key out, but then tried the handle. It turned easily and the door opened.

Inside, it was dark, but he knew the place like the back of his hand, so he didn't need the light.

Where would she be waiting?

He walked slowly forward, towards the living room door. It was ajar. Could it be a trap?

He suddenly rushed forward, slamming the door open and switching the light on. Then he stopped.

The woman was sitting on his couch.

'Hello, Harry,' she said. 'You look like you've seen a ghost.'

TWENTY-SEVEN

James McCallum sat in front of his large-screen TV, playing a game on his Xbox.

'Don't you get enough of that?' a woman said, putting her hands on his shoulders.

'What? I like playing games.'

'It's too much like work.'

He laughed. 'Can you pour me a drink, please?'

'Scotch?'

'What else?'

She squeezed his shoulder before walking over to the drinks cabinet and poured two glasses of single malt. Added ice from the little bucket.

'Oh, would you look at that? I got shot from behind. I hate when that happens.'

'Are you playing with other people online?'

'Yes,' he said. 'My nemesis took me out. I'll have to have a word with him.' McCallum smiled as he took the glass from her. 'What do you fancy for dinner?'

'I quite fancy that little Italian restaurant in Rose Street. The new place that just opened up. How about it?'

'I'd better forget about this then.' He sniffed the whisky and put it on a side table. 'Are they still in the hotel?'

'Yes. I checked.'

'Check again, please.'

She took her phone out and opened the scanner app. 'Max's phone is still saying it's there in the room, even though he's switched it off now.'

McCallum laughed. 'He's such a clown. I wonder what he's going to do when Melissa gets fed up with him?'

'His good looks will see him through.'

'Should I be getting jealous now?' He smiled at her.

'Of course not. Blue talks the talk, but he's as dumb as a log. Yes, he has friends in high places, but only because of his father. Otherwise, nobody would look twice at him.'

'My wife looked twice at him.' His smiled faded and he looked down at the carpet.

'Don't let her get you down. After tomorrow, it will all be over.'

'And yet tomorrow almost never came. You know, when I started out in this business, I knew there were a lot of people who would want to stand in my way, do whatever it took to destroy me, but I never saw it coming from my wife.'

'As you said, it will all be over tomorrow. They will see for themselves, and then we'll be able to move on.'

'I didn't think she would resort to murder.'

'I have to admit, I was surprised by that as well,' she said. 'And now Dave Pierce is dead too. I'm glad this is going to be over.'

James McCallum stood up from the chair he had been sitting in. He smiled at his companion. 'If Melissa could see me now.'

'How are the knees holding up?'

'Fine. The medical team are keeping quiet thanks to the huge bonuses we're giving them. Just wait till we unleash this on the world. You did a marvellous job with the software.'

'The benefits of working from home.'

'You're an absolute genius. And I am so glad that Melissa is only my girlfriend and not my wife on paper. I don't know why she insisted on calling herself my wife.'

'She wanted you all to yourself, James. But I want the real deal. I want it signed on paper.'

He walked over to her on legs that were even steadier than they had been before he'd had the accident. 'Of course. I want you beside me. We're a team. We're going to take the world by storm.'

'That's good to hear. I have so many more ideas. Now get ready. I'm starved.'

Maggie Carlton walked out of the living room in the big house on the Bush Estate. She loved James more than anything, and nobody, not even Melissa whatever her real last name was, would stand in her way now.

TWENTY-EIGHT

Harry stood looking at the woman. Young, blonde, slim. Just like Mia had said.

'Hello, Bea,' he said.

Bea Anderson stood up and smiled. 'Go and tell Alex it's safe to come up. I won't bite. I'm not really dead.'

Harry wasn't sure for a moment, but he took his phone out anyway and sent a text to Alex, his eyes flicking up and down from the screen as his fingers hit the digital keys. He hoped had Apple reconfigured what he'd typed and autocorrected properly.

He surmised that it had as he heard Alex coming up the stairs.

'Jesus,' she said, seeing Bea in the living room.

'I suppose that is an appropriate response, considering I did come back from the dead.'

'You want some chips?' Harry said, nodding to the brown wrapper Alex was holding.

'No, but you two go ahead. I'll put the kettle on, though.'

Bea walked through to the kitchen and Harry raised his eyebrows at Alex. *Run now, or get the hammer and stake out?*

'I know it's getting a bit late for coffee, but I think we might need it.' Bea opened a cupboard and took the mugs out.

'Should I be worried that you know where my mugs are?' Harry said, putting the wrappers on the table and fetching some plates. The little bistro table at the living room window was only designed for two, and Harry was glad of that. If Vanessa drove by and saw *two* women in his flat, she would go home and take some pills.

'We saw you being taken from the mortuary,' Alex said as they were sitting down, eating.

'We thought we'd knocked the cameras out, and for the most part, we did. But there must have been cameras that weren't on the circuit.'

'Correct,' Harry said, tucking into his fish and chips. 'I'm more concerned about who you and your friends are and what's going on.'

Bea had her hands cupped round her coffee. 'I won't tell you my real name, as that will only complicate things. Just keep using my cover name. But we work for British Intelligence. I've been working undercover for a few months now.'

'Who are you investigating?' Alex asked.

'McCallum Technology.'

'The helicopter crash,' Harry said. 'I read the article you left me and I did some research online. A name jumped out at me: Sean Carlton. I guessed he was related to Fiona and Maggie.'

'Their brother.'

Alex looked puzzled.

Harry explained to her. 'Bea left an envelope here with a newspaper clipping about a helicopter that went down a few months ago. It crashed into the woods, the pilots died and it was blamed on pilot error.'

'Except it wasn't pilot error,' Alex guessed.

'That's what we've been told,' said Bea.

'By whom?'

'Fiona Carlton. She couldn't accept it was pilot error. You see, her brother and the co-pilot didn't work for the MOD, they worked for McCallum Technology. They were test pilots. She just wouldn't let it go, even after it was deemed to be an accident. She worked there as a software engineer and she started digging around. Then she found a flaw. Something didn't add up. Something had changed in the schematics. She had worked on the original team and she knew for a fact that something had been changed. She then contacted us. The MOD are ready to put a lot of money into the new technology. Planes and helicopters flying with self-charging battery engines with AI doing all the work – it's the future. But if there's a fault, we need to know about it.'

Harry washed his fish down with some coffee. 'And that's when you were hired, working undercover.'

'Yes. It was a slow process. I couldn't go trampling in there.'

'How come they didn't find out you were in the government and didn't know the first thing about computers?' Alex asked.

Bea smiled. 'I was chosen because I am a computer expert. I studied software engineering before I joined British Intelligence; that's why I was handpicked. They couldn't send somebody in blindly.'

'So what next?' Harry asked.

'Fiona made contact with one of the other team members, Dave Pierce. She trusted him. His girlfriend was a friend of Fiona's too. Linda Smith was also a police officer. They got her involved, told her something was going on. Linda had aspirations of being a detective.'

'When we found Fiona, she had Linda's warrant card on her.'

'It was arranged for Linda to park her car in the Ocean Terminal shopping centre, and Dave put a mask on and broke into the car and stole her uniform. Fiona had ideas about wearing it, since they were about the same size, but then Linda got cold feet. Fiona just used Linda's warrant card after that.'

'Talking of which,' Alex said, 'what about the fake warrant card in my name that was found on you?'

'Sorry. But after you became involved, I had my team make up a copy of yours. It was a real one, just a duplicate of yours.'

Harry pushed his plate away, finished with his dinner. 'McCallum must have been on to you to have somebody try to kill you after Fiona was killed.'

Bea put a hand up to her forehead. 'Christ, that hurt. He came in and whacked me. I thought it was one of my team. They were going to meet me at Maggie Carlton's house. I just thought they were early. I had gone to the house to have a look around. Fiona said she had a room full of articles and cuttings. I wanted to see it.'

'Then you were attacked and left for dead,' Alex said.

'Yes. Luckily, my team turned up. The house was already on fire, but I said to leave me in the house, that it would look better if I was dead. One of the team gave me something to render me unconscious and then he turned up after the fire brigade took me out. He was right there before they started doing CPR, and he declared me dead. Then the mortuary van took me away. Scariest thing that's ever happened to me, and then I was put in the fridge.'

'That was a brave thing to do.'

Bea shrugged.

'What about the post-mortem you lot did on Fiona?'

'That was my boss's idea. It was a necessity. We had to check to see if she'd swallowed something. It was nasty, but it had to be done.'

'What about those guys breaking into my house?' Alex said.

'I obviously heard you saying you were going to take the laptop, and we had to have it. Fiona said she had some of the schematics on there, and the one that had been changed had been put onto a flash drive. Dave was going to meet her the night she died. To give her the flash drive. He had a room in a hotel. He was paranoid that he would be followed home after the meeting, so he wanted the hotel room to go back to. But he panicked at the handover and ran. Fiona wasn't about to let things go tits up, so she drove after him and then chased him. He gave the drive to her in the hotel room. One of my team was there. After we saw Dave running, we got to the hotel, but Fiona had neglected to tell him that we were working with them. It was only after he'd given Fiona the flash drive that he realised we were on their side. But by then it was too late.'

'But the bad guys caught her and killed her anyway.' Harry looked at Bea. 'Then they thought they'd killed you and now they've killed Dave too. Getting rid of the people they thought could bring them down.'

'It looks that way.'

'Did your people inflate my car tyres?' Alex asked.

'No. Why?'

'Because somebody did. And then my car was taken over. Just like Harry's was today when we were at the Bush Estate.'

'I know. I only heard a little while ago. That's why I knew I had to come here. Are you okay?'

'Yes. But I think today in Harry's car was a dry run. Tonight was the real thing. They're trying to kill us. I think we're starting to unravel something that went wrong at McCallum Technology and now they'll do anything, even resort to killing police officers.'

'Have you spoken to Maggie Carlton?' Harry asked.

'No,' said Bea.

'She moved into the apartment.'

'I know. We wanted to put her into protection, but she wouldn't hear of it. We'll watch her. One of our team will follow her to and from work. We think Max Blue is involved in this, but he stays on the property at Bush House. We have every exit covered. The McCallums are still there and so is Blue. If they leave, we'll know about it.'

Harry looked at her, then stood up. 'That mark on your head. Can I have a look?'

'Sure. It's where he hit me. God knows what he hit me with, but it was enough to knock me out.'

Harry stepped closer and looked at the mark.

It looked like an eye.

TWENTY-NINE

Alex was stiff and sore when she got up the next morning.

'How did you sleep?' Harry asked.

'Like I'd been in a car accident.'

'You should take the rest of the day off. I'm getting the team to come with me to McCallum Technology. And a whole scrum of uniforms. There's no bastard going to be touching any cars today. I want that arsehole Blue to come to the station for an interview. The PF is drawing up the search warrant right now. I was just on the phone with her.'

'You think I'm going to be in the house watching TV while you're out there having all the fun? I don't think so. I want to look that bastard Blue in the eye and slap the cuffs on him.'

They'd discussed the arrest warrant with Norma Banks, the procurator fiscal, and although they couldn't conclusively point the finger at Max Blue, they had enough to bring him in under suspicion.

'Okay. I made you a coffee. Once you're ready, we can get going.'

'I'll get showered and dressed. I won't be long.'

Half an hour later, they were at the office. They were all there, including a couple of detective constables from regular CID.

'For those of you who don't know,' said Harry, 'DS Maxwell's car was hijacked remotely last night. Some of you might have read about cars being taken over and the driver losing all input. This happened last night. We have an idea who is responsible, as it also happened to my car yesterday while DS Maxwell and I were leaving the McCallum facility. We think they're playing games, trying to warn us off. And for some reason, they think it's going to work. We're all going to show them today that it isn't. Any questions so far?'

A young female DC put her hand up. 'How do we know for sure this company is behind it?'

'Early this morning, I had a phone call from one of the techs who was looking through my burnt-out car, and they found a little box attached magnetically to the engine bay of my car. Whilst the fire destroyed most of the box, there was a fragment of motherboard left. With the name McCallum Technology microscopically engraved near some of the capacitors. It was a very complex little box, but having that name there means they were involved. So if there're no other questions, let's go get the bastards.'

They were getting into their cars and vans, preparing to drive to the Bush Estate, when Harry got another call. This time it was from a member of the forensics team.

'Sir, we found something interesting in the room at Dave Pierce's flat. Where the computer was located.'

Simon Gregg was driving, while in the car behind were Karen Shiels and the new girl, Eve Bell.

'What was it?' Harry asked the man.

'Splinters of wood underneath the computer desk, like somebody had broken something wooden over the corner of the desk.'

'Like what?'

'Not sure yet. But on one side of the wood there was a dark veneer.'

'Thanks for letting me know. Call me again if you narrow it down.'

As they drove up the road in a convoy, something was niggling away inside Harry's brain. *Wood. Veneer. What the hell?*

THIRTY

'This is it,' Melissa McCallum said to Max Blue. Her name wasn't McCallum, but she had called herself that ever since she'd got entangled with James. Thank God she hadn't legally married him.

'Now that the shares are at rock bottom, we can make a killing,' Blue said. 'And then we can move into our own place. I mean, this little house on the property has been fine, but I want to get the hell out of here.'

Melissa smiled. 'Don't worry. It will soon be over.'

'Where's James?'

'He left early this morning. He took a train to London. I knew he had this trip planned, to try to whip up some interest in getting investors of his own, not knowing we were going behind his back.'

'The fool. He doesn't know we're going to pull the rug out from under him.'

'Just concentrate on the job at hand, Max. The investors are here.'

'Okay.'

They were in her office in the lab above the underground testing facility. 'Let's go down and meet them,' she said.

Downstairs, the three women and two men were talking to one of the engineers. They turned when Melissa entered.

'Good morning, everybody,' Melissa said. 'I trust you slept well?' She smiled at them. They had better have slept well. The rooms at the Balmoral on Princes Street were costing her a fortune.

'Yes, thank you,' one of the women said. She was very rich and very powerful. She lived in Washington, DC, close to the Pentagon. 'Can we get on with the demonstration?'

Melissa smiled. 'Of course. My partner, Max, has gone down to the testing facility. He is going to be part of the demonstration. Then we can go to the conference room, where we can discuss business.'

'I'm looking forward to it.'

Of course you are, Melissa thought. *You're going to invest in a company that will be worth billions after this.*

They stepped over to the viewing window and Melissa gave the nod to the head engineer, who in turn spoke to his head technician.

'Through there, you will see two adjacent tunnels at each

end,' she explained. 'We have a train system running in a large loop, something like the New York subway. When the train comes out, you will see our new technology at work. If you look at the screens, you'll see a bird's-eye, 3D view, to give you a clearer picture. But from this viewing window, we can see directly across the level crossing.'

They saw Max Blue walk over to a small car. He turned around, smiled and waved at them. Then he got in the car.

'Max is a genius,' she said, smiling. 'He has brought so much to the technology in this company.'

'I just hope he knows what he's doing,' the woman replied.

Max started the car and drove it up onto the railway tracks.

'Those tracks are almost identical to the steel ones of old,' Melissa said, 'but they're made of stronger material and filled with sensors. If a car is fitted with one of our retrofit sensors, it will talk to the train. If it's an old car, then the train will be talking to the rails, and the rails will know if a car has passed over one set but not the other. Then all sorts of cameras come into play, but even if the train is working autonomously, it will know to stop. And here's our demonstration today, which we can watch, and then we can go and show you footage of some other applications of the AI we've designed.'

'Does that car have the AI in it?' the woman asked.

'Yes, it does. This is the brand-new autonomous vehicle

that we hope to have running on the roads within the next two years. Way ahead of the competition.'

They all stood and watched the huge arena below.

Max Blue drove the car onto the tracks. The software had been calibrated to perfection, he had seen to it himself, and what better way to demonstrate his confidence in the technology than to be a part of the demonstration himself.

Then his phone rang. Who the hell was this?

'This is a bad time,' he said to the as-yet-unknown caller.

'Max! James here! How are you enjoying your little stunt?'

'James? What's going on?'

McCallum laughed. 'Why don't you tell them, old friend? No, wait, do let me tell you: the train that is going through the loop right now is gathering speed and I have had its brain switched off.'

'What are you talking about?'

'Let me explain. I know what you did to the engine system on that helicopter. You killed those pilots and all the passengers. You had the investors running to the hills, didn't you, Max? You and my girlfriend. You know the one; she calls herself Melissa McCallum although we were never married. You don't think she wants you, Max, do you?'

'You're delusional, James.'

'Am I? I don't think so. You see, I found out about your investors. Once my stock had tanked, which it did, then your investors would jump in and buy up my company. Then when the military contracts came back, the share prices would go through the roof. Especially after you announced the self-driving cars were ready to go.'

'I'm not going to listen to this, James. You're finished. This is going to be our company by the day's end.'

'I want you to admit you tampered with the software on that helicopter, killing those people.'

'Or what?'

'The train has just entered the part of the loop where it's turned and is now facing you. In three minutes, the train will enter the tunnel and accelerate towards you. I have had my best engineer remotely take over the project. Nothing you can do at Bush will be able to stop it. The car has also been remotely taken over. You can't drive it or unlock it, and thanks to our anti-theft measures, you can't smash your way out of it. You have around four minutes to live, Max. The train will be doing over a hundred when it hits you. This is your choice. Detective Chief Inspector Harry McNeil is up in the viewing area, waiting. If you tell him what you've done, then the train will stop.'

'You asshole. My lawyer will get me off. I'm confessing under duress.'

'Wrong again. Your digital footprints are all over that helicopter crash. Hard to find, unless you know what to look for, but luckily for me, I have somebody on my team who does.'

'You're bluffing.'

'Am I? Well, we'll let Chief Inspector McNeil sort that out, will we? After the train hits the car.'

'He'll know this is murder.'

'He can't hear anything right now. But I'm about to switch the screen on. Oh, and when they look, they'll see you were the last one to calibrate the software. My engineer will cover her tracks by replicating your digital imprint. Just like you did to bring the helicopter down. Five seconds, then McNeil will see you. And so will I. Your choice, Max.'

He pulled and pulled at the car's door handle, but it wouldn't budge.

He shook his head. 'Go to hell, McCallum.'

Five seconds later, the little screen in the car showed him the view the others were getting up in the control room.

He opened a laptop and plugged it in to a USB in the car. He started typing furiously.

And in that second, Melissa could see her whole future going up in smoke.

Harry McNeil and the other officers were watching Max Blue hacking away at the keyboard on the laptop.

'What's he doing?' Harry asked.

Melissa turned to him. 'There's only one reason he'd be battering away at that laptop. He's trying to stop the train. Something's gone wrong.'

There was a kill switch in front of her, a big red button that she could smack her hand down onto, but she knew if she did that then the whole thing was over.

But she knew it was all over anyway.

The lights from the train were visible as it started its countdown towards the level crossing where Max Blue sat.

Melissa slammed her hand down on the big red button.

And nothing happened. The lights kept coming.

She turned to the chief engineer sitting at a desk a few feet away.

'Stop that train!'

'I can't!' he shouted back at her. 'Blue's just overridden the emergency software. Jesus.'

'Well, you override that!'

'I can't. I've been locked out.'

'Oh my God,' Alex said in a low voice as they got a view from inside the train cab. It was turning at the end of the loop before making its journey down to the level crossing.

'How long before that train hits?' Harry asked.

'What?' Melissa said.

'How long before the bloody train hits the car?' he shouted at her.

'Three minutes, maybe less if he ramps up the speed. Two minutes maybe. Why?'

Harry ran to the door marked 'Authorised Personnel Only' and opened it, feeling the change in the air. It was colder here. He turned around, looking for what he'd seen through the window.

Alex was right on his heels. 'Harry, what are you doing?' she screamed at him.

'Get back in there!' He ran to a door marked 'Maintenance'. A man was sitting inside.

'Your van keys! Where are they?'

The man was flabbergasted for a second. 'In the ignition,' he said.

The Transit sat back away from the track, a white vehicle with red and yellow chevrons painted on it. Harry jumped in behind the wheel and started it up. He could see the lights from the train.

He floored the van, going over the first crossing. The barriers were down on the second one, but he drove through them and hit the back of Max's car full tilt, smashing it off the track. The van stalled after the airbags deployed. Harry looked and saw the train bearing down on him.

The van wouldn't start.

THIRTY-ONE

For Alex, everything went into slow motion. She ran after Harry as he went into the small office. Then he came back out again, shouting at her, but she couldn't hear what he said. Then she saw him jump into the van and start it up. What the hell was he doing?

Then she realised what he was doing, but she couldn't quite grasp why.

The van moved towards the train tracks. It crossed the first level crossing, then smashed through the barriers of the second and crashed into the back of the car, pushing it off the tracks.

Then she saw the lights of the train as it came out of the tunnel.

The van stayed on the tracks. It was almost sideways to

her and she thought at first that the momentum had carried it off the tracks, but then she saw it was still on.

Alex was shouting and screaming, unaware of the faces that were watching through the viewing window. The train was approaching fast and still Harry wasn't opening the driver's door.

She ran towards the van, over the first level crossing, so focused on the driver's door that she wasn't even aware of the train now.

She said Harry's name over and over, her eyes locked on to the driver's door. It wasn't opening. Something must have happened.

Then she saw the figure coming from around the back of the van, running at her. She couldn't see who it was for the tears in her eyes, but then the figure was lunging at her.

Was it Max Blue? Jesus, he was coming to kill her, and Harry was in the van and the trains was about to kill them all.

THIRTY-TWO

Harry cursed himself. He had knocked the car off the tracks, but now he was stuck. The damn seatbelt wouldn't unlock. He yanked at it, pulled and tugged, but nothing.

The train was coming. He saw the lights in the tunnel and knew it was bearing down on him.

He took a deep breath and let it out slowly. *Keep calm or else you'll die.* His eyes locked on to the train lights.

He slowly pulled the seatbelt from the shoulder point, easing it through the clip until it was loose on his stomach. With his other hand, he lifted it up higher off his lap and started to pull his legs up. As he fed more belt through the clip it came a bit higher, then stopped. It had locked in place. He eased it up more, now not even wanting to see the train. If he looked, he'd panic and then it would be over.

He fed a little bit more through, then he was pushing

with one hand and he got his legs up and they were out, past the lap portion of the seatbelt, and he was suddenly lying half on the passenger seat.

He pushed and kicked and broke free of the seatbelt and his hand reached for the door handle. He pushed himself at the same time, his body shoving against the door, and then he was falling out.

That's when he saw Alex shouting and screaming. Other people running through the doorway. The new girl, Eve, in front, Karen behind and the big lumbering giant that was Simon Gregg, followed by uniforms.

Alex was approaching the track. She couldn't see him. He ran then, ran faster than he had in a long time, and threw himself at Alex as the train's lights came bearing down on them.

THIRTY-THREE

No more than five feet, Harry thought as he sat up. The train had stopped no more than five feet from the van.

'Jesus,' he said, his body aching. Then he looked at Alex, sprawled beside him, and the other team members running up to them. 'You okay?' he said to Alex.

'I'm fine. Sore, but fine.' She sat up and was helped to her feet by Gregg.

'Lying down on the job? You'll get written up for that,' he said, grinning.

'Shut up,' she said.

Then they watched as Eve Bell came across with Max Blue, shaken but not badly hurt.

'How did that train not smash into the van?' he said.

'Get him out of here,' Harry said as he stood up.

Inside, they found James McCallum standing up out of

his wheelchair, his face beaming. He turned to the other people, who were rooted to the spot. 'And, ladies and gentlemen, that concludes the physical part of the test.'

'What just happened, McCallum?' Harry said.

'You mean me being able to walk or –'

'The train. Explain what just happened.'

'As you can see, the train stopped. My engineers lied for Melissa's benefit. We had everything under control. Melissa invited these good people here thinking they were the investors, or at least people representing the investors. But they're not. They're from the MOD, working undercover. They went through everything yesterday and found what Max Blue did to the system on board the helicopter to bring it down.

'Melissa and Max had sabotaged the helicopter by replacing one of the parts, which Max then manipulated, causing the 'copter to crash. As a result, my shares went through the basement. He and Melissa wanted to get their own investors to snap up the stock at rock-bottom prices. And it almost worked. Until we had our own meeting.

'I told the investors that they would be working with a couple of murderers. I assured them I had fixed everything and the train would run perfectly. That's why when I cornered Max and tried to get him to confess, he thought he could go ahead and manipulate the system. As you can see, my top engineer and I had already put the new system in place. I just wanted to give the MOD a true demonstration. It was all a bluff. The train was going to stop. And you know Max will try to pin all of this on you, Melissa.'

McCallum turned to the MOD people. 'So, you saw for yourself, even with somebody like Max Blue's knowledge, the system couldn't be overridden. That train wasn't going to hit his car.'

Harry looked at Alex. 'Thanks for trying to help me anyway.'

'Right back at you. You thought the train was going to hit the van.'

The lead female investigator walked up to McCallum. 'We had reservations about Melissa. We put Bea Anderson in place after Fiona contacted us and Bea confirmed what we suspected: that Max Blue is a master manipulator. Thank you for showing us you've got things under control. I think I speak for all of us when I say we will be using you, Mr McCallum.'

'Thank you.'

'What about the legs?' Harry said to McCallum.

The man smiled. 'That's another thing we have to discuss. Not only the automotive world but the medical world too.'

Harry nodded. 'Who's the engineer you were talking about? I thought Fiona Carlton was your best engineer?'

'She was. But she had an equal. Her sister, Maggie. She's helped me through all of this. She and her sister were both friends with Dave Pierce's girlfriend. God rest his soul.'

'And Melissa had them murdered.'

Melissa turned to him. 'I know those pilots and passengers died because of us, but I'm not taking the blame for those murders. Fiona Carlton and Dave Pierce being murdered wasn't anything to do with us. We never touched them.'

'Do you believe her?' Alex said.

'I think I do.' *Splinters. Veneer.* 'Christ.'

'What is it?'

'I need to call Bea Anderson.'

THIRTY-FOUR

He walked along the side of the canal, just another punter out for a walk. Brisk autumn day. Nothing out of the ordinary. People passed him by but didn't give him another look.

He walked along to the gardens in front of the entrances that overlooked the canal basin. He took out the keys he'd acquired and opened the front door. Inside, he approached the front door of the apartment with confidence. This was the last one.

The front door opened quietly. The apartment itself was deadly quiet. He closed the front door and walked up to the living room. He didn't know if she would be in here or not, but considering what time of day it was, there was a good chance.

And he was right.

'Hello, Maggie,' he said to the young blonde woman.

She turned around. 'Hello. But my name's not Maggie.'

'Oh, I'm sorry,' he said, about to turn and leave. 'I was to meet her here. I got a call saying she knew who killed my daughter.'

'I know.' Bea Anderson smiled. 'That was me.'

'What's going on?'

'I think you know what's going on, Mr Smith,' Harry said from behind.

'I don't understand,' Brian Smith said, leaning heavily on his medical walking stick.

'I think you understand perfectly well. Are you really disabled?'

'You're about to find out.'

Harry thought Smith was going to attack him with the stick, but he turned his attention to Bea instead. He brought the stick up and was about to bring it down, but Bea was prepared this time. She stepped in to meet the stick, pulled Smith over and twisted his arm back.

The big bald man she worked with ran into the room and roughly manhandled Smith into a chair, taking his walking stick away from him.

'Move, and I'll bend this over your head. You hear?' he said to Smith.

Smith said nothing as the big man stepped to one side.

'Why?' Harry said, grateful the big man had stepped in. He was aching in joints he hadn't realised he had.

'They deserved it. Getting my Linda involved in that caper. They caused her death! If it wasn't for them, she wouldn't be dead! So, yes, I killed that stupid bitch Fiona Carlton, and Dave Pierce.'

'And you thought you'd killed Bea here.'

'Whoever the hell she is. Yes, I thought I'd killed Maggie Carlton. I couldn't let the three of them get away with killing my daughter.'

Maggie Carlton walked into the room. 'I am so sorry about Linda, but you didn't bring her back by killing my sister, or Linda's boyfriend.'

'Is that where you got the key for this place?' Harry asked.

Smith nodded. 'It was Fiona's. I took the keys from her the night I murdered her. But you lot deserved it. You might not have been driving the van, but you had her working in her spare time. Working on this stupid conspiracy theory you had going.'

Harry moved to stand next to Maggie. 'Why don't you tell them the truth, Brian?'

'What do you mean?' Smith looked at Harry with undisguised contempt.

'Tell them you were the one driving the taxi that night.'

Maggie looked puzzled. 'What are you talking about?'

Smith looked at her before answering. 'I don't know what he's talking about.'

'Because of her injuries, where she was struck on her hip, they thought that she had been hit by a van,' Harry said.

'Dave Pierce got it wrong that night. He said he saw a van driving away. He hadn't seen the accident happen, but when he got into the street, he saw a van driving far away up the road with no lights on. That's what he reported.'

'Is this true?' Maggie asked Smith.

'Are you going to listen to him? The police couldn't catch Linda's killer, so he's trying to come up with some cockamamie story about it being me.'

Harry continued. 'When we were in your house the other day, I saw a little leather pouch with a drawstring. I thought it was some kind of cosh at first, but then I remembered a friend of mine years ago had one. It's a little bag that a taxi driver carries his change in. It opens quickly and spreads out. Then you pull the drawstring. But you're disabled, Mr Smith. You couldn't be driving a taxi, surely? I had one of my detectives contact cab companies, and we narrowed it down to one company in particular where an owner had a taxi off the road a few months ago because his driver said a van had backed into it, smashing the front wing. But it wasn't a van, was it, Mr Smith? It was your daughter striking the front of your taxi that caused the damage. The owner confirmed that you rent a cab from him. Working on the side whilst claiming benefits.'

Smith's head slumped for a second, before it came shooting back up. 'If you people hadn't got her involved, she would still be alive.'

'If you weren't a benefits cheat, she would still be alive,' Harry countered.

'How did you know he was going to come for me?' Maggie asked.

'He knew he hadn't killed you in your house. He set fire to it anyway, thinking whoever he had hit was dead. But it was the mark on Bea's head. Fiona had the same one. In the shape of an eye. I thought it was very strange, and I was puzzled as to what would make such a mark. Then I remembered Smith there had a fancy walking stick when I first met him. One with a duck's head. He used it to hit your sister, to stun her before stabbing her. Same with Bea, but I think he didn't want to use the same MO. He just hit her and then let the fire take care of the rest. Then I assume you were told by Pierce that Maggie was still alive?'

Smith nodded.

'What about Dave?' Maggie said.

'He would have had the same mark probably, but I think the sharp duck's beak caught him, rather than the duck's face. And then something happened and the walking stick broke on Dave's desk. Forensics found some splinters with veneer on them. They were from the walking stick, weren't they, Mr Smith?'

'Yes,' Smith answered.

'That's when I saw him with the medical walking stick. I couldn't be sure, mind, but I had a good idea.'

Maggie shook her head. 'He kills his own daughter in an accident, then he blames us for it.'

'He tried to convince himself that he wasn't to blame. But this is all on you, Mr Smith.' Harry walked over to him.

'You're under arrest. Stand up.'

THIRTY-FIVE

'What's this?' Alex said, putting two plates down on the little table in the living room. 'More car brochures?'

'I'm still window shopping.' He looked up at her. 'What about you? Another Beemer?'

She sat down opposite him. They were waiting for the Chinese to be delivered.

'I'm not sure. I'm thinking of something different now. Don't laugh, but I'm thinking of getting one of the new Honda CR-Vs.'

'Now you're just having me on.'

She laughed. 'I'm not. They're great wee cars.'

'I know. I mean, so I heard. But we can't have the same car.'

'What about your classic?'

'The parts should be in soon, but it's not a car I'd like to go out driving in the winter. I might just stick with the ratty old pool car for now.'

'What? Away with yourself.'

'There's no rush. Maybe I'll get a Mercedes.'

'That's too posh.'

'One of those big four-by-four things.'

'You know nothing about cars, do you?'

'I'm learning.'

'I'll take you car shopping. Just so you won't embarrass yourself by buying a hairdresser's car.'

He smiled at her as they looked out the window, waiting for the delivery driver to call them to say he couldn't find the address.

'I can get my stuff together and move back along the road,' she said. 'Now that this case is over.'

'Whenever. No rush. I mean, I don't want you to think I'm kicking you out.'

'I know. Maybe at the weekend? I know you hurt yourself this morning throwing yourself at me, and I know it's been a long time since a man threw himself at me...'

'Here's the Chinese,' he replied. 'Throwing myself at you. If you'd bloody well done as I told you and stayed where you were...'

EXCERPT FROM DEAD BEFORE YOU DIE - DCI HARRY MCNEIL BOOK 4

CHAPTER 1

The weather was perfect for killing.

Snow came down from ruptured clouds, covering everything, making people lower their faces as the relentless storm battered everybody who dared to step out into the open. The wind was driving the snow into the unwary, chilling them to the bone. They kept their heads down, faces alternating between looking down so they wouldn't fall and looking ahead so they wouldn't die under the wheels of a bus.

He saw her, standing at the bus stop, just like he knew she would be. He'd heard her telling somebody she had to make sure she was out sharp, but he'd made sure that plan was scuppered.

The bus will be late in this weather, the younger man had said. Come to the pub with us.

He would have been the first to die if she'd accepted. His plans were not be messed with, but he knew there could be deviations and would need contingencies. Killing the smarmy sod with the funny haircut would have been an added bonus.

He pulled into the side of the road, ignoring the honk of a taxi horn. The cabbie looked at him as he drove by, and the man looked back. Almost willing him to get out and come talk to him.

Almost.

That would have meant his plan being rewritten, so he just stared until the taxi driver went on his way.

He rolled the window down and smiled out at her. 'Christine!' he shouted. There was nobody else in the bus stop or else he would have parked around the corner and walked up, pretending he had been in a shop and had casually bumped into her.

The snow was coming down thick and fast now. He could see she was shivering, gently stamping her feet in boots that looked cheap and nasty. Just like her.

She looked at him and smiled. Recognising him. She waved, unsure whether to walk forward or not. He kept the smile plastered on his face while his mind chewed her out. *You're letting the heat out of my car.*

'You want a lift?' Plan A or Plan B was going to kick in now, depending on her answer.

'Oh, I'm fine. My bus will be along shortly. Thanks anyway.'

It could still go either way, depending on how persuasive he was.

'Don't be daft! Hop in. The buses aren't running to any kind of schedule now anyway.' *Hop in now, or I'll fucking kill you where you stand.* One half of his brain told him to jump out and stick her, but the other half, the sensible half, told him to stay to Plan A, for the time being.

'Are you sure?' she replied, looking at him.

He looked at her blankly for a moment, his mind already setting the launch sequence for Plan B, maybe having to open the box on Plan C, but Plan C was only a rough sketch, one that would have revved up his anger level. He'd never had to use a Plan C so far, and by God, if this whiny bitch made him use one tonight, her chances of ever seeing her next birthday were very slim.

She's not going to see it anyway. Bloody clown, he reminded himself.

He almost burst out laughing but managed to cover it as a smile at the last minute.

'Of course I'm sure! There's nobody else here. Maybe the bus just left and you won't know when the next one will be along. It *is* after rush hour.'

After rush hour. He'd made sure she stayed late working tonight. Tonight was perfect; not only were the buses going onto an evening schedule – read *few and far between* – but the atrocious weather was making it worse.

'Oh, okay then.'

Score 1-0 for the psychopathic killer in the fancy car with the heated seats.

He was still staring with the fixed smile when he realized the door was opening.

'I really appreciate this,' she said, her hair wet around the edges under the hand-made woollen monstrosity that sat on her head.

'Not a problem at all,' he said as Christine put her seatbelt on. The car had four-wheel drive and sat higher than the other, lowly vehicles around him. Quality. That was what distanced him from the other plebs who were driving little hatchbacks with front wheel drive, or, God forbid, rear-wheel drive. People didn't learn. He laughed when he saw them stuck at the side of the road, sometimes *off* the road. Especially when the car wasn't an off-road vehicle. He'd honk the horn, wind down his window and make a face, sometimes followed by a string of obscenities.

Serves them all right.

'There's a heated seat button there,' he said, pointing to it. She looked around, like he'd just suggested she take over the controls of a crippled airliner. He gritted his teeth, again disguising it with a smile. He reached over and pressed the button.

'Ooh, fancy,' she said, making it sound almost sarcastic, but she smiled.

'Better than a ratty old bus,' he said, pulling away from the stop.

The big car cut through the snow like it wasn't even there. A radio station played in the background. 'You can change that, if you like,' he said.

'No, it's fine.' She looked at him. 'This is really nice of you to do this.'

I know. 'Don't mention it. This is a hell of a night to be standing about in.'

'You live out west a bit, don't you?' he said.

'Yes.'

'I'm going that way tonight. I can drop you off.'

She made another *don't be silly* face. 'No, it's alright. If you can drop me off close, I can get a taxi.'

He grinned again. 'I don't have much to do tonight. Just one thing I have to check on, and then I can drop you off at your house. No funny business though!' he said, laughing. 'Seriously, I'd rather you get home safe.'

He drove further on, leaving the lights of the city behind, but the snow filled in the shadows, making things lighter than what they normally would be. The headlights cut through the driving snow as he followed a smaller car.

'Listen, I'm going to look at a property I bought, but it's in a bit of disrepair. I just have to swing by to check and see if the contractor left some stuff I ordered. You know what they're like,' he said in a tone as if she really did know what they were like. 'Would you mind if we go there first?'

'Of course not. I'm nice and cosy and I can actually start to feel my feet.'

Ten minutes later, he was pulling off the road, bumping up an old track. 'The road will be paved last,' he said, smiling. The headlight beams cut through the darkness, bouncing off the trees. If she had looked closer, she would see there had been no other wheels up this track recently.

'It's not much further,' he said.

Then the trees thinned out. On the opposite side of the clearing sat an old mansion. It was rundown with boarded up windows. Pallets with building supplies sat out front, covered in snow. He pulled the car close to one.

'Great! He must have got here early. The tiles are marble. Come and have a look. See how beautiful they are.'

He smiled and hopped out of the car before she could argue.

Her smile slipped a bit. He could see her hesitate as he watched her through the windscreen. He smiled and waved at her. She undid her seatbelt and got out into the falling snow.

'See? In there? What do you think of the colour?' he said, pointing into the middle of the pallet. The headlights shone on the tarp covering what was underneath.

'I can't see anything,' Christine said, peering closer.

She didn't see any marble tiles because there weren't any.

She didn't see his gloved fist coming towards her face. All she felt was something connecting with her chin and then she fell sideways onto the snow-covered drive.

She didn't feel him lifting her and putting her into the boot of the large car.

He went into the passenger side and went through Christine's bag and took her phone out. Then he got back in behind the wheel. He would switch it off back down on the main road, further away from here, then take the battery out and put the phone in a bin somewhere. He knew where Christine lived so it would be close to her house. Where there were no cameras.

Then he would take her to her new home.

He drove carefully back down the road. The car did it easily. It paid to buy quality. Something Christine wouldn't understand.

At least she got a lift in it.

Even if it was her last one.

Lightning Source UK Ltd.
Milton Keynes UK
UKHW011835290722
406581UK00001B/4